Top Dog / Bottom Dog

Top Dog/ Bottom Dog

Coming to grips with power at home, at work, and in the sexual arena

BY ROBERT KAREN

DONALD I. FINE, INC.
NEW YORK

 Published in the United States of America
by Donald I. Fine, Inc. and in Canada by General Publishing Company Limited.

Library of Congress Catalogue Card Number: 86-46399

ISBN: 1-55611-035-9

Manufactured in the United States of America

10 9 8 7 6 5 4 3 2 1

This book is printed on acid free paper. The paper in this book
meets the guidelines for permanence and durability of the Committee on
Production Guidelines for Book Longevity of the Council on Library Resources.

For Thaleia

"If I am not for myself, who will be for me?
If I am for myself only, what am I?
If not now, when?"

—HILLEL,
The Talmud

Contents

PART II: THE REPLAY
Balancing the Power

PART III: THE PLAY
Maneuvers, Maneuvers, Maneuvers!

PART IV: THE REPLAY
Using Your Whole Self

PART V: THE PLAY
Three Characters in Crisis

PART VI: THE REPLAY
Making Fundamental Change

Foreword

by Paul L. Wachtel,
Distinguished Professor of Psychology,
City College and City University of
New York Graduate Center

TRUTH IN advertising demands that the reader of this book be given fair warning: It can become addictive. I myself innocently sat down one evening to glance at the manuscript for a few minutes before turning to other pressing commitments. What happened? I couldn't put it down. I ended up reading it through much of the night and the next day. The characters Robert Karen has created to illustrate his very useful psychological explorations are as vivid and three-dimensional as those in any novel, and I cared enough about them that I simply had to keep reading to find out what happened to them.

This is not the ordinary self-help book. Its vision of the world is complex and sophisticated and its psychological analyses extremely acute. The writing is wonderful. The hot breath of real human beings in action and in anguish can be sensed on every page.

Because the book tackles tough issues boldly, it is bound to be controversial. I myself do not agree with everything in it. Perhaps because I have not had to engage in the rough and tumble of the corporate world—where so many Americans must make their way each day—there are times I found the advice more adversarial and strategically minded than I would wish. But mostly I found myself nodding in agreement at the shrewd analyses and sensitive renderings of individuals in conflict and of the possible paths through which they might pass to a more successful and fulfilling life. Even where I disagreed, the book made me rethink questions I thought I had long put to rest.

I am afraid that to some readers this book may seem at first glance to bear a resemblance to those tracts which urge people to "look out for number one" or which in other ways exacerbate the rationalizing of selfishness that has marred our society in recent years. (I urged the author to change the title, which in my view does not do justice to the complexity—or the humanity—of his analysis). In fact this is quite a different kind of book. Karen's message is basically a healing and cooperative one that recognizes the common stake people have in understanding and being understood. It teaches measures of psychological self-defense for those who are too prone to be victimized; but it makes it clear that a life devoted to intimidation, domination, and competition is a shallow and ultimately unrewarding one.

Spend some time with Georgette, Martin, Jake, Marge, and the other full-blooded human beings who inhabit the pages of this book. Get to know them—their fears, their strengths, the ways they submit and the ways they fight back; and most importantly, the ways in which they learn to reach out to others from a core of self-respect. But please be forewarned; don't pick this book up if you have something important to do tonight and tomorrow.

INTRODUCTION

Interpersonal Politics

THIS BOOK is about the power struggles that take place between the lines of the most ordinary encounters, power struggles to which we are often oblivious even as they occur. It is about the ordinary business meeting, the telephone conversation with a parent, the disagreement about sex or money with a spouse, in which every second seems to writhe with tension and threat. It is about the subtle ways in which we put each other one-down in order to avoid ending up that way ourselves.

This book is also about vulnerability—in terms of the insecurity we feel about ourselves and bring to all our conflicts. It is about the terrible feelings associated with being one-down, the reason for them, how they tentacle their way like poisonous fibres into every corner of our being, and how they can be neutralized and turned into the raw material for growth.

Finally, this book is about change. It is about how to recognize and alter patterns of powerless behavior that invite subjugation, as well as strategic habits by which an unwanted domination is achieved. It is about how to survive with effectiveness and self-respect in a world where others may be obsessed with advantage or caught up in manipulations they do not understand.

One thing this book is not about is how to be a "winner" or to "come out on top." For the goal here is to do something infinitely better—to build relationships that are based on mutual respect.

In the course of defining this goal, a number of questions will be addressed:

What does it mean to have a balance of power between two people, and how can it be achieved?

Why does assertiveness so often fail?

Is it possible to be consistently open and strong?

Is ruthlessness ever justified?

How can you put into practice a vision of transforming your marriage, your company, or any relationship without being seen as a dictator or a dreamer?

How deeply can you reveal yourself to another person; when is it appropriate; and what can you accomplish by it?

Becoming attuned to these issues does not require putting competitive impulses out to pasture or giving up the pursuits and self-interests of a naturally striving life. Rather it means living with a greater awareness of your world as it really is. It means achieving command over interpersonal processes that are otherwise unconscious and out of control. And it means gaining a firmer conviction of your own worth and legitimacy.

About Paul Frisch

This book grows out of my work with the late psychologist Paul Frisch. When he died in 1977 at the age of fifty-one, Frisch had a large practice in Manhattan and Great Neck, Long Island. He had served as the secretary of the American Academy of Psychotherapists, had taught for twenty years in the prestigious psychology department at Adelphi University, and had been chief psychologist at the New Hope Guild Center, an innovative and widely respected clinic for the training of psychotherapists which he had helped to found.

Frisch was acutely sensitive to the microscopic events that go on between the lines of almost every human encounter. No subject was important enough to shake him out of his awareness of the way that subject was being discussed, maneuvered around, or played for advantage. He was an astute observer of interpersonal processes and he applied his observations to the smallest events.

Frisch believed that despite the advances in psychology and sociology in the last century, the social sciences have failed us. For they have skirted their responsibility to take a stand, to provide solutions to real everyday problems, to offer us an understanding of how to live in a world that has lost its traditional values and organization. He believed that our need for guidance goes beyond individual psychotherapy, which only helps a few and, even in those cases, only when distress is already severe. And so, with his wife and frequent collaborator, psychologist Ann Frisch, he began organizing workshops for the general public which he saw as a form of emotional education.

Frisch's main interest had been intimacy and creativity. But in the early seventies he came to see that in our power-obsessed society, where vulnerability is viewed as weakness, open and creative people were at a growing disadvantage. He concluded that an education in the skills and legitimate uses of power should be considered a basic training for modern life. That it was as crucial today as training in etiquette was in another time.

"If people want to be free," he once said, "if they want to grow, if they want to do anything in life that has any consequence above and beyond the routine aspects of everyday living, if they don't understand power their goals will never be realized. The most creative people—in living, in art, in science, in anything—if they don't understand how power works, their creativity will be a monster in their lives. The freedom people yearn for has to begin with an understanding of power. Otherwise, everything is wasted."

Shortly after I finished my own therapy with Frisch, he invited me to join his staff as a workshop leader. A few months before he died, he suggested I write a book about power. Because I've worked with this material so long, it would be impossible to say where Frisch's thought ends and mine begins. But I believe this book is consistent with his essential insights about power and insecurity and their unseen operations in our lives.

The Changing Social Climate

Sixty years ago when a boss ordered his secretary to buy underwear for his wife, it was generally a simple event. She followed his orders because one did not question a boss. She may not have liked the task, she may have felt it beneath her dignity, she may have detected a whiff of sexual innuendo in his tone. But she didn't have to question herself or plan an assertive response or consider a sexual harassment suit. Her mind, like her boss's, could be relatively free of self-doubt, fear, and calculation in these respects. She may have been oppressed, but her oppression was clearly not her fault and not within her power to change. It was written into the social code and shared to some extent by all her colleagues. There was some comfort in that.

Today we are freer but much more confused. We're not sure what it means to be a man or what it means to be a woman. We can't rely on society's conventions to guide or comfort us. The old sense of having a definite place, of knowing what is expected of us and what we have a right to expect from others, has evaporated. In courtship, business, and family affairs, we are on our own, and every moment is up for grabs. Even the social hierarchy is shaky. Authority figures no longer exude the same authority; and underlings have lost much of their meekness. Today, in everything the boss and secretary do or refuse to do, in the very way she accedes to or rejects his demands, precedents are being set and power is being jockeyed for.

Winning and Losing in the Emotional Combat Zone

Power is not necessarily about winning and losing. To define it most neutrally, it is simply the capacity to influence, to have an effect, to bring about desired goals. Parents exert a continuous power over their children, writers influence readers, friends each other. To alter someone's ideas, to sell a product, to criticize effectively, to woo someone in marriage are just a few aspects of the continuous flow of power that characterizes all social life. To partake fully of such power is to feel good, to be noticed, to get respect. Power is an essential nutrient of social living, and no one can survive without it.

And yet in an atmosphere of such uncertainty and instability, people don't assert themselves openly. Instead, they tend to maneuver. In recent years, certainly since the mid-sixties, but even as far back as Dale Carnegie's *How to Win Friends and Influence People* (1936), the importance of interpersonal maneuvers has become more apparent. As this knowledge spread, and as people came to sense that something was happening between the lines that might leave them feeling used or reduced, everyone's grown more antsy about small social encounters that were once taken in stride.

The power struggles we seem to worry about most are only indirectly related to common notions of success or failure. We argue bitterly with a friend who seems unavailable for the friendship. We become tense and hateful in a debate about who did what to whom in bed. We get into a spiteful standoff over small-time company politics. At stake in these battles is not so much who will carry the argument or get his way (although these things can certainly become important). More urgent is who will come out on top emotionally. Who will be under whose thumb. Who will feel like an okay human being and who will feel (there's no better word to describe it) like *shit.*

Although everyone is exposed to this desperate hidden game, not everyone is affected in the same way. Certain aspects of childhood training incline each of us toward the winning or losing position. So that after every incident, some tend to walk away limping and some tend to walk away erect. The limpers are not necessarily weaker or more neurotic people. But the long-range effects of being one-down can be disastrous for their personality and well-being.

Frisch called the top dogs in this system, those who tend to hold the emotional advantage, "subjects," and the bottom dogs, those who tend to hold the bag, "objects." "In almost every family," he once observed, "there is someone who feels like an object and someone who feels like a subject—that is, there is someone whose sense of security is based on someone else's insecurity."

Winning and losing in this emotional combat zone is still poorly understood. And, because of that, it makes us panic. It's like a wild card in human relations. Who's up, who's down? That is the fearful question hidden in one encounter after another. We don't know what the rules are or when we can feel safe. We see naked emperors with new tricks of winning instilling foolish awe. Should we be like them? Should we let them dominate us? Despite ourselves and what we may believe in, we get drawn into senseless games; and we become preoccupied with security, armament, and escape.

Our Fearful Responses to Power

In *Your Erroneous Zones*, one of the most popular self-help books of the seventies, Wayne Dyer wrote that "you make yourself unhappy because of the thoughts that you have," that "your worth is determined by you," that "self-love means accepting yourself as a worthy person because you choose to do so," that you can decide to "make nonacceptance of yourself a thing of the past." He wrote that "you can stand naked in front of the mirror and tell yourself how attractive you are," that "you're too worthy to be upset by someone else," that "people who *need* people are the unluckiest people in the world," that you can be completely free of guilt, free of anger, free of fear. None of this is true.

The mind is a powerful tool but it cannot will away the damage of childhood or the power of others. Nor can it undo the injuries we inflict on ourselves through bad habits and unwise relationships. If you're forty pounds overweight, you're not going to be able to stand naked in front of the mirror and fall in love with your own reflection, especially if you've just eaten a box of cookies for breakfast. By the same token, if your boss, your spouse, and your mother find fault with everything you do and say, so that you go to bed knotted with rage and self-hatred, you will not, because of something you read in a book, suddenly wake up and make nonacceptance of yourself a thing of the past.

The pains and struggles of life deserve more respect than this, and so do the people around us. We all need people and the emotional nourishment only people can give. Dyer's seductive portrait of someone with no erroneous zones—unflappable, above it all, autonomous—revealed a cultural trend. It illustrated our widespread desire to feel once and for all so "okay" that no one can bring us down. This fantasy of invulnerability is one response to the fear of losing and the insecurity of our times.

In recent years we've seen a plethora of programs promising release, each addressing the pressure cooker of winning and losing in its own way.

There are programs that toughen people and help them forget their self-doubts. Such programs may help us succeed at certain tasks, but they also make us less human and more prone to dominate others.

There are programs that concentrate on eternal truths about the unity of all mankind; that encourage self-knowledge, self-acceptance, tolerance, and love. But, because they evade the issue of power, they teach us to remain downtrodden or live an isolated life.

There are programs that show people constructive techniques for influencing one another, but the techniques are useful only as long as both people adhere to certain standards of fair play. As soon as someone pulls a fast one, it's back to business as usual.

The Whole Person Alternative

The problem of winning and losing is deeply rooted in the nature of social life. No simple formula can break it. But it must be penetrated and resisted with the checks and balances of skills and awareness if it is not to dictate the terms of our lives.

We want to be strong, we want to be good, we want to be authentic. And so we need an approach that is able to simultaneously interweave several concerns: the *pragmatic* ("I have to give my secretary orders and I want them to be followed"), the *ethical* ("I don't want to lord it over her or make her feel like two cents)," and the *emotional* ("She really knows how to get under my skin"). In short, we need an orientation toward power and insecurity with which both a sensitive and ambitious person can feel philosophically at home.

To develop this orientation, we will break behavior into its component parts, focusing on key interpersonal skills, with directions for how and when they should (and should not) be used.

Of the four broad areas of behavior we need to master, *strategic power* represents the largest as well as the most misunderstood, seductive, and perilous. It comprises all the indirect forms of influence—from image to defensiveness, from flattery to hidden punishments, from diplomacy to evasion—through which we manipulate, control, and signal each other all day long.

Personal power, equally important and frequently misused, is the simplest form of assertiveness, the ability to talk straight about what we think and feel in a way that reaches inside people and makes them understand.

Creative power is the ability to induce fundamental change in a relationship by bringing the other person along in a fully cooperative and equal effort. Subtle, profound, and largely unnoticed, it is an essential ingredient of leadership.

And finally there is *intimacy,* a process we simultaneously yearn for and fear—and often botch because of our ambivalence. A catalyst for healing, growth, and self-forgiveness, intimacy entails sharing our hidden selves with another person, including our darkest fears, doubts, and self-castigations.

Knowing how and when to use these skills has become especially critical in our complex and anxious world. It is a path toward integrity and mutual respect.

Mutual respect is the opposite of winning and losing. It is based on an understanding that we have influence over one another and a belief that that influence should not be abused. It says, regardless of our differences in station, in prestige, in abilities, in looks, in happiness, and regardless of what I *feel* toward you—dislike, fear, resentment, even disrespect—I desire to treat you fairly and respectfully, not as an object to be exploited.

Obviously, there are many pressures against living this way. We all have feelings of superiority and inferiority and are constantly acting them out. We harbor fears, habits, and unfounded predictions about other people's intentions that invite conflict. And when things get hot enough, we often prefer to do unto others before they can do unto us. But if we become attuned to the microscopic ways in which power operates, if we learn certain techniques of balancing the power, and make certain shifts in our emotional posture, we can become a force for mutual respect in all of our relationships.

How to Use This Book

A hidden question that haunts every book on personal growth is how much can people change without the help of good psychotherapy? The answer depends. Everyone is different and a book can do only so much. I've written this book to provide a roadmap. So that whether you're participating in a structured effort to change or are working through issues on your own, you can have before you a clearer sense of the direction you need to take, as well as the skills and awareness that comprise it.

To illustrate the interpersonal terrain of power and insecurity, I've created fictional characters whose stories I've woven throughout the book. Their struggles won't be identical to your struggles, but they will provide insights that I don't think could be had any other way. The fictional story also helps us around one of the key failings of much of the literature in this field. For instead of offering universal prescriptions that are supposed to serve all people in all situations, we will take into account the psychology and circumstances of each of our characters before making any suggestions for how they might make a change. In that way, I hope to show you how to apply meaningful solutions in your life.

Three segments labeled "The Play" will alternate with three segments labeled "The Replay." The "Play" consists of the story and analysis. Here we play out the entanglements and threats the characters face during a particularly conflict-ridden period in their lives, analyze their unthinking reactions, and explain the hidden causes and implications. In the "Replay", we see how each of them could have handled their troubles differently if they'd had a little more awareness and a little more skill. We then return to "The Play" and pick up the action where it left off.

Your job will be to find yourself in the characters, to see your struggles in theirs, and, through the process of analogy, to apply their lessons to your life. Ideally, you will see portions of yourself in each of the people who populate the book—from the two warring executives, to the office scapegoat, to the mistrustful lovers in bed for the first time, to the vulnerable wife and working mother, Georgette Grodin, who will now begin our story.

I.

THE PLAY

The Unwritten Record of Everyday Life

1.

"A Fat and Ugly Day"

Georgette, Martin, Marge, and Jake get caught up in a series of power struggles—struggles that become linked with inner turmoil and issues of self-worth.

"THE WAY I WAKE UP in the morning has always meant a lot to me. When I was a little girl, I remember waking up on winter weekends in my cold upstairs room, frost on the window and my cat snuggled up by the radiator, not a sound in the house because everyone else was still asleep, and a vast feeling of contentment. For a year or so after college, I often woke up with my ankles and toes anxiously flexing and my mind fixed on an unpleasant incident from the day before. Sometimes, just at those moments, I would recall how it used to be when I was little, and a wave of unhappiness would roll over me—if I couldn't wake up feeling serene, what was life all about? Nowadays I'm too busy to lie in bed and monitor my feelings. Being a mother pretty much takes care of that. But sometimes, especially on weekends or when my daughter Cindy is away, I wake up sad and become filled with remorse for a minute or two, remembering my frosty room and the old comforter and the cat.

"This has been a royal screw of a week. I work for a wealthy politician, a State Assemblywoman named Carmen Peccozzi who's about to announce for Congress. I'm what they call a 'community liaison,' which means I handle a lot of housing complaints and calls from people who were fired, abused, or hung up on by a city agency. For the last several months I've been killing myself to finish a report on the city housing crisis that Carmen needed as a position paper for the Democratic primary. It's the kind of thing you could spend years on. Until a few days ago I was so proud of it I was sure it would get me a promotion. Al, the legislative counsel, told me it was the best thing he'd ever seen on the subject.

"But now, a few words by a snot-nosed kid seem to have changed everything. Steve Friendly, Carmen's new campaign manager, found some typos and legal errors and started making comments, and before you knew it, the whole report was painted black. Somehow all the months, all the work, all the fuckin' *intelligence* of the thing didn't matter any more. All that mattered were those goddamned errors.

"When I finished that report, I felt like a hero. I could see myself triumphantly placing it on Carmen's desk. Then the other day at a staff meeting, she made a sniggering reference to it, and the last drop of good feeling I had about the report seeped out of me. For several months I'd been planning to press for a raise and for an official title. I'd been thinking, this is it, I've found my line of work. But now, if I could dig a hole and bury my report, and Carmen, and that whole stinking assembly district in it, I'd do it.

"The other day, at another meeting, up in Carmen's office, Steve comes up with a brilliant idea. Carmen should make animal welfare a campaign issue, because then the animal lovers will come out of the woodwork and volunteer for the campaign. Now I'm all for spay-neuter clinics and putting diapers on horses in Central Park, but the idea that Carmen is going to win votes during a budget crisis with speeches about stray cats and curbside dogs toilets is the most ridiculous thing I've ever heard—which is what I said at the meeting in a somewhat more diplomatic fashion. Steve turned his head sharply in my direction when I spoke, then turned away again as if bored and waiting for something of consequence to happen. Carmen continued doodling on her pad. Al, who I'm sure agreed with me, didn't say a word.

"Now the fact is, Carmen has a more relaxed relationship with me than with anyone else in that room. She likes to keep me late, to confide in me, to talk woman talk, and all that. I should feel comfortable speaking in those damned meetings. But suddenly all I could think about was that I was hired three years ago as a gal Friday, that I still didn't have a title, that my pay is not much more than her secretary's, that being a mother keeps me from putting in as much overtime as some of the others, overtime supposedly being the measure of one's commitment, and I felt horrible, as if I'd spoken out of turn.

"Yesterday Steve told me that the campaign committee needs to take over the space where I meet with constituents. He says it's essential for the volunteers. Maybe it is essential. I don't know. I feel like a wounded animal hungrily guarding a piece of meat. *But I don't want to give up that space.*

"Well, today is Friday, March second, my thirty-fifth birthday. I'm not going to work. I've called in sick. I'm depressed. Martin won't be around for dinner because Friday's closing night at the magazine, and Cindy's visiting her cousin for the weekend. Which is just as well—I was so horrible to her yesterday, barking, impatient. So my friend Marge and I will be celebrating my birthday this evening. That would be all right, I suppose, except something tells me Marge is not really into it. It's the way she's been acting lately—perpetual man problems, a guy named Chuck this time, I think.

"Sometimes I envy Marge her freedom. Whoever said that you were supposed to spend your life with one other person? Oh, *Martin*. I'm sick at heart about something that happened last night.

Martin came home distant and out of sorts. I could tell he was still doing mental battle with the managing editor, and I know that when he gets that way I should just let him be. But I thought, it's the eve of my thirty-fifth birthday, I'd really like to share that with him, he won't be around tomorrow evening, maybe making love will bring us closer together. But Martin obviously couldn't get out of himself, I didn't come, and when it was over, we were twice as far apart as when we started. It was awful.

"As I said, it's been a royal screw of a week."

Weak and Selfish

The speaker is Georgette Grodin who is having what she calls a "fat and ugly" day. It's a day when she finds it impossible to feel pretty no matter how pretty she is, impossible to feel like a valuable worker no matter how valuable she is, impossible to feel like a good wife and mother no matter how good she is.

Some people listening to her story will see only an irrationally depressed woman who needs to shake herself and get into gear before she hits bottom. Others will see a perfectly reasonable person under an extraordinary array of assaults. But let's avoid any judgment for now and watch instead, as she continues her story, for the ways in which her emotional make-up mixes with interpersonal events to create the crises that are ripping apart her life.

"I like sitting here alone, eating breakfast, looking out the window. I just wish I didn't feel like a loser. At thirty-five you'd think I'd be more clear about who I am and what I'm doing. Cindy is five now. I sometimes wonder if I shouldn't have just stayed a full-time mother and housewife and let it go at that. But about three years ago I got cabin fever. I decided that if I didn't go back to work I would lose my mind. So we became a hypermodern family with two working parents and a housekeeper who takes care of Cindy and makes dinner. I have a lot of regrets about that, a lot of guilt. I know Martin resents that I never cook any more, and in a way I miss it too. When I stay an hour late at the office or when I find myself pre-occupied with Carmen the Great and how to deal with her, I think: This is crazy, you're a mother, you're not thinking about your child! And after this week, I don't know what it's all been for.

"I was in therapy for a short time once, and if there's one thing I learned, it was how quick I am to accuse myself of being selfish. One of my early memories is running into the house after school and grabbing a piece of cake off the table. I was excited to see it because I was hungry and I thought it had been put out for me. My mother went into a fury and accused me of being a selfish little girl, of only caring about my selfish little desires, the usual litany. My mother always had an unpredictable temper (and turning alcoholic after my father died didn't mellow her any). I think she had a diabolical attachment to that word. *Selfish*. She loved the sound of it. And I grew up believing I was selfish—I still believe it!—because that's what she called me whenever I got in her way.

"Believing you're selfish is like believing you're fat. It doesn't matter how much you weigh or what you do. I could be a Trappist monk and I'd still believe I was selfish. It kills me to look back at all the things I've done to keep from seeming selfish. All the times I let friends and dates choose the restaurants and shows, let my boss tell me when to take my vacation. You think you've become assertive and gotten these things out of your system, but they hang on.

"Tonight I'm seeing Marge for dinner, right? I wanted to go to La Jardiniere. We can afford it, and it *is* my birthday. Well, I heard the slightest hesitation in her voice, so I quickly pulled back and agreed to make it 'some French restaurant.' So what does *that* mean? Beefsteak Charlie's probably. But the last thing I was going to do was press for something that might be inconvenient for Marge and leave me feeling like a greedy, acquisitive, *me-me-me* type.

"Or Martin. There was one thing I wanted from him this year. For my thirty-fifth birthday. A fur coat. I've never owned a fur anything.

In fact, I would say among our friends, those who can afford it, fur is considered somewhat rightwing and anti-animal. But we do go out on fancy occasions, and those women wear fur. It's not just status; it's *warm*. But talk about selfish, self-indulgent, middle-class, materialistic! You know, a few weeks ago we were kidding about what I wanted for my big three-five, and putting on a Mata Hari accent, I said, 'Mink, dahling.' Martin smiled and said, 'Yeah, and then a Mercedes for Mother's Day and diamonds for Christmas and you'll be able to hold your head high on Fifty-seventh Street.' I was glad I pretended to be joking.

"But you know what bothers me most about that incident? It was my timidity. What's the big deal about telling Martin I want a coat? The year before we had Cindy, I wanted us to go to Greece for our vacation. Martin ruled it out in his typical high-handed way for various reasons having to do with his job and his aerobic conditioning. He said there were no good tennis courts in Greece! So I said, screw him, I'll go alone. Martin was furious and hurt and couldn't stop trying to bring me around. But I pushed aside my doubts, I went, and I had a terrific time. You should have seen Martin when I came back. Chivalry lived!

"But in the last few years I seem to have lost whatever it was that made me do insane things like that. It could have something to do with being thirty-five and feeling, hey, this is it. I can't run around any more, youth is gone, et cetera, et cetera. My marriage isn't what I want it to be. We've settled into our routines, we make love without passion. It seems to suit Martin, but not me. Also, I'm tired of having to say 'screw him' and prove how strong I am. I want him to give, to devote himself more to our life and less to his job. But as soon as I get into that frame of mind, I run into the reality of Martin's priorities. And then I start to wonder if perhaps he isn't more mature than I am, more able to cope with life as it really is. I lose my spark. I get pessimistic. It's as if a basic weakness is emerging, as if, when you get right down to it, I'm some kind of need machine that can never be satisfied.

"Maybe I'm Crazy"

Power struggles and their ramifications are everywhere in Georgette's story. She's obviously in a fierce battle with Steve Friendly who's both belittled her report and made a play for her work space. She is not able to depend on Al, who appears to be her foremost office ally. Something peculiar is going on with Carmen, who values Georgette enough to depend on her for important work yet keeps her in a lowly position. She is having a problem getting a commitment from Marge. And, from vacation choices to mink coats to their sex life, she's struggling uncomfortably with her husband.

Something happens to Georgette when her needs and desires come into conflict with the needs and desires of others. Suddenly, she torments herself with questions and begins to lose faith. Doubts reach deeper and deeper into her identity, mixing and becoming one with doubts from high school, grade school, and early childhood—stupid things that she thought she'd long ago left behind.

"Well, I've got to get dressed. I'm going to go out and window shop and try to clear my head. You know what depresses me so much about last night with Martin? It's how close I came to faking an orgasm. That I could even think that way . . . But I remember telling myself, Christ, do it, *lie,* what difference will it make? Act as if things are wonderful and maybe they will be. At least I wouldn't have had to feel like such a bringdown. And then apologize. You think I was wrong to apologize? It *was* my fault. I knew he wasn't in the mood. Oh, *yech!*

"Okay, I was going to take stock today; no whining. You'd think if I was so selfish, I'd get my way more often. But it was my dread of being selfish and other unladylike things that ushered in my disgusting timidity in the first place. Whatever the boys wanted, I was willing to be! I had a friend in high school who used to complain that I was not outspoken enough. Those were my demure days. Over the years I became much more opinionated and generally stopped worrying so much about what people thought. In college they said I had a chip on my shoulder. But if you ask me right now, I'd say I'm still missing some basic element. There's a voice inside me that says, you're *weak,* you always *were* weak, you'll always *be* weak.

"What any of this has to do with reality—am I really selfish? am I really weak?—I don't know. All I know is I can't wait to get to Rumpelmayer's and have a croissant with hot chocolate. And they have those nice furry animals there, too!

"God, how do I get in these moods? Maybe I take everything too personally. There's a woman in our office named Beth, and well, alongside Beth I *do not* have a weight problem. A couple of times Beth has confided in me about how lonely she's felt since her husband left her. I said to her once, 'Beth, why have you let yourself get so heavy? You could be so attractive.' She said, 'Georgette, sometimes I'm sitting home alone, it's maybe ten, eleven o'clock. And I think, God, I want a *guy,* what I wouldn't do for a guy, just to be with, just to talk to. And then I think: I want a *cheeseburger*. . . . Hey, I can *have* that.' That's what she said. I really felt for her after that—which has become a problem in a way, because she's been knocking on my door a little too much since then. Anyway, if I don't pull myself together, the two of us are going to be eating cheeseburgers.

"It's not that I'm fat. It's my damned thighs. 'FTs' Martin calls them, 'fat thighs.' I know I eat when I'm down on myself. In fact there are times when a certain kind of thought goes through my mind and then, suddenly, I am famished. Thinking about sex with Martin last night, that alone is worth a small box of cookies.

"Since I've been married, the only times I've felt free from this insanity are those rare moments when Martin's been depressed—like three years ago, just after I got the job with Carmen, when out of the blue they brought someone else in for managing editor. Martin was so distraught about being passed over and about the nasty political scenes that followed that to get him out of it I became virtually everything I ever wanted to be. I made plans for the theater, I cooked magnificent dinners, I lost five pounds without trying, I encouraged Martin and petted him, and never had any problems coming when Martin was capable of making love.

"But when Martin started feeling better, I started feeling worse. I liked Martin when he was a little—I don't know—*subdued*. I remember telling him that he seemed to get colder as things improved at the office. But Martin looked at me askew and asked if there wasn't some connection between my being happy and his being in the pits. Boy that hurt. But maybe it's true. Maybe I'm just afflicted with a pathological need to be needed.

"Do you ever think about suicide? *Well?* That's the bottom line isn't it? Oh, I'll never do it. I have a child. But I do think about it sometimes. Just walking into the ocean and disappearing. Is that normal? It scares me, I have to admit. But when is life going to be free of these fucking moods! I sometimes wonder if it isn't a chemical imbalance. Martin suggested that Lithium might be the answer. Maybe that's what he'll get me for my big three-five!"

Georgette and Martin

Georgette Grodin has a bright sense of humor and a laugh that's blushing and unbuttoned. A top student at Vassar (though somewhat undisciplined), she has a sparkling intelligence that later made her a successful multilingual tour guide at the Metropolitan Museum. That was before Martin and motherhood. Her FTs notwithstanding, Georgette has a soft-edged prettiness that turns the heads of younger men. But what people respond to most is her impetuosity. When called back for a second interview with Carmen three years ago, she forgot Martin's coaching and blurted out as she entered, "I'm so nervous I don't know if I can sit down!" And Carmen, who was about to tell her she had the job, did so with twice the pleasure. When she is on good terms with herself, Georgette is like a girl riding by in a convertible with the top drawn down, waving to the fellows in the street, and ready to give anyone a ride.

She does have problems with power. She is often impetuous when she'd be wiser to calculate. Unless faced with a clear injustice, whereupon her anger can be fierce and efficient, she is slow to defend herself when she needs defending, and the thought of studying situations or people in order to measure advantage or monitor the giving and getting is an anathema to her. She is not good at asking for things. Dissatisfactions, which she may swallow for months or years, sometimes erupt in a way that shock the people around her. And when she gets nailed in a series of unfortunate incidents, as she has in the past two weeks, she agonizes over every innuendo, and her mind works overtime searching herself for flaws.

Except for a buried romanticism, Martin Grodin is very much the opposite of his wife. The national news editor of *Today*, the flagship magazine of a publishing conglomerate, he is, at 42, crisp, creased, and dynamic with an easy smile and grace that other men admire. Fiercely focused on his goals, he looks and feels as if no situation could ruffle him. He takes no chances with his appearance or his choice of words. He has a lot of energy and is always moving, managing to fit tennis twice a week and squash on Sundays into an already over-stuffed schedule. If a little question of doubt sprouts in him, whispering that he may after all have an Achilles heel, he turns from it with redoubled vigor, like a child stealing out of a haunted house and back into the daylit ruckus of reality.

Anyone who's spent time trying to say or do something in a safe way will understand what it means that Martin has made a science of it. He knows what will make him look good, what will break the stride of someone he perceives as a threat, how to get someone to offer what would be iffy for him to request, and how to appeal to individuals and groups without their knowing that he's appealing to them. He is so shrewd at perceiving prejudice and so subtle at playing to it that if all the compliments he's received were put end to end, they would circle the globe twice and describe the second coming.

Martin loves Georgette's fiery opinions, her natural way with Cindy, her bursts of laughter, so full of delight, now aimed at herself, now aimed at him. But she does nothing by halves, and when she starts showing signs of depression and overeating, as she has for two solid weeks now, he finds her intolerable. He would like to help her, but he feels impotent in the face of her overflowing discontent. Meanwhile, her moping and grousing threaten his equilibrium, an equilibrium he finds essential to smooth functioning in a high-pressured job.

On the whole, Martin's family feelings are waning these days, for Cindy, too, is beginning to get on his nerves. She strikes him as overly dependent on her mother, and she persists in certain distasteful habits. She won't wipe her nose. She has horrid table manners. She plays with herself.

Recently an old Harvard acquaintance of Martin's, who last fall was elected Lieutenant Governor of Connecticut, paid the Grodins a brief Sunday visit. Martin found himself inexplicably anxious about the impression he was making, and he was irritated with himself for that. Cindy, meanwhile, was displaying her usual ebullience—interrupting, mugging, asking a thousand questions. When told to be quiet, she wandered off to the foyer where she could be seen sniffing the Lieutenant Governor's gloves. Martin reprimanded her sharply and felt bad about it later.

Martin would like to be more tolerant. He tells himself he's too uptight. But, unlike Georgette, Martin's idea of change is not to torment himself with questions but to alter the conditions of his life. He sees women—stunning, intelligent, even famous women—attracted to him on the street, in the office, at cocktail parties, and he wonders about the necessity of his domestic anguish. He suspects that his problems might abate if Georgette took tranquilizers or if his daughter went to a therapist. But although his domestic dissatisfactions are threatening to poke a leak in the stable ship of his self-confidence, at the moment he has more pressing things on his mind.

Martin and Jake

Three years ago Martin's power base at *Today* seemed to evaporate when the founder and publisher died, leaving his son, Ed Roland, in charge. The young Roland was promptly faced with the duty of naming a new managing editor. Going against the wishes of his father, whose preference for Martin was well-known, Roland hired Jake

Donohue, a Pulitzer Prize-winning author and a senior editor at *The Washington Post*. Jake was a friend and at one time something of a mentor to the young publisher. He represented a chance for Roland to start fresh and put his own imprint on the business. Roland was also excited by Jake's proposal for editorial changes, which Jake insisted that Roland agree to before Jake would accept the job. Still, Roland was nervous about having bypassed Grodin, fearful of losing him, and uneasy about having violated his father's wishes.

Despite Roland's reassurances, Martin interpreted Roland's decision as a rejection and a humiliation. For a time he was not his old self. He mulled over offers from the *Times*, humbly made the rounds of old connections, and obsessed about the secret satisfaction the turn of events must have given several of his peers on the staff. He regretted every past snub, every little arrogance, every missed opportunity to demonstrate what a regular guy he was. He swore a thousand times he would never again depend on one man for so important a goal. And slowly, imperceptibly, he succeeded in attracting key executives to his camp and re-establishing his position as first among the senior editors.

Martin was never in as much trouble as he imagined. Indeed, if any of his rivals were inclined to see an advantage in his momentary predicament, they soon learned otherwise. For Martin is a good defensive player, and even at slightly diminished strength, he remained a sophisticated operator who could dunk a man into confusion and self-doubt while flattering or appearing to be helpful.

Now Martin's patience seems to be paying off, for in the last few months, Jake's editorial reforms have been causing him trouble. Conflicts have arisen that Jake has not handled well; he's experienced a sharp drop in self-confidence, and Roland has begun to fear that his former hero is a managerial milquetoast. Martin can feel the advantage moving in his direction.

On the surface, Martin has been on excellent terms with Jake, but Jake is aware of the threat that spices Martin's apparent good will, and on several occasions he's found himself having to dodge Martin's sarcasm. Recently Martin has begun to question the wisdom of Jake's policy of allowing reporters and writers greater editorial leeway, a policy which Martin, with Roland's backing, has yet to implement in the national news section. Martin's stalling tactics have been emotionally costly to Jake, and they have become a political problem, too. Many of the staff members are beginning to see Martin as Jake's imminent replacement.

"What a birthday present that would be," Martin thinks, as he enters the office building, smiling at the thought of embarrassing Jake (and overestimating his wife's interest in his maneuvers). His good instincts tell him that Jake will not be prepared for the upcoming meeting, and that one more bit of faltering on Jake's part will constitute a turning point.

"They're stunned that I've come in early," Martin notes as he watches the other editors cross the oak threshold. While feigning indifference, he examines the other men's faces and reads their thoughts: Martin Grodin, Mr. Smooth, Mr. Powerful, never early, never waiting. He's *early*. What kind of maneuver is this?

Martin smiles his mild, unrevealing smile and nods his perfect little nod, that nod being one of his devastating assets, the subject of worshipful observation by some of the younger men. Two of them have even practiced the nod in front of their bathroom mirrors. These two now watch the meeting gather, freed by their junior status from the intensity of the maneuvers about to take place.

In reaction to Martin's uncharacteristic punctuality, Jake, fifty-three years old, trim and stylish, but with a soft, round face, asks, somewhat nervously, "What's up, Martin?" and instantly regrets the question. He's gradually come to fear and dislike Martin. He's distressed by Martin's cozy relationship with the publisher and his seemingly invulnerable position as Heir Apparent. He feels stupid and weak for having made him the center of attention.

"Didn't you get the *agenda,* Jake?" Martin needles. Jake feels the giddy touch of panic. He's being drawn into something he's not going to win. Of course I got the agenda! I *wrote* the damn agenda! Why do I set myself up for him? Why did I stop taking tranquilizers before these damned meetings?

The two young editors wait for Jake's response. He's one of the most talented newsmen in the country, and he's always been generous with them. For once they'd like to see the nice guy finish first, but they are not optimistic.

Jake chuckles. Twelve men, Roland included, are now in the room watching Martin toy with him. He dreads exposing the fear he's experiencing. The key thing is not to *sound* upset. "I guess you can never tell what's going to happen when Martin Grodin arrives early," he says with a grin. The delivery was okay, Jake tells himself. Adequate. He looks at Martin to judge the response. He knows he shouldn't look, but his eyes have a mind of their own. He prays Martin will respond defensively.

Jake's stab is aimed at a tender target. If Jake could make an issue of Martin's strategy of carefully timing his entry into editorial meetings, he could make Martin squirm. But Martin knows that Jake will not pursue it, and so he now experiences only the slightest sense of threat.

Martin carefully lifts his arm and adjusts his glasses with a gentle touch to the rim. He then lowers his hand and turns his wrist to check the time. He measures his words: "This meeting *is* supposed to begin at eleven, isn't it, Jake?"

Jake's first impulse is to continue the repartee with a joke about Martin's habit of arriving at five or ten after, but Martin's serious tone seems to rule it out. The last thing he needs now is to sound juvenile. It occurs to him that he has already begun to sound juvenile—smiling broadly and bantering about what time a senior editor arrives at meetings. An image of himself as a silly man who laughs and drinks too much and plays anybody's fool flits through Jake's mind. He feels the heat rising in his body and looks furtively at Roland. He's afraid that any minute he'll say something that will reveal how important this exchange is to him. He imagines everyone looking at him curiously, or, worse, carrying him out kicking and howling accusations, as Martin watches, pretending to be confused, confidently waiting to take his job.

"Oh, right, eleven it is," Jake concedes, as good-naturedly as he can manage it. The five-sentence exchange has left him a temporarily defeated man. For the rest of the meeting he silently plays back his last sentence, trying to believe it did not sound as inane and laden with surrender as he knows it did.

Later, he wonders if the bad start accounted for the ease with which Martin succeeded in wringing a commitment from Roland to indefinitely postpone one of Jake's goals, the use of bylines in national and international news. It was an embarrassing turn of events, not yet fatal perhaps, but symbolically very bad. Jake has a drink before bed and barks at his wife when she protests. Sitting guiltily before the TV, he wonders whether he was cut out to be a managing editor, whether he should go back to Valium, whether he should retire and write books.

Martin, meanwhile, having just finished putting the national news to bed, is about to leave the office. He touches the rims of his glasses much as he touched them during the meeting and looks down at the traffic crawling across the Brooklyn Bridge. He savors his elegant moves from the meeting this morning. He loves moments like these; they are, he believes, his special state of grace.

Georgette and Marge

Home from her tour of Bendel's, Bergdorf's, and Bloomingdale's, Georgette has finally abandoned the hope that Marge will call to make plans for tonight and decides to make the call herself.

"Hello, Marge?" she says lightly, "are we on for tonight?"

"Oh, yes, yes," says Marge vacantly. "Uh, let me call you back in a few minutes, though—I just want to make sure we don't have any late meetings here tonight."

Downhearted by Marge's apparent lack of interest in her birthday, Georgette begins talking to herself. I'm just too sensitive. I know Marge cares about me. I shouldn't take this personally. If I tell her I'm upset, she'll just get defensive, we'll both become self-conscious, and the evening will be ruined. Besides, I'm not thinking about Marge. If I were a busy attorney instead of a glorified gal Friday, I might have some idea what real pressure is all about. But just the same, if I were a busy attorney and it was *my best friend's birthday?* Well, maybe that's why I'm not a busy attorney.

Marge calls back a half hour later. She sounds breathless but cheery. "Hi, George, what do you say we meet down here for a bite at Enrico's around seven-thirty? By the time these bigshots finish working me over, I'll be too wiped out for the trek uptown."

"But Marge, we talked about doing something a little more classy, remember? One of the French restaurants."

Marge's voice takes on a familiar, chiding quality that Georgette fears: "Oh, come on George, stop being so rigid. If you didn't think so much about food, you'd be able to move a little faster on the tennis court! Come on, the ride'll do you good. I'll see you at seven-thirty. Right?"

On Saturday morning, thirty-five plus one, Georgette wakes up the way she used to in college, her ankles churning. She remembers coming home depressed after dinner with Marge, finding Martin waiting for her with a big happy birthday hug, his present of two exquisite porcelain vases, his eager story about his editorial board victory, and his boyish disappointment when all this failed to more than momentarily raise her spirits.

Then she remembers dinner. She had felt so frumpy, so lifeless, while Marge was full of energy and élan. Her resolution to push aside the week, with its hurts and humiliations, and try to gain perspective vanished. "Gal Friday!" "Fat Thighs!" "Thin-skinned!" were resounding through her being like stampeding buffalo, while Marge talked about an important case she was working on and glanced at the men at nearby tables.

Not wanting Martin to see what a mess she's in or to give him any ammunition against Marge, Georgette says, "You go ahead to breakfast without me, honey. I think I'll sleep in a while."

Disgusted by her lifelessness and the phrase "sleep in," which has always rubbed him the wrong way, Martin feels fed up with trying to please her and flings one of his sarcastic jabs: "Exhausted from your evening out with the girls?" Wounded, shrinking into the pillows, Georgette stares at him in hurt silence.

"Oh, don't get that way, I was only joking," he says in a voice that teeters between appeasement and annoyance. "I just think we'd all be a lot happier, Cindy included, if you weren't so absorbed in yourself all the time."

Georgette turns her head to the wall and silently cries. Martin mutters, "To hell with this," and walks out, his mind tuned to his plans for the day.

2.

The Cries and Whispers of Shame

Understanding self-doubt and self-hatred—the hidden vulnerabilities, sometimes dormant, sometimes inflamed, that fuel all our power struggles and make them so distressing.

EVERYONE SUFFERS from negative feelings about the self. Millions seek some form of knowledge, love, applause, or therapeutic assistance to help expiate any question of inadequacy. But the essence of all this suffering is poorly understood.

If I ask you, "What are you ashamed of?" meaning what qualities of your circumstances or being, real or imagined, do you fear having exposed, qualities that bring forth painful feelings of shrinking self-worth, you may be hard-pressed to answer. You may be ashamed that at twenty-eight you're still living with your parents, that at thirty-eight you're still single, that at forty-eight you're not the success you once expected to be, that at fifty-eight you don't have a good relationship with your grown children, that at sixty-eight you're idle and unproductive. And yet the feeling of shame can be so anguishing you may deny its very existence.

We all have implanted within us troublesome voices—"pockets of shame"—which are like question marks or weak spots in our identity. The most painful and ingrained of these hateful self-concepts are usually the oldest, originating in childhood: "Stupid!" "Clumsy!" "Unwanted!" Although some people are more burdened with shame than others, prod deeply enough into anyone's emotional landscape and you're likely to awaken a whole gaggle of self-denouncing demons.

Often, such feelings of unworthiness are tied up with our most important roles—"Bad Mother!" "Weak Boss!" "Failed Husband!" "Thankless Child!" Many are linked to our physical selves—"Fat!" "Flatchested!" "Ugly!" "Crippled!" "Bald!" Still others can result from membership in a demeaned group—"Nigger!" "Female!" "Faggot!" All told, they form a hidden archipelago of the psyche where one aspect or another of our circumstances, physical traits, origins, or character can be suddenly spotlighted like a terrible stigma we alone possess.

On the surface there often seems no logic to the things that people feel ashamed of. They are ashamed of being very large or very small ("Amazon!" "Shrimpboat!" "Freak!"), of being intelligent ("Egghead!" "Brain!") of having big appetites ("Pig!"). They are ashamed of being sexy ("Cheap!" "Shallow!" "Animal!"), good-looking ("Pretty Boy!" "Dumb Blond!"), creative ("Dreamer!"). They are ashamed of being different in any way—even if their difference is their ticket to immortality. For they've been made to feel that there's something wrong with them, that they don't belong; and to not belong is one of the great agonies of any social being.

Georgette is ashamed of being "Selfish!" and "Weak!" Those self-denunciations are like ancient, unhealed wounds that she manages to live with much of the time without great discomfort. But when the wounds become inflamed, the accusing voices pierce her identity. Various personal crises can activate her feelings of shame, but nothing makes them surface faster than tension between herself and the people with whom she is close.

One minute Georgette is in bed with Martin, hoping that sex will revive their attachment. But after some awkward glances and false caresses, she wonders whether she was truly acting out of a desire to improve the relationship or whether she has been dishonest and manipulative, was really only thinking of herself, and was acting out of nothing but her bottomless pit of hunger. A pocket of shame has erupted.

One minute Jake is chairing an editorial meeting and, as always, finding the right words to put people at their ease. Suddenly he's involved in a threatening exchange with Martin, and an inner voice whispers that he has no balls and that all his sociable chatter is nothing but a craven attempt to suck up to everyone, even his enemies. A pocket of shame has erupted.

In these cases there happens to be a sliver of truth to the accusations Georgette and Jake level against themselves, but the accusations are exaggerated, incomplete, ferociously unsympathetic, and carry the implication that no proper human being could be so deformed.

If an inflammation of shame is not checked, it tends to swell, putting more and more of one's identity into question. Georgette, feeling inadequate as a wife because of a "pathological need to be needed," may turn to her happy relationship with her daughter for some reassurance of her worth. But a voice whispers, "Of course you're happy with Cindy, you've made her totally dependent on you," and the smile fades from her lips.

As the affliction spreads, it shows itself in one's speech, in one's eyes, in one's bearing. Other people sense it, get sucked in, exploit it. Now a cab driver, bank teller, or stranger in the street may enter one's life in a painful way.

The Damaging Messages of Childhood

Pockets of shame are not dealt out in a fair or equal manner. Some parents are more shame-instilling than others, and the children of such parents may struggle all their lives against the negative self-concepts developed when they were young. Society itself has prejudices, abuses, and class dominations, which result in the stigmatizing of certain qualities and the creation of ethnic scapegoats.

But, in fact, no one comes through childhood feeling perfectly whole and uncompromised. Shame is a powerful tool for training and controlling children, and all parents abuse it to some degree—with the result that their own hang-ups get translated into feelings of defectiveness in their children. Because Georgette's mother felt guilty whenever she said no, Georgette was made to feel ashamed of being selfish, a taker. Because Jake's parents could not tolerate conflict, Jake was made to feel as if a horrible ooze was seeping from him if he ever lashed out in his own defense. Because Marge's mother felt trapped by her responsibilities, Marge was made to feel ashamed of being needy. Because Martin's parents were uneasy in the presence of emotion, Martin was made to feel ashamed of spontaneity; and, to this day, any feeling that shows on him is likely to remind him that in some fundamental way he is unclean.

All these issues come powerfully into play when these people deal with each other in adult life.

Tangled Up in Doubt

Ideally, as adults, we should struggle to face our negative self-concepts and come to terms with them. But because shame is so painful, most of us organize our lives to avoid knowing it. The lucky ones seem to manage their ignorance with relative ease. But most of us live in various states of flight and anxiety.

Georgette has struggled. She has tried to see the truth and to grow. Her efforts have given her more self-knowledge than Martin, Carmen, or Marge, but the price seems to be that she is forever poised on the brink of defeat while they seem confident, content, and well-adjusted.

Is it any wonder she sometimes wishes she could turn off her mind and become a happy idiot?

Because she doesn't understand the dynamics of self-doubt, Georgette's inward search often makes her feel as if she is wandering through an endless maze. Her shame over being selfish seems unaffected by reason. When provoked—because of extra working hours away from Cindy or revealing a desire for a fur coat—it leaves her feeling ugly, defenseless, and powerless to master it.

She can avoid this inner accuser by resolving always to be helpful and agreeable, but that will cause another hateful voice elsewhere in the archipelago to squawk that she is not being aggressive enough, that she gives in too easily, that she is "Weak!" If she sits down with both accusers and tries to work out the truth, marshals everything she's learned from experience and self-analysis, she may only find herself deeper in troubled waters, surrounded by more and more of the old voices. They seem to multiply, divide, bring in brothers and cousins until she retreats in exhaustion and despair, fears her life is no good, and is finally consumed by the single primal issue, "Misfit!" She then fantasizes about walking into the ocean and eats cookies for an entire afternoon to kill the pain.

Throughout the struggle she never grasps the true nature of what she's up against, why at this moment she's vulnerable to such an assault, or how the surliness of a campaign manager or a quip about a fur coat could have triggered the whole thing off.

3.

The Hidden Chemistry of Power

How winning and losing works: The meaning of "playing for advantage" and how it is linked to self-doubt. The covert use of punishment. The significance of giving and getting. The difference between top dogs and bottom.

STEVE FRIENDLY, standing in mid-office, waves Georgette's report in the air, and makes a disparaging comment for all to hear. He tries to commandeer Georgette's work space for his volunteers. Marge brushes off Georgette's wish to eat at La Jardiniere and chides her, when she protests, for caring so much about food. Martin dismisses Georgette's request for a certain birthday present with a joke. He makes a snotty comment about her being exhausted. He implies that their daughter would be happier if Georgette were less self-absorbed.

Is Georgette being mistreated? Or is this the normal give and take? Did these events cause her recent depression? Or has her depression made every little pinprick appear to be a mortal attack? Is she going through what anyone might under the circumstances? Or is she excessively vulnerable?

In short, what are the dynamics by which powerlessness has overtaken her?

From Georgette's point of view, people like Martin, Carmen, Steve, and Marge seem surrounded by an aura of invulnerability. It is not so much that they *do* certain things, but that they are better constructed for the rough and tumble of the way life actually is, that they are not afflicted with lily-livered hesitations or hung up with self-doubts.

If we look at her fleeting encounter with Martin over whether he should buy her a mink for her birthday, we can sense how this concept of invulnerability is enforced. Georgette made a weak and self-effacing request, Martin fired a single volley, Georgette promptly retreated, and nothing more was said. But let's examine their relative positions more closely.

Shame: The Hidden Ingredient

Clearly, if Georgette is ashamed of her desire for a fur coat, she is going to present a weaker case and buckle under more quickly. But the situation is more complex than that. It is not just a question of whether she feels some self-doubt about wanting a mink; it is also a question of whether she reveals that doubt to Martin.

If Georgette makes wanting the coat seem the most natural thing in the world, the essence of healthy desire, something interesting happens. Martin's conviction weakens. He being to wonder about his motives. A voice breaks into his consciousness, suggesting that the real problem is not that he objects to killing little animals or that he believes mink is garish and wasteful, but that he is tight-fisted; or that he doesn't really love Georgette the way a good husband should; or that he's just plain unwilling to give. In short, that he is "Cheap!" "Fickle!" "Unloving!" and not a worthy husband. And so it turns out that both have elements of self-doubt just beneath the surface.

But take it a step further. Suppose that instead of being direct and pleasantly confident in her request, Georgette becomes manipulative, hints at the general inferior quality of Martin's gifts over the years, mentions that Marge Bernstein and her other good friends were all surprised when they found out that Martin had never bought her a fur coat. Then his inner doubts may begin to whir like sirens; he may feel his position slipping from under him and either abandon it in panic or escalate the conflict with shouts and overt accusations.

If the balance of power is such that the struggle lasts for more than a few seconds, they will each have time to marshal arguments in an effort to establish some universal right or wrong. Georgette may argue that it is scandalous for a successful man to refuse to buy his wife one measly mink when most of his colleagues have by now bought their wives much more. But the fact remains: Why should anyone give a present he doesn't want to give? Martin may insist that mink-farming is cruel, that fur is frivolous, that such self-indulgence is obscene in a world where people are starving. But considering the apartment they live in, the car they drive, the prevalence in their lives of meat and leather, his argument is clearly self-serving.

The real issue in this struggle is not whether a husband who makes fifty, seventy, or ninety thousand a year should buy his wife a fur coat in a world where other people have no food, but deeply personal feelings about money, giving and getting, respect, past hurts, and associated issues of shame, self-doubt, and inequality.

Neither Martin nor Georgette can be one hundred percent certain of the legitimacy of their own positions. This is true of all interpersonal conflict. They may argue forcefully, but inside lurk treacherous questions. Why am I really saying this? What am I afraid of? Am I the problem? Barring an open discussion of such questions, each attacks the other's weaknesses, trying to undermine his opponent by activating his self-doubts.

In the end, their struggle will be settled strictly on the basis of who caves in from an intolerable assault of shame and who is able, through between-the-lines exertions of power, to hide or suppress his own self-doubts while inflaming those of his opponent. This is the hidden chemistry of winning and losing. And this is the talent that distinguishes many seemingly indomitable people and gives them the aura of "winners."

In every interpersonal struggle like this, shame and the maneuvers around it are the secret ingredients that determine who will win and who will lose. In the struggle over the fur coat, Martin was able to ignite Georgette's self-doubt with a single sentence and wrap his attack in a smile. As a result, both he and Georgette believed not that he exploited her shame, but that he was essentially *right*, that it's obscene to own a mink, and that she is self-indulgent for wanting one. Although Georgette spent the rest of the day depressed, she never thought to blame him for it.

When we focus on the link between winning and self-doubt, upon who's playing for advantage and who's exploiting whose self-doubts, our normal pre-occupations change. Although women's rights, animal rights, or the rights of a giver to give the gift of his choice are important issues in other contexts, here they are just tools in a game of tag. It is a game in which the person who becomes "it" is afflicted with a crippling strain of powerlessness.

The Hidden Power of Punishment

When we examine the specific words and actions that yield a winning position, we find a seemingly interminable variety of strategic maneuvers involving image, innuendo, threats, silences, dissembling, and evasion. Marge's exuberance about her work, her eye-contact with the men at the other tables, Martin's attempt to sound sympathetic when he is actually annoyed, his imperiousness regarding vacation choices—all these poses and tactics are cut from the same strategic cloth.

But the single strategy that most quickly arouses shame and lies at the heart of winning and losing is punishment. In our story thus far we've seen innumerable examples of punishment. Guilt: "You selfish little girl!" Hostile criticism: "Oh, come on, George, stop being so rigid." Derisive innuendo: "This meeting *is* supposed to begin at eleven, isn't it, Jake?" And, of course, Martin's brutal "To hell with this," as he marches out of the house on Sunday morning.

But punishments are often not so apparent until we look at the emotional consequences. Carmen doodles silently when Georgette finishes speaking about the animal welfare legislation. Suddenly, Georgette remembers her low status in the office and feels ashamed, "as if I'd spoken out of turn." Marge fails to call about Georgette's birthday, she is evasive on the phone, and her tone is impatient. Suddenly, Georgette is attacking herself for being too sensitive. Martin implies that Georgette can only be happy when he's in the pits. Suddenly, her self-worth plunges and she wonders if she doesn't have a "pathological need to be needed." In each case a subtle punishment has been deployed.

Whenever punishment is used, it tends to be both safer and more damaging the more disguised it is. For punishment works most devastatingly in the dark, where the punisher can slip quietly out of the equation and the punishment can cut inward, unhampered by the victim's conscious scrutiny.

Martin, threatened by Georgette's closeness with Marge, finds himself irritated by Marge's energetic feminism. He doesn't become angry and say, "You irritate me, bitch!" That may be devastating, but it's too open, too prone to lead to an examination of Martin and his hang-ups rather than Marge and hers. Instead, he tries to undermine Marge without appearing to do so. He may use coolness, humor, some "helpful" criticism. He may use the strategy of isolation, implying that her feminist touchiness is irritating others besides himself. He may tell a pointed story.

"Why do you tell that story?" she says if she's really on the ball. "Oh, it just popped into my mind," says Martin, dodging her question. And if they are normally frank with each other, the dodging, too, is a punishment, perhaps the harshest of all. But he still hasn't reached the limits of subtlety, for a mocking smile or the dart of an eyebrow ("Uptight, Marge?") can make stiletto cuts that are so fine, that leave her so slightly compromised, she hardly knows whether anything really happened or a little breeze of insecurity just happened to flutter by.

Martin isn't fully conscious of his intention to hurt. An intuitive strategist, he plays to win simply by acting according to long-established, semiconscious routines. Whenever he's fearful, impatient, displeased, or angry, he unthinkingly reaches for some subtle punishment to bolster himself and undermine whomever is in his way. The effect is always to arouse shame.

Martin can make Georgette feel defective for not getting off on him sexually, for smiling a certain way, or not smiling that way, because of what such actions imply about her character. And if he does this (supposedly) on behalf of her intellect, her health, or her emotional growth; or if he does it "by accident," unaware that she was "so sensitive" in these matters; or if he was "only making a joke" or "blowing off steam," the knife he thrusts into her self-worth may be completely camouflaged, and she may be forced to conclude that her pain is the result of nothing more than her own inadequacies.

Because losing has such a high price tag, most of us invest more heavily than we know in the hidden game of tag, struggling to hold the high ground, with little thought to the kind of life that game implies. All Martin knows when Georgette starts talking about a fur coat is that he feels anxious and he wants the anxiety to go away. He reaches for some means of control, and the chemistry of the moment tells him he can have control through the expediency of a dismissive quip. Seen from this perspective, Martin is simply doing more skillfully and consistently what we all at times attempt.

The Agony of the Object

When Georgette is shoved into her shame, she *feels* like an object—a worthless rejected thing. An old wound has been inflamed and needs to heal. But if she tends to become an object on a regular basis, so that her pockets of shame are repeatedly inflamed and the self-castigation goes on unabated, the healing process cannot take hold, and no amount of inner strength will prevent long-range emotional damage.

The object condition is maintained not only by punishment; it works through withholding, as well. For whether it's measured in time, caring, respectfulness, or a willingness to compromise, the object invariably gives more. Georgette gives of herself fully to Carmen but is unable to get a fair return in the way of a proper title and salary. She is a devoted friend to Marge and yet finds Marge strangely inaccessible on her birthday. Even Martin's resistance to buying the fur coat reflects this inequality. For he is saying, in effect, I don't value you enough to give you what you want.

None of which is to say that Martin doesn't give to Georgette. Love, cooperation, even mutual respect still exist between them. But the marriage is structured to suit his needs, and in various hidden ways, his identity is nourished and prevails, while hers remains ill at ease and doubtful. From the moment, early in their relationship, when the seesaw tipped in Martin's favor, Martin began to relax his self-doubts and feel that he was an all 'round okay guy, while the painful questions began rolling toward Georgette. In the process, her energy, will, momentum, and health were all subtly sapped.

Why does she put up with it? Why does she keep ending up on the bottom? Because regardless of her strategic efforts, she returns to the place she was trained to accept as a child.

This is not to say that most of us haven't played both roles: A person may be a subject with women and an object with men, or vice versa. Marge is usually a subject with lambs and an object with bullies. But, generally, we follow the paths of our training. And for Georgette, in most cases, the path, slowly, imperceptibly, draws her downward.

Anyone can become an object for a moment, an hour, or a day as a result of walking unexpectedly into someone else's whirring blades. But when a full-blown subject-object relationship comes into being, we have to assume that both people are responsible for what they've created. Georgette may hate being oppressed, but no one could oppress her—not on a regular basis—if she were not somehow cooperating. The cooperation displays itself in little ways that seem to say, "I am a second-class citizen and it's okay if you treat me that way."

The Logic of Being on Top

Being a subject has many advantages. Master the techniques of winning, and people will laugh at your bad jokes, approve of your stupidest ideas, and give you the impression that your most embarrassing qualities are charming. Martin has pockets of shame that, if fully activated, would light up the World Trade Center. But because of his training to win and his expertise with power, he could say with near honesty that in his case shame does not exist.

Being one-up, of course, is only a mask for the subject's shaky identity. People do not put others one-down unless they are threatened, self-doubting, and feel somewhat impotent themselves. And although Martin's life is in many ways more comfortable than Georgette's, there are costs. He has to be willing, when the occasion demands, to cut himself off from his feelings, to ignore moral qualms, to turn his back on whatever doesn't go his way. That process alienates him terribly from himself and others.

For all his power, Martin never knows whether he's truly respected or whether his words carry weight because he's feared. He's terrified to look inward and know who he really is. And he is incapable of speaking honestly about what he feels or thinks, because to do so leaves him paralyzed by feelings of nakedness and fear. He's superficially very secure in his relations with others, but emotionally he's very alone. He's a prisoner of his winning moves.

Martin loves Georgette, but his love sometimes conflicts with his need to dominate. Whenever Georgette arouses feelings in him he does not want to experience or expose, he automatically puts love and consideration on hold and moves to gain security. Intuitively, he knows that if he can make Georgette the problem, prove that she is neurotic, keep her feeling inferior, he will not have to face his own feelings of inadequacy.

On Thursday night, Georgette and Martin made love with profoundly unsatisfying results. Afterwards, both experienced the impinging voices of shame whispering painful thoughts about their sexual and marital inadequacies. As Georgette lay there, upset with herself for having initiated sex at such a time and secretly hoping for reassurance, Martin moved strategically to push his self-doubt beneath the conscious membrane:

Martin: "How was it?" *(I'm terrified that I'm not a good lover.)*

Georgette: "Fine." *(I'm ashamed to admit I need more.)*

Martin: "You don't *sound* fine." *(You're ruining it again, Georgette.)*

Georgette: "I'm sorry." *(I hate myself.)*

As Georgette nestled into Martin's arm and as Martin set his jaw, angered over what he had to put up with, their subject-object tendencies were now fully in place.

4.

Looking Out for Number Two

How the fear of being a destroyer causes Jake to back off when he needs to take control. Trigger-happiness vs. powerphobia.

ON SUNDAY MORNING Jake Donohue puts on a tie and an old corduroy jacket and drives his wife into Manhattan where she will spend the morning with a friend. He then picks up a *Times*, buzzes over to an old working class diner in Chelsea he used to haunt as a young reporter, and sits down at the counter for a leisurely breakfast.

There's something aggressive about the way the husky short-order cook shoves outgoing coffees into Jake's counter space, but Jakes does his best to ignore the matter until the young cook sets a wet container right on his *New York Times*. Boy, this is not my week, Jake thinks, still unsettled from the editorial meeting Friday morning and the bedtime battle with his wife. He glances about, notices the crowd is sparse. I can hardly be taking up too much space—why does this hothead have it in for me? The only difference Jake notes between himself and the other early birds is his jacket and tie. Does he hate me because I'm wearing a tie?

Jake takes the container off his paper and moves it a few inches down the counter. But a moment later the belligerent cook challenges him with another container in the same spot. The cook's eyes flicker angrily, and Jake responds angrily: "You don't have to put it down on my paper!" "Yes I do!" the cook snorts, slapping it back on the opened page. "No, you don't," Jake says, shoving it away again, trembling with rage.

The man glowers and barks that this is a place to eat not read but stops short of launching another attack on Jake's *Times*. Jake looks away, pretending to be unaffected, but his stomach is constricted and he can no longer eat or read. As he stares through his newspaper, he has to fight off feeling degraded and wanting to kill.

The Powerphobic's Dilemma

Jake has managed to avoid being either a subject or an object most of his life. Through deft maneuvers he's usually able to maintain a sense of equality between himself and others even when the pressure to do otherwise is intense. He expends considerable energy deflecting winning moves and carefully refuses invitations to play the oppressor.

Faced with a dangerous, loaded question, Jake has been known to respond with cunningly evasive humor that makes an ally of his opponent. If he notices someone asking a question and not getting an answer, he feigns interest himself and supplies the missing response. If a young reporter puts his foot in his mouth at an editorial meeting, Jake will gently redirect the conversation to prevent a potential humiliation. Without knowing why, people feel safe and motivated around Jake.

Unfortunately, Jake is sometimes better at protecting others than he is at protecting himself. Some of the people who have been rescued by Jake feel little sense of gratitude or loyalty, because they are too insensitive to recognize what he's given to them. And it would never occur to Jake to point it out, for it would embarrass him to put them on the spot that way. This is just one element of Jake's powerphobia.

Until he took the job at *Today*, Jake had avoided the very top managerial positions in his field, despite several opportunities. His wife had always insisted that he should be in a leadership role. But Jake protested that a managing editor's job would give him no time to work on his own projects. He would be an overseer, giving orders. Nevertheless, Jake had frequent daydreams about being in control at the *Post*, or, before that, at *Newsday*. In his heart of hearts that was the role he wanted. But there was something forbidding about it, something he couldn't identify and preferred not to think about.

By the time Roland approached him, the issue had been stewing for years, contributing to Jake's small but steady drinking habit, his dissatisfactions, and his marital problems. Jake knew he had to get off the sidelines, and *Today* seemed a perfect vehicle. Roland's unequivocal support and respect would mean less time wasted in political maneuvering. True, there was the awkward matter of Grodin and Roland's irritating reminders about encouraging him, grooming him, not alienating him, and the like. But Jake knew Grodin's type. Always angling, always playing the game, and, beneath all that, utterly desperate for success. He would watch him. He would keep him under control. And yet, in a relatively short time, Martin has managed to force Jake to the wall.

Jake believes in being a diplomat, and to wage war, even in legitimate self-defense, seems a shameful thing. By avoiding the scramble for top positions, he intuitively knew he could avoid power conflicts that would throw him into a blind, scratch-and-claw struggle for supremacy. Now, confronted by just such a struggle, Jake places limits on what he will do in his own defense which amount to a voluntary handicap.

In most institutional imbroglios, Jake has generally been quick to make his stand. When dealing with inconsiderateness, negligence, or evasiveness on the part of subordinates or superiors, he can effectively assert his authority or his chagrin, thereby eliminating any hint of disadvantage. But when someone goes after him in a ruthless way, Jake will bob and weave and tie himself in knots without striking a telling blow.

One of the greatest causes of shame Jake knows is to be dragged through the mud of winning and losing. To act out of narrow self-interest, even when necessary, arouses self-indictments ("Small!" "Mean!" "Devious!"). To strike directly at someone's vulnerability or self-doubt, even when his own dignity depends on it, would make Jake feel like a crippled killer in a world of normal, healthy people looking out for their rights. Turning someone into an object can send him into days of agonizing self-examination. And yet to be made into an object himself is even more tormenting, for his pride is at least as great as his idealism.

Jake knows that power can be a seductive, addictive, and dangerous game, especially when it becomes adversarial. If you tend to see adversaries around you, you will become defensive and maneuver for advantage—and such behavior will certainly create adversaries even if they weren't there before. He knows that there's an animal inside him that would like nothing better than to destroy the person whom he perceives as standing in his way; and he keeps that animal on a very short leash. He has committed himself to assuming the best of people and always looking at both sides of any conflict. When colleagues are a little disrespectful or unfair, as they inevitably are in the course of things, he uses the minimal strategy needed to bring them back into the orbit of mutual respect.

But the question Jake never asks is, when do you finally decide that you are facing an adversary? When do you cross the line? When do you say, "My outrage is justified and I'm going to get tough?" The need to cross that line may come only once in a great while, but if you can't do it when the situation calls for it, your whole life will be soured. In Jake's case the failure will also sour his position as a role model for the younger executives who believe in a humanitarian style of leadership and want to see it work.

Jake is aware of his modeling responsibilities, and, as his losing struggle with Martin persists, somewhere in the back of his mind he knows he is blowing it. Indeed, he is sending his subordinates the worst possible message—for in his failure to respond to Martin with adequate strength, he is reinforcing the obnoxious folk wisdom that nice guys finish last.

Jake's inability to strike back at Martin marks him as powerphobic—so sensitive to the destructive effects of winning that he is inclined at times to ignore his own welfare when attacked. Powerphobia exists in everyone to some degree. It's the sensitive person's perplexed response to the senseless exploitation he sees around him. When strong enough, powerphobia keeps some of us from assuming responsibilities that are rightfully ours and causes others of us to work or live in isolation. Because powerphobia inclines anyone to tie one hand behind his back in a power struggle, it can easily lead to powerlessness. For most people, powerphobia is overshadowed by subject and object issues. Not for Jake.

The Downward Spiral

Thanks to the disastrous meeting on Friday, Jake has been sliding steadily downhill, one inner defeat leading to another. The skirmish with the short order cook was a mere symbol of that decline. Instead of brushing off the absurd public encounter the moment it began, Jake was drawn in and allowed it an exaggerated importance.

Why did the cook act as he did? Perhaps bitterness and self-hatred over his position in the world caused him to be filled with feelings of insignificance when a pointy-headed intellectual spread a Sunday *Times* across his counter. But whatever the cause of his hostility, the beaten set of Jake's features clearly offered too appealing a target to pass up.

Already infected by self-doubt, Jake was vulnerable to more abuse and unable to commit himself to his own defense. If he could have coolly dismissed the coffee incursions, as he might normally have done, or if he had put some money down and quietly walked out, the cook's secret feelings of shame might have exploded into an agonizing chorus: "Nobody!" "Servant!" "Trash!" But, although Jake held his own, he was obviously rattled, and for that reason the cook had only a minor brush with self-doubt.

The first thing Jake felt when the cook started punishing him was a horrible sense of deterioration. He is a man both accustomed to respect and unable to bear the lack of it. In recent years, he's been courted by powerful people. Last week he engineered a major interview with a foreign head of state visiting the U.N. and afterwards celebrated with champagne in the publisher's limousine. Now here was a total stranger whose behavior seemed to imply that an old, secret stain ("Kick Me!") had emerged on Jake's forehead, and that in some basic way everybody could see he was not worthy of respect.

By the time his breakfast was over, other dormant areas of shame—about being privileged, thoughtless, and hypersensitive—had become inflamed. As he drove back across town to pick up his wife, two incidents from four decades back were flickering through his mind. In one, a gang from another neighborhood is intercepting him on his paper route, one smiling member of the group approaching him and delivering him a punch in the mouth. In the other, Jake is going along unthinkingly with a group of friends who are humiliating a timid boy in the lunchroom. He was barely aware that he was reliving those memories—or mixing them with fearful fantasies about the magazine and the guilt he felt over his treatment of Grace on Friday evening when she scolded him for taking a drink. But those incidents and others like them and years of subsequent determination never again to be bullied or cruel in any way represent pockets of shame that were now highly aroused.

Grace Donohue was in a good mood when she hopped into the car and asked her husband how he enjoyed his breakfast. Jake shrugged off the question, and feeling rejected, Grace was cool to him for the rest of the day. The hounds were really howling now; the sense that *there is something wrong with me*, that *I am the problem* was cornering Jake, while the defending voices, charging the cook, his wife, Roland, and Martin with various malfeasances, sounded defensive and self-pitying by contrast. Jake wanted to approach Grace for some sort of help, but he was too proud, and, in any case, he hardly knew what to ask for. Reading alone in his room, he felt that his weekend was ruined, that his marriage was on the rocks, that there was no pleasure for him in his work, that he should leave everything and move to California.

"This is the lowest I've been in years," Jake says aloud. Hearing his own voice is a strange relief after listening to the inner ravings for hours. "How the hell did I get this low?" He notices that he's been reading the same page all afternoon. He stands and paces. He thinks about his bout with alcoholism so recently concluded, how feelings like this were responsible for his drinking, how imperative it is that he snap out of it.

"Grace, I've got to talk to you," Jake says. He tells her about the meeting and the breakfast incident and the regrets he has about the way he spoke to her. Gradually, he looks less beaten, and the keenness and humor return to his eyes.

Grace, feeling tender toward him as she always does when he confides in her, quickly recognizes the source of his misery. "You've got to deal with Grodin," she says.

"I know."

5.

Getting Sucked In

How inadvertently the power scramble can begin and how devastatingly it can end. Haunted by the fear of losing we act defensively and fire the first shot. Marge's trouble with men and the single life.

MARTIN AND GEORGETTE are married and have problems that stretch back twelve years. Everything they do reverberates with past hurts and grievances and with the silent contracts they've established. Martin and Jake are rivals. If they'd met only two weeks ago, they'd already be engaged in threatening maneuvers, because they want to do each other in. But, power and insecurity being what they are, even strangers, strangers who have no cause to dislike each other and may in fact be attracted, find themselves getting sucked into needless conflict. The problem shows up again and again with single people as they flirt, proposition, and date.

When a twenty-eight-year-old unemployed history professor named Chuck Meyers spots Marge, dark-haired and slender with bright eyes and broad gestures at the Urbanorganic Gallery in Tribeca, he doesn't tell her that the sight of her backside made his heart leap into his throat, that he is so hungry for a woman he can barely stand up, or that he is quaking with insecurity at the thought of asking her out. For such forthrightness may be perceived as inappropriate and instantly lead to judgment, rejection, and shame. Instead, he chats her up, smiles, flatters, tries to win her interest with calculated impressions, maintains a respectable distance, and assesses her reactions. He keeps his image guard high, and he is careful not to give too much (by showing the extent of his interest) without getting some indication of interest in return. These strategies are standard to the dating role. They give Marge the time to look Chuck over without feeling on the spot.

Traditionally, the ability to understand the little rules and expectations of everyday life has been the first step toward social power—not power in the exploitive sense, but in the sense of taking a respected place among other members of society. In our society there is a general feeling that formality and convention are dead, that complete personal freedom is just around the corner for anyone who dares to grab it, that Chuck can go up to Marge and say, "How would you like it, vertical or horizontal?" and walk away a hero. But here's where Chuck's problems begin. For while Chuck is free from the rule of old standards and authorities, his inner freedom is minuscule. He is governed by a vast array of hidden imperatives, many of which he is barely aware of. They have been implanted along with his shame and are enforced by every person he meets.

The old social standards—about how to dress, how to speak, whom to respect, what to say to a strange woman—offered a sense of security, because they told you very specifically what was expected of you in almost every social context, and no one could take that away from you. You knew that if you followed the rules, you would be accepted as a proper person, regardless of what you might be feeling.

As the old standards have deteriorated, new standards have evolved which tell Chuck what he should *feel*, what he should *be*, what impulses, desires, and capacities he should have. Because Chuck is particularly concerned with approval and acutely sensitive to moral fashion, he constantly experiences a pressure to prove himself intelligent, confident, efficient, talented, articulate, independent, assertive, attentive, sensitive, considerate, open, able to take criticism, able to be a winner, and—not to be forgotten—original, spontaneous, sincere, and self-accepting as well.

So while Chuck may risk being totally outlandish in his opening line, this burdensome recipe for a proper human being makes him very vulnerable to Marge's disapproval. He shouldn't try too hard. He shouldn't monopolize the conversation. If he's unhappy, if he's depressed, if he's anxious about having an affair with a woman who's seven years older, he shouldn't let it show. If it comes out that he's unemployed and living with his parents, he shouldn't act as if all that has made a dent in his ego. With Chuck's insecurity running particularly high since he lost his job, he is sometimes so fearful of a wrong move that he feels frozen in place.

In the end, no matter how hard he tries and how well he does, Chuck won't be sure of his performance until he reads Marge's response. A rejection—or any sign (a glance, a yawn) that he may read as rejection (Ho-hum, another suitor)—may tip his fragile balance away from self-worth. That is the way vulnerability works.

Marge is caught in a similar predicament. After one date with Chuck, she may want to call him, to tell him she likes him, to take his hand when they're walking, all of which she sees as perfectly acceptable for a liberated woman and, indeed, her *duty* if she truly believes in being who she is. But if she does any of these things and runs into an awkward or uncomfortable response, a feeling of "Uh-oh, I'm doing something inappropriate" burns through her; it ignites various rebukes along the way ("You shouldn't crowd him, you dope!"); until finally a voice explodes with the cry "Needy!" and she feels she has exposed a subhuman quality that lies at her core. Anticipating this, she swings toward playing it safe and either hesitates to call or rings him up in a manipulative and controlling way.

In the absence of the old-fashioned social regulation, it's becoming harder to know what's acceptable. And this makes us extremely sensitive to the feedback we get. Chuck, sensing Marge's uncertainty, can make her feel that phoning him after their first date is the most natural thing in the world, or he can make her feel that she is moving in on him. Of course, if Chuck signs on with an awkward coughing hello, it may not be intended as a rebuke. His mind may be elsewhere. But Marge will interpret his cough according to her own fears and assumptions and will respond in habitual ways.

Sooner or later Marge's and Chuck's vulnerabilities will get raw enough and their mistrust hot enough that they will no longer be able to view each other with the delighted eyes of potential mates. Given their psychologies and the tenor of the times, winning and losing will enter the picture, unwanted, uninvited, but inevitable.

Taking Her Problems Public

On Sunday evening, two weeks after her third date with Chuck (and two nights after Georgette's birthday), Marge experiences an unpleasant incident with a stranger. Wearing jeans and an old sweater, she is waiting on line at the Trailways station for the bus that will take her from New Paltz, where her brother lives, back to Manhattan. She is protective of her place on line because in this hip student community the old rules about waiting your turn don't necessarily apply, and she has been burned up several times at the sight of latecomers finding friends at the front of the line to talk to and slowly merge with. Marge is not only worried about getting a seat, but about getting on the bus altogether, because it is sometimes already half-filled when it arrives here from Kingston.

Minutes before the bus is due an erect old woman, wearing a sable coat and a plumed hat, steps quietly in front of Marge, half in and half out of the line, and starts talking to the woman alongside her. Marge has no reason to believe the two are connected in any way. "The line forms back that way, ma'am," she says, gently touching the woman's sable shoulder to get her attention. The woman glances at Marge's finger, looks her quickly up and down, says, "I know," in a scolding, irritated tone, and turns away.

This makes Marge very agitated. Is she playing games with me? Is she not really planning to take the bus? "Excuse me, ma'am," Marge persists. "If you're waiting for the bus, the end of the line is back there." "I *know*," says the woman more firmly and more irritably, and again shows Marge the back of her head. Marge has the urge to grab the old crone and heave her out of the line. In a premature flash of retribution and guilt she sees the woman sprawled on the ground as scores of accusing eyes search Marge for character defects. Anger crackling through her words, Marge persists: "Lady, you're cutting ahead. I suggest you move before the line gets longer." The woman looks her square in the eye: "*What*, are you afraid of not getting a seat?" "Yes!" spurts Marge, and with a dismissing glance the old woman marches off toward the rear.

Marge cannot understand why she does not feel good about her victory, except for the uneasy thought that she wasn't dressed well enough for the encounter. The bus arrives, and she is the last to get a seat. She is pleased now at having stood her ground and feels vindicated on that score. But as she sits on the crowded bus, her arms folded over the bundle in her lap, she is still dismayed by sour feelings. The day at her brother's wasn't the happy reunion she'd hoped for; she's made an old lady miss the bus; she's going home to an empty Sunday night. Beneath these depressing thoughts are vague, barely conscious shifts in her self-image—of being larger, louder, more Jewish than usual. As she stares past the Madonna look-alike sitting next to her, hypnotized by the oncoming traffic on the expressway, she is jolted by the realization that she wants to see Georgette again. I should have agreed to that French restaurant, I really should have. Why was I so pigheaded? I'll call her as soon as I get back.

Marge's friends know little of her struggles because she likes to present a happy front. If we ask Marge if being single arouses self-doubt in her, she says, "Of course not! I'm proud that I've made it on my own and didn't have to lean on a man to survive." But if we press her, she might reluctantly admit that there is a little voice in her head that accuses her of not being able to love or be loved, of not being as good as Georgette. Each little scuffle, with Chuck, with her brother, with a stranger on a bus line, causes the voice to grow louder ("All alone!" "Can't Love!" "Defective!") even as Marge busies herself to keep from hearing it.

The faster she runs and the further she gets from herself, the worse her vulnerabilities become. New encounters stir additional pockets of shame, some of them long forgotten and seemingly healed. Now we find that Marge, who is successful, who moves in powerful circles, who lives in a city where her heritage is respected, has self-hatreds we would never expect, that she is vulnerable to feelings of ethnic shame, and when a haughty, elegantly dressed woman with an aristocratic bearing belittles her, a buried chorus of inner voices makes her feel like a pushy, unwashed, Yiddish-speaking immigrant right off the boat.

As the pressure builds to unbearable levels, Marge seeks Georgette, because she is the one person with whom Marge can unbosom herself of her depression and fears. Others prefer their favorite chemical, a vicious tennis game, or twenty minutes of deep relaxation; while those seeking the final solution enroll in Scientology, est, and other emotional training programs to kill off vulnerability for good. But very few know how to live with their vulnerability in a creative way. Very few know how to be honest with themselves about who they are, open or shut with others as the situation demands, quick enough to catch potential problems before they arise, and able to respond to power moves in a way that suits their best interests and allows them to be themselves.

Review 1

1. We all have *pockets of shame* which make us feel separate and unworthy.

Self-hatred ("I can't stand these horrible, defective qualities in me") and certain forms of *self-doubt* ("Maybe I'm not good enough," "Maybe I'm the problem") are both experiences of shame. They represent highly inflamed and milder versions of the same condition.

2. Interpersonal experience helps determine how inflamed our sense of shame becomes. And because we know this, we often operate in a strategic way, falling into a game of tag whose purpose is to make the other person "it" before he can do it to us.

Am I a horny, grasping, sexually graceless man? Or are you a frightened, frigid woman? Am I a rigid, inconsiderate boss? Or are you a lazy, rebellious secretary? These are some of the issues of shame at stake in power struggles we might stumble into any day of our lives. In such struggles, one person often gains a sense of security by establishing his self-worth at the other's expense. This is called "winning."

3. *Winning* does not mean achieving your goals by convincing others that those goals are worthy. In fact, it does not always mean achieving your goals. It has nothing to do with such traditional sentiments of competition as, "May the best man win," or the truest idea prevail, or the most efficient product succeed. It has only to do with

coming out on top. In this sort of winning the sole value is winning itself, the security of being one-up.

4. Winning is achieved through subtle strategies. Subjects, like Martin and Carmen, may be riddled with terrible self-hatreds. But they operate in a way that always puts the other person's inadequacy at center stage. As long as they can do this, they feel safe, secure, and okay about themselves.

People who tend to maneuver strategically for advantage do so because they are on the run from their own self-doubts. In most cases, they were trained to live this way as children. In our society playing for advantage is widespread. It is often approved of and rewarded.

5. The strategy that is most likely to arouse shame is punishment. It comes in many forms from guilt ("Maybe you just can't be happy, Georgette, unless I'm in the pits") to humor ("And then you can hold your head high on Fifty-seventh Street"). Punishment is generally most shame-inducing when it is covert.

6. *The subject-object relationship* is built on incidents of power in which the object's shame is exploited. Both people may maneuver for advantage, but their interpersonal chemistry requires that the subject generally comes out on top. As a result, he feels more comfortable and secure, while the object becomes the problem.

7. Georgette feels inferior to Martin, Marge, and Carmen. They, too, feel she is inferior. But such judgments are nothing but the spoils of victory. When Martin was feeling like an object three years ago and his secret sense of inadequacy was burning, he saw Georgette as a model human being—competent, happy, loving, easily giving and open—while he himself felt unfit to sleep with pigs.

Subjects don't like to see their responsibility for the object's pain. They prefer to define that pain as sickness.

8. Georgette is an object not because she is inferior and not because she has a heavier burden of shame. She is an object solely because she was trained to take that role as a child. When conflicts arise and her object tendency is activated, she suffers depression, illness, cookie lust, paralysis of will.

9. Just as Martin is able to bring out the object in Georgette, she is able to bring out the subject in him. While one person may be at fault in individual instances, over the long run they both share complicity in having produced a subject-object tilt in their life together. Lately Georgette has been creating subjects all around her by broadcasting object invitations.

10. *Fear* is pervasive in interpersonal politics, and it generates struggles where they needn't exist. Marge and Chuck are attracted to

each other, but they are fearful of the other's intentions, fearful of having their inadequacy exposed, fearful of coming up a loser.

They have just met. Neither wants to play for advantage. But they've already begun maneuvering in such a way that win-lose incidents are likely.

11. Jake is a responsible, ethical man whose caring spirit reaches into arenas others are happy to ignore. But he is also *powerphobic*—so fearful of being destructive or exploitive that he avoids situations where he may have to be aggressive in order to defend himself. His avoidance becomes costly when there are sharks in the water. Now he is sucked down and chewed up in one defeat after another.

II.

THE REPLAY

Balancing the Power

6.

First Things First

How Georgette could have dealt with the abuses she encountered. Immediate counterstrategies, not for fundamental change, but for holding one's own and preventing the erosion of one's position.

IN OUR STORY THUS FAR, Georgette has been confronted with several examples of outright abuse. Steve Friendly ridiculed her city housing report in front of other members of the staff. Martin made her feel like two cents when she failed to burst into song after sex with him on Thursday night, and then on Saturday morning he mocked her wish to stay in bed.

Obviously, Georgette's problems go much deeper than these affronts:

• She has self-esteem problems and habits of mind that keep her acting like an object. They must be confronted.

• She has old contracts with the people in her life, contracts which allow them to give her less than she gives them. Those contracts must be altered.

• She's allowed herself to tread water in her career, accepting a low status and salary even though these concessions are playing havoc with her self-worth. She needs to mobilize herself to change that.

But the instances of abuse represent an immediate challenge that must be tackled if she is not to feel damaged, demeaned, and set back in her other goals.

Mindless Maneuvers: The Ruinous Unconscious Arsenal

Georgette does try to counterattack when she feels put down. She withdraws, she withholds, she employs various techniques to make people guilty. But her weapons emerge from an unconscious arsenal of automatic responses, responses that have not changed since she first learned them as a child. They gain her nothing but short-term satisfaction.

Unhappy with Martin's immersion in the magazine—and too ashamed of being selfish to tell him so in a direct and persistent way—Georgette becomes petulant and uncooperative and fails to do the little things, such as making Sunday breakfast, which Martin once took for granted. She covers herself by attributing her withholding to lack of time or important professional commitments.

Martin is defensive. How can he oppose his wife's legitimate career goals, especially since she already does more than he around the house? Although he's hurt by the change, he is unwilling to risk an open discussion, which might lead to God-knows-what revelations or new demands. So, instead, he begins fault-finding in totally unrelated areas and stabbing her with jests.

Now Georgette starts losing interest in sex. Martin misses more dinners. Georgette attacks him for never seeing their daughter. And so on.

This mindless series of maneuvers is standard in many marriages. It does nothing to alter the status quo, which makes it a bad bargain for the object. It's a futile merry-go-round, and Georgette must get off.

To use strategies effectively, Georgette has to use them consciously. She will have to stop her knee-jerk maneuvers based on childhood training and habits, get her subconscious calculations into the forefront of her mind—where she can make evaluations according to adult principles and understandings—and take responsibility for what she does.

I. Countering Abuse

There are many ways to deal with abuse, the most obvious being a direct counterattack. How can it be deployed effectively?

Weak strategy: powerless punishment. On Saturday morning, when

Martin sneered: "Exhausted from your night out with the girls?" Georgette responded by staring at him in hurt silence. She would say it was an entirely spontaneous act, but in some small way Georgette knew that a wounded look would make Martin feel guilty. It's an age-old female maneuver, and, like crying, very potent. A club of guilt and shame ("Insensitive!" "Mean!" "Brute!") bludgeoned Martin's forehead. Even though he managed to go off and do as he pleased, guilt clouded the rest of his day.

But Georgette gained nothing by attacking Martin this way. Martin did not think, "Wow, I'd better watch out—if I step out of line with Georgette I'll get it!" No, he escalated the level of punishment ("To hell with this!"), and he walked out the door disgusted with her. Her powerless punishment invited an even bigger punishment for which she was completely unprepared, and the subject-object tilt in their relationship worsened. Let's replay the incident.

Strong Strategy: punishments that take control. 1) Imagine that instead of looking crushed, Georgette gets out of bed, goes to the bathroom, and without saying a word, snaps the door sharply behind her. The slap of silent anger startles Martin. He tries to make her talk, but Georgette leaves of the bathroom, gets dressed, and goes to the kitchen, still silent.

Martin now maneuvers in various predictable ways. He asks innocently: "Hey, what's the matter?" He kids: "What's got Georgie's goat this morning?" He becomes irritable: "What's with the silent treatment, Goddamn it!" But as long as he maneuvers like this, she ignores him. Not until he heaves a sigh and says, "I'm sorry," does she begin to talk.

2) With stern but muted anger, Georgette now insists that Martin account for himself. He caused her pain; he is going to have to own up and right the balance. "Why did you speak to me that way?" she says. Martin mumbles that he was in a bad mood. That is not good enough. "What's going on with you? Come on, let's have it!" Georgette's struggle is not over until Martin seems genuinely concerned over the pain he caused. When he does, Georgette will begin to feel the sting coming out of the wound.

3) The guilt-making power of the wounded gives Georgette an authority with which she can pressure Martin until he is more forthcoming. Then it's important that she let him out from under her thumb. The abuse has been neutralized.

4) If Martin is able to open up to the point of acknowledging what lay behind his disparaging remark ("I've been down on you lately, because. . ."), Georgette may expose some of her feelings as well.

There's nothing necessarily wrong with Martin being upset with her; what's wrong is acting it out in a disrespectful way. If things go exceptionally well, they may even find themselves talking honestly about many of the feelings they've experienced in the days leading up to her birthday.

Here then is a series of conscious maneuvers carefully designed for a purpose. To make it work, Georgette has to be sensitive to when she feels abused, sensitive to the methods she uses to respond, and sensitive to when a balance has been achieved. The creation of a balance is a key moment which calls for a softening of posture. But: *until the balance exists, talking openly is futile*.

II. Evading Abuse

Subjects and objects are always hooking each other. Georgette cries, or she says, "You never hold my hand any more," and Martin, zapped with guilt, starts churning and doing his tricks. Similarly, Martin gives a sigh of exasperation, or he acts a little impatient, and Georgette, zapped with self-doubt, starts churning and doing her tricks. Neither one knows how to evade the other's hooks, so they're always getting into trouble.

Weak evasion. After making love on Thursday night, Martin hooked Georgette by asking, "How was it?" Georgette attempted to evade the question by saying, "Fine." But her evasion lacked conviction and she was soon snared in Martin's trap.

Strong evasion. Georgette's evasion would have been more effective had she fully committed herself to it and pulled out all the stops. "Something's been on my mind, honey," she might have said. "We must talk about it."

Martin thinks, "Uh-oh, it's about sex. She's not having orgasms. She wants more foreplay. She wants me to do something I don't want to do." But Georgette says, "It's about Cindy. I don't think she's adjusted well to this new teacher." With good acting, this change of topic would be hard to reverse.

Georgette's evasion is dishonest, not because Cindy isn't having problems, but because she is hiding all the distress she feels. What she's decided, in effect, is: I have a major problem in my marriage, but I'm not going to fight it out here over a trivial issue where I can only get hurt. In short, she evades the hook; she evades a confrontation she doesn't want; she evades his prying maneuvers.

Martin (penetrating): "Are you sure nothing's bothering you? You seem a little down."

Georgette (shrugging pleasantly): "No. I feel fine."

Martin (incredulous): "Honest?"

Georgette (amused): "Yeah."

If Martin were to press on about sex ("So, do you still think I'm macho?"), Georgette should intensify her evasions. "Honey, I'm really *upset* about Cindy" will place her concerns above his humorous-sounding question. If he still persists in pawing over their sexual experience, he will begin to sound a little obsessed. It now becomes possible to move the focus to him: "What's the matter with you, Martin? You don't seem yourself tonight."

Does all this seem too ruthless? Would you rather have Georgette say, "Let's talk about it another time, Martin"? That might work with a less controlling man; but Martin would not understand, his anxiety would go berserk, and he would become more insistent.

But how can one be so deceitful in the context of a close personal relationship? To ask that question is to misdefine the context. Because what's going on between the lines is not close and personal at all. Martin, without the dimmest understanding of his motives, is trying to force Georgette into a degraded position. She must spare them both that conclusion.

III. Defensiveness

Defensiveness is an unpleasant quality when we have no control over it, but because it can serve as a protective wall which shelters us from attack, it must be available as a potential strategy in special situations.

Weak defensiveness. Weak defensiveness comes in many forms from lame excuses to reflexive rebuttals to unsolicited attacks. Georgette said, "I thought we were going to eat at one of the French restaurants," and Marge, defensive, replied: "Oh, come on, George, stop being so rigid." This was a weak response. Marge was acting out something she felt she couldn't speak about—her faltering interest in their date. She could have been open but chose to play it safe and hurt Georgette unnecessarily in the process. Her defensiveness said, "I'm fine. If there's anything wrong with you, that's your problem."

Strong defensiveness. A few days before our story began, Steve Friendly waved Georgette's housing report at Carmen and said,

"We'll be killed if we publish this thing!" The entire staff was in earshot. Al looked at Georgette with a worried expression. Georgette got a pain in her stomach and her body became hot. She wanted to kill Friendly. But an inner voice said, Be open to criticism, Be reasonable, Listen to his point of view. Don't be defensive.

Defensiveness would indeed have closed her to Steve's criticism. But Steve's criticism was not legitimate. He didn't take Georgette aside and point something out to her or respectfully suggest she check her legal references. He dismissed the entire report, he held Georgette up to public ridicule, he undermined her standing in the office. What was really going on was not criticism at all but the most primitive kind of power maneuver. Georgette was being made into an object and, if, in the days to come, she continues to stand for it, she will be reduced to someone whom the entire staff is free to use for target practice.

Shrewd defensiveness does not defend the report; that would be weak since the value of any report is debatable. Rather, it attacks the disrespect; that is not debatable.

"I *beg* your pardon!" Georgette might have said, rising to her feet. (That alone could scare up an apology.) "The nerve!" she says in a tone of moral outrage. And suddenly everyone in the room, Carmen included, shrinks a little and thinks better of thinking the worse of Georgette's report. Al suddenly finds himself emboldened and considers voicing his own high opinion of the work.

If Steve continues playing to win, Georgette must mobilize her anger, search for Steve's weaknesses, and remind herself that it is her dignity more than the report that is at stake. A defensive Georgette has only one goal: to assure that if anyone feels bad for the rest of the day, if anyone tortures himself over whether and how to make amends, if anyone goes to bed in a state of turmoil and doubt about his position in the office, it will be Steve and not her.

In all likelihood, the exchange will end quickly. Carmen will intervene, suggesting that Steve and Georgette hash out their differences in private. Georgette will have salvaged a potentially dangerous loss of prestige, while putting Steve on notice that she is not an old bag he can bat around at will. But if Carmen says nothing and more hot words are exchanged, Georgette will have to go after Steve's vulnerabilities—his newness in the office, his divisive influence, his violation of the chain of command, his attempt to brownnose the boss, the manner of his delivery—anything that can be seen as a violation of the normal standards of office propriety.

"If you have criticism of my work," she says fiercely, "I expect you to address them to *me*."

He protests: "I'm sorry, Georgette, I was only trying to prevent a disaster." The word "disaster" kills the apology.

She presses him: "If you have a problem with anything I've written, *address it to me*. What exactly do you accomplish by blurting it out in the middle of this room?"

Georgette is older than Steve. She's been around longer. She can play on that. She is a grown woman scolding a little boy. He comments on her excitability; she keeps the focus on him. She uses her anger to maintain her momentum; she doesn't falter if her logic sounds a little off or her verbal constructions faulty; she keeps the spotlight on Steve's inappropriate, disrespectful behavior.

Throughout all this, Georgette doesn't worry about Steve's feelings. She does nothing to protect him from the embarrassment of being scolded in public. She does not look at Carmen or anyone else to determine if they approve. And she certainly never laughs at herself if she stumbles. Meanwhile, she resists *ad hominem* attacks—or anything that may be construed as inappropriate on her part. And she does nothing that might mitigate her image of moral outrage or allow her energy level to fall beneath his.

Having succeeded in clubbing back an attacker, Georgette must resist the temptation to beat him into submission. That's where legitimate self-defense turns destructive; and it will certainly come back to haunt her later. If Friendly gives adequate indication of contrition, she can accept it and assure him that there are no hard feelings. Once the power's been balanced, there's no need to bear a grudge, make an enemy, or hold an advantage of her own.

Skill Begins With Awareness

There are times when Georgette is hypersensitive, when a simple "no" makes her feel like two cents. But as she pays attention to strategic assaults, she will find that she can tell the difference. A real assault has a characteristic sting. She will know it by her physical reactions, by the atmosphere of threat, by the way someone is using the truth rather than seeking it, by the poisonous self-hatreds crowding her consciousness.

Seeing through the strategic camouflage of Martin's snide innuendoes ("I'm just reacting to your irritating downness") or Steve's public attack ("I'm just doing my job") and recognizing that she is facing an adversary will, of course, not free Georgette from having to deal with them. Their assaults will still hurt and still tend to arouse shame. Even with awareness she may be defeated. And if defeated, she will suffer.

But as long as she realizes that an adversary was involved, she will know, *It's not just me;* and that knowledge will keep her from turning entirely against herself. She will not buy the unconscious message that because she's being abused she must have deserved it. If this knowledge reaches Georgette before the struggle with Steve or Martin is over—if she can say to herself, "I'm in a power struggle and I'm under assault," she can halt the spread of shame in time to plan her counterattack.

7.

The Inner Game of Power

How to restructure our emotional posture so as not to think or act like an object. This chapter is not about getting rid of self-doubt but about keeping it from running our lives. *Breaking the habit of losing.*

GEORGETTE THINKS like an object. Her object assumptions tell her that she cannot walk tall and still get the love and connection she needs. They whisper, "If I stand up for myself, I will lose all my friends." Anyone who thinks like this cannot possibly succeed with the strategies we've just discussed. One way or another she will always be communicating that she can be had.

Object consciousness reveals itself in these three postures:

1. *The great need syndrome.* When Georgette went to bed with Martin on Thursday night, her hunger for love and approval was so great it was almost impossible to think about anything else. By initiating sex with Martin when he was acting cold and uninterested, she was asking to be crushed. She emphasized her emotional needs at the expense of her self-esteem.

It is painful to push aside a longing for contact. It is painful to walk away from what you need. It is painful to maintain a formal, "how-are-you-everything's-fine" posture when you crave connection. But there are times when it must be done.

2. *Compulsive intimacy seeking.* Some people always feel compelled to reveal things about themselves. "Nice to meet you. I'm really quite insecure—how about you?" Or, "Can I take you out for a drink?—or better make that a cup of coffee, I'm too much of a lush as it is." This kind of openness makes others uncomfortable and leaves

one overexposed and overly vulnerable. It can arise in any of us when we feel an intense need to express our pain.

Georgette, who's never at ease until she's taken off her shoes, who, figuratively speaking, flings off pieces of clothing with abandon, does not want to believe that even with the people closest to her there are times when image must be maintained. But during moments of conflict, Martin or Carmen or Marge's carefully polished image can make her feel defective, while her foibles are readily available for discussion, evaluation, and exploitation.

3. *The fear of a break*. The third posture that typifies the object is perhaps the most common: an unwillingness to risk a break in a relationship. This is dangerous because when someone senses that your commitment to him is such that he can be a monster without losing you, he may be drawn to test the thesis, and, in any event, he will certainly lose respect.

Notice how Georgette has slipped into this posture at work. Prey to the self-doubt that afflicts many women who have taken time out for motherhood, she fears that if she can't cut the mustard at Carmen's, there will never be a place for her in the working world. Controlled by this fear, she is a little too timid with Carmen and generally unable to act with complete confidence and self-respect, something that Steve Friendly sensed on their first meeting.

Georgette cannot immediately free herself of her lack of self-esteem. That's a gradual process that results from an expanding self-awareness, intimate exchanges with a friend or a therapist, experiments with new ways of being, achieving certain successes in personal and worklife, and refusing to let herself be mistreated. But there is something she can do that will immediately affect how she feels about herself, and that is to refuse to take an object posture.

If Carmen or Martin or Marge react to Georgette's new behavior with coldness or anger because they expect her to play a meeker role, she will learn, by waiting them out, that most rifts are temporary and that everyone—even a subjects—values connection and fears its loss.

The first thing Georgette must do to alter her posture is look at herself squarely and see that she is an object. This may be hard, a) because it's not pretty and b) because it will require acknowledging her own responsibility for so much of what goes on.

But, if she admits that she is an object, she will be able to inhibit her tendency to act like one. It will be easier to stop giving off the signals that invite oppression—the nervous laugh, the "little-me" phraseology, and other emblems of objecthood—because she can intercept them before they leak out. And, she will have a better chance of avoiding the object postures. This is the first front in Georgette's battle to break the habit of losing.

The Second Front: Catching the Object Spiral

Georgette rises on Thursday morning, the day before her birthday, and senses that this is going to be a lousy day. She then proceeds to make it so.

As she climbs out of bed on Thursday morning and readies Cindy for kindergarten, Georgette decides to skip a shower, to save her "good" dress for another day, to put off certain errands and calls, to let Cindy put two scoops of sugar on her cereal. When Cindy tests her further, Georgette overreacts, loses her temper, and then hates herself for it. She allows herself to come into the office forty-five minutes late. She ignores a message from Carmen.

As Georgette stumbles down the spiral staircase, she acts out her object invitations, arousing the subject tendencies of everyone she encounters along the way. Her wan smile, her hesitancy, her vacant expression, her eagerness to please, her disheveled appearance all suggest to her family, her co-workers, and the people she meets on the street that she is available for mistreatment. Finally on Saturday morning, Martin, who has observed the process since it began, complete with sloppiness, depressions, and cookie consumption, says, "To hell with this!" and shoves her to the bottom of the pit.

Breaking the object spiral is the second front in the object's efforts to reform. The moment she wakes up and smells depression in the air, Georgette must mobilize herself against the slide. Though she feels less than whole, she should make an effort not to announce it to the world through her self-diminishing mannerisms. She must wear the good dress, be on time, keep Cindy in line without becoming a tyrant, and refuse to allow herself a single act of sloppiness.

If depression is settling in, she may have to go further—schedule an important lunch, make an important purchase, do something significantly opposite to the nothingness that engulfs her. Such mobilization will halt the downward spiral and buy her time.

The time should be used to locate the origins of her descent. Is it the approaching birthday and her feelings about being thirty-five? Is it the horrid exchange with Martin about the mink? Is it the nasty Mr. Friendly? Georgette can work out these smoldering issues in the privacy of her diary or in an intimate conversation with Marge—

rather than by acting them out in her general behavior.

It's important to note that for many people neither the diary nor a good friend like Marge will do. They need the help of a therapist to achieve this degree of awareness.

The Third Front: Mobilizing for Major Change

Making a major change can be crucial to getting out of a powerless rut. But major change is exactly what the depressed and powerless person feels least capable of. Look at Georgette. A raise and a title would transform her life, make her a different person not only at work but at home and with friends. Her obsessive eating, her self-denigration, her clinginess, much of her current mire can be attributed to letting these two things slide.

But there is a mush at the center of the object consciousness that says, "There is no point in my launching anything until I feel stronger." Such an attitude is rarely valid. In Georgette's case it's an alibi.

When Georgette first began the job search that led her to Carmen's office, she was in a similar frame of mind. She felt overwhelmed by the odds (there are so many more qualified people), by the summer heat, by the poor quality of the available positions, by her lack of credentials, by her doubts about leaving Cindy, by the approaching thermonuclear destruction of the world, by the sheer boredom of it all. Why bother?

But after three futile months of lackadaisical job-hunting, she became disgusted with herself, and the disgust mobilized her. She consulted a job-search specialist and carefully followed her advice. She read the want ads with gusto and went to the employment agencies and job interviews with a forethought and care that she lacked before. She let herself be selfish. She acted as if she had a right to seek the job, whatever it was, and her determination and commitment to herself showed in ways that image can only approximate.

She hired a full-time housekeeper while she was still searching, a financially bold move at the time, which further hardened her commitment. Her mobilization showed, and wherever she went, it made her a respected prospect.

Momentum has curative powers. It is a potent antidote to stagnation, to self-doubt, and to procrastination. It keeps you from getting drawn into meaningless struggles and from overlooking impending disadvantage. Momentum is the opposite of a power vacuum. People sense it and pay it respect.

Georgette has reached a juncture today that requires renewed mobilization. She must get the title and the wage she deserves. Doubts about being a working mother, about her motives in seeking the promotion, about whether she really deserves the raise have no relevance here. Georgette deserves a proper salary because she is doing a proper job. And she needs it, because without it she is a second-class citizen in the office, with effects that reverberate throughout her life.

8.

Tackling Carmen

How to plan and execute *a complete strategic campaign*. Sizing up a complex situation, using allies, neutralizing foes, breaking large objectives into small chunks, uncovering hidden objections, going for the close.

GEORGETTE WAS ORIGINALLY HIRED by Carmen to be a "general assistant," with the promise of more responsibilities within a short time. She quickly began handling most of the community work, and within a few months that niche was hers. Thrilled to be doing what she wanted to do, she put her dissatisfactions about making $4000 less than the "senior aides" (with whom she was in every other way on equal footing) on the back burner. Besides, she was being strategic. She was a newcomer without experience in this field, and she wanted to be accepted.

But today, no one, Carmen included, can deny that Georgette has a right to be making as much as the others. If Georgette steers her ship shrewdly, she can get what she wants. But the course is tricky.

For one thing, Carmen respects power and power alone, and although she doesn't understand why she acts this way, she doesn't like to give unless she is forced to. Once she sees she has no choice, she accepts the inevitable and gives more or less happily and with no hard feelings. But first she tests and tests and tests to satisfy her inner compulsion.

Another issue that keeps Carmen from dealing openly with Georgette is the high cost of her re-election campaign. To give

Georgette the wage she deserves will mean not just an ordinary raise but a whopping increase—and for that she is not emotionally prepared. Carmen would be willing to give *something* now; but she's afraid that once the topic of Georgette's salary is opened, she won't be able to close it without losing her shirt.

Every time Georgette tries to raise the issue, Carmen becomes a whirlwind of evasive maneuvers. She churns herself into such a distracted and hyper state that she effectively discourages Georgette from pursuing her. When Georgette screws up her courage and tries to pierce this shield of maneuver, Carmen finds a way of brushing her off by acting the charming bully or saying she can't talk about it now, or "Let's both think about it"—and nothing happens. This has now gone on for months, establishing a slight subject-object tilt to the proceedings, and the very existence of that tilt has created a new barrier for Georgette.

Having successfully maneuvered around Georgette, Carmen has hardened her position. Over the last few months Carmen has unconsciously come to see Georgette as less worthy of the raise precisely because she hasn't been able to get it. If Georgette were to make a wrong move now, become too aggressive, blurt out an accusation, stupidly start a war, Carmen's nebulous judgments might condense, causing her to tell Georgette where to get off and perhaps putting Georgette in a position where she has to quit to salvage her dignity. This would be a terrible error on Carmen's part and would represent neither her true desires, her real feelings toward Georgette, nor the best interests of her political operation. But it could nonetheless occur.

The months of evasion have had their effect on Georgette, too. Her position has softened. She feels mousier, more like a pest, less deserving of the raise. Her reactions, although illogical, are nevertheless real, and capable of mixing with Carmen's judgments in a disastrous way.

Finally, there is the complication of Steve Friendly. By taking advantage of Georgette's weakness, he has accentuated it both in Georgette's and Carmen's eyes and made Georgette feel even more hopeless about the possibility for change.

Clearly, given all this, Georgette has a difficult course to navigate. But, despite all the obstacles, she can do it.

The purpose of this chapter is not to demonstrate how to get a raise but how any complex strategic problem can be analyzed, understood, and corrected. Georgette may not be able to sail into the harbor in one outing. She may have to move forward, lose some ground, replot her course. But in all that follows, we will not assume any changes in Georgette except one—a mobilization of her will.

Advance Work:
Allies, Enemies, and Other Preliminaries

Having failed to react effectively when Steve Friendly first struck, Georgette will now have to play a defending game. In chess, when you fall behind by a pawn or lose some positional advantage, there is often a temptation to try something rash in order to recoup your losses. The result is generally devastating. The smart player is patient. He plays a defending game. He lives with his disadvantage, protects against further erosion, and waits for his opponent to make an error.

Georgette's anxiety about having been bested may tempt her to walk into Steve's office and belatedly give him a piece of her mind or try to have an open talk with him in order to "iron things out." It would be best to do nothing and wait for Steve's next move. Then she should be ready to establish that she is a person to contend with.

It will also help to keep her "paranoid" assumptions in check. Steve is not the sort of person who steps on everyone. He's young and unsure of himself, directing his first Congressional campaign, and eager to make an impression. He quickly saw that Carmen's office was a free-for-all with an uncertain chain of command and an explosive leader who rules through blame, temper, and preposterous demands. Like anyone caught in the whirlwind of strategic maneuvering, hungry to make it, fearful of becoming the next scapegoat, and not troubling over the interpersonal fine points, Steve sensed a power vacuum and moved in. But he's no monster.

As it turns out, their next conflict has already been drawn. You may remember that Steve wants to appropriate the space Georgette uses to interview constituents about their problems. Under no conditions should he be allowed to get it. To defeat him, Georgette need only use his own tactics against him.

When Friendly demands Georgette's space, he doesn't say, "I want to establish that I'm top dog here," or "I want a space as big as the one Roy Hartmann's campaign manager has." No. He says that the election must take priority, that his volunteers need a place to work, and that Georgette can meet constituents in the reception area for the duration of the campaign. In other words, he is very careful to clothe his demands in appropriate-sounding rationales.

Clearly, Georgette is not on the firmest ground if she counters by saying that she has been working here much longer and will feel belittled by the loss of this space (does she put her seniority or personal feelings above Carmen's reelection?); by insisting that once she gives the space up she'll never get it back (selfish and paranoid); or by threatening to quit (hysterical). To be most effective, she must, like Steve, use appropriate-sounding reasons; she must embody the Good Team Player. She must emphasize that she meets with constituents in this space. To ask constituents—the voters!—to talk to her about their personal misfortunes in a public waiting area would be an insult that would jeopardize Carmen's standing in the district and therefore jeopardize the campaign itself. And on that basis she refuses to move. If she plants her feet on that ground, her motives are beyond reproach and she will be difficult to budge.

The next problem is Al.

In every group, people are concerned about their power base—who is on their side and who will support them in a conflict. Al is Georgette's chief ally in the office. They think alike, confide in each other, and look out for each other's interests. For Al to let Georgette twist in the wind at a meeting, as he did when the animal legislation was discussed last week, is a breach of that allegiance, and he must be confronted.

Heavy punishments are not in order here. Georgette need only catch his attention with a stern voice and a touch of guilt so that when similar situations arise in the future, he will think twice about failing her. Al will probably be so mortified and regretful at Georgette's slightest reproach that she will have to spend the next five minutes reassuring him of her friendship.

Georgette has to get her head screwed on right about Carmen, too. Why did Carmen doodle when Georgette spoke at the meeting? Why has she said nothing favorable about the report? Why has she been so evasive about meeting to discuss a raise?

It is tempting to take all this evidence and assume Carmen has written her off. But Georgette must guard carefully against falling victim to such a deduction. The best thing she can do now is assume the report is acceptable unless she hears otherwise; recognize that she made a strategic error by presenting it in the sloppy way she did; give up on getting the applause she wants and deserves and might otherwise have gotten; and spend a few days in a passive watchful mode to satisfy herself that her fantasies about having fallen into disfavor are unwarranted. Meanwhile she can begin to turn her full attention toward tackling Ms. Big over the critical issue of her raise.

Preparation

A confrontation with Carmen deserves some thought and rehearsal. Georgette has to calculate what looks right as well as what is right. She has to size up the shop: What wages are actually being paid to others? Is more money available? Is this in fact a good time to press the issue? In fact, because of the upcoming campaign, the timing is not ideal, but as time passes, Georgette's second-class status will only become more cemented, and the incline on which Georgette labors will steepen.

Negotiating Position. The more thoroughly she can calculate her own position, the better off she'll be: What am I willing to settle for? What am I willing to give up? What offers will I refuse? How can I refuse them without looking unreasonable or unwilling to compromise? What counterproposals can I make to keep the negotiations alive? If it comes down to it, how can I accept a low offer without seeming to bear a grudge and without pretending a satisfaction I don't feel? If I lose my handle on the negotiations, is there a way to bow out gracefully so that I can return again the next day?

Strategic Strengths and Weaknesses. Everyone has a strategy that he is best at, and in Georgette's case her ace in the hole is "rewards"—that is, she knows how to make people feel good. People like her, they like to like her, and she should use that to the hilt.

She should also assess what her soft spots are and how Carmen might try to poke them in order to detour her. She has to remember what she does when her doubts are tapped—does she talk too much? begin making jokes at her own expense? become frozen with a blank open stare?—and program herself not to to it. It will be useful, too, if she prepares several short, pat phrases that will enable her to change the subject if Carmen starts moving in on her.

Finally, she should identify her safe ground—the inequality of her wage—and remember to keep returning to it if she becomes confused or out maneuvered.

Knowing Whom You're Dealing With. Carmen, of course, has her sensitivities, too. Georgette may feel that Carmen is in the driver's seat, but Carmen is still a vulnerable person with her own fears and concerns, and Georgette has to be mindful of that. She doesn't want to arouse too much guilt or make her too uncomfortable, and she certainly doesn't want to insult her. She simply wants to apply a steady, good-natured pressure and be prepared to control Carmen with a touch of guilt if she becomes too rude or familiar.

With a person like Carmen some form of aggressiveness is essential. Without it, you can't get through to her. You have to be persistent, and you have to keep demanding commitments. And, since she is the boss and you have no right to demand that she slow down, you have to maintain an energy level that matches hers. You can't deal with a person on a motorcycle while you're riding in a rocker.

Aggressiveness is obviously not Georgette's strong suit, so she has to give it some thought. She must avoid assuming overly aggressive postures to compensate for having acted meekly. "Carmen, I insist!" "I will not stand for it!" "Not another stitch of work!" Such tactics will make Georgette look foolish and extreme, and her behavior will become the issue rather than her legitimate right to a raise.

Aggressive posture does not have to threaten or irritate. It can be subtle—a tap on the arm, a forceful repetition of what's already been said, a refusal to hear no, an apparent unwillingness to leave the room, a slightly raised voice. Combined with humor and rewards, it can break through the aggressiveness, obfuscation, evasive maneuvers, and heavy maternal charm that Carmen uses to wiggle away.

Putting Irrational Assumptions on Hold. Georgette tends to believe that if she makes demands and requests she will be opposed. Her "adversary assumption," because it is unconscious, has a subtle but firm grip on her. It causes her to give in and accumulate secret resentments (as she's done for years with Martin) or to go her own way without exploring the possibility of compromise. If she gets treated badly enough, she may even end the relationship in a blaze of recriminations. This adversary assumption must be anticipated and studiously suppressed.

Georgette could calm her adversary fears by packing a sharp word or two in her pocket. If Carmen gets a little nasty, Georgette will then be prepared with an appropriate weapon reestablish a balance. But Georgette should remember that Carmen is genuinely fond of her. To be excessively preoccupied with how she'll act if she and Carmen come to verbal blows will nurture her irrational fears and make them grow.

Living Through Anxiety. Because she assumes she will be attacked or abandoned, Georgette becomes particularly anxious whenever she makes demands. Carmen, ever-sensitive to insecurity, will play on this, flexing her muscles and shrewdly attempting to aggravate Georgette's fearfulness. And something in Georgette will want to put her tail between her legs and run. She has to be prepared to live through the moment.

Anxiety tend to make us spew forth weak and self-destructive maneuvers, but it doesn't have to; it can be controlled. It really doesn't matter if Georgette is anxious as long as she can contain it and not allow it to make her do the things it normally makes her do. If she can live through her anxiety just ninety seconds longer than usual, she may find the resources to react to Carmen's strategies in a measured and effective way. It will be helpful if she can identify in advance the strategies that are most likely to rattle her, identify the sorts of reactions she wants to inhibit (nervous laughter, stammering), and be prepared with specific alternatives (like pacing the floor and acting pensive) to disguise what she's really feeling.

Taking One Step at a Time. Finally, Georgette should see her campaign as a series of small objectives.

Her first objective is to get Carmen to agree to a time to talk.

The second is to get her to talk under sheltered conditions—not in the stairwell, not with others present, not while Carmen is talking into her dictating machine or taking a dozen calls.

Her third goal is to see whether Carmen has a hidden objection to giving Georgette the title or the raise, an objection she is for some reason embarrassed to speak of. Is she dissatisfied with Georgette in some way? Is there some precedent she's afraid of setting? Is she planning to phase out the community operation? Georgette has to know what she's really up against.

Her fourth goal is to close the negotiation within a reasonable time so that her power isn't dissipated in endless talk.

Once her objectives are broken down this way, the first steps are less daunting. If Carmen acts a little bullyish and rude when Georgette asks her for a time to talk, Georgette will not be thinking, "How can I justify a four thousand dollar raise?" but merely, "I have a right to ask her for an audience and to be spoken to respectfully." Such a perspective enables her to counter with a properly measured strategy ("Carmen, you're being rude") rather than becoming hysterical and reaching for the ultimate weapon ("I quit!").

As for the ultimate weapon, it is only powerful if it is never used. Carmen knows what the bottom line is. She knows she may lose Georgette if she doesn't treat her well or give her what she wants. It's a possibility that keeps her negotiating and keeps her respectful. At a certain point in the negotiation, when Carmen seems intransigently committed to a paltry offer, Georgette may respond by saying "I'm still dissatisfied," and then wait. This may fluster Carmen, but because she doesn't want to lose Georgette, she'll keep trying to accommodate her. But for Georgette to mention quitting is to destabilize the relationship and force Carmen's hand. Georgette should carry herself at all times as if she belongs here and will be here tomorrow.

Getting the Commitment

Carmen sees it coming, of course, the minute Georgette approaches and asks to see her for ten minutes. "What's it all about," she asks, "and why the serious face?" Georgette wisely resists giving the information at first, but Carmen persists. "It's about my status here," Georgette concedes, at which point Carmen starts moaning about the primary, the speeches she has to make, the rent strike at Oasis Park, the awful pains in her feet: "Let's wait till things ease up a bit, honey."

"Carmen," Georgette says in a mock scolding voice, "I need you for ten minutes, and I'm willing to come in early or stay late or stop by your place while you soak your feet."

"Okay, Georgie, I'll work it out."

This is an intense moment for Georgette. She's made a demand, been bolder than usual, and was given a small assent. Glory hallelujah, be satisfied, duck out, don't push it, don't become a pest! But Carmen hasn't given her what she wants—a commitment to meet. She's still operating under the old contract—Georgette can be evaded, Georgette is a sweetheart, the whole thing will blow over, I'll give her a nice bonus at Christmastime. So it's crucial for Georgette to make the extra effort now and demand a definite time; or in two weeks she'll be back at the bottom of the hill, and have to go through the climb all over again, feeling more the pest, and bearing a bigger bag of resentment.

"Let's set a time now," she says in a reassuring voice. Her tone bears no trace of adversary posture, but rather seems to caress and care for Carmen. She does well to use few words, for the longer she talks, the more likely she will reveal her insecurity or anxiety and give Carmen hooks to hang her evasions on.

Carmen looks at Georgette with endearment and nods her head with a few rapid strokes. She didn't think it would take this long. "So you want to pin me down, is that it?"

"That's it," says Georgette with a grin.

"Okay, let's get Lynn in here with my calendar," Carmen says, thus proving what a softy she really is.

A Strategic Initiative

Georgette knows Carmen well enough to understand that she lives in a world of maneuvers, always seeks the advantage, and only allows a real balance when she has no choice. Although Georgette has no illusions about Carmen's giving her a $4000 increase all at once, she decides to take a strategic initiative by asking for it anyway. Her demand not only establishes her ultimate goal, it is technically justified and thus cannot be exploited as inappropriate. It helps smoke out Carmen and gives Georgette some cushion, something to give up.

"Well, Carmen," she says softly, every bit the sweet Georgette, "there are two things I want. The title—community liaison. We've talked about that. I want it printed on my new cards. And the same salary as the other senior aides. I think it's about time, don't you?"

Carmen's fears are confirmed. (The woman's become unreasonable!) Her motors start revving, but she exhibits perfect control. "The title's no big deal one way or the other," she says. "I mean what's a title?" A false argument and a strategic hook by which Georgette should not allow herself to be snared. "So let's get down to brass tacks. What are you making now?"

"Twenty-two thousand."

"Okay, I'll give you twenty-three—and you can have whatever title you want except boss. All right? Can we get back to winning this campaign now?" She stands up and smiles as if the whole thing is over.

Georgette should not be caught in Carmen's ploys—the decisive offer, the seductive humor, the suggestion that precious seconds are being wasted, the implication of generosity. She has to counter them all in some way that does not actually confront any of them. It would be helpful at this point if Georgette used a little shrewdness of her own—a little image, a little humor, a little sign of play—just to show that she's on top of things and that her disagreement is not hostile.

"Well, so far we agree on the title."

Carmen begins to panic. Someone is making her do something she doesn't want to do. She's being backed into a four-thousand-dollar corner. The fear of losing Georgette and her much heralded community operation right in the middle of her big campaign compounds her anxiety. She unloads some heavier maneuvers.

"Georgette, I don't understand you. Here we are in the middle of an expensive campaign, the bottom is going out of the market, my funds are drying up, and I'm offering you a thousand dollar increase. Come on!"

Resist escalation. "The economy is hurting all of us, Carmen."

"But, Georgette, your husband does very well, I can't believe you're under financial stress, you only have one kid, you're constantly running home to take care of her. I mean, what's going on? Did Martin put you up to this? Are you in therapy?"

A three-ring circus of strategic assaults. The first thing Georgette thinks is: It's true, caught in a lie, I don't need the money, I just want it for my pride. Then: I do take off more time than the others, I do get special benefits, I don't deserve the same salary. Then: Martin did push me to do this, she can see his hand at work, my fraudulence is showing!

Now is the time to resist defeat (Run! Run!), resist becoming argumentative or defensive ("I didn't know you resented my taking care of my sick daughter"), resist pulling a bomb out of her pocket ("Perhaps you shouldn't have a community liaison if you can't afford it").

If Georgette has prepared herself well, she's thought about these soft spots and recognized that they do not undermine her position—equity. With this in mind, she does not need to counter any of Carmen's wild accusations. To do so is to be distracted from her goal. Let Carmen stick her with a few pins. Getting the raise will erase the pain.

Still, despite the most lavish preparation, she may be hooked by all this and, if so, she may have to buy time. She can do this by remaining silent for a moment, by standing up and pacing, by repeating herself, by asking a few stalling questions, by temporarily diverting attention ("Goodness, Carmen, are you spilling your tea on the rug?"), and waiting for the fog to pass. Each of these cool manuevers will require fighting off her anxiety, for anxiety tends to make hysterical demands—"Respond! Defend yourself! Go for the bait!"—which we tend to unthinkingly obey.

Smoking Out the Hidden Objection

"Carmen, may I ask you a question?" A nice strategy at this moment. It diverts attention, seduces Carmen out of her tank, breaks the adversary atmosphere, and invites her to give Georgette her full attention.

"Yes?"

"If you were in my position, would you be satisfied with my salary? Honestly."

The conversation is returning to safe ground. Georgette fashions the question so that it is impossible to oppose and, at the same time, invites Carmen's identification. Carmen struggles for a moment, unwilling to concede the point and unable to come up with a convincing lie.

"If you were in my place," says Georgette with a touch of anger, "you'd be earning forty thousand by now!" Flattery works with Carmen, especially if disguised by an adversary tone. Georgette notes the change in Carmen's face and softens her voice. "All I'm asking for is the going rate. It's not that I don't appreciate your offer—I do. I know you're concerned about my welfare. But is there any reason why you can't do better?"

"Yes," says Carmen, adopting for the first time a thoughtful, honest tone. "My funds are tight right now. Contributions haven't been everything I expected. And I'm worried—worried about the overhead."

Georgette continues to smoke her out. "You have no objection in principle to paying me on a par with the others?"

"No. In principle, none."

This is a major concession. Georgette is in the harbor now. She only has to find her berth.

Closing

"Can I suggest," she asks, "that we set up a schedule to put me on a par?"

"I'll tell you what, Georgette. I'll give you twenty-three-five now and twenty-four next January if we're still in business. That's the best I can do for now. I hope you'll accept it."

The generous concession, the tone of conciliation, the big show of turning her pockets inside out, the image of utter sincerity make this a strategic speech of the first order.

"On one condition," says Georgette.

"Yes?"

"That in a year from January I'm earning the same as the other senior aides."

Georgette has to make this point. Otherwise the second class citizenship will not be expunged, there will be meetings when someone will give her a nasty look and she'll wonder all over again whether she has an equal right to speak, and resentment will once more set in.

Carmen thinks. What objection can I come up with now? Well, that is a long time away. Anything can happen in eighteen months. I really can't say no after saying I had no objection in principle. It would surely cost me twenty-six thousand to replace her. And I certainly can't afford to look around now. I guess it's fair. Still have a good deal, really.

She picks up her head from her calculations. "You sure drive a hard bargain, Georgie!" she says smiling. And then she stands to give her a hug.

9.

Tackling Marge

Although it can be used as a punishment, anger need not be destructive. How Georgette can modulate and control her expression of anger so that it becomes an effective tool for balancing the power with Marge. *Confrontation without overkill*.

PUNISHMENT IS a loaded word. People punish each other incessantly—with anger, silence, pointed criticisms—but no one likes to own up to doing it. There's nothing necessarily wrong with punishment. If you can't punish, you can't defend yourself, train a child, or maintain a position of authority. But punishment is a hot topic, and you'll have to overcome our cultural prejudice against the word to fully appreciate what follows.

Human beings are very sensitive. They feel the slightest signs of dislike, disapproval, or disrespect and they are hurt by them. But as fragile as many of us are, we are often heavily armed and trigger-happy. Even with children, we can be heartbreakingly careless with our weapons. If Georgette tenderly but firmly reminds Cindy that because she didn't eat her vegetables she will get no dessert, the punishment will hit its mark with more than adequate force. But if Georgette speaks harshly and irritably, her tone is much more punishing than the withheld dessert. For instead of steering Cindy's behavior (You must eat your vegetables), she seems to reject the girl herself, thereby arousing feelings of pain and defectiveness.

Punishments are a special tool because they have the power to train people, but they don't always work in the way that's intended. If Martin is testy whenever Georgette questions him about his feelings, if he flicks pointed humor at her whenever she asks for something he doesn't want to give, if he becomes exasperated when she's not the life of the party after sex, she will be trained by such responses. Without knowing it, she learns not to question him about his feelings, not to be direct in asking things of him, and never to be too solemn after sex. For gradually she associates those ways of being with the pangs of shame induced by his punishments. Martin gains the immediate security of being one-up by training Georgette to be docile. But Georgette is also trained not to be honest with him, to seek intimacy elsewhere, and to see sex with Martin as something of an ordeal.

We've already seen Georgette effectively use punishment against Martin and Steve in Chapter 6. But let's look now at Georgette's problems with Marge and at the subtle ways in which anger can be put to good use.

The Four Phases of Constructive Confrontation

Although Georgette and Marge always patch things up, Georgette frequently feels one-down with Marge. She gets punished, but she doesn't know how to respond in such a way that both her self-respect and the friendship are preserved.

Marge was depressed around the time of Georgette's birthday dinner. She was afraid that if she spent too much money on dinner, or left work too early, or got home too late, or had a rotten time for any reason, that she would become even more down on herself than she already was. Her fears put her in a rigid and controlling mood. She probably would have gone along with the original plans if Georgette had pressed her to do so in a forceful way. But Marge is accustomed to getting her way with Georgette, and when Georgette presents her with a power vacuum, she gets drawn in and maneuvers for control.

Why didn't Georgette simply blurt, "Oh, Marge, I'm so miserable, are you about to back out of our date"? Or why didn't she let some anger show? "Damn it, Marge, do we have a date or don't we!" Either response would have been perfect. Georgette has done both many times, and they've worked. But once her feelings have become extreme, Georgette chokes on her words. To make things worse, they're talking on the phone, and Marge is at work, sounding formal and rushed.

If Marge stands her up, Georgette has a broad range of reactions. The most extreme punishment is to withdraw from the friendship. Less extreme would be to tell Marge to forget about dinner if she's not interested. Still less extreme is to reprimand Marge for backing away from her best friend's birthday. But what has Marge done to deserve any of this? So far all she's done is hedge.

PHASE ONE. *Reality Check*. The first thing Georgette has to do is stifle her negative assumptions. She assumes that Marge doesn't want to be with her on her birthday, or that Marge wants to choose the restaurant herself, or that she doesn't think Georgette's birthday is important enough to warrant the cost. Georgette must put all such thoughts on hold and get to the truth by smoking Marge out:

"What's on your mind, Marge?" "Are you opposed to a French restaurant?" "Is money the problem?" "Are you really not in the mood?" Spoken with care, these questions assure Marge that whatever her feelings, they will be respected. If Marge answers honestly, Georgette will no longer feel bullied, and the two of them will be able to work something out.

A more aggressive approach—"Hey, what's going on here! It's my birthday and I can't even get you on the phone!"—may be just as good, or better. But overly hurt or hostile tones will only elicit defensiveness.

PHASE TWO. *Assertiveness*. "I want to go to La Jardiniere. It's important to me." This can be said straight, without anger. It's an important step, because it may be the first Marge has heard of how much this dinner means to Georgette.

If Georgette chooses to contain her anger at this point, she should still not forget that she feels it. For the feeling itself will lend a force and concentration to her words.

PHASE THREE. *Mobilization of Anger*. If Marge continues to sound impatient or to make snappy, evasive, or dismissive comments, Georgette should begin to mobilize her anger more forcefully.

"Marge, I'm angry." To say that one is angry in a nonpunishing way is a powerful tool. It can wake Marge up without making her defensive.

"Marge, goddamn it, I'm not going to Enrico's for my birthday!" This is a little punishing, because now the anger is expressed in the tone. But it is still tactful and can be further modulated with the merest suggestion of irony.

"Listen, we made a date. Doesn't that mean something to you? When it was your birthday—and not even your thirty-fifth for Christsakes—I ran around half the day!" A fiercer statement because she's introduced guilt. Again the tone is everything—stern, but not vicious or hateful.

PHASE FOUR. *Direct Punishment.* At some point, if Georgette does not get the explanation she has a right to expect, if the discussion turns into an argument, or if Marge becomes derisive ("Oh, come *on*, George, if you didn't worry so much about your stomach . . ."), Georgette has to go beyond the moderate expression of anger and punish Marge by breaking the date. "*You* go to Enrico's, Marge, we'll get together another time."

True, if Marge doesn't acquiesce, this is the end of the party for Georgette, too; but at a certain point she has to see that she's failed and let go. Only an object holds onto something that isn't worth keeping.

And that's as far as the punishments need go. Marge will get the message and the effect on the long-term restructuring of their contract may be salutary: You cannot take Georgette for granted; you cannot treat her with disrespect and live comfortably. Given the closeness of their friendship, they will probably talk it all out later.

Marge may have failings, but she is also a good friend. She could be an even better friend if Georgette would measure moments more carefully and pay more attention to her rights. Marge values people who are forthright in their demands and who stop her from playing the subject. For with them she is free to be who she is without having to constantly monitor herself for fear of taking advantage.

The Measured Use of Anger

Most people assume that anger is something they will let out in an explosion, act out through constant seepage, or doggedly contain. It is better to think of anger as a powerful emotion that can be channeled and used as a tool.

Between the two extremes—1) swallowing your anger and denying it even to yourself (which shrinks your whole being and assures your powerlessness) and 2) lashing out with uncontrolled rage—there are a near infinite number of tones and positions to take. The important thing is to strike the right note for the moment at hand. Some guidelines:

1. *Stand Back.* There are ways of expressing anger that invade another's identity, and there are ways of expressing it that simply demand attention in a forceful way. There is dignified anger and there is shrewish anger; there is respectful anger and there is anger that kills, and the only way of controlling it is to stand apart from it—to

save some piece of your mind for observation, assessment, and calculation. To become one with anger is to lose the ability to regulate it. And uncontrolled anger mixes with self-doubt to produce venom.

2. *Know when to have it out*. Sometimes when friends blow up at each other, the angry words are cleansing. In the calm that follows, they talk intimately or make love, and their connection is renewed. They can afford to be openly, even uncontrollably angry because they have faith in themselves and in each other. But unsheathed anger can just as easily be a tool for subjugation or a knife that cuts a relationship to shreds. If Georgette had screamed, "You ungiving bitch!" and then hung up on Marge, the result might have been happy or sad, but it certainly would have been out of Georgette's control. She would have made herself very vulnerable, she would have felt like a mental case, and if Marge had not called right back and been understanding, she would have become a candidate for six hot fudge sundaes.

3. *Protect the Opposition*. Anger gets out of control for several reasons. 1) We hold it back too long. 2) We're ashamed to punish and thus become twice as angry at someone who forces us into it. 3) We jump to conclusions about what the other person is up to and how he'll react if we express our anger. And 4) we allow today's small hurt to mix and become one with all the hurts of yesterday.

Georgette has experienced a lot of pain over various hurts that go back to childhood, and she is in a lot of pain at the moment because of a string of recent setbacks. Even if Marge is clearly in the wrong, Georgette must recognize that Marge's insensitivity resonates with much else that's hurting Georgette already. How easy—and how destructive—it would be if, because Marge made one wrong move, Georgette blasted her with the accumulated pain of the week. She must protect Marge from the extreme emotions she feels.

Besides Georgette does not want a defeated Marge to celebrate her birthday with her. She wants only to awaken her to her needs and to Marge's responsibilities as a friend. Her purpose is to right an imbalance so that the flow of their friendship can resume.

4. *Avoid Emotional Contamination*. The fear that you are doing something wrong makes it difficult to express anger gracefully. Anger does not mix well with self-doubt, approval-seeking, self-justifications, or pleading. Once you decide to express your anger, get behind it and do it cleanly. The other person will feel less manipulated and more likely to listen to the message. And, if he believes you're wrong, he'll be better able to tell it to you straight.

Remember, too, that anger can be expressed without threats, without "or elses." When you are clear on the issues, your anger will generally accomplish its purpose without the need for coercion.

5. *Use Guilt Carefully.* The ideal way to instill guilt when dealing with the peccadilloes of everyday life (as opposed to major interpersonal crimes) is a pinprick insertion, clear and undisguised, followed by immediate removal. You want the person to get the message ("I was thoughtless") just as the pain of the delivery is receding. The common alternative, shoving it in again and again with insistent twists, serves no purpose. It's the strategic style of someone who's lost in a childhood rage or who's feeling guilty himself about what he's doing.

The guilt strategy is not enhanced by hurt tones. Keep it dignified. Keep it straight. Keep it short:

- "Listen, we made a date. Does that mean something to you or not?" A simple reference to the contract.
- "When it was your birthday, Marge, you had no trouble getting me on the phone." A stinging understatement, which reminds Marge of all she's gotten from this person to whom she's now so reluctant to give.
- "And it wasn't even your thirty-fifth!" Emphasizes the imbalance. A tinge of humor will keep it from being too strong.

6. *Avoid Escalation.* When applying guilt, escalation may easily creep in through exaggerated statements. Georgette will be most effective if she aims for the violation of the moment ("I'm angry that you take this commitment so lightly"). The alternatives—attacking a pattern in Marge's behavior ("You never adhere to your commitments"), aiming for a quality in Marge's character ("You care only about your own needs"), or combining the guilt with isolation ("No wonder everyone finds you so difficult")—are excessive. The punishments are too big for the crime. Such artillery should be saved for real battlefield conditions.

"I'm feeling so rotten today and now I get *this!*" is an irrelevant and undignified use of guilt. Marge is not responsible for Georgette's rotten day. Violently hanging up, meanwhile, even without denunciation, gives Marge the happy opportunity to play victim herself.

7. *Be Sensitive to the Other Person's Vulnerability.* One person is mortified by public displays of emotion. Another is destroyed by icy withdrawal. If Georgette knows that Marge is crushed by a raised voice, she has to take that into account.

8. *Watch for Signals of Openness.* A softened tone, a reflective quality in the voice, a loss of defensiveness on Marge's part indicate that Georgette's anger has succeeded. Now is *not* the time to drive her point home and win the argument. Now is the time to move from

the spirit of contest to the spirit of sharing and bring her own feelings to the fore.

9. *Know When to Quit*. If Georgette doesn't get the apology, the understanding, or the changed behavior that she seeks, it is best to walk away and trust that in some long-range sense, her anger has been effective. She shouldn't get hung up on achieving the type of success she originally envisioned or trapped into playing to win.

Listening to Anger: A Word for Marge

Clean anger deserves attention and respect. There is something satisfying about being dealt to from a straight deck. Marge would do well to drop her defensiveness, if she can, and try to respond to Georgette with honesty.

But what if Georgette goes too far—gives Marge a bitter tongue-lashing laced with poisonous accusations? Now it's Marge who must balance the power. The simplest statement can accomplish this task: "Georgette, I don't think you're being fair." If Georgette is intransigent, Marge may try to smoke her out: "Do you feel I'm always insensitive to you? Can't I blow it once in a while? Have I built up no credit for any of the good things I've done in the past?" Finally, "*Hey*, give me a break!" or some other bit of aggressive humor may hit the right note and break the spell.

As long as Marge keeps her focus on the overkill (and doesn't try to salvage her position on the French restaurant or prove that she was somehow right all along), she will be on safe ground.

This, then, concludes our first section on balancing the power—confronting abuse, overcoming the object mentality, launching a complex strategic campaign, and using anger with effectiveness and grace. Now, after a short review, we'll return to our story.

Remember, all that has happened in these replays is only what could have been, not what was. As we get back to the real world of our characters, we find them just as they were four chapters ago, with Georgette still an object at home and at work and Marge still hung up about a guy she last dated a week before Georgette's birthday.

Review 2

1) *Beware strategic habit*. Social life consists of an almost continuous strategic dance in which we manipulate, control, signal, and support one another with shorthand messages of approval, disapproval, acceptance, rejection, requests of all kinds, and assertions of authority. Like any form of influence, strategies can be weak or strong, elegant or clumsy, ethical or unethical, courageous or cowardly.

Unfortunately, we rely more on rigid strategic habits developed in childhood than on carefully considered moves that suit our real needs. The best strategies are exercised in a conscious way, and tempered or abandoned as soon as a limited objective is reached.

2) *Confront abuse*. Georgette cannot come to terms with issues like selfishness and weakness while she is being shoved into her shame about them; and she cannot come to terms with the key people in her life when she's one-down. If she is an object, self-hatred comes with the territory and forces her to believe the false logic of shame—that she is a bad person who deserves whatever she gets. Balancing the power is thus her first priority.

To deal effectively with abuse, she may have to confront it with carefully measured punishments or take a fierce defensive posture. At other times it is wiser to evade abuse by refusing to go for the "hook."

Tactful evasion is one of the toughest strategies to master, because our individual psychologies can make going for the hook irresistable.

3) *Punishments* vary greatly in style and intensity. When someone belittles Georgette, she may walk away, stare coolly, come back with a rebuke of her own, demand an apology. The response depends on what works best for her. But somehow the other person must be made to know that if he stings he will be stung. A little such knowledge goes a long way.

4) *Fight off the object mentality.* In order to operate effectively, Georgette must overcome object-think. This requires a) facing the fact of her object condition squarely, as well as her own responsibility for it; b) halting the object spiral the moment she spots it; and c) mobilizing herself for a much needed change.

She must also learn to stop placing her need for emotional contact, her need for intimacy, and her fear of losing the relationship ahead of her self-esteem.

This inner game of power does not require that Georgette feel different about herself. It only requires an act of will. Some degree of improved self-feeling will inevitably follow.

5) *Analyze, plan, rehearse, execute.* When facing a complex strategic task, like Georgette's effort to get a raise and a title, you have to analyze carefully before you act.

• Georgette has to be sensitive to her allies and opponents and where she stands with them.

• She has to prepare her negotiating position, assess her own strengths and weaknesses, put her irrational assumptions on hold, and prepare to live through anxiety without acting it out.

• She will find her task easier if she breaks it into small objectives and keeps in mind the legitimacy of her position each step of the way.

• Georgette will also do better if she knows what to expect from the people who give her trouble and works out the likely moves. Rehearsing is extremely useful; as is reviewing incidents later.

6) *When angry, remember your goals*. Anger can initiate a fair fight between intimates. It can open an honest discussion between friends. It can cause a cessation of abuse between co-workers. But it rarely works without sensitivity, diplomacy, or shrewdness.

To fine tune the degree to which you display this important but dangerous emotion, you must: a) be sensitive to what you're feeling; b) not doubt your right to feel it; and c) be clear about what the situation allows.

Quiz

This quiz will help you review the material in Part II while assessing your own skills and power needs. Try to pick both the answer that most reveals you, as well as the one you think is best. What does your first choice say about your strategic habits?

PROBLEM. Marge, recently separated from her boyfriend and feeling rather down, accepts an invitation to go sailing with a casual friend, Jerry. "We need a fourth hand," Jerry says, "and it will be just what you need, too." Marge considers saying, "Strictly platonic, Jerry," but she doesn't want to be presumptuous or insulting. Once out to sea, Jerry begins to change from the sympathetic supporter into the relentless pursuer. As Marge's gentle rebuffs become firmer, Jerry becomes nasty and insulting. When she complains that he's hurting her, he says, "Oh, don't take me so seriously," and continues the attack. Two days from port, Marge is in agony. She doesn't want to spoil everyone's vacation with her rage. She wishes she'd been more careful not to lead Jerry on. She can't wait for the doomed voyage to be over. If you were in her shoes, what would you do?

1. I'd apologize to Jerry for not having been more explicit about my intentions, assure him that it was not personal, and ask if we couldn't resume our old friendship.
2. Realizing some mistakes can't be undone, I'd try to make the best of a bad situation and spend as much time as I could with the others.
3. I'd fight fire with fire, using innuendo, barbed humor, and other punishments to make life as difficult for Jerry as he's making it for me.
4. I'd tell Jerry, "I'm ceasing all activities as a member of this crew and not manning another shift until you change your attitude."

SOLUTION. This is an open and shut case of abuse, and Marge needs to do something dramatic to balance the scales. 1. May be worth a try, but, given the way Jerry has been acting, will probably be brushed off. You made a mistake by not getting the contract straight in advance, but that doesn't doom you to abuse. You don't owe Jerry an apology, not after the way he's behaved. A weak response. 2. Escapist; too willing to accept defeat. Sometimes you think you have no options because you're afraid to recognize the one option you do have. 3. Too little too late. Jerry already has too much momentum. And he'd love an excuse to escalate. This is where Marge would typically get herself in trouble, relying on banter where it isn't useful. 4. Bold and effective. Cracks the atmosphere with a truly relevant threat. You risk standing alone and being seen as a spoiler, but you need to take control to regain your dignity. This action may salvage the vacation.

PROBLEM. You walk into the grocery store and say good morning to the grocer. As usual, he goes on doing what he's doing and doesn't respond. What do you do?

1. I say, "To hell with him," and do my shopping.
2. I vow never to come to this store again, even if it is the most convenient.
3. I wonder what it is about me that turns him off, and spend the rest of my time there figuring out what I can say to get on his good side.
4. I assume he's busy and tell myself that I'm stupid to have any feeling about this at all.
5. I add an edge of aggressiveness to my voice when speaking to him.
6. I say politely: "You know, Mr. Jones, I've been shopping here for years, and yet whenever I greet you, you don't respond. Is there any reason for that?"

SOLUTION: This is a small-time rejection by someone who has little importance in your life. If you feel wounded, you should ask yourself why you are so vulnerable and carefully examine more critical areas of your life. As for the immediate problem, it doesn't matter too much how you handle it, or whether you handle it at all. 1. Fine. 2. You're taking this too personally. He probably treats everybody this way. Besides, you're punishing yourself more than him. Ask yourself where all this pain is really coming from. 3. An object response. 4. Fine, but don't ignore your feelings; get them into perspective. 5. Okay, but are you getting too involved? 6. If you can do this, you are very rare. Suggests great composure and self-confidence. Might even achieve something.

PROBLEM. Your mother, who lives in the neighborhood, has a habit of showing up on weekend mornings unannounced. A friend is due over shortly, and you have a full schedule for the rest of the day. When you tell Mom that you'd like her to call first, she becomes angry and says, "I hardly see you any more! Is a mother unwelcome in her own child's house?" You would reply by:

1. Telling her that you love her, but explaining that you have to ask even the people you love to call first. You then politely excuse yourself and promise to call her soon.
2. Denouncing her for trying to make you feel guilty.
3. Apologizing and inviting her in.
4. Trying to talk the problems out with her.

5. Stating forcefully that you saw her just two weeks ago, that you don't get to see your best friends more, and that there's nothing wrong with making a phone call.

6. Inviting her in for coffee, using the occasion to firmly express your point of view, and not giving up until she acknowledges that her behavior is unacceptable.

SOLUTION: If this is Mom's habitual style, then the problem is probably more her abusiveness than your lack of consideration. She plays hardball with guilt—and you're likely to get hooked into an habitual response. 1. A skillful evasion because it gets rid of Mom without getting snagged by her hooks. It consists essentially of a reward (There, there, I love you, I'll call soon). It also keeps you in the role (loving child). 2. Swallows the bait. You end up looking like the crazy one, and a vital relationship is kept in a destructive mode. 3. Unless it's done out of pure generosity and good will, an object's response. Mom obviously knows how to control you. 4. Unless Mom is the rare sort of person who easily moves from strategies to openness, you're making the error of trying to be direct with someone who's playing to win. 5. Logic is on your side, but defensiveness is not useful here. With Steve Friendly it could work because the relationship is more formal. Here it simply acts as a hook, inviting further strategic moves. 6. Gracious, effective, strong. The power is getting balanced because Mom is giving you a commitment. If she later reneges, then you have to move to a less accommodating strategy, such as standing in the door and repeating, "I'm sorry, Mom, but I'm busy now" to whatever tactics she employs.

PROBLEM. Sarah is an assistant editor in Martin's office. Since Martin is often abrupt and rarely generous with his praise, she's sometimes unsure if he's satisfied with her work. When she asks for feedback, he cocks an eye and says, "I didn't know that you liberated women needed stroking." If you were in Sarah's position, what would you say?

1. "Martin, I was here till ten o'clock last night, and this is the kind of comment you make when I ask for an evaluation?"

2. "Excuse me, but I can't talk when you're like this."

3. "You're the one person here whose feedback would mean more to me than just stroking."

4. "Well, I wouldn't call it stroking. What I'm asking for is your evaluation. How do you feel about my work?"

5. "You! What do you know about women's liberation?"

6. I'd be angry but say nothing. But I'd stop giving my all.

SOLUTION: Sarah needs something that she's not getting. When she asks for it she gets evaded with derision. In responding, Sarah has to be especially careful, because she is a subordinate. 1. Guilt. He deserves to be made guilty, but this move is inelegant. It fails to deliver the message that as an employee you need feedback, and as a boss, it's his job to give it. May be effective in the short run, because he will feel he owes you one for staying late. But does it set the tone you want?

2. Dignified punishment in the form of withdrawal. Effective if he knows what you're getting at based on previous confrontations. Otherwise, it accomplishes little. 3. Flattery; very manipulative; too transparent. A good tactic for someone like Carmen when she's on a steamroll, but dangerous with someone who can smell it out. 4. A direct, non-strategic response (except inasmuch as you're playing innocent). Shows an ability to put negative assumptions on hold and to persist in going after what you need without being snagged by his hooks. A wise move for someone in the subordinate role. None of which is to say that you should forget your hurt and anger if you go this route. Just don't show it to him as yet. If he persists in being snide, you can apply a touch of guilt: "I work hard trying to give you what you need. Is there any reason you wouldn't want to let me know how I'm doing?" 5. Humorous banter in the Marge style. An effective evasion of his hook (the putdown), but that's all. 6. Powerless punishment. If your typing deteriorates or if you come in late, he will have real cause to punish.

Further Exercises for Self-Awareness

Use these questions to bring the lessons of the book into your daily life. Don't try to answer them all at once, but rather come back from time to time and select a new one to tackle.

• Observe with a more detached eye what goes on between you and other people. Write about it in a notebook. Refer to yourself in the third person, if necessary, to get more distance. What was really happening? What do you usually tell yourself about it? What strategies were used? Which of your self-doubts were at stake?

• Determine whether you tend to be more an object or subject. Does this apply with men? With women? At home? At work? Do you tend to seek subject or object mates? If you were a member of the opposite sex, what sort of mate would you choose? (That's a good one to think about, for it often reveals the hidden object in the subject, and vice versa.) Can you identify powerphobic inhibitions and the times when they arise?

• What are some of your major self-doubts? How do they get played out in your relationships?

• Notice how easy it is to dominate the people you dominate. What makes you do it? What do you gain? What do you lose? What are you hiding? What are you afraid of?

• Notice how easy it is for certain people to dominate you. Identify your object qualities and the qualities in others to which you fall prey. When struck by awareness of winning and losing, subjects typically feel guilt and remorse, objects feel anger and resentment. Those reactions are natural and legitimate. But consider also that each party has responsibility; each party contributes. What is the most effective avenue to change?

• What object posture do you take? Are you afraid of risking a break in the relationship? Do you seek intimacy inappropriately? Do you let your emotional needs undermine you?

• Can you maintain a private agenda when you need to? And drop it when you don't?

• Which strategies do you use most often? Image? Guilt? Flattery? Humor? When do you use them well? When do you use them poorly? Which strategies are you unable to use at all? Why not? Can you think of times when you might experiment with them?

• What powerless or misplaced strategies do you use when under duress? Can you see how they evolved from your childhood relationships?

• What strategy do you rely on excessively? Do you always turn on the image, pretending to be okay and unaffected, when you could be direct about what you feel? Do you keep trying to smoke out the other person's feelings, when you need to get angry and express it? Do you filibuster when you'd do better to listen? Do you dodge and divert attention to avoid answering a delicate question? Do you always confront with guilt or denunciation, hoping to change the culprit once and for all, when a policy of occasional flattery would accomplish far more?

• Which strategies are you most susceptible to? How do you react to anger? To a very slick image? To someone who takes without giving? Do your reactions to such behavior betray you at times? How might you act differently?

• Can you find someone to talk to in a nonjudgmental way about power and insecurity? If there are subject-object issues between you, can you put them on the table?

III.

THE PLAY

Maneuvers, Maneuvers,
Maneuvers!

10.

Power With a Proper Stranger

How insecurities, self-doubts, poor self-awareness, hang-ups about what we should be, and the fear of being direct can all lead to disasters in bed. The saga of a short but volcanic love affair.

As soon as Marge becomes involved with a man, she begins to judge him. She hates clumsiness. A man may be generous, talented, artistic, knowledgeable, but if he's timid about handling things in her apartment, if he doesn't know how to put a cassette in the tape deck, if he fumbles when reclosing a box of crackers, she finds herself beginning to fume. Ashamed of her impatience ("Bitch!"), she controls herself and tries to focus on his fine qualities, all the while hating herself for not being able to do so. Eventually covert fragments of abuse begin to leak out, which she quickly denies or explains away with defensive statements like: "Oh, I'm still a little edgy from the office," or "Easy, easy, I was only teasing." Or else he acts like a nerd once too often, and, unable to control herself any longer, she clobbers him one between the eyes; whereupon they agree that perhaps they're not quite right for each other.

"Why am I like this?" she asks in distress. And goes through a million permutations about her parents, about philosophy and values, about what she wants in a man. And yet she misses what's really bothering her. The things she calls clumsiness all have an element of powerlessness about them. And inadvertent displays of powerlessness—of fearfulness, hunger for approval, lack of self-respect—are for Marge an irresistible invitation to abuse. If a man were totally incompetent around a tape recorder but was genuinely at ease about this shortcoming, if it didn't make a dent in his self-assurance, she might smirk and shake her head and put the tape in herself, but she would respect him all the same.

If Marge tends to become a subject with some men and judge them as weak (Uch, incompetent! Uch, too eager to please!), with other men, she tends to become an object and judge them as exploiters (Uch, what a bastard! Uch, what a pig!). In each case, her judgments eventually provide her with a convenient means of escape.

Every so often Marge finds herself with a man who is more like herself, someone who successfully uses image to mask his self-doubts and who has a talent for studiously pleasing others without seeming to sacrifice his own identity in the process. With such a man she is slower to judge. Unfortunately, no matter how much they enjoy each other, and no matter how much they sense they have in common, their thick layers of image are a barrier. Who's going to open up first? Who's going to break with the banter and the blasé and admit some genuine interest? Who's going to reveal feelings that might indicate a lack of complete command?

To each the other looks crisp, cool, and confident. One moment Marge wants to show him exactly who she is; the next she feels she's gone too far and suddenly must prove that she's happy, healthy, and on top of everything. As she pours on the air of well-being, her date feels required to do the same, for, as with all uncontrolled maneuvering, there is a built-in tendency to escalate.

They go to a party. Her date talks and dances with other women, some of whom are very attractive, and Marge feels possessive. But in the context of such a new relationship, her possessiveness seems inappropriate. Besides, they've both leaned so heavily on presenting themselves as self-reliant, confident, and emotionally secure. How can she be jealous after just a few dates? So she covers her feelings with breeziness. Unaware of Marge's inner turmoil, her date begins moving closer to her later in the evening, showing affection and hoping for affection in return. But when he gets breeze in return, fear whispers through him—"Uh-oh, I've gone too far"—and he begins to blow some breeze of his own.

The tendency to see manipulation everywhere is now hard to resist. Each senses the other moving away and makes assumptions about the reasons why. Their self-doubts become inflamed, and they escalate their strategic messages. Painful rough edges start poking through their banter. Marge jokes that she hopes he got the telephone number of a certain woman at the party—the one who made her the most jealous. He interprets her nonchalance as a warning that she does not want an exclusive relationship, at least not with him. He stops touching her and his smile becomes forced.

In the beginning the strategic escalation operates entirely between the lines, and Marge and her date may cooperate in the pretext that everything is fine. But as they proceed to build a relationship on these subterranean messages, they create a house of cards. They each feel hurt, suspect that their hurts are the result of their own insecurities, and retaliate in covert ways. Little signs of weakness—a false laugh, a fallen face, a momentary paralysis—are shingled over with wisecracks, loving gestures, and outright lies. Finally, somebody goes too far, the hidden hurt becomes unbearable, a terrible breach is committed, and the house collapses in a rumble of abuse. Such escalation can happen over the course of months, or, as in the case of Chuck Meyers, in the course of a single evening.

The Date According to Marge

Marge's disastrous third date with Chuck triggered a downward spiral in which she has been immersed since our story began. The events of that evening, over a month ago, were so laden with the shame-stirring effects of interpersonal strife that she has made a major unconscious effort to suppress the memory, an effort that has tightened the texture of her life. She's been stalked by feelings of loneliness, pessimism, and fear. She's felt excessively vulnerable to little power incidents like the old lady cutting ahead of her in line. She's been unable to give of herself to the point of stinginess. She's been inclined to grasp for control lest some unexpected twist of events plunge her back into her darkness. And she's been so obsessive about her image that her morning make-up ritual has pushed breakfast off the agenda, while her customary attempts to appear light and breezy have reached compulsive levels.

Submerged as she was in her own turmoil, Marge felt acutely uncomfortable about how much Georgette was depending on her for a happy birthday. The contrast between Georgette's expectations and her own ability to give was stark. Marge never actually sat down and tried to get to the bottom of her internal conflict, but she sensed that something about her posture regarding Georgette's birthday implied she was an inadequate friend. In response to these stirrings, she subconsciously began to reduce the birthday to manageable proportions: What's a birthday? No big deal. I'm not planning anything special for my birthday. So we'll be together and that will be that. And even: Georgette always was a little wimpy about these things.

Georgette also felt uncomfortable. As she became more and more despondent about the events of the week, she found herself increasingly concerned that at least her birthday dinner with Marge work out well: One more rejection, one more layer of *shit* and I've had it! As a result, she became deferential whenever she talked to Marge. And Marge, as she is prone to do, picked up the pathetic, powerless quality and became irritated by it.

Marge was expending so much energy suppressing her own pain, pain she detested and despised herself for, that hearing the pain in Georgette's voice and the message, "I need you," was more than she could manage. She began to believe she was being manipulated and to resent it. Only later, sitting on the bus, overwhelmed by sadness, did she take a different view of things.

Marge and Georgette are meeting for lunch at a restaurant in Murray Hill midway between their offices, a date Marge arranged after her unhappy bus ride. Marge has volunteered the subject of Georgette's birthday and apologized for vetoing La Jardiniere. In a display of openness, insight, and reversal for which Georgette has always loved her, Marge has explained that she was all wrapped up in herself, that she took out her anxieties on Georgette, and that "I really acted like a creep. I'm sorry. I was just in too much pain to deal with anyone else."

The exchange warmed them to each other. Soon Georgette was talking about what a rotten week it had been and why she had behaved "like Little Miss Clingsville." As she spoke, Georgette revealed a resilience for which Marge has always loved her. For even as she talked of being clingy, she was full of laughter and sparkle and obviously back on her feet. She seemed to have the ability to let herself hit bottom and then, in a way that Marge admired, to talk about it, shake her head, and be herself again.

Georgette is now listening sympathetically as Marge begins to relate a series of unpleasant incidents and searches for the source of her depression. For Marge the search is always difficult, for when she gets anywhere near bottom, she feels so sullied by it, she finds it hard to experience anything save a sealing depression.

"What happened to that fellow Chuck, that twenty-eight-year-old you were raving about a few weeks ago? Whatever became of that?"

"Oh, God," says Marge, "are you sure you want to hear about it?"

"Sure, why not?"

And so, with some uncertainty, Marge begins, speaking soberly, almost grimly, at first, gradually becoming more and more animated. "Okay, well it's true, I was excited about him. Very excited. He was tall, attractive, a little receding hairline maybe, but otherwise pretty terrific looking. And he seemed strong. So many men I meet are so weak. He wasn't always trying to please me in one way or another. But let me qualify that. A lot of men don't try to please you because they're bastards. They don't give a shit. What I liked about Chuck was that he didn't seem so hung up on proving what a man he was. He seemed to be his own person."

As usual, Georgette is impressed with Marge's ability to read volumes between the lines, to know by the depth and timing of a man's smile or the way he shakes her hand whether or not she can respect him. And preoccupied as she is these days by issues of power, Georgette listens closely.

"Okay, so much for my brilliant first impressions. So I went out with him once. We didn't make love, but there was passion in the air. We talked about how we felt about meeting a new person, about the problem of going to bed with someone on the first date, about the whole AIDS thing, about how much we both liked self-reliance. We were connecting so much that the conversation alone turned me on. I kept having this fantasy that when we got back to my place we would lose control of ourselves and, despite everything we said, do it right on my living room floor.

"So we walked back, we kissed some more, and then I pushed him away at the door. And a half hour later he called to tell me what a terrific time he'd had. You can imagine how I felt.

"The second date wasn't so great. A party at my friend Joan's. He danced too much with one of her friends and I didn't like that. But when I saw him again the next Saturday—I guess that was about two weeks before your birthday—we both knew we were going to sleep together. We went dancing. I must say, Georgette, it was hot. He had his hand on my ass, I had my hand in his pocket (!)—I've never done anything like that. He was drooling on my neck. I couldn't tell you what anyone else in the place was doing or whether they were all just standing around watching us. Well, afterwards, we didn't walk back to my place, we took a cab.

"The first thing that bothered me is that he wasn't interested in undressing me. He did something in that direction—yeah, he unbuttoned my blouse—but then he went to work on his clothes and I did mine. Not very romantic, but I figured, well, maybe that's just kid stuff anyway. This is a relationship with a mature man. You've finally met a mature man. This is the way a mature man does it.

"The next thing that bothered me was the way he kissed. He kissed very aggressively, it even hurt a little, but I didn't feel that he was kissing me. I like to kiss tenderly at first. It's more loving, more caressing. But again I thought, it's just your insecurity. You've got a hot number on your hands. The tenderness stage passed hours ago. Let yourself go, get into it, stop being a teenage girl. And, of course, while I'm thinking all this, he's practically ripping my flesh off. Every minute of the way I felt I was half a step behind because of the stuff that was going on in my mind. So much of what he did I normally like, but I just, I couldn't—oh, how can I put it! When he was kissing my legs, I was still hung up about trying not to be self-conscious when he was biting my ass!"

Georgette shakes her head. "Marge, I've been in that situation a hundred times! All the times I've felt uncomfortable and never said a word. Why can't we say we need to talk? Why do we keep going through with it?"

"But how could I say anything?" says Marge, glancing at Georgette to see if any criticism was implied. "If I told him I felt self-conscious, that I wasn't really with it, I would have had to admit I'd been acting the whole time. And, besides, I didn't want to ruin it. Either he'd think he doesn't turn me on and feel rejected and withdraw, or else he'd think I have some kind of hang-up about sex. I guess I just didn't want to give him the wrong impression right off the bat. I mean here was this terrific guy, *supposedly,* and my entire act is falling apart. I didn't want to look like a sniveling little neurotic."

"Oh, Marge, you're not a sniveling little neurotic," Georgette says emphatically. Marge glances at her and then takes a poke at her foot. This is a difficult moment for Marge. Whenever she comes close to revealing what's really going on with her, she fears the judgments that might be made. Will Georgette re-evaluate me? Begin to feel that she's healthier than I am? Assume I'm wrong when we have arguments? "Oh, this must seem ridiculous to you," Marge says. "I mean it's nothing like married life."

Georgette senses the emotional pulling back that Marge's last statement represents, and she interprets it as a demand for reassurance. Feeling she must have done something wrong, not been sensitive or sympathetic enough, she immediately complies. "Oh, no, Marge, I've been there, I assure you." They both feel awkward after that and return to their food.

They are eating in a small Middle Eastern restaurant off Lexington Avenue in the Thirties. They look out on a garden of sorts, a little brick patio, and the backs of tenements on the next block that are mostly obscured by ginkgoes and wisteria. One of the windows in the nearest building is boarded up, and on the ledge two pigeons are engaged in some sort of interpigeonal activity. They begin by pecking at each other's beaks; now one seems to be getting on top of the other from behind; wings flutter about, they are down, wrestling, one biting the neck of the other; until the bottom bird breaks loose and flies away, floating for a moment in the light breeze, and stopping on a higher sill.

"Why can't it be that way with people?" says Marge, reviving the conversation. "You kiss, you screw, you grab, you fight, you get angry, you run away, you unruffle your feathers, you collect yourself, and then you start all over again?"

"That sounds exactly the way it is with people!" Georgette says, smiling and pleased with her observation.

"That's right, the men grab and then the women run away and unruffle their feathers!"

"And then come back for more!"

The two friends laugh like school girls until Georgette sees Marge's mouth and eyes slowly sadden. "What's the matter?" she says.

"Georgette, are you really like that?" asks Marge, in a downcast voice. "Do you really recover so quickly?"

"No, never. Never," says Georgette, touched by Marge's display of vulnerability. "I have a story to tell you, too. Martin and I . . . Well, you finish. What happened with Chuck?"

"All right, so where were we? He was biting my bottom and I was self-conscious. Well, then he started to get on top of me. I was sort of relieved. I figured, let's get this one over with. Then maybe we can relax, talk a little. I'll feel like I'm with him again, like I know who he is, and then maybe we'll, you know, get back into it again. Slowly this time, gently. I kept thinking, the poor guy is so hot he's going to blow apart pretty soon."

"Oh yes, the poor guy."

"But it turns out, no, he's got other plans. He wants to achieve a higher state of erotic intensity. He sort of moves up so he's straddling my stomach, so that his you-know-what is pointing you-know-where. He was kissing my forehead, and mussing my hair with his hand, and pulling, trying to lift my head where he thought it ought to go, as I hadn't figured out where he thought it ought to go. And I guess that was when I first started getting angry. No, no. I *wasn't* angry. Maybe I should have been. I'm angry now. But then it was, you know, again: this is just natural; if I were really into it, I'd be all over him, he wouldn't have to coax me. But, Christ, you know how it is when you're not into it: It's, Yech! Get that thing away! So I give it a little kiss . . ."

"Oh, yes, the little kiss!"

"Right, and then I looked up at him and put my arm around his neck and tried to kiss his mouth and get him back into screwing position. Well, he pretended to comply. He was still in high gear, all hot and bothered. He kissed me, he stuck his tongue in my ear, he breathed hard, but—oh, yeah, I remember—suddenly he puts his hands on my shoulders as if to pin me to the mattress, he sort of reared up, and there I was with his thing pointing at me right between the eyes!"

Georgette starts giggling and has to put her napkin over her mouth to keep from spraying food.

"You laugh—I cried," says Marge.

"Why?"

"I felt humiliated. Here I was with a completely strange man trying to force me to suck his cock. I know, it's ridiculous to think that way, but I was getting deeper and deeper into something *I didn't want to do*, and it made me feel dirty, Georgette. Well, it took the creep a while, but eventually he noticed that I was crying. He didn't ask me what was wrong, which was a relief in a way—I figured he understood. He just became very tender, kissed my eyes, wiped my tears, slid down a bit, kissed my breasts, and for the first time, I felt sort of with it. And so finally he got his condom and started doing it." Water begins to fill in along the bottom ridges of Marge's eyes. "I still didn't feel good about it, Georgette, I still don't."

"Well, why should you? How could you?" Georgette asks.

Marge again scans Georgette's eyes to check for unspoken judgments. She's worried now that her story suggests a self-destructive streak in her and that a healthier person would have known that sex with Chuck could not have proceeded comfortably even after he'd wiped her tears. Again Marge has reached the limits of what she feels is safe to express. Feeling a little compromised, she says: "Well, I don't know. Haven't you ever been carried away by the moment against your better judgment?"

Georgette instantly senses Marge's fears and, ignoring the defensiveness in her voice, reassures her: "Of course, I've been carried away," she says gently. "Everyone gets carried away."

Relieved, Marge continues. "I kept trying to go with it and I couldn't. I suppose he thought I was all there. He certainly seemed all there. Huffing and puffing. And I remember thinking, I just wish he would stop for one minute. Ask me how I felt, talk to me. Maybe I could have come around. I just waited. After he came, I stroked him a bit on the back of his head. I thought, well, I'm glad it's over, maybe now we can get back to getting to know each other again. But for the life of me I couldn't figure out what to say.

"So suddenly he says, 'Hey, I'd like to take a shower.' That seemed kind of strange, but I figured, okay, make yourself at home. I was still hoping the night would turn out as originally planned. I still wanted to really make love. I'd been so turned on earlier. So I thought, maybe we'll go to sleep and we'll wake up feeling sexy in the morning. But the whole time he was in the shower, I was stewing. A part of me was thinking, you son of a bitch, aren't you going to show any interest in my feelings? I thought I could hear him humming, and that got me even more agitated. And I began thinking back to how we met, how there was never any reason for me to believe he was interested in anything but sex. I couldn't help thinking I'd acted too hungry, that maybe this guy was just playing me for another horny New York woman. But all that seemed like paranoia to me at that point, because, technically speaking, what had he done that was so bad? He didn't undo my bra? He wasn't perfectly sensitive the first time out? And what was so wrong with a shower? How many times had I wanted to take a shower after making love and not done it because I was afraid of what the person I was with would think? Maybe I'm just afraid of his independence, of his self-confidence. That's the way I was thinking. And then he comes out of the shower, and he starts to dress.

"I said, 'What are you doing?'

"He said, 'I want to go for a walk. You want to come?'

"I couldn't believe what was happening. He kept repeating that he wanted to go for a walk, and he said I could come too, if I wanted. But I didn't for a minute believe that he wanted me to. He just wanted to get out. He really thought I was a *whore*. 'You're just going to walk out of here at five a.m.?' I said.

"'What do you mean?' he said.

"'I mean all those fancy words about sex and sensitivity and getting to know somebody, and you just get your rocks off and split? What about me?' I said. 'Didn't you happen to notice that there was another person in the room? That there was another person in bed with you? Did you think you were just having a wet dream?'"

Marge suddenly stops and looks around. Her face is moist and her eyes storming. A wet strand of hair is stuck to her forehead, and she looks slightly deranged. A couple at a nearby table continues to eat as if nothing has happened. "Do you think they heard me?" she says. "No, no, you were only whispering." Georgette reaches across the table and touches Marge's hand.

Marge is nervous about how far she can allow her confession to go. She's on the edge of a landslide of shame. Words like "Horny!" "Out-of-control!" and "Desperate!" are washing insistently onto the shores of her consciousness.

"God, Marge," Georgette says, trying to pull her back to safe ground, "This guy really triggered something in you."

"Yes, an oath of celibacy. I mean, to think, for this I risked my life!"

"So what did he say? He must have been stunned."

"He tried to pretend he wasn't. He said he didn't know what I was talking about. He said, 'I thought I was making love to you. What did you think?' I said I thought he didn't give a damn about me or whether I had an orgasm or whether I got any satisfaction out of the evening. He got what he wanted and now he was leaving. And I didn't say this, but it was killing me now that he'd used my shower and dried himself with my towels and probably left the whole bathroom a mess. So he says, 'Let's take a walk and talk about it.' But I tell you, Georgette, at that point, to take a walk with him—to do anything his way—would have made me feel totally exploited, like some little honey he was twirling around his finger. I was so furious. I said, 'What's your rush to get out of here? Are you afraid I'm going to rape you if you fall asleep?' I remember this moment especially, because he was standing there looking at me with that big blank face and then he sat down and started lacing his shoes, forgetting that he hadn't even put his pants on yet. He said, 'So you didn't come,' very sullenly, as if it just dawned on him. He said, 'You have to come every time, is that it? If you don't come, then you kill.' And that did it. I mean here was this guy who talked such a mean line of intimacy, and then goes about and does exactly what he pleases without a goddamn thought to my feelings—honestly, Georgette, he never demonstrated the slightest sensitivity once we got to my apartment—and then, and *then,* he tries to lay the whole goddamn thing on *me!* On my unfair sexual demands! He didn't see a demand the whole evening! He wouldn't know a demand if it came up and sat on him! I mean, I'm not perfect, Georgette, and I don't mean to say I didn't make any mistakes—I know I get hurt easily and . . ."

Georgette's attention drifts at this point. Her mind tends to wander whenever someone begins to justify himself so furiously. She would have preferred it if Marge weren't so intent on building a case, on making sure Georgette sees it exactly her way. Even if Chuck is not the complete pig Marge makes him out to be, Georgette would not be any less sympathetic. Such wild feelings come into play whenever sex is involved, Georgette thinks. Especially between strangers. What would have happened if Marge had told him she needed to stop? Perhaps the whole thing would have ended differently. But to say anything like this to Marge seems impossible now. Gradually her mind wanders back to Marge's bedroom. She can see the rumpled ruby sheets, the pre-dawn light on the wicker furniture, and the two strangers trying to salvage their dignities as the hurt feelings stomp around the room like Nazis.

"I mean what do you think, George?" says Marge. "Wouldn't you have been furious? Tell me. Honestly."

"Yes, certainly," Georgette answers.

"So anyway," Marge continues, "I started screaming that he should get out, that I never wanted to see him again, that he should make his walk a very long walk, that he should bone up on his masturbation because that's probably what he did best—I'm afraid I said a lot of terrible things—and, well, he just got up and left without saying another word. He just picked up his pants and his jacket and"—she flicks her hand—"he split. The end. I went into the bathroom afterwards. He had hung my big bath towel over the shower rod. It was hung at a slight angle, and I don't know why that got under my skin, but just seeing it made me so upset, I grabbed it and jammed it into the hamper and ripped off a piece of my thumb in the process." She shows Georgette the wound, which now consists of a big scab on the knuckle.

Georgette takes Marge's hand, rubs it a little, then lets it go and says, "You mean he left without his pants on?"

Marge shrugs. "I guess he put them on in the hall."

The Date According to Chuck

Walking didn't help Chuck this time. He spent much of the morning jogging, even though he was exhausted and had an important obligation later in the day for which he needed his wits. From the moment he had met Marge, her slick appearance, confident manner, important job, and sexy adventuresomeness gave him frequent rushes of, "I'm in over my head." The contrast between her position in the world (rising lawyer, good salary, Gramercy apartment) and his (history instructor, unemployed, living at home in Queens) struck him as irrelevant on the rational plane ("I know what I'm worth as a person"), and he sensed that Marge would respect him all the more if he didn't seem affected by it. But he was affected by it. Despite his better judgment, it aroused insecurity ("Second-rate!" "Egghead!") and touched feelings of remorse he didn't even know he had. In response to all this he redoubled his image efforts, for he didn't want to ruin what was shaping up to be a good thing.

After the excitement of the dance floor, Chuck, like Marge, felt he had to maintain an up quality. By the time they got into the cab, he was experiencing his role of Third Date Lover as a delicate straight jacket of delicious excitement that any feeling which seemed in the least bit inappropriate would destroy. Under such zealous self-control, the delicate excitement withered.

Back at Marge's apartment his clandestine struggle with forbidden feelings reached the point where kissing and touching were no longer the thrill they had been before. He wanted to tap his sexuality quickly now for fear that he'd lose it altogether.

But each time he picked up on Marge's lack of involvement, all the doubts that her image stirred in him started squawking. He began to wonder whether Marge thought he was a lackluster lover, whether she wished she were elsewhere, whether she was an uptown woman slumming with a young guy she took for a stud and was now disappointed. All this, despite the fact that he is obviously a substantial and educated person, and that he is generally quite appealing to women and frequently pursued.

As a result of his fears, Chuck's energy got turned around and he began having trouble maintaining his erection. Until they'd landed in bed, both he and Marge, buoyed by the sexual excitement, had been full of confidence and high spirits. They'd joked about namby-pamby couples who clutch each other out of desperate dependency, about the poseurs at the single bars. They were flying down the highway without brakes, and now he was losing his erection. To Chuck there was only one solution: get it back.

He reached for some oral sex, a semi-conscious recognition on his part that he needed more involvement from Marge. To maintain the image he'd sold himself on, he pursued his objective aggressively, hoping to conceal his self-doubt. When Marge dodged him with her little kiss, his insecurities gained the upper hand again, and he was consumed with certainty that his cockman's image was fading ("Phony!" "Reject!" "Inchworm!"). Meanwhile, sprouting within him was a kernel of resentment. Why isn't *she* more involved? What is *she* doing? If push came to shove, he could use that resentment to bury his self-doubts and make Marge the issue.

Then, to his surprise and relief, he saw that Marge was teary. She had feelings, too. She wasn't just standing back, evaluating him. He felt drawn to her, started kissing her gently, and as he did, he found himself emerging from his vortex of doubts, forgetting his embryonic resentment, getting more aroused, and—lo!—in possession of a rock-hard erection again. He wasted no time in using it.

Chuck assumed that Marge did not want to discuss her tears any more than he wanted to discuss his doubts. He thought that his kisses achieved a meaningful communication ("I care about you"). Once they resumed making love, however, he noticed that he again seemed to be flying solo. Once more the shame voices rose up in him, he succumbed to impotency panic, and to maintain his erection, if by nothing but friction alone, he furiously accelerated the pace. This caused him to come sooner than he would have hoped and made him ashamed of his performance.

All Chuck knew when it was over was that he felt "fucked up" and needed to get out of that room, take a walk, and clear his head. He'd recently resolved that when he felt this way he would be true to his feelings and not be a slave to pretense. (Although, in fact, he'd been a slave to pretense all night.) And so he saw his manner of departure not as an act of great insensitivity, which it was, but as a free man's rebellion against propriety. Until his decision to leave, nothing he'd done had openly violated the role of Third-Date Lover as Marge interpreted it. But leaving was a wrong move, the clear violation that suddenly made all her rage legitimate. The image maneuvers were over; it was time for war.

Despite having dealt out a fair share of the punishment, Marge was hurting. She felt diminished by the whole event, despondent over her own behavior, and haunted by Chuck's parting blow—"If you don't come, then you kill"—because her ranting made that accusation look plausible. She regrets having made that an issue. It had nothing to do with why she was dissatisfied, but in her pain and humiliation, she had reached for the nearest weapon, and there it was. And he, doing the same, had nailed her to it.

Now, having shared much of her grief with Georgette, Marge feels relieved and no longer on the run. But she's sorry she didn't reveal some deeper thoughts, strip away more of her cover, and, in particular, acknowledge the choking pain she still feels over Chuck's final calumny—rather than having worked so hard to prove it wrong. She senses she could have gone further with Georgette, and something about doing so touches her with bittersweet longing.

11.

Fears, Habits, and False Assumptions

How we are conditioned by shame and become slaves to an array of "shoulds." How we develop irrational expectations of what others will do. How our automatic pilot steers us into power struggles.

IF LIFE WERE SIMPLE and people were direct and trusting, many of the conflicts we've witnessed would never have developed. Marge would say, "Chuck, I don't know what happened, but I don't feel like making love any more." Chuck would say, "Gee, what's the matter?" or "I've been faking it for the last ten minutes myself." They'd start to talk. They'd learn more things about each other. And then they'd shake hands and say goodnight, or likely as not, slip even more passionately back into what they were doing.

The excessive maneuvering that Marge and Chuck get lost in is typical of many unwanted struggles. It results partly from efforts to maintain control: Neither wants to do anything that might elicit the wrong response or in any way shatter the moment. It results partly from strategic habit: It would never occur to them to be honest about their desires or loss of desires regarding the embarrassing subject of sex. And it emerges partly out of fear—of getting out on a limb, experiencing rejection, being pushed into their bad feelings about themselves. Trying to play it safe, Marge devotes more mental energy to figuring out where she ought to be (sexy, independent, unhung-up) than where she is (confused, turned off, upset). Thus preoccupied, how can she explain to Chuck, or even to herself, where she's coming from or why she feels the things she feels?

Both Marge and Chuck are caught in patterns of behavior and emotion that were established in them as children, patterns that make them feel perpetually on the brink of powerlessness and fearful of being direct. One of the contributing elements is Marge's conflicts about sex.

Once, when Marge was five, she played "I'll show you mine if you show me yours" with a little boyfriend who lived nearby. Marge was both excited and anxious about what she'd done, eager to share it with her mother and to get some sign of approval. But her mother, who disliked sex, fixed Marge with a harsh, disapproving stare, then looked quickly away without speaking. A few months later Marge and the same boy were sitting in the school assembly. He asked her, smiling and a little abashed, if she'd remembered their secret game. She fixed him with a harsh, disapproving stare and looked away.

Marge learned from her mother that there was something unclean about her sexuality. That unconscious knowledge, that pocket of shame, has always affected her relationship with men. She drew the conclusion that sex was only justifiable if it were kept in its proper place, which meant love and marriage. In order to be comfortable having sex with a man, she has to convince herself that they are in love and embarking on a serious courtship. Then she is safe from shame.

But there are complications. For all her prudery, Marge's mother was also a flamboyant extrovert. Marge, who is naturally more private, grew up believing that there was nothing worse than being a "Dormouse!" (which she knew she secretly, shamefully, was) or better than being a *bon vivant* (which, of course, she wasn't). And so, despite the imperative that sex be attached to love and marriage, Marge has other imperatives, to appear carefree and uninhibited (even when she feels the reverse), and to fling herself into bed with a man without getting all hung up about her feelings. Either way, she loses.

Marge's fear of shame constantly leads her into false and contradictory positions. And when she is with a new man, it often seems that every step of the way there are new bits of herself to avoid and more ways to be that she's not.

Like Marge, Georgette, too, is controlled by shame and by unspoken imperatives which relate to events that happened long ago, yet seem as fresh as yesterday. Let's look closely at how this straightjacket of shames and shoulds comes into being.

The Shame-Should-Shame Cycle

The shame instilled at an early age ("Selfish!") is the beginning of a reverberating cycle that goes on for years. A pocket of shame is surrounded by inhibitions: Georgette feels, I should not take, I should not ask, I should not calculate on my own behalf. The inhibitions sometimes manifest themselves in social situations as symptoms, such as becoming immobilized or stuttering; or as "shoulds," like always being very "good" or manipulating to get her needs met. The direction she takes depends on which alternative avenues are allowed, encouraged, or modeled by her parents.

Look at Georgette as a child of six who feels a knife go through her every time her mother calls her selfish. Desperately trying to adjust, she develops unspoken rules: There are certain things I must never do, and certain things I must always do in order to never appear selfish. The threat of having her defect exposed, of having that second head pop out of her shoulder with "Selfish!" written all over it, forces her to be as giving and agreeable as she possibly can.

So she makes nice all the time. She keeps giving even when her giving is not reciprocated, and she pretends to be satisfied even when she's not. At a certain age, terrorized by the fear of shame, she's one of those girls who's always polite, always does what's right, always sits with her hands folded in her lap.

Inevitably, some adults get turned off, and children resent her. They call her "Goody-two-shoes," and "Phony!" The comments hurt. They form a burning hot spot inside her. In fact, there is something a little phony about Georgette as a result of her not wanting to be selfish. But when the spot gets heated up, she feels not that she behaved a little falsely but that Phoniness is in her blood. It tells her that she is not as worthy as the other children, that she doesn't belong, that she's defective.

And so, the very "shoulds" and "should nots" Georgette adopted to escape the shame her mother injected bring on more shame. That is the essence of the shame-should-shame cycle. The "shoulds" of the cycle have nothing to do with morality or values or useful social conformity. They are inhibitions, symptoms, blind imperatives. They become part of a layered fabric of self-hatred and unnaturalness that skewers the trajectory of Georgette's life.

A compliant little girl can run into a lot of problems besides being called a Goody-this-or-that. Always agreeable, Georgette is easily taken for granted. It's just human nature that people give less to those who make fewer demands. And that too causes Georgette to feel that there's something wrong with her. Why else would people neglect her, or choose her last, or give her the smallest piece?

Feeling powerless to cope with her troubles outside the home, trained to be a good girl and to submit to an object position, Georgette begins developing another prominent pocket of shame—"Weak!" And for years afterward, the fear of being dominated or experiencing herself as weak in any way propels the cycle onward. In class debate when she feels unsure of her position, she becomes pigheaded and refuses to acknowledge uncertainty. In college, boyfriends tell her she has a chip on her shoulder. And these events also arouse self-doubt ("Difficult!"). As an adult, she finds the issues of selfishness and weakness to be hot spots that almost defy rational examination.

None of this means that Georgette's life is miserable. From the time she is very young she has a spontaneous side that is never entirely suppressed and many other superb qualities that stand her in good stead with others. She has her circle of friends, her share of popularity, her dreams. But there are always painful periods and always a sense, often remote, that somehow she is not quite worthy.

People are complex, and their layers of shames and shoulds have many tangled and contradictory elements. Despite her problems with giving and getting, Georgette becomes in many respects an aggressive and expressive girl, reflecting in part the unrestrained atmosphere of her home. But in school, where many of her classmates come from more well-to-do homes, she sometimes experiences herself as lower class and crude. These feelings become worse in adolescence when her teachers call her boy crazy. Her mother, who pooh-poohs such criticism, is a weak ally, for her alcoholism is itself becoming an embarrassment to Georgette, who is taking on more and more of the household duties. "Ill-bred" "Over-sexed!" and "Drunken Mother!" combine to inhibit Georgette's spontaneity and push her toward refinement, a major obsession of her teenage years. Today, all her spontaneous qualities—her laughter, her sexuality, her emotional accessibility, in short, all her most wonderful traits—are apt to become a cause for shame.

The cycle of shames and shoulds is universal in our society. Inhibitions, awkward and rigid ways of living, emotionally safe rituals and routines, and obnoxious habits from boastfulness to false affection may all emerge from this process. Even in adult life, the cycle continues, adding new islands to the archipelago of doubt and new imperatives to be and to do in ways that bear little relation to who we really are.

One of the tasks of adulthood is to bring the shame-should-shame cycle to a close and to begin to come to terms with the pockets of shame implanted in childhood. But coming to terms with oneself and one's shame is a demanding, often painful process for which society gives no guidelines and few rewards. Besides, there are many socially approved alternatives—constant busy-ness, circumscribed friendships, pleasure drugs, free sex, and dominating others—alternatives that may work surprisingly well for long periods of time. With all these options, why pause to come to terms with aspects of the self that may seem disgusting or illegitimate?

And so, in many ways, we continue to run from ourselves, to refuse to know who we are. The shame-should-shame cycle rumbles on, and so do its corollaries—the fears, habits, and irrational assumptions with which we approach other people.

Strategic Habits

One of the first things we're made to feel ashamed of is being dependent. Dependency is something of a taboo in our culture, and even the most sensitive parents are bound to make a child feel ashamed of some of his needs and demands. But the child's needs do not go away. He learns to express them in covert ways. He thus develops his first strategic habits.

Cindy, having been told to play in her room until both hands of the clock are on the twelve and not to bother her mother until then, begins testing every aspect of her prison. "Mom," she says, standing outside Georgette's door and speaking in a querulous voice, "where are you?" Georgette, ashamed of her own needs, feels a pang of guilt. The poor child is all alone! "I'm in here, Cindy." "Where, Mom?" "I'm in my room. I'm working."

They thus become involved in a conversation, and Cindy has found a way to maneuver to get the attention she wants, even if for only a few minutes. If her efforts grow more sophisticated and continue to be rewarded by Georgette, she may discover her mother's soft spot regarding selfishness and learn how to make her feel guilty by acting afraid. In later years she may find that acting frightened gets her warmth and attention from other people besides her mother, and she will have no sense that her fearfulness has a strategic design.

Dependency maneuvers are rampant in adult life. Marge learned that she could be most effective in getting what she needed from her mother if she became sick, Georgette if she used sweetness and flattery, Martin if he churned out the charm and image—and they keep using such maneuvers today. When Jake Donohue shrugs off his wife's question about how his breakfast went, he is acting out a dependency maneuver (stoic pouting). He now expects that Grace will come to him and start petting and appeasing (which, fortunately for both of them, she refuses to do).

As children experiment with speaking their minds, they quickly learn that expressing their needs is not the only risky transaction. They are punished for criticizing, or competing, or saying no, and they become ashamed of any feelings that may cause them to do such things. They develop new inhibitions about being direct, and in each case a strategic habit—based on what is approved, what is modeled, what works—is the symptom, or the should, that replaces forthrightness.

As a result of such unfortunate early experiences, many people feel powerless when it comes to expressing themselves directly. They find it hard to say no, to express dissatisfaction, to ask for something, to apologize, to convey bad news, to disagree, to compete, to give criticism, to question authority without maneuvering in some way.

Instead of giving someone a simple no, they refuse to answer his calls; or they say yes and then resent him; or they punish him for asking. Instead of disagreeing in a considered way, they say, "Oh, come *on!*"; or they smirk and walk away; or they remain silent and think, "What an ass!" Instead of approaching someone with an open request, they make it awkward for him to say no; or they ply him with hints; or they sneak around and take what they want in a presumptuous and infuriating way. Instead of openly questioning authority, they submit, or rebel, or both.

The interpersonal lives of many people are riddled with these disconcerting habits. They don't express dissatisfaction; they don't apologize; they don't accept or give honest feedback; Instead, they become critical or cute, cuddly or cold, manipulative or vindictive. Given such tendencies, is it any wonder that Marge and Chuck ran afoul of each other in bed?

False Assumptions

All this maneuvering is a constant source of misunderstanding. Marge, for instance, may have lost interest in sex just when she thought she shouldn't have and she may be too ashamed to reveal it. But if she weasles away from Chuck every time he tries to get things going again, what is he supposed to think? Will he assume that Marge still likes and wants him despite the hurtful evasions?

But the potential for misunderstanding is even greater. For not only do Marge and Chuck communicate through confusing and unreliable maneuvers that operate according to primitive childhood habits, but the maneuvers are interpreted in a primitive and unreliable way, according to childhood assumptions about why others act as they do. Thus, although someone else, more secure, might stand back from Marge's evasions and try not to assume too much, Chuck assumes a great deal—specifically, that Marge has turned off to this inept young bozo and can't wait till he's out of the house.

For his part, Chuck does not openly voice such assumptions. Because to do so is to leave himself open to charges of being insecure, paranoid, hypersensitive, or insulting. Instead, his assumptions about the meaning of Marge's maneuvers spawn countermaneuvers of his own, which are also subject to misinterpretation.

Generally, we misinterpret others based on experiences with our parents, and we project motives based on our own fears and secret desires. In the heat of power exchanges, three assumptions about others take on special significance: that they are manipulators, incompetents, or adversaries. Often, these assumptions become self-fulfilling prophesies.

The Manipulative Assumption. Marge tends to see people as manipulators, for that is what her mother is, and that is what her mother assumed her to be. As Georgette's birthday approaches and Georgette starts acting pathetic, Marge assumes that the pathetic quality is meant to control her. Marge counters with manipulative acts of her own—breeziness, distance, forgetfulness—in order to play down the importance of the date. Now Georgette maneuvers to disguise her hurt and anger, and before long they are tied in a manipulative knot.

Manipulative thinking is so ingrained in Marge that she virtually lives between the lines. She is always nudging, suggesting, squeezing, circumnavigating. Many of her manipulations are playful and harmless, but people are prone to experience Marge as having a thousand tentacles that tickle, pull, push, and twist them in every which direction. They get sucked into her games with moves of their own, until Marge feels that nothing simple and direct ever happens in her life.

The Assumption of Incompetence. To Carmen, most people are weaklings, jerks, or bumblers. As soon as she feels frustrated, she begins to find fault, and her fault-finding erupts in little digs and jokes. Her children, her husband, her employees are pained by her jabs and become frightened of making a wrong move. They get into the habit of letting Carmen do it, of going to Carmen for advice, of thinking of themselves as not quite up to any task where she may be the judge. This only increases Carmen's impatience, her smirks, and her jocular scolding, and it further convinces her that she is dealing with idiots.

"Against stupidity the gods themselves toil in vain!" she cries aloud, as she walks away from Beth, her press secretary, after a disagreement about the headline on a release. Fearful of inducing another wave of Carmen's pointed humor, her loyal underlings become more inhibited. They second-guess themselves, they lose their concentration, and they make errors, which to Carmen, of course, only further proves their incompetence.

The Adversary Assumption. When Martin looks between the lines, he sees adversaries where they don't exist. He reads disagreement as opposition, criticism as condemnation, a simple request as an intentional effort to put him on the spot. An open conversation with Georgette about what she wants for her birthday or whether they should take their vacation in Greece can make him feel as if he is being controlled and has lost his options.

Georgette does things that upset Martin. She allows herself to be exploited by Carmen. She talks with animation to strange men who obviously find her attractive. She keeps smiling and saying hello to the surly man in the bakery even though he never smiles or says hello to her. But Martin doesn't say, "It bothers me that you let Carmen exploit you like that"; or, "It makes me jealous when you talk to other men that way"; or, "Why do you keep saying hello to that creep when he never says hello to you?" He is certain that if he puts his cards on the table, he will be opposed, so he maneuvers for control instead. Georgette, who might agree or at least give his views a sympathetic hearing if she didn't feel so threatened, turns defiant, refusing to acknowledge the legitimacy of anything he says. She becomes the adversary he predicted.

12.

Right Moves, Wrong Moves

Deep inside a marital squabble where each partner worries about forbidden feelings and desires and the ways he might be judged. How we are often most punishing when we think we are just standing up for our rights. *The tyranny of guilt and image.*

IN THE WEEKS since Georgette's birthday, power maneuvers and bolts of self-doubt have been shooting through the Grodin household, as Georgette takes what she sees as a persistent and aggressive stand for her rights and Martin tries to withstand her. She snaps, she scolds, she wins some concessions, but she reaches no deeper than an inch or two into the mire of the relationship.

It's a Wednesday evening, and Martin has come home early from work in an effort to contain his wife's testiness. After dinner they begin discussing an apparently harmless subject, where to hang a lithograph that Georgette's brother gave her for her birthday. Martin is very solicitous, pouring on the old charm. He wants to lift the marriage out of its recent pit, and he's willing to forget his own dissatisfaction to achieve some kind of accord.

But gradually he grasps that Georgette wants to hang the lithograph in their bedroom, which is upsetting to him because it portrays a woman who reminds him of another woman whose thighs he has lately found more appealing than his wife's.

Unable to admit his discomfort and convinced it will interfere with their sex life (especially if, as Georgette suggests, they hang the thing at the foot of the bed), Martin tries to make the best of an awkward situation by pressing for the living room. Georgette resists, and being in an assertive mood, she gives sound reasons for her preference. Martin feels the image of those illicit thighs edging closer to the surface. Because he feels guilty about his forbidden desires and wants to suppress them, her disagreement causes him great anxiety, and, thus consumed, he states his preference more forcefully.

Georgette notices something cold and authoritarian creeping into Martin's tone and begins to feel punished and humiliated. She tries to nail him with guilt: *You may be a dictator at the office, but you're not going to be a dictator here!* Her strategy inflames a pocket of shame ("Rigid!" "Ruthless!" "Uncaring!"). Despite all his good intentions, Martin is furious now and begins making irrational assumptions (She's doing this just to be stubborn!).

Fueled by self-pity and bitterness, Martin waits for the perfect moment and then tries to nail *her* with guilt: *Georgette, I do my best to understand you, but you don't seem interested in making the same effort for me. Go ahead, hang it where you want.* Now Georgette is stung ("Selfish!") and doubts the legitimacy of what she's doing.

For the next half hour they continue this way, hitting upon increasingly personal issues (if *you* weren't so defensive; if *you* weren't so uptight). In each accusation a grain of truth is exploited, and each attack inflames more shame.

Among the subtler uses of guilt that arise in such conflicts are the citing of *promises* ("Didn't you say we were going to make this decision together?"), *precedents* ("You were able to choose where you wanted to hang that portrait of your grandfather"), and other contractual arrangements. *Isolation* is also used by bringing in an outside opinion ("Dr. Ruth says that a picture like this in the bedroom can be ruinous to your sexlife") and thus making it two against one.

Such tactics can feel overwhelming. After all, an objective opinion is an objective opinion. How can it be opposed? A precedent is a precedent. We've agreed that that's how things will be done. A promise is a promise. It can't be violated. But no matter how reasonable these arguments sound, their sole purpose is control. In a climate of trust, an entirely different negotiation takes place.

Forbidden Feelings

In the argument over the lithograph, both Martin and Georgette are harboring knots of forbidden feeling. In Martin's case, his recent lack of sexual desire for Georgette, his doubts about the marriage, his attraction for this or that other woman are feelings that seem beyond the pale. They are not what a Good Husband should feel. Such forbidden feelings automatically constitute a vulnerability. They are like an embarrassing physical trait—a bald spot, a birth mark, a runny nose—which he tries to hide by turning this way and that: Let's hang it in the living room; let's talk about it later; I don't think it goes with the bedroom decor. His efforts to conceal his shameful feelings lead him into countless battles for control.

Georgette is in a similar bind. She is motivated initially by a desire to hang the lithograph in the bedroom, then by a deeper desire to get her way for a change, and finally by a determination to be dealt with respectfully. But she can't bring herself to talk about her underlying motivations. For her experience with Martin is such that whenever she expresses a discontent, it somehow turns out that she's the problem. So she reverts to maneuvering instead. She expresses her dissatisfaction between the lines, and, once the power struggle is underway, her goal of being treated respectfully becomes a vulnerability that must not be exposed. Because if Martin finds that she's been pressing the issue so forcefully for reasons that have nothing to do with the lithograph or where it hangs, he will become exasperated, paternalistic, and shake his head.

So she too gets drawn into a spiral of maneuvers. She too forgets her real motivation. She too experiences a desperate need to control the argument and stick to her official positions.

Guilty! Guilty! Guilty!

Maneuvering around shameful, forbidden feelings generates power struggles that are so subtle, involving such small and easily overlooked stabs and wounds, that the sense of hurt and rage can build up imperceptibly to tremendous proportions. And this rage too feels forbidden. It, too, seems inappropriate. But finally someone, in this case, Georgette, makes a wrong move, says one thing that so blatantly violates the role of Wife, or Fair Fighter, or Loyal Friend, that all of Martin's wrath seems suddenly legitimate.

Trembling with hurt and befuddled by her raging self-doubts, Georgette forgets that all she wanted was a fair negotiation and flings herself toward victory: "Martin, if the picture hangs in the living room, I *sleep* in the living room!"

"Now who's being the dictator!" he barks. And for the next forty seconds he fumes with such righteous anger and makes such a convincing case against her, that finally, in a masterpiece of guiltmongering, he storms out of the room, deeply indignant over the treatment he's received.

In conflicts like this, a "wrong move," like refusing to sleep with your husband in a way that makes you look shrewish, is the kiss of death. Any act that leaves you open to accusations of impropriety or vulnerable to the strategy of guilt, a wrong move works like a magnet, attracting all the pent-up anxiety, hostility, and anger that a power struggle generates. In truth, it is not necessarily immoral or even unkind. It may be an act of honesty or generosity. But in the hidden court of world opinion, it looks bad. It's our way of settling upon the villain and forgetting what went before.

Shame vs. Guilt

Often, when we say we feel guilty, we actually feel ashamed. The difference between shame and guilt is this: Guilt has to do with right and wrong, whereas shame revolves mainly around feelings of being inadequate, inappropriate, or illegitimate. Guilt arises from judging yourself immoral, whereas in shame you experience yourself as subhuman or defective. Guilt and fear of punishment also get confused, but true guilt always results from violating your conscience.

Society has changed greatly in the last century. Our culture no longer has a stable consensus about what is right and wrong or even about the existence of right and wrong. The things that arouse "guilt" in us today are generally not morality issues but conformity issues, *shame* issues. Nevertheless, the word "guilt" is still useful to describe shameful or fearful feelings associated with something we've felt or done or been. And making others feel "guilty" remains a primary strategy for control, even if shame is what we really make them feel.

The Tyranny of Image

Much of what Georgette and Martin consider right and wrong shifts frighteningly from moment to moment. They know that a cunning strategy, a graceful act of diplomacy, or a wrong move can turn someone from a swine to an angel and back again, while his true intentions remain unknown and the effects of his behavior unexamined.

Georgette is dimly aware of this phenomenon, but the awareness is cause for much anxiety and fear. If black can become white and white black—if one minute she can be engaged in a legitimate struggle for her rights as the owner of a new birthday lithograph and the next be revealed as a neurotic, controlling shrew—then even extreme piety can't save her from the pits of self-hatred.

Facing this phenomenon repeatedly, Georgette will naturally tend to redouble her strategic calculations and to invest more of her self-worth in winning the little encounters (or at least not being defeated). After a while, she will begin to see losing as a cause for self-hatred, and the mere presence of self-doubt will be shameful. Under the circumstances, image takes on a scary imperative.

Image is, most obviously, our packaging, the impression we convey about ourselves by what we wear, what we say, how we move. It is an inevitable response to feelings of inadequacy, to the necessities of business, to the fashions of social life. Martin acts sensitive in order to be treated gently. He acts charming in order to be liked and to avoid punishment. He acts tough in order to be feared and respected. All this is pretty standard image stuff, the only liability being that Martin often doesn't know where his image ends and his real self begins.

But when the air is electric with winning and losing, image can become a particularly insidious way of life. In her battles with Martin, Georgette, who's normally quite authentic, gets locked into playing parts—like Wounded Party or Assertive Woman—that cut her range of being down to a pathetic caricature. True, her real feelings often explode through, but frequently in the form of a wrong move that finally undoes her.

As Georgette's dissatisfactions begin to seep out in the form of depression, overeating, unhappiness, and petulance, Martin's attachment to his lifelong pose that everything is fine in Martinland accentuates her feelings of defectiveness. His polished image pushes her toward powerlessness and keeps the lid on any inclination she might have to speak openly of what's on her mind.

Meanwhile, as Georgette continues to spew forth misplaced punishments and manipulative signals of distress, she reinforces Martin's disrespect and encourages him to adhere all the more rigidly to his line.

13.

A Supplicant and Junior Grade Person

How we can sink to the bottom of the pecking order where others are able to mistreat us at will. The destruction of Beth reveals how the nicest people can become subjects.

IT WAS a cool Sunday in May. Martin was playing squash. Georgette was downtown doing some errands, glancing in the windows of the East Side shops, thinking about getting home before Marge arrived for coffee at noon, when she stumbled upon Beth Billingham, her fat friend from work.

Georgette was hoping to get to Bloomingdale's before they ran out of Spoletti's Imported chocolate chip cookies, the latest rage. But in the course of their hellos, Georgette detected in Beth a note of unhappiness and longing, and she didn't want to rush off without some show of friendliness. Still, she feared that given the opportunity, Beth would talk her ear off for the next three hours, and Georgette was not prepared to endure that. She stuck closely to the role of an Office Friend making light conversation on a city street, even though there was some basis for interpreting their relationship as being closer than that. Meanwhile, she tried, indirectly, to convey her degree of unavailability and to test the level of Beth's distress.

Beth was extremely depressed and saw Georgette as a possible godsend. She would have liked to suggest that they stop and have some coffee. But she felt embarrassed by the desire, both because of the great emotional need it represented and because of the shameful implication—sharpened by the distance Georgette was maintaining—that she had no one closer to rely on. She could not bring herself to say, "I need someone to talk to, Georgette. Do you have time for coffee?" The request would have made her feel exposed, and to be turned down when she was feeling so vulnerable by someone who is, after all, little more than an acquaintance, someone she would have to live with every day in the office, would have been crushing. So she too maneuvered and tried to get a reading on Georgette.

The push and pull of their subterranean messages quickly propelled them into an incident of power. Georgette was making small, evasive gestures, punishments really—a calculated lightness of manner, a quick glance at her watch, a failure to look directly at Beth when she spoke—evasions whose purpose it was to maintain the social distance that Beth's hungry eyes were trying to close. The gestures were accompanied by equally slight rewards—a smile, a show of enthusiasm for something Beth said, an exclamation of delight over the coincidence of their meeting—rewards whose purpose it was to camouflage Georgette's true feelings, to assuage her guilt, and to divert the conversation away from serious topics. For Beth the most painful aspect of the encounter was the way Georgette secretly glanced into her eyes, for at those moments she felt scrutinized, as if Georgette were worried about her mental stability and afraid she might go off the edge.

Because of the prevailing emotions, the little diplomacies that normally carry Georgette through such awkward moments were not working. Beth, hoping against hope, failed to correctly read Georgette's rejecting messages. She continued to chatter and ask little questions, only to find herself walking into bigger punishments. As Beth plowed on in the face of Georgette's rebuffs—a slight yawn, an overly laconic response, a sour smile—she became engulfed by feelings of shame ("Fat!" "Boring!" "Reject!"), while painful juices invaded her stomach. Georgette, meanwhile, her impatience waxing and her capacity for sympathy spent, was beginning to feel revulsion and disrespect (Get this woman away from me!).

Although neither of them intended it, they had slipped into a subject-object position. Georgette saw through Beth's false efforts to look self-contained, saw through her little attempts at humor and reward, found them annoying and manipulative, and took an irritable pleasure in wrangling herself away—while Beth's identity plunged toward supplicant and junior grade person.

Beth's Story

A guest entering the Billingham household when Beth was six would have seen a heavy, drab, self-conscious girl, vacillating between self-absorption and awkward efforts for attention, while nearby her adorable baby sister monopolized her parents' attention. The baby was proof of the parents' ability to produce something beautiful. Beth was evidence for a side of themselves and their marriage they wished to forget.

Beth's father was coarse and open at times in his disdain for his older daughter. Her mother, while sometimes struggling to be fair, was generally too involved with her petty intrigues and manipulations to realize that Beth was a little person desperately in need of care. Beth became a pawn and her object behaviors a target. Beth was seen as the problem person in the family, the source of her own unhappiness and a distress to everyone else.

As an infant, Beth was in the way of two warring and unhappy young people who constantly sought distractions outside the home. Shunned when seeking attention and love (*this child is too dependent!*), she became markedly inhibited in her demands. When the rejection occurred at mealtime, Beth discovered that something comforting happened if she began to overeat instead of seeking attention. Not only was the pain muted, but her parents, happy that she was no longer clawing at them, sometimes showed pleasure and approval that she was stuffing herself instead.

Later, when chubby Beth tentatively approached her father, he continued to reject her, for he found repulsive the symptom he had helped to create. Besides, he had another little girl now who did not have such symptoms, and her existence allowed him to justify and harden his position. Each year Beth's shame ("Unnatural!" "Unlovable!"), her inhibition (don't approach), and her symptom (eat) were reinforced.

From the very beginning Beth was trained to be an object. No other avenues were open to her. While she could find ways to alleviate her feeling of self-hatred, she could find no way to alter her status in the home. Her mother's affection was available only as long as Beth was well-behaved and did not protest her second-class citizenship. "Better to be a second-class citizen than no citizen at all," was the understanding Beth extrapolated from this. It would become a guiding principle throughout her life. To this day, if she gets into a row, she may reject herself in anticipation of what others will feel.

Inevitably, Beth was made ashamed of being fat. At school she tried to carry herself so that her profile wouldn't show. She looked awkward whenever she was called up to the blackboard, and she felt so self-conscious that she couldn't grasp the teacher's question and often gave the wrong answer. Her teachers were frustrated and irritated by her performance. Her classmates sniggered. New pockets of shame developed: "Stupid!" "Graceless!" "Jerk!" And her basic sense that she was unlovable and did not have a rightful place in the world grew stronger.

Fearful of unpredictable abuse, Beth tried to hide. As her shyness was repeatedly pointed out to her, her shame over her timidity grew. Hating herself for being timid she found it impossible to accurately measure when she had gone past another person's span of interest. Once she got going, her mind filled with noisy admonitions not to be timid, and a new symptom developed. People now commented on her garrulousness. They yawned. They looked at their watches. Her father accused her of yapping. Her ex-husband called her a motor-mouth. She became ashamed of being a "Bore!" and her belief in her own words was undermined.

Although she found an intellectual niche in college, realized she was much brighter than most people she knew, and even became something of a snob, she was not able to translate any of this into a feeling of self-worth. Subjects like Carmen sensed that they did not have to look at Beth or acknowledge her when she spoke.

Beth's compulsive talking is one of the emblems of her powerlessness. When she disagrees with Carmen, tries, for instance, to explain that it's inappropriate to give the political reporters gifts for Christmas, her object fears activate the talking symptom. She keeps talking long past having made her point. She dissipates her power in a verbal avalanche which says, in effect, "I do not feel worthy of your respect."

Failing to get a response from Carmen, Beth makes little jokes at her own expense, another emblem of powerlessness, like putting on a dunce cap. Carmen studies her and says nothing. More fearful, Beth mumbles and loses track of her point.

As an adult, Beth continues to have problems with her mother. Mrs. Billingham is a weak person who sees herself as a victim. The fact that Beth keeps reaching for her love means nothing to Mrs. Billingham except that here, at least, is one person over whom she has some control. The harder Beth tries, the more her mother uses Beth's efforts to gain bits of leverage. When Beth attacks her for an obvious act of uncaring or an obvious favoritism toward her younger sister, Mrs. Billingham is just bewildered: Why is Beth such a malcontent?

Beth's object quality is connected to her effort to win her mother's love, for she constantly sees her mother in others, constantly sees their acceptance or approval as just beyond her grasp. Whenever she is faced with rejection, her desperate desire for love and approval compel her to go into her "Feed Me" dance, spinning off object invitations right and left. She sucks up with humiliating rewards. She alienates with guilty insinuations.

The subject quality in almost everyone finds it very hard to resist the object hook. In a scapegoat like Beth the hook becomes so prominent and seductive that object invitations are broadcast to one and all. Somehow the scapegoat manages to communicate, "The world treats me like shit," and even the neutral observer can't help but wonder if the world doesn't know what it's doing.

The Vortex

A self-effacing, eager to please, low-paid woman, who knows exactly which reporter is right for which story, Beth is the ideal press secretary for a State Assemblywoman. But in recent months, as Carmen has come closer to announcing her Congressional candidacy, fears and anxieties of all kinds have begun to haunt her. She feels she needs a different sort of press secretary, one who would never be ruffled, who could be tightlipped and lie convincingly, whom the reporters would find threatening enough to respect.

But Carmen's in a bind, because Beth has been a model worker. To dump her now seems treacherous. So she's postponed a decision for several months and tried to put the problem out of her mind. But as the pressure has built up within her, it's begun to spill over in punishing ways. She's felt stuck with Beth and has blamed her for it. Gradually, her irritability has assumed the form of a hidden agenda—to provoke Beth until she does something that justifies the axe.

An element of abuse has always characterized Carmen's relationship with Beth. While Beth has been intellectually unbent—"I cannot worship you, I cannot agree with you when you're wrong, I cannot make a fool of myself by sending out press releases with smile faces on the envelopes"—she has obviously been bent in spirit. And Carmen, never able to resist kicking a cowering dog, has found that while it's difficult to subdue Beth intellectually, it's easy to control her with sharp tones and impatient glances. This hasn't made her feel like a model boss or a model person, but she keeps herself going eighty miles an hour just so niggling doubts of that sort won't get too strong a grip on her.

The more Carmen attacked Beth—for the headline on a press release, the timing of a story, the small showing at a press conference—the more inadequate, incompetent, and unappealing Carmen found her. And the worse Beth felt about herself as a result of

Carmen's attacks, the more trying she found her work. Each morning the fog in her forehead thickened, the cigarettes and cups of coffee increased in number, and the emotional incline up which she dragged her spirit grew steeper. Carmen was finding real errors now, real lapses in judgment. And then two weeks ago, Carmen lost control.

Carmen, Steve Friendly, and Beth were outside City Hall with several other local politicians and their staffs at a rally and press conference to denounce the city's rent control policies. Carmen was in her highly mobilized state, smiling, shaking hands, making small talk with well-wishers. Her eyes were like car beams, every cell in her body quivering with alertness and momentum, when she spotted Beth, bearing an armful of press releases, chatting cozily with an aide to City Councilman Manny Figuero. Suddenly Carmen felt disgusted that that fat, frumpy, slow, *powerless* woman was her press secretary. Knotted with fury, she approached her through the demonstrators.

"And what are you doing?"

"Waiting for the festivities to begin," Beth said with a difficult smile.

"Why aren't you handing out those releases?" said Carmen.

"There's no press here yet."

Carmen glanced quickly around. "Well, here's a press, for Christsakes!" she said, pointing to a WINS reporter standing nearby, fiddling with his tape recorder.

Beth, whose job consists in part of achieving a comfortable and respectful relationship with reporters, walked over to the young man, smiled apologetically, and handed him a release. He looked at her curiously.

"Circulate, goddamn it!" Carmen called after her. "Go inside, go to Room Nine, get those reporters out here!" What's *wrong* with that woman? she sighed and turned her attention to the crowd. Then, as she chatted with a district leader about an impending judgeship, she saw Beth walking towards her.

"Carmen," Beth said, "we called the conference for eleven. It's only five after. Give them a chance. They'll come."

"Goddamn it, if you're afraid to go in there, I'll go in and get them myself!" And with that, she grabbed Beth's releases and marched up the steps of City Hall and across the Rotunda. Entering Room Nine, she cried, "Come on, boys, there's work to do outside!" At which point a half dozen reporters stopped typing and kibbitzing and followed her back to the rally. Beth watched, hemorrhaging pain.

The Vulnerability Spreads

After the press conference, Beth came to work each morning with such pain in her chest she could barely function. If I quit, she thought, there's nothing left for me in life. I will have failed everywhere. She tried to believe there was some hope of improvement. Perhaps she could talk with Carmen. If Carmen is dissatisfied, if I can do anything . . . .

But Carmen gave her the brush off whenever Beth approached, and the thought of pushing through the resistance and risking another barrage was unthinkable. She treaded water, kept hoping for an opening, and prayed that the recent unpleasantness was a temporary symptom of Carmen's election anxiety.

Beth's co-workers could see that she was off. Her face was long and haggard, her eyes frightened and evasive, her smile ingratiating and unreal. She often sat at her desk with her back to the others, not turning to talk for hours. Thwack! A bundle of mail landed in front of her. Roseanne, the receptionist, dropped it as she walked by, never pausing to say good morning. It was a typical Roseanne gesture—adolescent, insensitive, defiant. But Beth, armorless and raw, experienced it as a knife in the belly.

Fueled by Carmen's open disrespect toward Beth, Roseanne's guerrilla tactics multiplied. Beth looked toward Al at the next desk, hoping for an ally with whom to share a reassuring smirk. But Al, a frightened man who marches to the loudest drum, sensed that Beth was contaminated and kept his distance lest her contamination spread.

"Roseanne," Beth said, "When I get a call, please ask the caller his name before buzzing me. I expect that courtesy."

"I'll do it when I have time," Roseanne said curtly, "you're not the only person who gets calls here."

"You little bitch."

"What did you call me?" Roseanne shrieked, as if she'd never heard the word before. Beth looked at her with hatred, and, biting her lip, walked away, aware of everyone's eyes.

Becoming "It"

Beth has never felt perfectly at ease with the other people in the office. Unlike most of Carmen's staff, she does not enjoy more than a minute or two of office gossip, and she cannot feign excitement over trivial things, like Carmen's birthday or the appearance in the office of Carmen's grandchildren.

Beth is out of step with the times. As someone who likes to talk philosophy, to think about religion, to keep a journal, she has virtues that her career-absorbed friends lack; but she suffers from a dearth of purpose and momentum, which most of them seem to have. When she feels secure, she feels above the others, and judges them as narrow or stupid. When she's insecure and hungry for connection, she listens to their chatter and feels like a helpless child in a world of socially competent adults.

Many people feel different or separate from the group, but Beth's differences are accentuated because she's never been one to disguise them. She cannot force herself, as Georgette does, to smile, to dodge, to feign interest, to stroke, when her seriousness puts her at odds with the frivolousness of her colleagues. She does not fortify her differences with a powerful pose like cynical self-confidence, amiable efficiency, or indulgent maternalism. Ashamed of phoniness or fraudulence, she resists being political.

Still and all, she has managed to fit into the office scene for two and a half years, has worked hard, and gotten by.

But as object consciousness began to envelope her, the situation changed. Her pain began to seep out in inappropriate acts. Beth laughed in the wrong places to cover a rush of shame. She made quips that did not suit the moment or the relationship. ("Do you think Carmen will get a facelift for the campaign, Al?") in a desperate attempt to make an alliance. She dropped her sentences midway when she feared her words revealed her inadequacy.

Beth's behavior was extremely annoying and discomfitting to her co-workers. Except for Roseanne, who was inclined to be cruel, they expressed their dissatisfaction by wrapping themselves in formality, by drawing in the boundaries of the appropriate, leaving Beth stranded outside in a pool of impropriety. Al looked down without a smile, because a legislative counsel is not supposed to respond to a farcical dig at the candidate. Carmen scolded Beth for insulting Roseanne with "street language." Steve played the part of the campaign manager who is too busy for someone who laughs inappropriately and either talks too much or doesn't complete her sentences. They were each playing the subject in their own way.

Again and again Beth found people taken aback by her impropriety, as if she were an embarrassing barbarian in their midst. There were times when she wanted to say, "Look, Al, you and I, we're just people. We don't have to play games, do we? I'm having a little trouble here, and I could sure use a friend."

Other times she felt so wronged she wanted to go through the office with a machine gun. On several occasions she threw caution out the window and made a direct accusation, only to find that she'd made a wrong move. Sure that Roseanne was not taking her messages, she screamed at Roseanne as if the girl were her husband or mother. Although nothing compared to what Roseanne deserved, her outburst was a totally inappropriate display of emotion for an office setting. Roseanne folded her arms and shook her head.

In almost any conflict, her co-workers found an easy target in Beth's manner or her loss of control, so that the truth or falseness of her words became irrelevant. There were moments when Beth felt as if she were a wild animal that people in business suits were calmly spearing.

Beth swung turbulently from passivity and resignation to primitive self-defense. People started saying she was crazy and walking around her. There was no question any more of right or wrong or how it all began. The only question was Beth's disturbing and inappropriate behavior. And as Beth descended into the vortex of powerlessness and became a convenient target for everyone's old, bottled-up dissatisfactions, an aura of good feeling spread throughout the staff.

Hell

Outside the office, Beth conferred with friends, received as much comfort as her friendships could afford, and managed to pull herself together for a day or two. She'd go into the office and be perfectly proper; but the awkwardness of the effort was apparent, especially to Roseanne, who said, "Look, she's like an ape with a ribbon in her hair!" At other times Beth abused her friends for not caring or doing more for her. They became guilty, defensive, and enraged. Her habit of monitoring friendship and loyalty and meting out guilt accordingly, grew extreme, pushing people further away.

The more self-pitying she became, the more inclined she was to be defiant, to do things that would invite abuse. And the very presence of the abuse-inviting impulse within her was itself an ugliness that cried out for abuse.

Her stomach now had a permanent pain the size of a canteloupe. She spent a lot of time lying in bed unable to read. She spent many hours dulled before the television. A week ago, dining with friends who invited a single man for her to meet, she found herself dreaming, even before she met him, that he would ask her to marry him. She prayed that he was in pain too. But he was cheerful and seemed happy, and she thought, Oh no, I can't handle it. Seeing her own thoughts, her self-esteem took another plunge, and the canteloupe grew hotter.

Georgette was so involved in her own projects, which had kept her out of the office, that she had no idea how bad things were. Beth would occasionally look down the long, narrow row of filing cabinets and cluttered desks and wonder, Should I approach Georgette? After all, they had exchanged some intimate words a few months back. But she decided she was fortunate that Georgette was out of it, for how on earth could she expect that Georgette would react any differently than the others? Besides, everyone loved Georgette, and to risk counting her among the opposition by saying something stupid or presumptuous was more than she could bear. Now, after their encounter on the sidewalk this afternoon, Beth was convinced: Georgette knows I'm paranoid and out of control. She's been warned to avoid me; she's on the other side. With such thoughts, Beth abandoned her last hope for an ally, someone who would touch her, someone who would reassure her, someone who would contain her pain and give her the blessed light of reason by saying, *It's not just you*.

That afternoon Beth began to fantasize that she would be hospitalized. Oh, to be carted away and taken care of. But then she had a frightening thought and the pulse in her neck throbbed heavily. They would give her a label. They would see that she was fat and out of control, and lacking a husband, and not wealthy, and they would conclude that she was seriously defective. What a victory for Roseanne!

She feared that the stigma of hospitalization would stay with her forever. Whenever she overate, whenever she had a fight with someone, whenever people turned against her, she would recall that she'd been a mental patient, and a dogged inner voice would cry, "It's *me*, it's *me*, it's *me!*"

Her mind reached for other forms of deliverance. She thought about her niece in Reverend Moon's menacing army of glee. Her vision was flooded with the forced smiles on the faces of the saved. Were they really forced?

The telephone rang. But when she answered, there was only an ominous click. She was frightened. She felt alone and persecuted. A constant tapping made by a Con Edison work crew beneath her window seemed to be sending her a message.

Her fantasies turned to suicide. She imagined her indicting note, how she'd rip into the bastards—her mother, her father, her sister, Georgette!—how mortified they'd feel. Meanwhile, quietly, she ate herself into oblivion.

14.

Dr. Aggression and Mr. Charm

Martin gets depressed, throws a tantrum, comes back cute. The top-dog style of relating when he competes, when he can't get his way, and when he wants forgiveness without having to own up.

WHILE GEORGETTE WAS DOWNTOWN, bumping into Beth, Martin was playing squash at the Columbia University gym, as he does every Sunday. He played with a group of men he's been friendly with since undergraduate days, most of them professionals, including Frank Caruso, who went to high school with Martin in New Roses, Connecticut, and is still his best friend. Martin and Frank never burden each other with the dreams and illusions that Martin once saw as the coin of an ideal friendship, but they have a similar facility for one-upmanship, and that forms the basis for a distant sort of camaraderie.

Frank heads Columbia Medical School's video technology department. He is as light and swift as a frisbee, with a wry, easy sort of humor and a record with women that Martin admires and marvels at. He's never married and at forty-two seems no more concerned about the matter than he was at eighteen. His great loves are sex, technology, the latest mind-altering substances, and vacations in Sufi ashrams, approximately in that order. He's never at a loss for words and derives great satisfaction from teasing Martin for his ambition and competitiveness. Since Martin is never at a loss for words either, they circle around each other, unthreatened, fascinated, constantly teasing, and, in a backhanded way, thoroughly supportive. "Frank is like a Chinese dinner," Martin likes to say, explaining his ability to spend so much time with him, "he never fills you up." "Because he's utterly empty himself!" Georgette rejoins, to which Martin only raises one eyebrow.

The men were playing a round-robin tournament this morning in which Frank came in first and Martin second. As winner and runner-up, they were both due a free lunch at The Balcony, but to his buddies' consternation, Martin decided that the prudent thing to do would be to go home and spend some time assuaging the feelings of his increasingly testy wife.

"Problems with the little lady?" said Frank with a broad, goading grin. The comment was so obviously meant to get the better of Martin and so obviously a move in their perpetual game of interpersonal chess that it was almost painless. "Hmm-hmmmmm," Martin said in his long cynical drawl, his mouth gathered at one corner, his eyes cocked into a mocking stare that said, "*Wise guy.*" Frank chuckled with satisfaction as Martin hailed a cab and entered it without ever changing his expression.

Martin arrived home from the match, disgruntled about having come in second. He planned to go straight to Georgette and start pouting. But as he turned the key, preparing to taste her reassuring pets and delicious digs at his oversized ego, he heard the sounds of Marge's Brooklynese emanating from the kitchen.

Because he regulates every minute of his time, one of the few things that can undo Martin is the undoing of his plans. With Marge in the kitchen, ruining his fantasy of this afternoon, he suddenly feels empty. He feels a fool for having given up brunch with the guys. He remember's Frank's quip, feels rankled by it ("Pussy-whipped!"), and gets angry. Objectively, of course, there is no one to blame. And yet he feels angry all the same, the more so for its lack of justification.

Being a subject, Martin does not ask, What does this threatening feeling mean? He does not open the trap door to a self-examination that may lead who knows where. He certainly does not confide such a feeling, ask for help with it, or acknowledge the irrational anger it induces. Rather, he seeks to discharge the sense of threat with an act of aggression. As Martin enters the kitchen, trying to sustain his unflappable image, he is cocked, loaded, and ready to fire. The only thing he lacks is a legitimate target, for which duty Marge soon makes herself available.

" . . . and I think you're going to have to be more assertive," Marge is saying. "Maybe you should remind Carmen that she's being hypocritical to take a stand for women's rights when she underpays a key female staff. . . ."

"Rabble-rousing, Marge?" Martin teases as he ambles past them. He turns and looks disdainfully at the bag of cookies the two of them are dismantling. His every gesture, his whole body is provocative.

Marge stiffens. He's going after her again. "Why? Do you feel they pay her enough at that place?"

Martin continues to drawl off-handedly as he plucks a Perrier from the fridge. "No, I just think you're making a big mistake if you turn this into a women's issue."

"I'm not turning this into a women's issue," Marge says emphatically as she cranes her head for a glimpse of Martin's averted face, "it *is* a women's issue."

"Well," he smirks, opening the bottle and still not looking at her, a trick he taught himself twenty-five years ago, "I personally would rather get the raise than deliver a dissertation on the history of sexual oppression."

At this, Georgette begins to gather the remaining cookies and stuff them into a jug.

"Martin, you talk as if you're the only one here who's ever operated in the real world," Marge says defensively.

He smiles and wags a finger: "Defensive, defensive."

"Well," she says, slightly stung and putting on a display of overdone sarcasm, "all I can say is I don't see that Georgette's gotten so far on the advice you've been giving her."

"That's where we differ, Marge," Martin says, redoubling his cool as he finds his target. "I don't try to run Georgette's life."

Marge is hurt and starts to sink. Her pulse and breathing quicken and her armpits grow damp. She sensed from the beginning that she was caught in a no-win contest. Now she feels as if she is a worm that a sneering giant is calmly crushing underfoot. She hates him, and she hates herself for succumbing to him. "You don't *have* to try," she mutters.

It's a sloppy, defeated move, a wrong move, which puts her plainly in the ring with Martin and leaves her open to accusations of interfering in the marriage. In effect, Martin has succeeded in provoking her to step outside the boundaries of what is appropriate for someone in the role of Guest or Family Friend to say. Her breach of propriety puts "world opinion" on Martin's side. Now he can kill.

At another time, Martin would have looked at Marge steadily, nodded, and left. But this afternoon he is in a mean mood and wants more than his usual two-percent advantage.

He glares at her. "And what's *that* supposed to mean?" His sharp tone, his hawkish expression of total conviction throws Marge into a frenzy. He is standing over her now, defying her to get off the canvas and put up her dukes.

Trying to regain an appropriate posture and recognizing the need for a tactical retreat, Marge pulls herself together and pours on her brand of maneuver. "All I mean, Martin," she says in a rational and reassuring tone, "is that you are a very aggressive guy and taking charge comes naturally to you. A little while ago I was having a conversation with Georgette about her job. I'm sure you're not trying to run anyone's life, but now here I am having a conversation with you instead."

At first, Martin is struck with the feeling that he has underestimated the opposition, and he starts to scramble. "Well, it seems to me that what you're saying is that if I try to offer a suggestion, then I'm interfering. Isn't that what it comes down to?" He tries to vaporize her with his eyes, then turns to his better half. "Do *you* think I'm interfering, Georgette? Do *you* think I *run your life?*"

Fearful, divided, and angered at being used as a pawn, Georgette laughs nervously and feigns indifference. "I'm going to make some more coffee. You guys let me know when you figure out who's won."

Feeling betrayed, and furious that Georgette has slipped out of his control, Martin finally abandons all pretext of reasonableness and reveals the level of punishment that always lies beneath his easy-going authority, "Goddamn it, Georgette," he calls after her, "people who get promotions usually know how to take a stand!" Then addressing Marge in a calmer, more derisive tone: "If your advice were any good, she'd be able to tell you directly, *assertively,* how little you understand about marriage." And he walks out.

Turning to Georgette, looking devastated, with her mouth hanging open and her face gone white, Marge says she feels as if she's done something awful, as if she's violated their marriage. Georgette, holding down her own distress, assures her that nothing of the kind has happened, that Martin was not himself, that he probably lost at squash, that she'll make sure he never acts that way again. With that, Marge wipes her tears and her self-hatred subsides.

Bought Off

By the time Martin calls Georgette from a phone booth to see if Marge has left, he's decided against playing the injured party. Having blown his cool and so openly displayed his hostility, he will be hard-pressed to maintain his innocence. Better to cut his losses than risk renewed warfare. The self-deprecating humor with which he accepts Goergette's reprimands, the little hints of flattery and flirtation are all calculated to win her forgiveness and divert her away from any suggestion that he apologize to Marge.

When he returns home later that afternoon, he finds Georgette on the phone taking care of the business that often spills over into her weekends. Still peeved, she pays no attention to him beyond a single glance. She is in a state of high efficiency, a sight Martin loves. He even savors the slight rejection her aloofness implies, because it puts them on more equal terms, makes him feel less the boss and more desirous of her.

She is all concentration, busily telling Mrs. Rios, an embattled tenant, how to handle two relocation goons banging on her door. ". . . And nothing happened when you dialed nine-one-one? . . . Okay, let me give you the number of the precinct house . . . . That's okay because I'm going to call them, too. . . . Yes, that's right. . . . That doesn't matter. No one has a right to bang on your door. That's harassment . . . . Don't worry, I'm calling Cynthia McCormick of *The News,* too . . . . I know it's terrible, Mrs. Rios. It's a horrible, horrible thing. I can't tell you how much I admire you . . . ."

When she hangs ups, Martin, who is familiar with the case and all the work Georgette has put into it, says, "Christ, why don't they *move?*" a question he knows will put a little more heat under her collar.

"Martin, I can't discuss it now." She begins dialing, and Martin watches with pleasure. She speaks to the cops with a forcefulness and manipulative charm she rarely uses with him. She cajoles her reporter friend by playing on her idealism and enticing her with an exclusive. She then sits down at the kitchen table and begins jotting notes in a file labeled "536 E. 13." Martin feels more drawn to her and sexually aroused than he has in weeks. If only she could be this way all the time, he thinks. Why does she let herself get so bogged down, so doubting, so intimidated? It isn't *necessary.*

"Now if you could only be that way with Carmen," he says smiling as if to indicate his comment is made more out of admiration than criticism.

Georgette begins to shrink. Then, remembering Mrs. Rios and the things she still has to do today, she suppresses her self-doubts and counterattacks. "You always say the nicest things, Martin."

"Come on," he says, circling behind her and putting his nose into the back of her neck. "You know why I say that." "Yes, Martin, I know, so that I should never forget what a *shnoid* you think I am." "Come on, come on," he says with a touch more petulance, massaging her breasts and nuzzling her as he speaks, "I don't think you're a *shnoid*. I think you're terrific. You had that cop wrapped around your finger. You should be the one announcing for Congress next week. You practically run that office yourself anyway. That's why I can't understand why you let that dyke bully you."

Georgette stares at the ceiling in an exasperated pose as he speaks. He's after something and she's hesitant to give it. She doesn't know whether to respond to the content of his words, which is absurd, or to the overall tone, one that more or less demands, according to precedent, that she accept Martin's pleading and cooling justification as a legitimate truce offering for his transgressions. She decides to stretch his discomfort.

"So you think I should be announcing for Congress next week instead of Carmen?"

"Oh, you know what I mean," he says. "*Yes*, I think you should be. You're smarter and you care more, you're more honest, and"—he pauses—"you've got much nicer boobs." He strokes them and snuggles her in an exaggerated way.

Georgette remains aloof: "And the national news editor of *Today* sees that as an important factor?" she says, smirking.

"It couldn't *hurt*."

"And what would I do when I got to Congress if people like her started bullying me?"

"Hmm, well . . . ." He smiles, aware that he's being buried in his own logic. "I guess you'd just have to go topless. Yeah," he adds, aroused by the thought, "the Topless Congressperson. I can see the campaign now!"

"Martin, I'm asking you a question!"

But by now he has her shirt off and is leading her off down the hall.

Review 3

1. As we follow our characters through this period of conflict, we see that they are all controlled by the *shame-should-shame cycle* and the habits that follow from it. Their fears of being seen for what they really are and punished for it, their long-established habits of maneuvering, and their unconscious assumptions about what other people are up to constitute a hidden dimension of their personalities, a bundle of tendencies and perceptions that are mostly unexamined and out of control. The relationships they form under the auspices of these fears, habits, and false assumptions are loaded with implicit contracts which are remembered and held onto like precedents in a court of law. All this makes change very difficult.

2. In a strategic environment, you have to worry about the *wrong move*—an inappropriate-looking act or statement that invites defeat. It is not necessarily wrong in any moral sense; it just *looks* wrong and is thus a great strategic liability. It is often an unconscious act of self-destruction.

3. Instilling *guilt* entails shaming someone by making him feel he has done something immoral or inappropriate, that he has violated the norms by which proper people live. Guilt can be used judiciously to force a person to reconsider what he's done; but more often guilt is used with thoughtless aggression—to make him feel that he is socially deformed and that his deformity is showing.

4. *Image,* a necessary tool of everyday life, is also part of the defensive barrier we create around ourselves. In this age of insecurity, image has attained a particularly ferocious hold on many people.

5. In an environment where "winners" are applauded for the ability to stay on top and "losers" are looked upon with disgust, emotional *vulnerability* becomes a frightening burden to many people. Weakness, hurt, doubt, defeat, even self-hatred itself may become grounds for more self-hatred. When Chuck stalks out leaving Marge feeling like a frigid killer, the mere fact that she has lost the battle and is in pain causes her to feel yet more pain. It's as if, at the moment of Marge's defeat, the whole world is divided into two classes: hearty, happy, well-fed, well-sexed Farrah Fawcett smiling faces, and Marge—a grimy, misshapen slug who deserves only to be stepped on and forgotten. The same feeling threatens to re-engulf her at lunch with Georgette and keeps her from being more open.

6. Beth tends to become a *scapegoat* because she sends out object invitations to almost everyone. That these invitations are hard to resist is no excuse for accepting them. Her office mates are all responsible for the subject role they take with her and partly to blame for her downfall. She is the outcast we all dread becoming, and she represents an aspect of our lives we prefer to disavow.

7. For all our characters, change is possible if they are willing to examine themselves deeply enough and struggle to expand their repertoire. Balancing the power is obviously important. But, as we are about to see, so is diplomacy, forthrightness, and intimacy. With these skills, they can prevent power struggles before they begin, achieve a level of communication that is impossible with any kind of maneuvering, and finally come to terms with who they are.

IV.

THE REPLAY

Using Your Whole Self

15.

Finessing It

Subtle maneuvers to circumvent unwanted conflicts. How to gently administer guilt, flattery, humor, rewards, image, manipulation, and smoking out. *The little diplomacies of daily life.*

ON SUNDAY AFTERNOON, under the pressure of Martin's kitchen offensive, Marge's world was destabilized: Is he mistreating me? Have I done something wrong? Is my secret dislike for him showing? Is he just being insensitive? Am I being paranoid? The role of Guest and Family Friend, normally so free and informal for her, narrowed to a perilous tightrope where almost anything she said could be used against her. With Martin's final blow, Marge tumbled and was engulfed in self-hatred.

Her vision of herself changed from a competent, attractive person who knows how to get along in the world into that of a slovenly, meddling pig. She saw herself as pushy and insensitive and unable to deal effectively with strong men. She felt she had no future as a lawyer and very little as a human being. Only Georgette's allegiance quieted the screaming voices and lifted her out of the pits.

Martin's upper hand in this fight was based partly on the fact that Marge was in his house and was obliged to pay respect to his authority there: A Guest and Family Friend is not supposed to be presumptuous or meddlesome. Martin kept provoking Marge until she made a wrong move and he was free to clobber her.

But the same legalistic attitude toward right and wrong (How dare you criticize the way I live with my wife!), the same exploitation of role proprieties that enables Martin to make Marge "it," can be turned against him. Martin may have the home-team advantage, but, just like the visitor, he can be reminded of certain limits and responsibilities. A Husband should not alienate his wife's friends; a Host is expected to offer hospitality. As soon as Martin's tone turns hostile, it represents a violation of the social expectations governing *him,* and, if Marge can keep her cool, that is where she can nail him.

The Diplomatic Use of Punishment: A Surgical Strike with Guilt

Martin: *"Well, I personally would rather get that raise than deliver a dissertation on the history of sexual oppression."*

This is a derisive statement. Martin has acted inappropriately. He has violated the role of Host and is therefore out on a limb. If Marge lets this one go by (as so many of us would be prone to do), the advantage passes to Martin, and Marge knows all too well what he will do with it.

Marge: *"Excuse me, Georgette, perhaps we'd better talk another time. It's getting late."*

Marge, perfectly cordial, purports to be leaving because of the hour. This is a necessary cover, because Martin will go right after her if she openly protests his intervention. ("What's the matter, Marge, aren't I allowed to join in?") But between the lines she is subtly making Martin feel guilty for what he's done.

Georgette: *"Oh, Marge, please stay."*

Martin: *"Yeah, come on, hang around a while."*

He makes it sound casual, but he now realizes the spot he's in. He can't say, "You only want to leave because I'm getting under your skin" without looking hypersensitive and paranoid. So he lays on a little image and tries to act friendly instead.

Marge: *"No. Thanks anyway. I've got to be going."*

In this version, serious conflict is avoided. Marge retains her dignity and, if anyone feels a little sour, it is Martin. He'll probably get a talking to from Georgette and be more considerate in the future.

Note that Marge has to let go of something in order to achieve this victory. She has to be willing to give up her time with Georgette. If holding onto that is more important than her self-esteem, then she is trapped in an object posture and bound to fail. Note, too, that Marge punished Martin in both the actual incident and in this replay. But in the replay her moves are conscious and disciplined, and she is careful not to leak inappropriate punishments that could be used against her.

It is a cool and forceful act of diplomacy that balances things while leaving her perfectly free to return to the Grodin home.

There are many other areas in our story where a timely act of diplomacy would have prevented unnecessary conflict. In most cases, unlike this incident with Martin, there was no hostility, but rather clumsiness—clumsiness that led to conflict or escalation or some hidden sense of winning and losing. What was needed was a way to smooth out the awkwardness. And for this chore a whole set of mild strategies are available.

Using Humor

Humor is a strategy that works well in combination with other strategies. It can camouflage a punishment ("Ha-ha, I was only kidding, don't be so defensive"), but it has many moderating influences as well. Let's observe it in its weak and strong configurations.

Weak humor. Early in the story, Georgette said, "Mink dahling," in her Mata Hari voice in order to make light of her desire for the mink coat. The humor was self-denigrating. She was serving herself up with a smile and a prayer to be squashed or patted on the head as Martin saw fit. She would have been better off asking for the mink in a straightforward manner, without smiles, shrugs, or other strategic embellishments. Once she belittles herself with humor, she gives Martin license to do the same.

Strong humor. 1. When Georgette and Martin are fighting over the lithograph, Martin is in a bind, and his skills fail him because of his guilt. He's certainly not going to rekindle any tender feelings by telling Georgette that he's hot for someone else's thighs, and, besides, that's not the real issue between them. He has problems with Georgette that he should be talking to her about, and the thigh obsession is simply a manifestation of the distance between them. For now, he just needs to get by. "I don't know, Georgette, a picture like that in the bedroom would begin to feel like a *ménage à trois*." The joke suggests in a harmless way the inappropriateness of another attractive female in the bedroom. It gets Georgette's attention without making her feel jealous or bullied.

2. Early in our story, Georgette stated her views on the animal welfare legislation and nobody responded. Such moments cry out for smoothing over. Georgette might have salvaged the situation by screwing up her face and saying: "Well! Don't everybody speak at once!" Delivered with mock indignation, with all vulnerability bur-

ied, as she stared challengingly about, a comeback like that might have gotten her through the meeting and slowed her object spiral.

Humor like this takes an apparent setback and says, "Hey, I don't feel vulnerable about this at all!" It thereby dissolves the anxiety of all those inept colleagues who see her vulnerability and don't know what to do about it. Liberated from their awkwardness, they rush to the side of the spunky speaker, and celebrate her ability to slide out from under impending doom.

Using Manipulation

"Manipulation," like "punishment," is a word that has such bad press, it's hard to talk about it in a positive light. But manipulation is an important tool, and we should be clear about what it can do.

Weak manipulation. Georgette often complains that Martin is not seeing enough of Cindy. Recently she told him in a loaded tone that the kindergarten teacher seemed concerned about Cindy's ability to relate to male figures. This is a case of pure and unhealthy manipulation. Although what she says is not necessarily untrue, Georgette's underlying purpose is to make Martin feel guilty about spending so much time at work; the idea being to get him to spend more time with her.

There is something inherently undignified (not to mention destructive) about Georgette's maneuvering to get someone—her husband no less—to spend more time with her and using their daughter as a pawn in the game. It creates another knot in the Grodin's marital web of dishonesty. Georgette should tell Martin about her concerns for Cindy, but cleanly, independent of whatever she's doing for herself.

Strong manipulation. Georgette is in a competitive conflict with Steve Friendly. He does everything he can to put her in a bad light, but couches his moves carefully so that Carmen remains unaware. Steve is a destructive influence on the staff, and it's in Georgette's interest to make Carmen know that. But Carmen is so caught up in strategies that Georgette cannot sit down with her and talk straight. She has to be very careful because if it looks as if she has an axe to grind, her opinion of Steve will be instantly discounted. Besides, she does not want Carmen to know that she sees Steve as an adversary, because she'd rather not convey the impression that there's anyone in the office she's unable to get along with.

Georgette has to wait for a moment when she can casually plant a seed of doubt. Such a moment could arise during one of their late afternoon sessions, when Carmen uses Georgette as a sounding board. Toward the end of their time together, Carmen typically tries to motivate Georgette by telling her what a wonderful job she's doing with the constituents and how important her work is to the reelection campaign. Here is the perfect opportunity for Georgette to express her appreciation and, with apparent innocence, ask Carmen, "Does Steve feel the same way?"

Carmen cocks her head, considers for a second, and answers, "Oh, sweetie, I'm sure Steve appreciates your importance to us."

Georgette says, good, she's happy to hear that. But she has managed to plant the suspicion that Steve may be hindering her in some way. Carmen will now see certain incidents in a new light and listen more carefully when Steve talks about moving Georgette out of her work space.

Smoking Out Feelings

Because Beth never knows where she stands with Carmen, she needs to smoke her out. She may not be able to get Carmen to tell her everything, but she can get enough useful information to transform many of the little transactions between them. Some guidelines:

Get the apology. An apology is worth more when it's aboveboard and on the record. When the ever-devious Carmen throws a twisted, unclear apology her way, Beth should carefully massage it into its proper shape:

Carmen (smiling): "We had ourselves a little row this morning, didn't we?"

Beth (firm but gentle): "It was worse than a row."

Carmen (jocular): "Well, you know how it is, trying to be a saint all the time."

Beth (smiling slightly): "Is this an apology, Carmen?"

Carmen (contrite): "Yeah, I guess."

Beth (straight): "Thanks."

Get the criticism out in the open. Let Carmen take responsibility for her criticism and not try to slip it between the lines, so that she remains safely outside the equation. If she has a problem with the headline on one of Beth's press releases, she should say so openly rather than make oblique comments. The more open her criticism is, the more she'll have to take responsibility for it—including suggesting how it might be better. "Are you criticizing?" is thus another important smoking-out question.

Get the request "in writing." When dealing with an emotionally withholding person like Carmen, you want to get her to ask for whatever she wants openly rather than hint. Let the need and the giving be acknowledged. "Are you suggesting I go back to City Hall to retrieve your purse?" leaves Beth in a much better position than if she reads her orders between the lines. Forcing the request onto Carmen's lips makes Carmen feel the importance of the request as well as the natural sense of obligation that goes with a favor rendered.

"Are you saying no?" (If so, let her say it.) "Why do you say that?" (Don't let a pointed joke go by without explanation.) "Is that what *you* believe?" (Don't tell me what so-and-so says, tell me what you say.) Each of these questions combats various forms of evasive maneuvers.

Warning. Questioning has its limits. Beth would be asking for trouble if in response to Carmen's jabs and cuts she tries to get to the bottom of it by finding out what Carmen's overall feelings are toward her. Vulnerable Beth will be approaching armored Carmen and get wounded again by Carmen's automatic fire. In her position, she should only smoke Carmen out on specifics, where Beth can be secure in her position and Carmen is out on a limb.

Using Rewards

Rewards are as powerful a tool as punishments for controlling and training people. Listening, showing concern, doing favors (and making them seem like trifles), laughing in the right places, remembering people's names, their children, their awards—all these things have a strong, seductive effect on people.

Rewards consist of any form of giving to which an attempt to influence is attached. If you do it right, such giving is like putting money in the bank, because the recipients will be inclined to give to you, to like you, to side with you, to relax their scrutiny of the interpersonal balance sheet.

Rewards can be used up front as a means of winning friendship and good will, and they can be used as reinforcements to motivate people, maintain allegiances, and otherwise encourage the sort of behavior you want.

Weak rewards. Jake (at the editorial meeting where Martin unmanned him): "You can never tell what's going to happen when Martin Grodin arrives early." Jake was trying to be friendly. He was hoping that if he was cordial to Martin, Martin would be cordial to him. That's usually a sound enough approach, but it is stupid and weak when someone is out to get you. The obvious rule is never to reward someone for punishing you. A diversion of some kind—like ignoring Martin and asking a question of Roland—would have been stronger.

Strong rewards. 1. Anyone in a position of authority has rewards and punishments at his disposal, and they should be leaned on heavily when his authority is under attack. In Jake's case this might include: a) making assignments based on loyalty. Editors who support him get the special reports and other plums; editors who don't find their perks drying up. b) Suggesting that Roland write a special essay in the business section. Roland, who has always aspired to be a writer as well as a publisher, will be flattered (assuming, of course, that he does not detect that flattery is Jake's intention).

2. Chuck should have been more open with Marge from the beginning about his feelings. But by the time he took his shower, there was so much static between them and so little basis for rapport that in order to save the night, he would have had to be extraordinarily in touch and eloquent about what he felt. In fact, he was so muddle-headed at this point that any attempt at openness on his part would have made the mess worse. What he needed to do was praise Marge a little, recall aloud the magnificent time he'd had dancing with her, lie with conviction about how much he was looking forward to seeing her again, ask when she was free next, and say something perhaps about how much more wonderful a new person can be when you get to know her better. Then he might have gotten away unscathed. His situation demanded massive diplomacy.

3. One of Georgette's most effective rewards is pleasantly putting up with some of Carmen's unfair criticism. She acts like a devoted pupil, thanks Carmen for her help, and Carmen loves her for it. Beth, by contrast, who is proud and defensive about her work and hates unfair criticism no matter how insignificant, is never able, even in the best of days, to get to first base with the boss.

Warning. Georgette uses rewards to be liked and included. They show up in her attentiveness to group expectations—in never forgetting a colleague's birthday; in occasionally supplying cake for the coffee break; in her way of making others feel good around her with her jokes and compliments; in the way she babies Carmen and attends to her emotional aches and pains. Such rewards are powerful until one of two things happens. She finds herself giving more than she's getting, or someone starts treating her with disrespect. Then rewards must be restrained and other strategies—punishment, smoking out, balancing the giving and getting—must come to the fore.

Once the power is out of balance, rewards, if used alone, will generally look obsequious and make the imbalance worse. Unfortunately, people who are adept with rewards are often unable to stop them. Instead of being a tool, rewarding becomes a permanent fixture of the personality, in peacetime a barrier to honesty, in conflict a barrier to success. Making people feel good is a strategic skill that will take us a long, long way. But we must guard against its becoming a habit. Once it feels like an essential piece of our being without which we will not be accepted, the reward habit may be our undoing.

Image: Playing the Part

Power struggles create an emotional climate in which it becomes perilous to lean openly toward any feelings that don't conform to social expectations. When Georgette is evading Martin after sex, her cover story has to be that she "honestly" has nothing to say. Because, technically, it's unseemly to withhold feelings from your husband after making love—and the whole world operates according to such social technicalities. When Jake maneuvers at an editorial meeting, it has to be for the good of the magazine, not because he's trying to save his own skin. When Marge gets back at Martin, she must stay within the role of Guest. Being right doesn't matter in strategic struggles; it's looking right that counts.

Let's go back to that moment early in our story when Georgette submitted her housing report with typos and a few legal facts unchecked partly because she was rushed, but also, unconsciously, in order to withhold something from Carmen. Georgette felt that she was always giving and not getting enough in return, and here was a place to take a stand. She foolishly indulged in a typical powerless punishment, for her anger was acted out in a context that did her no good.

Using strategic power effectively requires that one wrap oneself in the flag of whatever roles are involved—in Georgette's case the essential role being that of Employee and Devoted Follower. She must appear cooperative, "positive," loyal, eager, painstaking—postures she normally assumes without thinking. Of course, the typos were an unconscious blunder, but not so unconscious that they were totally beyond her control. If, in general, she makes a concerted effort to stick to her role in circumstances like that, she will pay better attention, and such "illegitimate" impulses will automatically be flagged.

She can then recognize that she is about to act out her anger and carefully restrain herself.

The strategy people use to play the part, to seem to be exactly what a proper person is expected to be, is, of course, image. Image is the umbrella under which all other strategies march. Image lends an element of sincerity and conviction to the most calculated maneuvers. Image means correct appearance, acceptable motives, and, above all, good acting. If Marge were as attentive to image and role propriety with Martin as she is at work and in bed, the kitchen debate might, as we've seen, have ended differently.

Warning. Like all strategies, image has its liabilities. Take Marge. She looks attractive and sexy to elicit favors and desire. She acts cool, uses buzz words, and wraps herself in the role of the expert in order to gain acceptance, credibility, and respect. All this can be rather harmless until it becomes a tool for domination or so routinized and ingrained that Marge herself mistakes the surface for reality.

Even in strategic terms, image can be a problem. Nervous about playing the Healthy Normal Person on her dates with Chuck, Marge puts so much energy into regulating the impression she makes that she leaves little room for personal connection. Threatened by Marge's slick image, Chuck doubts himself and shrinks away, creating an emotional distance that leaves Marge feeling rejected and alone. Indeed, she's so good an actress that Chuck has little appreciation of her fragility, and, in the end, she does not receive the benefit of his caring when she needs it. And because image accounts for an excessive part of Marge's strategic arsenal, when hostilities erupt and her patina is pierced, her power fades with terrible swiftness.

Nevertheless, if you look back over all the successful strategies, you will see that image of some kind—"I'm just being playful," "I'm just being helpful," "I'm just doing what a person in my position must do"—has always been a factor. Like strategic power in general, image is a double-edged tool, and mastering its appropriate use must go hand-in-hand with avoiding its dangers.

16.

Playing It Straight

Throughout our story people have maneuvered or dumbly sought advantage when they could have been direct. The skills that turn forthrightness into *personal power:* How to be open and strong.

WHEN JAKE FIRST DISCUSSED the managing editor's job with Ed Roland, the young publisher of *Today,* he described the editorial reforms he wanted, changes that were unprecedented in the industry. He was articulate. He demonstrated an inner conviction. He was sensitive to Roland's needs and concerns. And he was able to persist in a clear, straightforward way at times when Roland was skeptical, critical, or even slightly dismissive. In the end, he convinced Roland to try the unusual experiment.

That is power.

The ability to sustain your point of view without self-effacing humor, barbed innuendo, trial balloons, and other strategic crutches is as important as any other kind of power. But in our calculating, maneuvering, insecure age, the heartfelt statement is becoming a lost art.

Martin does not say: "I can't buy you a fur coat, Georgette. I'm sorry. It's something I haven't wanted to talk about. But the way you've been lately and the way I've felt, a gift like that doesn't feel right."

Georgette does not say: "I'm dissatisfied, Carmen. I love my work here, and I would like to make it my career. But I feel humiliated by my salary level, my lack of title, and my secretarial duties. And I'm disappointed with you for failing to support me against Steve Friendly's attacks."

Roland does not say: "Jake, I have a problem with the reforms we agreed to when you became managing editor. I don't want to usurp your authority, but I am getting nervous and I think we'd better talk."

Instead, some aspect of what they feel is communicated through hostile or inelegant strategies. Martin makes a sarcastic quip. Georgette hands in an uncorrected report in order to convey, "I'm not a secretary, I don't do shit work." Roland becomes unavailable and distant and uses Martin to help him stall.

As we've seen, certain situations preclude our being straightforward. But much of the turmoil we've seen could have been avoided with honest communication. For in each case there was at least one person who was in a secure enough position to be open.

Look again at Marge on her second date with Chuck, when the style of their relationship is forming. Chuck dances with other women. Marge pretends to be independent and not to mind. Before they know it, an uncomfortable distance separates them.

If Marge's purpose is to influence Chuck in such a way that he freely and without guilt begins to turn his attention toward her, the most powerful thing she can say would be, "Chuck, would you spend more time with me? I feel out of things over here," and to say it without a tone of anger, accusation, or self-effacement.

The thought of making this statement, which looks so harmless on the page, may arouse great anxiety in Marge. It may be unlike anything she's ever said. She may feel as if she's putting herself at his mercy. It certainly will not have the power to force him to do what he doesn't want to do. But if she speaks evenly and allows him the freedom to move, Chuck will seek to accommodate her in some way. If, on the other hand, she controls him with a hard-to-get image, calculated rewards, and teasing, punishing words about dancing with other women, so that for reasons he doesn't quite understand he never leaves her side, she will have initiated strategic vibrations that will reverberate throughout their relationship.

In all such situations, the irrational and unexamined assumptions we habitually make about other people are a primary barrier to being direct. Marge's assumptions tell her that Chuck has already rejected her and that his roaming is a way of sending her a message. The reality is that Chuck is unaware of her feelings, that he is trying to prove himself as independent as she seems to be, and that he would be pleased to know she cares. Only by putting her assumptions on hold and being direct can Marge test her fears against reality. She may even learn something from Chuck about the intimidating signals she normally transmits.

Forthrightness cannot give you control. No matter how eloquently you express yourself, people may still be disappointed with your decisions, think poorly of your motives, refuse your requests, get hurt, or become irrationally angry. All the same, open communication can achieve great influence—much greater in many ways than punishment or manipulation. To speak confidently from your center without strategic embellishment is a rare and compelling capacity. If people trust and respect your words, your message can reach inside them and affect them in a profound way.

The ability to make forthrightness powerful is called *personal* power. It is similar to what we normally call assertiveness, except that assertiveness, as it is often taught, includes various strategic postures and techniques. Here we want to emphasize the skills involved in being perfectly direct.

I. Establishing Your Context

Perhaps the greatest task of personal power is to be more aware of your feelings, your motives, your desires. Why, for example, does Ed Roland feel frustrated with Jake and want to slow down his editorial reforms? This is a question Roland has never clearly put to himself. Does he wish to go back on their agreement? Does he want to diminish Jake's authority? Has he totally lost faith in Jake and decided to replace him? Or does he simply feel frightened about setting off on this new course and want to satisfy himself that Jake is sensitive to his concerns?

Roland must define this issue for himself—he must establish his own context. For unless he is truly aware of where he's coming from and makes that clear to Jake, everything that happens between them will be distorted by his doubts and fears. As Roland tries to speak, self-doubts will fog his mind, protective strategies will undermine his words, he'll wander into contexts he would have avoided if he'd given them any advance thought, and the two men will be off on a disturbing round of maneuvers.

Marge has a similar problem at the party with Chuck, for she doesn't know her own cards well enough to know which ones to put on the table. Has she already become pitifully dependent on Chuck (as her self-doubts suggest) and hopelessly jealous when he dances with other women? Or does she simply want his company and (given the newness of their relationship) want to get to know him? If Marge could define her context for herself, she could establish it with Chuck, and her manipulative games would be unnecessary.

Note that even if Marge is feeling inappropriately dependent, the presence of such a feeling does not invalidate Marge's perfectly appropriate desire to have Chuck by her side. But she has to make some effort to define and separate the two issues before she speaks.

Martin is unhappy with his wife, but whenever he glances inward, he sees such a hodgepodge of impulses and desires he has no idea how much importance to give to what. There's his recent attraction to other women, his fantasies about separation, his disgust with Georgette's depression. He feels ashamed and afraid that Georgette would reject him if she knew his thoughts. He feels guilty about neglecting Cindy and about the amount of time he spends at work. And he is certain that if he expresses his own dissatisfactions he will have to entertain Georgette's dissatisfactions, as well. What kind of context can he make of such a swarm?

To dump all these feelings on the table or allow himself to get drawn toward the most negative, most shameful material simply because it seems most true is to make a regrettable and punishing mess. The idea of personal power is to be open in an effective way, not to carelessly confess one's must hurtful or self-incriminating thoughts.

Weak Personal Power. "Georgette, I have other women on my mind all the time, and I just felt I should tell you about it." Martin is speaking the truth here, he is being clear and direct, but this is hardly a necessary communication. What is his goal? If it's to place the burden of his guilt in Georgette's lap, he's certainly succeeded, but that's a strategic goal. If it's to talk about the pain he's feeling over his extramarital desires, he'd do better to confide in someone who's not directly involved. To use personal power, he must consider what message he wants Georgette to get and then speak it in the clearest possible way.

Strong Personal Power. "I'm upset about the distance between us." Excellent beginning. "I'm having a lot of trouble communicating with you lately." More to the point. "It's hard to be around you when you're in the dumps. I feel as if you've shut me out." Better yet. In these three sentences we see Martin's central and legitimate themes. If he can hold onto them, he won't get sidetracked by self-doubts.

Legitimacy in this case does not mean that Martin is right and Georgette is wrong, that she should not be depressed, that he has a right to abuse her, that the advantage is now his. Legitimacy simply means that it's not shameful for a husband to have the feelings he has or underhanded, cruel, or inappropriate to express them.

II. Avoiding Strategic Contamination

Strategic habits can be so subtle we hardly see their insidious effect. Without knowing it, people who think they are being absolutely straight and "just expressing their feelings" use strategic devices to shore themselves up. But even a small strategy—a raised eyebrow, a tone of voice, a loaded word—can be ruinous to personal power.

Weak personal power. Martin gives Georgette advice about how to deal with Carmen. His words sound fine: "Look, you've got to get her alone and have a serious talk. Nothing is going to happen otherwise." But imbedded in his delivery is displeasure. He is upset with Georgette for being exploited, and he thinks that may have something to do with why she's been depressed. By evading his real context (dissatisfaction) in favor of a false but easier context (helpfulness), Martin ends up making Georgette feel put down. Georgette resists speaking to him about Carmen; Martin becomes hurt and angry to see her accepting inferior advice from Marge; and their marital skirmishes open on a new front.

Strong personal power. "It bothers me that you let her treat you that way, and I think it brings you down, which also bothers me." No matter how nicely Martin says this, Georgette may still get pissed. But he's put real cards on the table in the straightest possible way and has nothing to feel guilty about. A honest talk is now possible.

Of course, Georgette may not be willing to talk. In that case, Martin should let the things lie for a while and see if anything changes. People often come around in quiet ways.

Notice the difference between the strategic posture and the forthright posture. When Martin is strategically motivated, his primary interest is not in *reaching* Georgette but in *steering* her. His words are measured, first, for their effect on her: Am I pleasing her? Displeasing her? Working in enough flattery and affection to control her? Second, for their impact on the unspoken contracts of the relationship: Am I setting a precedent? Implying a commitment I may not be able to keep? Giving so much that I'm out on a limb? And, third, for the way they make him look: Am I coming across sympathetic? Generous? Responsible? Etc.

Using personal power, however, Martin would be focused much more on some aspect of his inner sense of things. Where am I coming from? Let me be exact. Let me describe it in the most effective way. Let me find an analogy that will make it absolutely clear. He would still be sensitive to whether his words were reaching their audience, but would not alter his message to gain acceptance or control. He would simply speak his truth as effectively as he can and let it sit.

Unfortunately, our insecurities constantly urge us to take some cover. And unless we are aware of that impulse and able to control it, various forms of strategic contamination will emerge:

• *The flawed criticism*. Georgette tells Marge, "You've got a problem with being late," when what she really means is, "You're frequently late with me, and I don't like it."

• *The subtle isolation*. Roland tries to tell Jake about his anxieties but instead talks about what others have said. The temptation to rely on the comments of the advertising manager or an unnamed editor seems so innocent, but the effect is to handcuff the victim. Once you've brought in allies, an open, one-on-one exchange is impossible.

• *The anxious filibuster.* Martin wants to tell Georgette that he's unhappy with her being depressed, but hearing his own words, he panics at the thought of what she might say and tries to explain. His explanation goes on and on, frustrating her attempts to respond.

• *Pleading neurosis*. Marge manages to tell Chuck she needs to stop making love, but nervously adds, "I get so hung up about sex." Chuck senses that something is being evaded, and the evasion becomes the issue in his mind.

• *Loaded words*. Georgette tries to tell Martin why she's upset with his style of debate over the lithograph, but, carried away by her anger, starts out with, "You always . . ." or "You never . . . ." The rest of her sentence falls on defensive ears.

• *Excessive anger.* Anger that is fair, modulated, and without venom has a legitimate place within personal power. But if Georgette tries to be direct with Martin and injects anger from past situations, her message will be wasted.

Even charm is a liability when you want to be direct:

Weak personal power. "I guess I got a bit of a bee in my bonnet this afternoon, huh?" This is Martin's cute way of acknowledging he did something wrong.

Strong personal power. "I'm sorry I drove Marge out of the house. I'll apologize to her." That's much more direct. "I was feeling depressed and jealous and wanted you to myself," takes the communication a good deal further.

III. Reaching the Other Person

Georgette worries that she is simply not good with words. But if she were in touch with her context and not preoccupied with fears of disapproval, her words would carry weight. Verbal artistry is rarely as important as emotional and interpersonal issues. The same applies to Martin. Some key factors:

Brevity. If Martin wants to reach Georgette in a new and open way, he would be foolish to keep talking after her eyes have glazed over. The best he can do is open with a headline—"I'm upset and I'd like to talk," or "I want to apologize for the way I behaved this morning." Martin's anxiety may push him to cover all his points at once. But he is wiser to stop and allow his first piece of information to register, see how Georgette responds, and only then proceed with more detail.

Maintaining a balance. If Georgette seems evasive, Martin can gently try to smoke her out. But he should be careful not to get hung up in eliciting her position, for he may soon succumb to one of his favorite tricks—expose, criticize, and conquer. He must remember that his goal is to speak his truth, not to find something in Georgette to get angry about.

Strategic Back-up. While it's true that strategic leakage destroys personal power, it's also true that even a subject like Martin will feel vulnerable if he tries to be straight where he has never been straight before. He will feel more secure knowing that certain devices—such as smoking out an evasive Georgette—are available to him should her defensiveness cause him to sink.

Anticipating and Meeting Objections. Personal power depends on the receptivity of the listener. If, as Martin talks, Georgette thinks, "This is another maneuver," all the eloquence in the world will be lost on her. Martin needs to sense the possibility of this objection and respond before it derails him.

Martin: "Please don't think I'm trying to justify my own behavior. I don't want to lay the problem on you. I only want to do whatever is necessary to end this state of emotional divorce."

The need to neutralize mistrust is particularly important when previous maneuvering has soured the atmosphere. Roland: "I have a lot less experience than you in this business, Jake. I'm not about to claim that because I inherited the magazine I inherited the expertise too. But I still have to make certain decisions, and I have to be satisfied that they're right."

Anticipating objections requires the ability to sense what the other person may be feeling. But telling him what he's feeling ("You think I'm just trying to manipulate you") is a bad move. It will only set his teeth on edge.

Persistence. Even after your context is established, doubts linger. They suggest illegitimate aims: To question is to interfere; to ask for attention is to be possessive; to express dissatisfaction is to be a lout and a bringdown.

The other person's reactions may resonate with these doubts in a debilitating way. Jake responds, "Are you trying to get out of our agreement?" Suddenly Roland has to struggle to hold onto his point of view. Chuck says, "I was only away for a couple of dances." Suddenly Marge has to fight off feeling defeated. Georgette says, "I didn't *choose* to get depressed." Suddenly Martin feels as if he's made an accusation and now feels compelled to defend it.

The defensiveness we face at such moments can hardly be avoided. After all, if Martin is being straightforward for the first time in years, Georgette will naturally be wary of what he's up to. Persistence in the face of such wariness is crucial.

Persistence also means not getting hooked by small strategic signals—the slightly defensive tone in Chuck's voice, the way Jake folds his arms across his chest, the dull look in Georgette's eye. To become involved too quickly in such signals is to play to the listener's unreceptive side and to turn your apprehensions into self-fulfilling prophesies. Think instead: He is not playing for advantage, trying to manipulate, or incapable of understanding. He simply has fears, doubts, and habits, just like me.

IV. Maintaining A Respectful Distance

In trying to get our point across without being misunderstood, we may become too emotionally entwined with the other person. If, instead of presenting his point of view in the voice of an equal, Roland begins to plead for understanding or explain himself as if he were on trial, he places Jake in the position of a judge. On the other hand, if he impatiently exclaims, "While you sit there willfully misunderstanding me, I'm trying to open a dialogue!", well, needless to say, the dialogue, such as it was, is probably concluded.

The fine line between approval-seeking and advantage-seeking, can best be described as "maintaining a respectful distance," a distance that is particularly useful when feelings are running high.

The situation in the Grodins' home is volatile. Anything Martin says could cause a flare-up. Trying to say something honest about his dissatisfactions, he's best off thinking of Georgette as a completely independent person over whom he could not possibly have any control. Picture it like this:

Martin is on one side of the table and Georgette is on the other. Martin places his lead cards between them and awaits Georgette's response. He does nothing that might involve himself in the nature of that response. He doesn't seduce or cuddle her or issue subtle threats. If he feels a judgment forming in his mind or a self-doubt squirming in his stomach, he disregards it and returns to his context (I have a dissatisfaction; I want to communicate it). He keeps his distance and refuses to allow a hunger for Georgette's approval to rule his behavior. If Georgette should slap him with a dose of guilt—"What I could use right now is a little sympathy, not criticism!"—Martin's respectful distance will lessen his vulnerability and allow him to either proceed or temporarily back off without getting into a fight.

Of all the difficult things that people have avoided saying to each other in this story, none is more onerous than what Carmen has avoided saying to Beth. She not only has to tell a loyal and excellent worker that she's fired, but she has to do it in the face of grave self-doubts regarding the morality of her decision. Here, too, a respectful distance is essential.

Should Carmen get up the courage to be straight with Beth, it's not hard to figure out the humane approach. She should invite Beth into her office, tell her that she's decided to hire a new press secretary, ask for an opportunity to explain why, and offer Beth the option of staying on in some temporary capacity until she finds a position elsewhere. The tougher question—which Carmen fears and which causes her to torture Beth slowly instead—is what does she do if Beth becomes angry or argumentative or makes Carmen suffer unbearable pangs of guilt?

The solution is to stand back, respect Beth's feelings, contain her own guilty feelings, and not get caught in the emotional whirlwind. That's the only way Carmen is going to be effective in fulfilling her goal of replacing Beth in a halfway decent manner.

V. Managing Anxiety

The transition from manuevering to personal power is difficult, because strategic habits represent emotional security, and a threat to security creates anxiety. Anxiety is awful because it is fear combined with the unknown. And when anxiety arises in the context of a threatening exchange, where clouds of disadvantage and shame gather in the distance, the fastest way to get over it is by winning or losing. Unconsciously, we may even prefer losing to prolonged irresolution. Interpersonal struggles thus become a lightning rod through which anxiety is discharged in destructive ways.

To use personal power effectively, we must live with the anxiety. Tolerating anxiety can open the door not only to cleaner communication, but greater self-knowledge as well. For anxiety forces us to ask, where does this fear come from and what does it represent? What's going on inside me?

Let's turn to that deeper question now.

17.

The Intimate Alternative

Because Marge almost never experiences the feelings that are most troubling to her, she neither learns from them nor gets the help she needs from others. How she can stop running, speak her truth, and come to terms with her shame. Using intimacy for healing and growth.

PEOPLE ARE NOT FREE. They are deeply conditioned, perhaps as much today as at any time in history. Modern conditioning simply has a different face, much of it smiling and subtle and full of talk about freedom.

Much of the self-help industry is built on the notion that we can dump all bad habits and create freer selves at will. This scurrying to make change before we've taken the time to become familiar with who we are is a kind of self-betrayal. It says, in effect, "I cannot bear to know myself until I can make myself acceptable."

The rush to change exemplifies the way our society panics at the thought of shame, imperfection, or pain of any sort. Ultimately, it is ruinous to the hope of real change, for it is equivalent to throwing the ball before catching it.

Genuine change begins with passivity, with goallessness, with doing nothing but experiencing what you really feel and who you really are—and then carrying that truth around for a while. As the philosopher and teacher J. Krishnamurti put it, "The very perception of 'what is' brings about its own mutation."

Moving Inward

Until now we've talked about shame as a residue of childhood training and a horrible aspect of being one-down. But shame is an essential part of being human, and it can also be understood as the fluid surrounding our hidden selves. We have to learn how to move voluntarily into that fluid in order to know the secret of who we are and to come to terms with the layers of shames and shoulds that have constricted our lives.

Moving inward assumes a determination not to be controlled by the fears and anxieties that overwhelmed us as children and keep us on the shame-should-shame treadmill. You look at this thing called "Selfish!" and how your fear of having it exposed has controlled you. With repeated exposures, you gradually stop running from it, take it in, and see what's rational and irrational in this tyrannical voice.

Even if you discover that there's truth to the accusation, that you are selfish and do place yourself first in an obsessive way, there are grounds for self-forgiveness. For you see that, although the selfish pattern may be shameful in some respects, the pattern was born of certain childhood reactions that were inevitable at the time, and that far from being a core deformity, it is a common human affliction and within your power to change.

The experience that is most likely to bring about this kind of awareness is intimacy. Intimacy generally implies the natural openness of people who trust each other and are very close. Thoughts can be expressed, "improper" or unkind feelings exposed, and self-doubts revealed without any of the political considerations typical of everyday image and defense.

Aside from defining a relationship, intimacy can also be thought of as a specific type of event, one that has the power to heal wounds and catalyze change.

The intimate event represents a voluntary emotional undressing in which the only purpose is to share our true self with another. We get in touch with embarrassing traits in ourselves that we don't approve of and generally don't even want to see and reveal them to someone we feel has the depth and the compassion to understand.

An ongoing involvement in intimacy of this sort is one of the surest means to slow the wheels of the shame-should-shame cycle and, over time, to come to terms with all that we run from in ourselves.

People often believe that intimate moments come on their own schedule and cannot be reproduced. But, actually, intimacy involves skills, much like the power skills, which can be learned and improved. Marge these days is desperate for a healing dose of intimacy. But before we replay Marge's story and see how intimacy could work for her, let's look a little closer at how her habits of image and defense derail her.

Marge's Running Life

Marge is almost never at rest. She is always running just ahead of shame and sorrow so that she knows pain only in moments of defeat. To voluntarily allow the pursuing question marks to gain ground on her seems the height of folly. And so she leads a perpetually busy life, racing along with fear in the driver's seat. She is a slave to her conditioning, and, because she cannot be still, life seems to slip through her fingers untouched and untasted.

Tricks of "positive thinking" help Marge to excise her little torments. When a looming birthday, her thirty-fifth, darkens her spirits, she reminds herself of how firm her body is in comparison to the others in the gym, and her spirit is revived. But in evading her sadness, she evades a message her heart is sending about the sorrow she feels about reaching her mid-thirties unwed. There is an ancient saying that a dream unremembererd is like a letter unopened. What would the ancients have said about a feeling unfelt?

Constant action, even what might normally be considered growth-oriented action, provides Marge with a bubble of self-enforced ignorance. But just beyond that bubble, feelings of shame, like banished ghosts, have free reign over her unconscious. And so Marge lives in a constant low-grade panic, forever fearful of unknown implications. Should one of the pursuing question marks overtake her—"Why are you really alone, Marge?"—the protective membrane is pierced and her whole identity is thrown into question.

When Marge is hurt, as she was on her third date with Chuck, and self-hatred comes knocking at her door, her need to run becomes more intense. If the pain is particularly deep, she looks in the mirror and sees a collection of ugly features. She spends hours making herself up, glimpsing herself in shop windows, buying new clothes, getting haircuts and facials, all to no avail.

At times like this, she will not let herself be alone for a minute. If she tries to talk about what she's going through, she becomes embarrassed about being "too self-involved" or "stirring around in my own mess." Every encounter with a man conceals a secret inner debate over whether she is the sexless clod she fears she is or the slinky goddess she has labored to become; as the debate heats up, she pours on the slink with more energy (and falseness) than before.

Marge dreads her periodic attacks of loneliness or sadness because both imply failure and defectiveness. (How can she be lonely or sad in the singles utopia of New York City?) And so she structures her life to avoid these feelings. When Marge is with friends, she is concerned about the awkward moment when two people run out of things to say, an empty space opens between them, and feelings—who knows which ones!—threaten to surface. She does her best to avoid such moments by being late, thinking up agendas, filling in pauses with bursts of humor or enthusiasm. She justifies the time spent with others by the potential for romantic involvement or business advancement or an opportunity to talk about her problems. When someone touches her unexpectedly, really touches her, she dispels her anxiety with a joke. None of this keeps her friends from valuing her energy, her company, or her insights. But it does keep her at a distance from them and, more important, from herself.

Something in Marge knows that if she paused in her constant quest for comfort and self-improvement, if she let herself be still, she would be flooded with self-knowledge. But she's frightened. The longer you evade your feelings, the more forbidding they become. Dare to look inward and it's not the ecstatic, or self-enhancing, or even bittersweet truths you see; the banished ghosts are the first to greet you.

What is the price Marge pays for never experiencing her loneliness?

First, and foremost, she is cutting off a part of herself. Whatever her loneliness means (and whatever she fears it means), she has a right and a need to experience it.

Second, she is telling herself, "I don't want to know you," as if she had a harelip and was ashamed to look in the mirror. This keeps her from seeing her good traits as well as her bad, and denies her the comfort of knowing her value.

Third, she is turning herself into someone with something to hide, and this increases her need for control, increases her vulnerability, and makes it difficult for her to be open.

Fourth, she is imprisoning herself in the shame-should-shame cycle, for, if she cannot know about her pain, she must submit to the habits that help her to deny it.

And, finally, by refusing to experience her loneliness, Marge is unable to learn from it. She is unable to know what she most deeply needs, what course her life must take. She is sealing off an avenue of growth. In ten years she may awake as if from a dream and wonder why she never stopped the automatic march of her life long enough to prevent reaching middle age alone.

Marge is the first one to talk about "knowing yourself" and being "centered," but her noisy life makes it impossible for her to be centered. She assumes that jogging, meditating, psychoanalytic bull-sessions with friends, and occasional weekends in self-improvement workshops provide the necessary allotment of in-touchness. But, in fact, they are a piece with her striving, reaching, achieving style of life. Their sole purpose is to keep her strapped into the safety of useful routines.

Because passivity does not come easily to someone like Marge (except with the help of drugs or distractions), she has to cultivate it. Knitting, watching a fire, taking a walk, sketching, or writing in a notebook can serve this purpose for many people. And if you have a friend like Georgette, slowing down is simpler yet.

Letting Go: The Skills of Intimacy

Marge's mistake when talking to Georgette about the disaster with Chuck was her failure to expose more of her self-doubts. She was so involved in getting Georgette to be an ally against Chuck, and so anxious about the judgments Georgette might make about her, that she missed an opportunity to experience the healing effects of intimacy.

Intimacy is devoid of attempts to influence. It is devoid of concern for appearances. There is no effort to get sympathy or reassurance, to prove anything, or to reach a mutual understanding. The only goal is self-revelation. To make intimacy happen, Marge has to do several things:

• She has to let go of the inner debate with Chuck over who's right and who's wrong. Her need to stay with that debate is a spinoff from an unseen assumption—that she is a reject with no rights to her humanity or her feelings if, perchance, she was indeed somehow wrong. She can't allow that assumption to rule her any more.

• She has to stop worrying about her image and relinquish her investment in Georgette's seeing her as the dashing, attaché-bearing, on-top-of-it "new" woman.

• She has to abandon any idea of maintaining a superior position in the relationship or monitoring Georgette's repsonses for any wavering from the party line. Openly sharing herself is incompatible with being better, above, or in control. In intimacy there can only be equals.

• Finally, she must honestly seek out whatever is stirring within her. There will be a moment when Marge sees that Georgette is holding onto a flattering image of her. Her defensiveness will say, "Let it pass, life is easier when Georgette looks up to you—and who knows what will happen if you give her cause to look down?"

There will be a moment when Marge comes face to face with a piece of herself that has been long hidden and seems too horrible to express. Her defensiveness will say, "This is not important to your story. Forget it—God knows why you thought of it in the first place."

There will be moments when Georgette asks her a question that takes her someplace she hadn't wanted to go. Her defensiveness will say, "Just like Georgette to ask an irritating question like that."

There will be moments when the conversation could easily go off on a tangent. Her defenses will say, "Okay, you've exposed enough, how about some fun before Georgette thinks you're a drag?"

Her defenses and her image anxieties will give her every reason to get off the track of self-discovery and onto something less meaningful instead. She must resist them and allow her feelings to surface.

To put the feelings and thoughts that arouse self-hatred into words—even in a notebook or a letter—would be for Marge the beginning of a healing process. To speak those words to Georgette, however, is the most powerful healing force available to her. Let's look back at her lunch with Georgette and see how she might have done it.

"My Disgusting, Disparaging, Unforgiving Self"

When Georgette first asks Marge how she's been and what happened to that guy she was dating, Marge feels threatened. "I don't want to talk about it," she says sadly. "The whole thing was too hateful."

But with some encouragement from Georgette, she makes a stab at it. From the very beginning, it's clear that this is a painful story, even if at times it does cause them to laugh. And all the while, Marge does nothing to retain her image of a flashy woman who's successful with men.

As she gets into her story, Marge stops repeatedly to work out a feeling that comes over her. "I've been so *down* on myself! It's two weeks since this happened and I still can't handle the fact that I blew it. I know, what's the big deal, too many fish in the sea, and all that.

But I don't believe that. I feel like I've become all thumbs with men. Nothing I do with them seems to work any more. No, that isn't true. 'Any more!' I've *never* had a decent relationship with a man."

It's important to note that Marge doesn't speak this line in a whiny, plaintive way. She doesn't pull for reassurance. ("Boo-hoo, I can't do anything right!" "Oh, sure you can. Marge!") That's not intimacy; it's a game, which would take them off in another direction. What Marge does again and again in this imaginary re-enactment, is to try to express what she feels with the greatest honesty she can muster. There's no melodrama, no manipulation. She's simply trying to face something, something she's only admitted to herself on the rarest occasions, if at all: Nothing's been working with me and men.

"I keep telling myself that I was just being assertive and standing up for my rights. That's all I've been thinking for the last two weeks. You know, until this minute I didn't even realize how obsessed I've been with that? But it's true. I've been constantly replaying that scene and constantly arguing my case: I was okay, he was a rat, et cetera, et cetera. And I had to keeping saying it louder because"—a deep breath—"I didn't believe it. I felt like a shrew. I was just like my mother! And, ooh, God, that is the only thing I do not want to be."

She shakes her head and stares at Georgette for a moment, pursing her lips froglike. "And I cannot stand the fact that I might have been in the wrong! Ooooooh, that kills me."

"Well, I hate being wrong, too. And, believe me, it happens a lot when you're living with someone who's perfect."

Marge glances at Georgette and smiles. Georgette is often more protective of Martin, and Marge appreciates her opening up on this score.

"I don't know what Chuck is like," Georgette continues, "but it sounds as if he was pretty hung-up about something. He certainly didn't make it easy for you."

"I know! I mean, can you imagine? Leaving at five in the morning? Saying he wants to go for a walk! Needs a little fresh air! Nothing like the need for fresh air to make a girl feel just, well, so *secure*." The two laugh, and for Marge it's a wonderful laugh, every bit as good as a cry. Indeed, for a moment, she's not sure which it is. The good feeling encourages her to look inward again and see what else is cringing there.

"I couldn't believe it," she says, charged up again, "when we first started getting into bed and I started finding things wrong with him. It's like my disease. Making judgments. I thought I wouldn't be down on this guy. But right away, he's not being this enough, he's not being that enough. You know, I have this thing. This idea—that I'm like, frigid." She squinches her shoulders and her hands fly out nervously. "I know it sounds ridiculous. But I always get turned off."

"You've got problems, Marge, but you're not frigid. Frigid is . . . *frigid*. You're passionate. But, you know, the funny thing is I think of you as being so free with men. When we were in college, I thought, how does she do it? She has whomever she wants, sometimes more than one at a time."

"But, Georgette, for Christsakes, I've told you a hundred times how tough my relationships have been! Why do you keep seeing me as this free spirit?"

Marge's flare-up does not scare Georgette. She feels no twist in it, no blade. "You're right. I don't know why I do that. Maybe it's my insecurity. Or maybe I want you to be that way. Maybe I don't want to think of you as having a hard time."

"What do you mean?"

"Then I don't have to be pained for you. But, you know, that's not the whole thing, either, because I often feel that I want to see your vulnerabilities and you won't let me."

"It's not just you. I don't let anyone see them. I don't let *myself* see them. . . ."

"That makes it hard, you know—for both of us."

Marge nods her head and looks Georgette in the eyes. For a moment a wave of self-doubt comes over her and an axe rises, about to chop off her head for all the times she's been imagey and maneuvering with Georgette. But she brushes off the temptation to sink into self-rejection. It doesn't feel right to lacerate herself or start getting on her knees and pleading for forgiveness, not with genuine feelings so close by, and so she returns to them.

"You know, it's not that I'm frigid," she says and then laughs—"to pick up a refrain! What it is is these *situations* I get myself into."

"That was an incredible situation. For Chuck, too, by the way. I mean the guy was uptight."

"Yeah, he was," says Marge, "and it's really easy for me to forget that. But, but that's not the point." Again, she returns to the feeling, refusing to get sidetracked into excusing herself, refusing the temptation to talk about Chuck. "You see, maybe we shouldn't have been in bed so early on in the relationship—that could have been part of it—but the real thing is, it was so fraudulent. I mean we never stopped impressing each other for one minute. Just thinking about it is exhausting. But you know—it's hard to say this—I really wanted him. And I was so afraid he wouldn't like me if he saw who I really was.

And the age thing. I couldn't stop thinking about the age thing!"

None of this shocks Georgette. Despite her tendency to fall for Marge's image, she knows that Marge has not been able to keep a relationship alive in recent years and that the failures have pained her. Drawn into Marge's intimate orbit now, Georgette dares to ask what she's often wondered:

"What *are you* that he's not going to want when he sees it? What is it that you think is so bad?"

The question touches a fat, dull pain in Marge's stomach that she chooses not to fight off. "That I'm a fraud. That I'm not a live wire. That I'm insecure. That I get extremely *dependent*."

"You're so worried about being dependent. What's so terrible about needing somebody? Your mother, the great independent woman, she doesn't need anybody—"

"—and despises anyone who does!"

"Right. But normal people do. I remember when we were in college, someone asked Roberta Flatley if she was your best friend. And Roberta said, 'I sure hope not—for Marge's sake—because I don't feel as if I know her at all.' And I remember thinking, Roberta really was your best friend. And why couldn't you open up to her? I thought well maybe you did it with men."

"No, I didn't do it with men." Marge looks at the table for a moment. "Oh, college was a struggle for me. I was trying to *be* a certain thing and constantly fighting off the feeling that I wasn't that thing. It wasn't until I became a lawyer and saw what I could do that I found something to really feel good about. That has been just a terrific part of my life." She beams. "But relationships, forget it."

Marge is pleased to see that Georgette is smiling. She is usually careful not to sound too positive about her career for fear of arousing Georgette's envy. But in this open context such restraint seems out of the question, and she lets the full pleasure of her work life radiate throughout her. It's been months since she's felt it. Georgette, having seen the whole picture, has no inclination to begrudge Marge her happiness. To her own surprise, she beams for Marge, too. It's an important moment for them.

"I don't know if I ever told you about what it was like for me in junior high. Until ninth grade, I was tall, and kind of fat, and we lived in a Waspy neighborhood and I just felt very, tchhhh, *klutzy*. I was a klutzy, brainy Jewish girl, and I hated myself. I kept my nose in my books (I figured that's where it belonged, considering its size) and didn't dare think I could ever be with a boy. Well, then—I mean it was a miracle—I lost weight, my shape changed, they said I looked like Cher—that's what they said!—and I was *popular.* Well, I just wanted to erase the past. I find it hard even now to remember exactly what it was like before I became attractive. But I still didn't know how to talk to boys. I still felt awkward. And I still do."

"Is it that much different from what everyone feels? I haven't had as much experience as you, but I remember first dates as being torture."

"Maybe it isn't that different. Maybe I just think it is. Maybe it's just that for my mother you always had to be on top of things. But I've always felt fraudulent with men. Like I'm putting on this big show and any minute they're going to see I'm just a socially retarded klutz."

As Marge talks to Georgette like this, her feelings toward herself go through a transformation. When tears come to her eyes and she feels like a lost little girl, her heart goes out to herself. She feels the sympathy and understanding that she would feel for a hurting child—rather than the coolness she reserves for a defensive adult.

There is also something about confiding in Georgette that makes her feel cared for, as close and warm as the best of family feeling. And exposing her innermost, negative emotions takes a bit of the edge off them. They don't seem quite so horrible once she's put them into words. The shame still exists, but she is no longer one with it. She has some distance.

Georgette naturally wants to know how things ended with Chuck, and that brings Marge back to the most painful moment: *If you don't come, then you kill!* Says Marge, "I don't think I'll ever forget that as long as I live."

"It was a horrible thing to say."

"But I guess I feel I deserved it."

"Why? You don't think it's true?"

"No, of course not. I mean, gee, if it were true, there'd be a lot of dead men around."

Georgette giggles and squeezes Marge's hand. "So why does it sit with you like this?"

"Because I was so obnoxious. You should have heard me. And besides it hurts. Whether it was true or not it hurts!" At this, Marge bursts into sobs and puts her face on the table. Georgette pulls her chair around and strokes Marge's hair. It's amazing to her that Marge is speaking this way. And it fills her with a love for Marge she has not felt since they were in college.

"Oh, Marge. I know how it feels to be hurt like that." And then: "Besides, you really liked him."

"It's true. I really did. I had such a crush on him. And, God, I wanted him to like me. As soon as he said he wanted to take a shower,

I knew he wanted to get out. Not just out of the apartment, but *out.* And I'd invested everything in that stupid lay! Can you imagine? That was going to be the big test. And if I passed that test, he'd be my boyfriend and my life would be okay. It's amazing how dumb you can make yourself. That's probably why I was so hung up about having sex in the first place. So, then, he's in the shower, and the whole time I'm praying for a passing grade. And then—Jesus!—he starts putting on his shoes!"

"What a disaster!" Georgette pushes up her bottom lip and shakes her head at Marge sympathetically.

By now Marge's intense anxiety and edginess have been almost entirely drained from her system. The engine of her running life has come to a dead stop. She feels exhausted and raw, but she does not feel bad. The barriers have fallen between herself and a whole cluster of self-hatreds that normally operate in the dark.

After some silence, Marge says, "I'm so lonely."

Georgette nods. "You've been alone a long time."

"I know you have your troubles with Martin, but being married makes such a difference. Just to have someone around. I get so down on myself for never having done it. Even if it didn't work out. Even if it was a fiasco! Just to be able to say, 'I've loved someone and been loved by someone. That we cared enough to make a commitment.' I'm thirty-four, and I can't say that."

As Marge gets more and more in tune with herself, each feeling she touches is coated with shame, and at each point she is tempted to run. She hates the way she behaved with Chuck and is ashamed of what that implies about her. She's thirty-four and still single. What defect has prevented her from joining her life to another? She's lonely and hungry—how disgusting! She hates the way she's conducted her relationships—the maneuvering, the lies, the failure. And she's ashamed of talking about it—stirring around in her mess.

But somehow, in this timeless moment with Georgette, talking about her "disgusting self" seems like the most natural thing in the world. As she finally lets herself feel what she feels, she experiences a release from the nightmare that shame becomes when she's running from it. Suddenly, surprisingly, that unforgiving part of her that labels her "disgusting" when she is merely struggling with being human seems to have lost its power.

As she and Georgette continue to talk, Marge loosens up more and more, and her freedom to explore grows. As her trap door slides open and her mind receives hot signals from long-tensed muscles now relaxing, she slowly adjusts her gaze toward center and eyes a truth she spends every day of her life burying: Gawky, brainy Jewish girl with a garish insensitive mother. At first she wants to cry for being dealt a raw deal. The old lament. But then she becomes thoughtful. Tears form again. She pities herself for her self-made prison and the years she's toiled to build it. Dare she make common cause with that Jewish girl? Dare she take a piece of her rejected self to heart?

The Intimate Partner

Of all the characters in our story, Georgette runs the least, and the door to her feelings is almost always ajar. Sometimes, as we've seen, she keeps it open when it would be better for her if it were sealed. But during intimate moments, or when she is sitting alone watching the river, she lets the door slip open in a lovely way, and feelings emanating from the deepest parts of her being radiate throughout her body.

Georgette is a perfect partner in intimacy. Feelings expressed by another person touch resonating spots within her, and she is not afraid to go to those spots and experience them. She is not judgmental; nor does she take the occasion of Marge's openness to even old scores.

Georgette does not encourage Marge to start running again ("You're just not circulating enough, hon—they're plenty of good men out there"). She does not give advice ("Maybe you should try to be more honest with men, Marge"). She does not launch into a frenzy of reassurance ("You weren't wrong! You're not a fraud! You're not like your mother! You should be delighted with the life you have!"). She does not bury Marge in compliments about her beauty or her grace ("And if men don't see that, they're idiots!"). She does not get overly involved in Marge's inner debate ("Stop thinking that way—it'll only make matters worse!"). She does not get hung up in analysis or fill every silence with helpfulness.

Her exertions of power are minimal. When something comes up that bears on their relationship, Georgette doesn't hesitate to have a forthright exchange. But she keeps it short. When she senses that there is an important detail Marge wants to forget, she urges her to recall it. When she feels Marge is becoming overwhelmed by pain, she helps her to understand the source and offers some comfort. Because she has faith in the value of feelings, whatever they are, she becomes a catalyst, helping Marge's hidden self to emerge.

The Aftereffects of Intimacy

An intimate experience does not guarantee fundamental change. But it is an antidote to losing, for it releases the poisonous, frozen anxiety that follows an abusive struggle like the one Marge suffered with Chuck. It frees her to feel again and to let down the defenses that have militarized her emotional life.

Over the course of time, intimate exchanges have the power to go much further, getting into the very center of Marge's negative self-concepts and weakening their hold. Change can be very difficult, even under the rigorous conditions of therapy. But, ideally, if Marge keeps at her efforts to stay in touch, the inner signals of self-reproval that cause her to flee or don disguises, will eventually become less compelling.

As she stops running from one area of shame, others can be penetrated more easily. "Am I a dependent person? What exactly does that mean? Where does my shrewishness come from? Am I really like my mother? How is my anxiety about being unwed causing me to live? To behave with men?" Such self-examination helps Marge gain a truer sense of who she is and a greater freedom from the fear of shame. As pockets of shame dissolve, or at least fade in their power, the symptoms, inhibitions, and guilty imperatives that are linked to them also weaken. Gradually, she is able to make the strength of her true being felt in the world.

Marge's childhood training and her culture both deny the value of her most significant traits. She is by nature cautious, loyal, and thoughtful, with a subtle but strong sexuality. These qualities have not been nurtured. She has grown up believing she should be "on" all the time, the life of the party, a vamp. The ramifications in her dating life are immense, to say the least.

Unlike Georgette, whose sexualilty flows readily, Marge is slower. Yet she sends out enticing glances, makes frequent sexual innuendoes, and dresses to the nines. Men who are sensitive enough to register the disparity feel uncomfortable or threatened and pull away. Less sensitive men plow forward, out of touch with themselves and with her. She then wonders why the men she goes with are oblivious to what she feels.

Because of her fears, Marge never allows herself the chance to evaluate what is happening. She's still living out the childhood program. Intimacy can change that.

The self-knowledge that comes from intimacy also has the power to make Marge less vulnerable (in the negative sense) and less trigger-happy. For the closer Marge lives to her center, the less likely she will be to topple over. When she is hiding less from herself, she is less fearful of being ambushed by unexamined truths.

Once Marge knows she can handle hearing the voice that cries "Sexless!", her image and her defenses in that area will be less automatic. She will find it easier to define her context and be forthright about her needs ("Chuck, let's stop"). She will also be more able to spot the strategies, innuendoes, punishments, and disguised personal signals ("I need to stop") of others—and to have a more balanced view of what they represent.

There is no end, necessarily, to the inward movement that intimacy promotes. Beyond the brainy girl are other self-doubts of a personal nature; and beyond them are things that all people run from—the life cycle, the pain and tragedy of loss, the knowledge that many dreams will never be attained, the certainty of death. To live close to those issues is to be most fully alive.

For now, though, if Marge can allow the eighth-grade girl, who's ashamed of being gawky and out of place, some life inside her, the way she lives with men will change. The lower center of gravity and the new elements of forthrightness will present themselves with the glow of dignity. Marge may discover that she has real weaknesses, but that some of the qualities she's been running from are among the very best she has. She may discover that the brainy girl has a lot to give. That she is the kernel of a woman who can be the flywheel of a relationship, keeping it alive and rich. One day, Marge may even come to love her.

18.

Beth Revisited

Can I walk erect even as I suffer with pain and self-doubt? Can I survive and grow even with enemies who hate me? How Beth can face these bottom line issues of interpersonal politics.

WHEN WE CONSIDER how Beth might have handled the office scene, we must begin by assuming some avenue for intimacy. She needs a context, therapy or otherwise, in which to bring her life patterns—particularly her misguided search for love and acceptance—into focus so that she can prevent re-enacting them with Carmen and the staff.

Intimacy, even in doses of a few minutes at a time, is also critical to drain some of the pain that accumulates very quickly when Beth's been exposed to anything that feels like rejection.

It is important to remember two things. First, that no matter how effectively Beth acts, she is still going to be a person with deep wells of unresolved pain. Second, that a person in pain, even a person with built-in scapegoat circuitry, is not compelled to act in self-destructive ways. Although Beth's burden of shame is great, and although there is no way, certainly no quick way, to rid herself of it, she does not have to be an object.

**When the Crisis Begins:
Standing Back, Playing a Defending Game**

Let's replay the early weeks of the campaign when Carmen first started having doubts about Beth and began acting a little mean, more so than usual. What Beth needs right now, in addition to an intimate, is a sounding board, someone who can listen and perhaps give her some useful feedback, as well. Beth needs to get the office experience into perspective as soon as it starts hurting. Unlike her chance encounter with Georgette, in which she had no purpose other than a vague and desperate hope for connection, she needs to make a direct effort for assistance and be clear about what she needs. From the resultant conversation, several things might emerge.

First, Beth might see that although she tells herself she is terrified that Carmen might be trying to get rid of her, her real fear concerns what will happen to her self-respect if she gets dragged through a humiliating office experience at this vulnerable time in her life. She is frightened of becoming the office scapegoat, a pattern she is quite adept at provoking once she feels wounded.

If she looks at the situation objectively, though, during these opening moments of the crisis, it's apparent that she has not yet reached any such point. Roseanne's been acting a little bitchy toward me, Beth concludes, but she does that with everyone; she may not have consciously put me in a separate category yet. Georgette seems to have been avoiding me and acting a little strange, but it would certainly be premature to say she has made me *persona non grata*. Al is no different than he's ever been. The only problem I'm really sure of is Carmen.

Any honest evaluation may also help Beth to see her own responsibility in causing some of her co-workers to be less than completely warm toward her. After all, hasn't she tended to remain aloof? Might they not have sensed the judging and superior quality in her aloofness?

With this new awareness in place, Beth plans to go into the office the next day with a watchful attitude. To stand back a little, to make no assumptions, to see how things really stand. She will play a defending game—cover herself carefully at all times; do nothing to rock the boat; watch for openings. She will not punish anyone for what's already happened, and she will not be too eager to be anyone's friend. She's going to be like a chess player who's made an error and fallen slightly behind: play a defending game, don't panic, don't rush to recoup the losses—for such moves will make a small disadvantage grow.

Beth dresses for work with care. She treats the day as a significant event. She walks into the office carefully suspending her victim assumptions. It's strange to notice that everything is just as it always is. She doesn't get a warm hello from anyone, but people don't turn on their heels at the sight of her either. Had she entered with her scapegoat predictions, she realizes, the same scene would have looked like a conspiracy.

She works as efficiently as she can. Her work has a clear purpose now: self-preservation. No, she doesn't care whether Carmen wins re-election. But this is war, a very personal war, and she's going to cover every base for her own sake. If Carmen should act surprised or pleased, Beth will resist sucking up. She'll just thank her pleasantly and let it pass.

Three incidents stand out this morning. First, Beth overhears some contentious voices: Roseanne is having a tiff with Carmen's secretary, Lynn. Second, around 11:30, Beth notices some maneuvering which seems to indicate that two other staff members don't want Al to join them for lunch. Third, shortly afterwards, Lynn stops at her desk. She has to give Beth some notes from Carmen for a speech Beth is writing. Lynn pauses to say a few words. It occurs to Beth that Lynn may be seeking an ally against Roseanne; or maybe Lynn has always been friendly and Beth has never cared to notice. They speak for a while and Beth feels very good afterwards. All three incidents leave her feeling less isolated.

Beth looks around the office. Nobody seems available to have lunch with her. She resists the inclination to maneuver her way into one of the pairs, to eat with Al, which is always a drag, or to become self-pitying and resentful. She decides to treat herself to lunch at Faulkner's, something a little better than the corner coffee shop. She is careful to order a light lunch. Under no conditions will she return to the office her keenness cut in half because she's stuffed.

Georgette enters Faulkner's moments later, appears to catch sight of Beth, but sits alone. Again Beth has to restrain her assumptions. After lunch they meet at the cash register, and Georgette acts surprised to see her. "Oh, were you here all the time?" she says. "Yes," says Beth, aware of Georgette's fraudulence, but speaking without a hint of innuendo. "In fact, I saw you come in, but I had the feeling you might want to be alone." "Yeah, that's probably true," Georgette concedes, happy to be off the hook. "I've just come back from Mrs. Rios's and I have a lot to figure out—this rent strike is in trouble."

As they walk back to the office, they make small talk about the Rios case, and some part of Georgette registers that Beth's insidious guilt-making machinery is pleasurably silent. She ever so slightly adjusts her opinion of her.

That afternoon, Roseanne flips some envelopes on Beth's desk. This is now the second time Roseanne has bordered on discourtesy, but none of the ugly incidents have yet occurred. "Excuse me, Roseanne," says Beth when they are alone. "Is there some reason why you threw the mail on my desk like that?" Beth asks the question with complete purity of tone and posture. Her image, pure calculation, says: I make no assumptions. I am simply concerned. I am the very spirit of cooperation, the sort of person who cannot imagine staff relations being anything less than respectful. By contrast, Roseanne feels unclean. The adolescent nature of what she's done seems to be written in neon. She turns red. "No," she says.

"No? Oh, okay," says Beth. She let's it drop at that and turns away. Roseanne waves her hand like a fan to cool off her armpits. Beth feels buoyed for having taken care of business.

Beth and Carmen have only minor contact. But as she observes Carmen with a cooler eye, she feels more confident of her earlier perceptions and less inclined to accuse herself of paranoia. There is clearly an adversary aspect to Carmen's behavior. It pains Beth to see this and to realize that she may be in for trouble and misery on this score. She feels anxious, and she is tempted at times to sink into lamentations. But having struggled so well on her own behalf, she feels more ready to face whatever must come next.

The Carmen Factor: Confronting Abuse of Authority

When someone in authority abuses his power, guilt is often the ideal counterstrategy. Which brings us, of course, to Carmen. A boss has a right to fire. A boss has a right to express dissatisfaction. A boss has a right to criticize. But a good boss is expected to fire with just cause, to complain without humiliating, to make guidance and constructive feedback a part of criticism. Carmen's abusiveness is a violation of her responsibilities, and with carefully chosen words Beth can make her know it.

"Carmen, I expect you to criticize my work, but is there any reason you feel the need to be abusive?"

What can Carmen say to this? She instantly feels guilty and ashamed and wants to apologize.

Notice that it is strategically weak to mention the underlying issue ("You're trying to get rid of me"). Beth's power lies in her ability to keep Carmen from breaking the norms of propriety. This technique, which will cause Carmen to feel ashamed of abusing her authority, may eventually move her to reconsider dumping Beth, or, at least, to be more open. The moment she says, "Beth, you've been a good worker, but I'm not sure you can handle a Congressional campaign," a fair negotiation can begin.

As things worsen between Carmen and Beth and the adversary aspect of their relationship becomes pronounced, guilt is no longer the useful tool it was before. Beth can no longer make Carmen feel ashamed for having behaved poorly as a boss. And, by the same token, Beth can no longer afford to worry, to the extent that she did before, about what Carmen thinks of her or whether she looks presumptuous or disloyal. Her thoughts must now turn to another set of strategic concerns: What do I have that Carmen needs? What can I do that Carmen fears? How can I remind her that I'm still holding some cards without actually playing them?

Beth is holding two big cards. One is the possibility of a law suit, especially if Carmen hires a man to replace her. A sex discrimination case would look very bad for Carmen just now, especially instituted by someone in Beth's position. Her second card is the general ability to create negative publicity in the midst of the campaign. Beth knows all the inside dope, she knows how to make it look embarrassing, and she knows the press. This is such an obvious fact that she probably does not even need to allude to it. Just by standing firmly for her rights, by refusing to accept insults, by refusing to follow demeaning orders, by insisting on certain conditions if Carmen wants to let her go, by adopting a more aggressive posture across the board, Beth will be saying, "I'm not afraid of you." Let Carmen's fears figure out why.

Once Carmen starts acting nasty on a regular basis, there's no disadvantage any more in adopting an adversary posture and letting it show; although it would be wise to keep it measured—just short of Carmen's own adversary posture. Even now a wrong move is possible. Always let Carmen be the one who is creating the conflict, Beth the one who is merely defending her dignity as a human being.

Whether or not Carmen alters her position, in the end Beth will feel better about herself for having fought. Because most people don't like to have enemies around—especially enemies who have a proven will to fight—Carmen will probably be willing to work out a deal. Even if that deal includes Beth's departure, and even if it is hammered out in an atmosphere of hostility, Beth will be able to leave with heightened energy and momentum and with her dignity intact.

The Bottom Line:
I. Carrying Your Burden With Grace

Beth exhibits several important strategic deficits. She refuses to play the game, to live in a political style, to be shrewd in her use of image and reward. She lets herself become immobilized. And she lacks an organizing principle in her life ("Lose weight," "Recover from the separation," "Find a direction or career into which you can throw yourself wholeheartedly"), something that will give her a purpose and direction of her own. Each of these liabilities contributes significantly to her powerlessness. But if we had to isolate one element that serves as the linchpin of her object syndrome, it would probably be her inability to carry her pain with dignity.

A typical example. When Beth, in her unhappy state, is visiting friends for dinner, she fails to be attuned to the ways in which she puts everyone ill at ease by acting out her pain. There's no taboo against talking about what she's been going through or even crying, but to tug desperately at her friends' lapels, to sarcastically refer to the help she hasn't been getting from certain people, to bitterly refer to the unfair disparities between their lives and hers is to live without dignity. By displaying her pain so shamefully, as if she is covered with smut, she not only alienates her friends, but transforms herself from a wounded person—to which no stigma need be attached—into a cursed person, a pariah.

Even the cursed feelings themselves—the envy, the regret, the bitterness, the spite—need not decay her identity if they are not acted out. They can all be revealed and expressed during intimacy. As long as she can discuss such feelings without becoming one with them, they will not be self-destructive.

And yet Beth is driven to self-destruction. Why?

Clearly, Beth is straddled with a burden of shame that is very great. Even if she gets the therapeutic treatment she needs, she is not going to stop seeing her rejecting parents in authority figures and lovers; she will not stop seeing female co-workers and friends as her favored younger sister; she will not stop seeing herself as inadequate. No matter what happens, she will carry that burden for many years. But does her burden have to break her?

Beth hates herself for being fat, for her compulsive talking, for all the time she's lived as an object. She senses that the sheer weight of her self-hatred makes her different from other people, and she is bitter over the raw deal she got. But the cruelest twist, her deepest sin against herself is this: *She is ashamed of her burden of shame. She hates herself for being a self-hating person. She cannot forgive herself for being in pain.* That is the curse of the "loser." And that is what keeps her life on a negative incline, always causing her to slip deeper into her depressive hole through self-destructive acts.

There is nothing shameful about being insecure or bearing a heavy burden. No amount of self-hatred makes Beth a second-class citizen, makes her inferior, makes her unworthy of respect. If Beth could understand that, she might begin to carry her burden with just a little more grace and dignity and get on with her life in a more serious way. And that, along with certain of the strategic efforts discussed in this chapter, might be the beginning of the end of her scapegoat syndrome.

Something else must be added here. In a society like ours that labors under a tyranny of happiness, where everyone scurries to hide his pain and where Keeping Up With the Joneses has become a grotesque emotional masquerade, carrying one's burden of self-doubt with dignity is a socially significant statement. In our world today, we are constantly inclined to use our bad feelings about ourselves to fuel advantage, abuse, slavishness, and self-destruction. We find it hard to experience pain or to realize that we feel small in certain ways, and yet continue to walk erect. Beth, by carrying her shame with dignity, would be setting a rare example.

The Bottom Line II: Enemies

One doesn't always catch problems when they begin, and Beth's failure to put out the office fires when they started has left her to deal with, among other things, a viperish Roseanne.

Everyone, at some time or another, must face an enemy. Your landlord wants to evict you and decides to play rough. Your ex-spouse launches a malicious custody suit. A colleague wants your job and is willing to do almost anything to get it. Suddenly you are faced with cruelties for which you have no ready response. You are barraged with verbal insults, threats, and the loss of heat and hot water. A summons arrives without warning demanding your presence in family court. A piece of work you feel deeply about is sabotaged.

For people who lack experience with such adversity, these conflicts can be crippling. There's nothing quite like the feeling of being treated like prey or vermin or dirt. If you believe in living a peaceful life and treating people with decency, if you are sensitive to others and tend to listen to them, the first reaction is often complete paralysis. For days afterwards you feel debased without fully knowing why. You may find it inconceivable that an obviously sick or corrupted individual could affect your feelings about yourself. You may identify with the pain of the attacker and find no similar basis to sympathize with yourself. Or you may, like Beth after she was run through by Roseanne, blame yourself for having failed to come more forcefully to your own defense.

After the first attack, Beth relives the moves again and again, wondering what she could have done differently. And meanwhile she dreads the next encounter. At the sound of Roseanne's footsteps, Beth experiences a churning in her stomach. Every molecule in her body says, "I cannot oppose that person."

To avoid having to arm herself and move into military footing, Beth may now entertain various futile notions. She thinks to ask Roseanne if "we can talk this out like human beings." This is pointless. "Talk what out?" Roseanne will ask.

Another temptation is appeasement. Beth wonders if she can reassure Roseanne of her good intentions and likableness. Maybe a smile or nice gesture and Roseanne will let bygones be bygones. But nice gestures are the height of absurdity when dealing with malice. To smile encouragingly is to tell Roseanne, "You can attack without fear of reprisal."

To prepare herself for this conflict, Beth has to evaluate the situation with a keen military mind. She has to think out all the moves, like what she will do the next time she encounters Roseanne. Will she say hello? Will she remain silent? Will she avert her eyes? Will she ride in the same elevator? How will she respond to pleasantries? These considerations may seem petty and stupid, but they are real, and throwing herself into such calculations is not only strategically useful, it's good for the spirits.

As for the combat stage, that too is important, even if Beth never reaches it. Verbal warfare demands that she pack a weapon—often a single sentence will do—that can penetrate her opponent's defenses. "Everything they say about you in this office is true, Roseanne." Said with simple intensity, this statement skewers the poor girl. She knows she has a tendency to be bitchy, she just had a spat with Carmen's secretary, she cares very much about what everyone thinks of her, and she can't bear the feeling of isolation. Beth doesn't have to say what the others think, or even know what they think, to slice Roseanne in two.

By knowing that she has this potent sentence available to her, Beth is better able to face the struggle with poise.

In her scrapes with Roseanne, Beth must be willing to become cold and calculating and exchange some blows. If she is able to land a few, she will not feel so much the object and her wounds won't seem so deep. Her fear of opposing Roseanne will decrease, and she may take some pleasure in noting that Roseanne, by placing the mail on Beth's desk with less than her usual insolence, is steering clear of another scene. In this way the confidence levels balance out, and new possibilities open. Indeed, sometimes the most hardened adversaries become fast friends once the air has been cleared with a few purging blows.

On and Off the Ropes

To mobilize oneself into an adversary posture may seem like a bleak task. To fill one's head full of counterattacks, denunciations, moves, legalities, alliances; to squander precious resources of time, energy, and money on wasteful conflict; all this can seem like the end of life itself. But one can live well in an adversary state. Once you feel the security of preparedness, you can go about your life without the dread of surprise attack. You can forget about the conflict for much of the time—something that's impossible for the unmobilized and the fearful. And doing battle has other benefits. It's invigorating. It overcomes internal discord, quiets self-doubts. It feels *good* to be thoroughly on your own side, to be going all out for yourself for a change. In the end, conflict tends to teach you that your worst fears are groundless.

But the main thing is you have no choice. The whole world knows someone who is unwilling to stand up for his rights, and it is merciless in punishing his weakness. Enemies are an occasional fact of life. They are a challenge that should not be shirked.

The object mentality, which exists in all of us, dreads a fight and is certain of imminent defeat. The subject mentality, which also exists in all of us, relies on this to feed its confidence. But defeat is never foredoomed. There is a way out of almost every strategic jam. We may feel that we are on the ropes, but fate is fickle, the fans are fickle, the opposition is full of fears, needs, and doubts that do not always show on his face, and the count is much longer than we think.

Review 4

1. Punishment is effective in countering abuse. But in most other situations where a strategy is needed, diplomacy, in the form of humor, gentle manipulations, and rewards, is much more powerful. Diplomacy achieves results without dominating or arousing mistrust.

2. A certain minimal level of *image* is necessary to strategic success, for image is the quality that enables you to stay role-appropriate. But image is also the enemy of every kind of openness.

3. *Personal power* is straightforwardness that works. It achieves what no amount of strategic power can—true communication of thoughts and feelings. Personal power depends first on self-knowledge; without that it is an empty exercise.

4. When you break a habit, *anxiety* is aroused, and the temptation to retreat is enormous. If you wish to use personal power where you've relied on strategic habit before, you will have to tolerate anxiety.

5. In personal power the goal is some kind of influence. We want to get something across—a position, an explanation, a proposal, a question. *Intimacy* is a very different kind of openness, for it seeks no influence at all.

6. In intimacy all the barriers come down. Concern for roles and propriety ceases. The only purpose of intimacy is to explore and to share oneself with another, allowing the implications to fall where

they may. Intimacy is the best tool we have for coming to terms with shame and all the conditioning of childhood, for achieving greater self-acceptance, and for getting in touch with what we feel. It also creates the deepest bonds.

7. Because intimacy helps us to know and accept ourselves, it also broadens our area of personal power. Generally, if we have a regular outlet for intimacy, we will be able to express a greater range of feeling. We will have less need of habitual maneuvers and will find it easier to take the risks involved in being straight.

8. *The intimate partner* has faith in feelings. He is not made anxious by the exposure of pain; he does not feel compelled to run from things that cannot immediately be fixed. Rather than attempting to repair, soothe, advise, or deny, he responds with his feelings. He is able to care and to love without being compulsively helpful.

10. *Getting in touch*, whether through an intimate experience or a walk in the woods, is built on passivity, simply letting ourselves feel. Getting in touch is the only means to halt the wheels of the shame-should-shame cycle and to locate the core of oneself, the spiritual center, which is independent of all conditioning. From that core some new and truly self-directed activity may emerge. Without it, change is trivial.

11. *Enemies* are a special case. Generally, if we're skillful and sensitive, we try to balance the power without hurting the other person. We keep our irrational assumptions on hold, remember not to take every hurt personally, and avoid escalation. But once in a great while someone makes himself into a genuine enemy and is only interested in doing us in. Then it's time to pull out all the stops and play to win. The key considerations:

• Size up what he can do to you and what you can do to him. Who holds which cards? Who has what vulnerabilities? Plan your moves accordingly. And be prepared.

• Never let your behavior become the issue. The skillful fighter does not act out his rage. He is cold and calculated and operates with precision.

• Measure carefully. You may want to kill, but a sharp slap may be all that's possible, appropriate, or just.

• If you care about decency and are unaccustomed to hostilities, you may dread stepping across the line into military thinking. But when it's truly necessary to do so, it's not such a bad place to be. Better to mobilize than to cringe.

• An enemy may change his colors when he sees you can't be walked on. Watch for opportunities for rapprochement.

Quiz

This quiz will help you assess your skills and habits. See if you can spot the answer that most characterizes you, as well as the one you think is best. Use the exercise to help you spot your fears, habits, and faulty assumptions.

PROBLEM. You have been dating a man (or woman) for several months. You like him enough to fantasize about marriage, but these dreams are tarnished because you're dissatisfied with what goes on in bed. He seems unwilling to do certain things you enjoy, and when it's all over he virtually disappears emotionally. The whole subject is so upsetting and embarrassing that you can't imagine how the problem will be resolved. What do you do?

1. I'd ask him to show more affection or enthusiasm in lovemaking. I'd remind him of what I do that he likes and offer to help him work out the problem.

2. The next time I was dissatisfied, I'd let it show. I'd have faith that revealing my true feelings would help change things for the better.

3. I'd realize that he is just timid, and I'd do whatever I could to loosen him up—a drink, a joint, an erotic movie.

4. I'd try to discuss sex with him at times when we were relaxed and had nothing to do. Just try to open the subject up for conversation. Ideally, I'd try to ask him how he felt about those things I like that he never does.

5. I would become a little less available in order to force him to stop taking me for granted and to think more about my needs.

6. I'd talk about my own problems with sex and what a hard time it can give me. If I opened up and became intimate, I'd be inviting him to do the same.

7. While we were making love, I'd make a stronger effort to let him know what I like and what I want.

SOLUTION. This is obviously a delicate problem that must be addressed or your dissatisfactions will eat away at you, causing you to abandon the relationship or retaliate with misplaced or powerless punishments. 1. Guilt-making. Asking for what you want is fine, but loaded words like "considerate" will induce resentment and resistance. Reminding him of what you give is also an attempt to control. By the time you get to the word "problem," he may be ready to explode (not sexually). 2. Letting your dissatisfaction show can feel as if you're being very open. But it's hard to imagine it not being hurtful here. Besides, your "true feelings" are an accumulation of months of dissatisfaction and not really true to that moment. 3. Good-hearted intentions, and perhaps worth a try, but could backfire, especially if he feels manipulated.

4. This could work very well, as long as you don't put too much of the burden on him by being vague or asking too many questions. Ideally, this gives him a chance to talk in a non-threatening context. At some point you have to be able to say, "I really like x, how do you feel about it?" 5. Too passive. A misplaced punishment that leads nowhere. You haven't gotten your irrational assumptions under control. 6. Just goes to show how we can fool ourselves into believing that manipulation is intimacy. 7. Fine, as long as it's done sensitively.

PROBLEM. After moving into her new office, Marge has to use a colleague's phone for several days until hers is installed. He's a prickly sort of man who does nothing to make her feel that her intrusions are forgiven, and she's already begun to pick up bits of irritation in his grunted greetings. If you were Marge, what would you do?

1. I'd explain with great feeling that I am really sorry to be bothering him, and that I can't thank him enough for his putting up with these impositions.

2. I'd just smile and keep coming back. I didn't create the problem and there's nothing I can do about it.

3. I'd make a joke: "I think I should just move in. Do you have an extra desk for me?"

SOLUTION. This is a minor but nagging problem. A lot depends on your personal style and how exactly you perceive the person you're dealing with. 1. Okay, but may come out a bit overwrought. Could sound like pleading for approval, begging the guy not to be so unsmiling. He may take it as a reward manipulation rather than genuine personal power. 2. Fine, if you're comfortable with it. You could always achieve his friendship later. 3. Might work the best. Gently apologetic, charmingly grateful, you retain your dignity while possibly disarming him of whatever irritation he may feel.

PROBLEM. You are a new editor at a publishing house. Young and unsure about the security of your position, you are replacing a man fired after twelve years with the firm. An important aspect of your work is making certain that your books are properly promoted. You are supposed to feed your ideas to the publicity director, Will, a man in his fifties who is entrenched in the firm. But Will, who was a close friend of your predecessor, invariably takes a few days to return your calls and sometimes forgets entirely. When you finally reach him, he's professional and gives no hint of being purposely uncooperative. Each week, as urgent messages go unanswered, you vacillate between fury and fear. What do you do?

1. I'd find Will in his office and say, "Perhaps the success of this company's books is of no great interest to you, but it is to me, and I would appreciate it if you would return my calls."

2. The next time we spoke, I'd try to be a little more personal: "I know my predecessor was a friend of yours and that you were sorry to see her go. But I wish you wouldn't hold it against me."

3. I'd use humor: "You may not enjoy speaking to me, Will, but if we're going to get these books promoted, I'm afraid you'll have to. So why put it off?"

4. Will needs things from me, too. My predecessor was working on a number of books before she left, and Will's secretary calls me for information regarding their production and sales. I would start being unavailable.

5. I would find an opportunity to say, "Since we've been working together, Will, I've found that you often take a few days to return my calls. Is there any reason for that?"

6. I'd wait until some time when Will and I were engaged in a casual conversation and find a way to work my feelings in. If he talked about how busy he was, I'd say, "You must be. It takes forever to get a hold of you."

7. I'd ask him forcefully, "Will, why don't you return my calls?"

8. I wouldn't say anything to him. The man is very busy and I shouldn't let that trigger my paranoia.

SOLUTION. You need to be direct and tactful. 1. A heavy-duty wrong move. By charging in with your untested assumptions, you risk coming out the overemotional troublemaker. Overloaded with anger and guilt. 2. You're telling him what he feels. Be careful about assigning motives or becoming personal before you've explored the surface. 3. You may take the edge off by saying this humorously, but why put him in an adversary position? You still have no idea of what's really going on. 4. You're opting for combat before you've discovered if Will is an enemy. He may have no understanding of why you've stopped cooperating and retaliate in a whole new way.

5. An ideal use of personal power. You're putting your dissatisfaction on record, asking a direct question, and giving Will plenty of room to respond. 6. Much too indirect. You're leaving it to Will to interpret your context—whether you're expressing a serious dissatisfaction or just making a quip. If he's a very sensitive and caring man, he'll make it work for you, but you shouldn't depend on that. 7. Very

aggressive, and certainly direct, but success depends on what Will is like. This could raise his hackles. 8. In this case, putting negative assumptions on hold becomes an excuse for evasion. You're upset. You should find a way of dealing with it.

PROBLEM. In Marge's new law firm, she has a group of aggressive male colleagues. Periodically she meets with three of them to determine how to proceed with an important case. They all talk loudly and interrupt one another, shouting each other down, and dismissing any point of view they don't agree with. Marge, who is new and wants to make a good impression, finds that her statements are hardly noticed. Lately she's begun to feel like an inferior member of the group, that she is not respected by the men. If you were Marge, what would you do?

1. I'd find the right moment to say, "Excuse me, but I feel my points are being ignored."

2. I'd mock them: "Come on, loudmouths, let a softspoken girl get a word in edgewise."

3. I'd persist in politely stating my point and not falter if I had to repeat myself again and again.

4. If one of them shouted me down, I'd say, "You have a hell of a nerve. Let me finish."

5. I'd walk out if I were consistently ignored and take it up with our superior.

6. I'd express my views in a memo, thereby avoiding unnecessary confrontations so early in my new position.

SOLUTION. This is an important strategic problem. Marge is not faced with abuse, but she could end up in an object position if she is not careful. She has to prove herself with men who may be a little wary of her and are certainly doing nothing to make her feel at home. They may even be harboring negative assumptions about what it's going to be like to have a female on the team. If Marge begins to feel like a lesser member of the group, she will eventually let a little object tendency show, which will then naturallly get linked up with whatever subject tendencies exist in her colleagues. She needs to be direct, but she also needs to lay a little carpet down for her message.

1. Done right, this could be terrific. But it would take some special twist, like a particularly feminine arch to her voice or a very appealing flash of eyebrow, to drive home the point that the men can't be such bulldozers when dealing with this delicate (but very savvy) newcomer. Done wrong, with a twist of self-pity or guilt, this could be disastrous, arousing the men's defensiveness. They'll think, "We're not ignoring the dame. She doesn't know how to speak up!" And she will have an

even more difficult struggle. 2. If this is said with humor and if these guys have a sense of humor, the strategy could break the ice and open up some space for her. With a humorless group, it could be a disastrously wrong move. 3. Weak personal power. She'll probably be seen as a drag. 4. Instead of being diplomatic, this is asking for a fight. They may listen, but they'll be resentful, and they'll talk about Marge negatively among themselves. 5. Marge can't depend on higher ups to make the system work for her. She has to find a way to deal with the style of her colleagues. 6. To put her position in writing is to create a permanent record she may regret later. It also separates her from the group. Marge has to hang in there and be resourceful.

PROBLEM. You've just driven your date home and she's invited you in for the first time. In one fluid motion, she switches on both the lamp and the television, tosses her keys on the bed and plops lazily alongside them. For the next two hours you try in vain to wrestle her out of her clothes. Nothing works. What do you do now?

1. I'd get myself out of there. Why expose my desire any more to someone who doesn't want me? She probably invited me in to be polite.
2. I'd show a little anger. Why is she acting like such a kid?
3. I'd say, "Hey, wait a second. I'd like to spend the night with you. How would you feel about that?"

SOLUTION. 1. This doesn't accomplish anything (although it's probably better than more of the same). You haven't exposed yourself so terribly much, and your decision about her is just a guess. 2. A touch of anger could break the whole thing open. But it could go either way. It depends on whether you can use anger in a nice way and know how to invite a clean fight. Otherwise, she may feel blamed and defensive. 3. Can't lose. A good use of personal power.

Further Exercises for Self-Awareness

These exercises cannot be done in one sitting. Check back on them from time to time.

• Try to trace the strands of your shame-should-shame cycle. How were your attitudes formed about yourself—regarding sex, money, authority, competition, success? Think about your parents. What were their illusions and dissatisfactions? What were they trying to escape from? How did their problems translate into their behavior with you? Is there someone with whom you can share this information? Can you keep the awareness of pain with you, rather than discarding it at once when you go about your daily routines?

• How do you feel when told that a new supervisor will be placed between you and your current boss? Do you expect him to be an adversary? A manipulator? An incompetent? Are these attitudes and expectations typical of you? Can you see how they may have developed out of your relationship with your parents? How do they affect you in other nonwork-related areas of your life?

• How capable are you of being absolutely straight? Do you have a good sense of when it's safe to use personal power? What trips you up when you try to be direct? Which signs of manueuver or resistance hook you? What do your doubts and assumptions whisper? Could you keep your personal power alive for a minute or two longer than usual and withstand the attendant anxiety?

• Are you able to be direct about expressing dissatisfaction? Can you say no without barbs, hooks, or backpedalling? What about making a request. Disagreeing? Debating? Questioning authority? Apologizing? Listening to criticism? How do strategies sneak into your communication in each of these areas?

• What do you do when someone starts speaking about his troubles? Do you welcome the opening or leap to cover it up? Do you know someone with whom you feel you can absolutely be yourself? Could you be even more open with that person in the future?

• What do you feel about yourself that no one else knows? Can you imagine coming out of the closet with it?

• Are you able to be alone?

V.

THE PLAY

Three Characters in Crisis

19.

Jake—The Powerphobic's Story

High on the corporate tightrope, where image counts for more than substance; and where a man with inner strength can be destroyed if he hesitates to play for keeps. The power struggle at *Today*.

IN THE WORLD in which Martin and Jake operate, strategic power is the coin of the realm. At every level of corporate affairs, strategic considerations make it difficult at times to distinguish product quality from sales, talent from image, strength from the appearance of strength. A lapse of editorial judgment—a tasteless choice of words, a photograph that humiliates a public figure, a failure to doublecheck an important piece of information—is still a lapse of judgment, but it only becomes a liability if it cannot be successfully camouflaged or stone-walled.

At Today, Inc. a kind of formality exists that makes every role very rigid, and the slightest act of spontaneity may prove to be a wrong move. This formality is not the old European formality based on manners, deference to authority, and carefully ordered ritual. It is a peculiarly modern formality based on strategic values, in which people are judged appropriate almost exclusively on their image as winners. Here, image often becomes more important than the substance it is supposed to imply.

Among the executives at *Today,* how they dress, where they eat, whom they associate with is considered with secret care, as if mixing a magic formula. The formula for success changes somewhat from season to season, and the constant shifts in fashion and the appearance of new books and theories on the subject keep adding new twists and subtleties. You should never wear a certain brand of shoes (Loser shoes!). You should never eat or drink with too much gusto at a business lunch (Loser lunch!). You should never be the first to excuse yourself and use the men's room at an important business meeting (Loser bladder!). But *careful*. You shouldn't follow fashion too closely either. Because to look as if you're playing by the book, as if you *care* about all this stuff, is to violate the first rule of the game, that the moves mustn't show. And this, too, will cause people to smile knowingly.

Cooperative human activity still proceeds in this atmosphere. Real thoughts are expressed, policies debated, criticism offered, kind words exchanged. But even the simplest communication is conducted through a thick shield of image and manipulation. And the higher you go in the hierarchy, the slicker and more beguiling the shield becomes—slick fellowship, slick "openness," slick expressions of idealism or anguish—allowing less and less substance to squeeze through the layers of calculation.

Tuesday Morning: The Cover Conference

Martin's ability to thwart and upstage Jake without doing anything overtly offensive—that is, without making a wrong move that openly violates the role of subordinate—enhances his already strong position in the power struggle. Although Jake has tried to strengthen his posture since the unfortunate meeting at the beginning of the story, he has not been able to stop Martin from making small but dangerous inroads. The young publisher, Ed Roland, is influenced by this trend (which he of course helped to foster), and there is a growing anticipation that if he doesn't remove Jake entirely, he will pressure him to establish another assistant managing editor's post for his chief rival.

The subtle power shifts are evident at the Tuesday morning cover conferences, one of the editorial meetings that Roland, much to Jake's displeasure, occasionally attends. The editors no longer perceive the meetings as a three-pointed affair between Roland, Jake and his lieutenants, and the others. They now perceive that Martin occupies a corner as well, that his word carries weight with Roland and is cautiously supported by those who perceive the advantage moving in his direction.

At this morning's meeting it is assumed that the cover choice will be "Dr. Jenkel," the *nom de terreur* of a much wanted international assassin. As a result of informal meetings they've had with Jake and the cover editor in the last few days, the senior editors know that Jenkel is Jake's choice. Also being considered is Palmer Brian, the director of *Scare Your Pants Off!*, a new sex-and-horror film that's grossed over $40 million in its first month.

"This is a terrific shot of Jenkel," says Jake. "He's practically snarling. I think we should go with it."

"I'm with you," says Roland. "There's nothing else on the boards this week, and Brian is already on the cover of *Rolling Stone*, *Penthouse*, and *New York* magazine."

"How do we look," says Martin, "if we go with Jenkel and *Time* goes with Brian? Are we going to take a beating at the stands?"

Roland looks at Martin, obviously concerned and interested.

"Are you suggesting," says managing editor Lester Chase, Jake's first lieutenant, "that we have another set of matching covers with *Time*?"

Martin, bordering on politeness: "No, that's not what I'm suggesting." He stops, allowing an uncomfortable silent moment that seems to slap Lester Chase in the face.

Jake, with level authority: "What are you suggesting?"

Martin, firm but respectful: "I think we should reconsider the earthquake story, Jake. It raises and answers a lot of questions in people's minds."

Before Chase can protest the lack of an adequate earthquake cover, the science editor, glancing nervously, reveals that, indeed, some new shots have come in this morning that makes the earthquake cover "conceivable." He passes several transparencies to Jake, who holds them to the light, nods, and passes them to the cover editor, who silently projects them, one by one, onto the screen. They are sensational.

Had Jake been a foolish man, he would have insisted on Jenkel for what everyone would have taken to be personal motives. Had he been a powerless man, he would have mumbled his approval of the earthquake shots and displayed his emotional deflation. Had he been a frightened man, he would have panicked as if in the midst of an earthquake himself. But he would have had to be a blind man not to see that he had been upstaged, that he had not yet found a means to halt the erosion of his authority.

"Well, gentlemen, we have an embarrassment of riches," Jake says and rises to adjourn. That afternoon he calls in the science editor and questions him on the surprise photos. The man swears up and down that the photographer handed them to him minutes before the meeting. Jake nods and dismisses him, unsure of what to do next.

Creativity Without Power: The Vulnerability of Commitment

Jake's problem can be traced in part to his commitment to the editorial reforms. About ten years ago, having established that he had energy and ideas, that he could hold substantial jobs, that he could motivate and train subordinates, Jake thought, Okay, now what? The answer was obvious. He wanted to influence the way things were done.

Jake had strong feelings about journalism and the way it should work. He believed that standards of objectivity had to be changed, made more exact really, so that reporters would have the freedom to say, among other things, that a public figure was not speaking the truth. A reporter had to be able to interpret, or at least draw extremely evident conclusions. He should not have to manipulate the reader through the careful loading of opposing quotes or, worse, to play the role of partisan.

Reporters have an important role to play in today's society, Jake argued—not to express their points of view, but to see through the increasingly managed facade of political and social life to present a true, unbiased story. This would be objectivity taken to a level of high craft.

This was one of Jake's major reforms. But such changes require huge shifts in the operation of a large institution. Everyone must be prepared and reassured. New responsibilities require new guidelines and new training. Certain editors have to cooperate in a process which may look to them like a loss of power to reporters and writers. And the institution must be prepared to take heat from outside. After all, Jake is tampering with a decades-old formula. The magazine will no longer have its familiar feel of homogenized infallibility; and many people will be outraged over assertions that have never before appeared in serious news columns.

Trying to bring about fundamental change requires proficiency in every sort of power—strategic, personal, and what we will call "creative"—the ability to bring others along in a cooperative effort. Jake has all the skills needed for such an endeavor. He's shrewd, he's eloquent, he's sensitive. But he's neglected one element. He hasn't cleared the field of land mines; his authority still faces pockets of resistance. And so, instead of looking like a leader, he looks like a fool.

Where winning is king, commitment to anything other than self-advancement can look wishy-washy, old-fashioned, and naive. And so within the institution, Jake's reforms always had a slightly curious ring. They were not designed to scoop the opposition, to boost readership, to increase ad pages—although naturally these are all hoped for byproducts. The reforms were designed instead with a purpose that, in business at least, is completely unfashionable—to do something better, to make the magazine more useful to society.

Jake's reforms were high in quality, low in gloss. But unfortunately, in the corporate environment, image without substance will always defeat substance without image.

That does not mean that Jake's policy is doomed. But to succeed it must be chaperoned by the same bodyguard of allegiances, public relations, rewards and punishments that he's used in the past to push through staff reorganizations and other less revolutionary measures. He must cover himself on every front, make the success of his plans personally worth the while of people in key positions, make any opposition among subordinates, beyond open and legitimate disagreement, costly.

But to put all that together takes resolve, and Jake's has been slipping. He had begun this venture with grains of self-doubt he hadn't previously experienced. Who am I to alter the course of journalism? Who am I to tamper with an institution like Today, Inc.? Because they were shameful and therefore unexamined, these doubts threw him off his game.

Without realizing it, Jake had begun several months ago to seek a more than normal level of consensus among his subordinates. He found himself excusing certain behavior among the senior editors that he normally wouldn't tolerate. He allowed Martin to expand his independent power base. He didn't go the extra mile to pin down Ed Roland about the source of the subtle discord that had grown between them or to oppose Roland's encroaching editorial involvements.

Meanwhile, a nervous current was running through the senior editors, like the current that runs through children when they sense uncertainty in their parents. Jake's allies were getting worried. Jake's old friend, Kevin Collins, the culture editor, whom Jake has always protected, secretly played ball with Martin. As the opposition to Jake grew and as Martin became more ruthless, Jake's powerphobia kept him from responding forcefully.

Shameful, Unleaderly Fear

Early signs of trouble appeared last summer when Jake instituted the first of his changes, the elimination of the star system among writers, a system whereby the lead story in national and international news was assigned to the writer who was "hottest" that week. Jake opposed the system because it induced unnecessary levels of insecurity and competitiveness, and it tended to sacrifice substance for jazziness in reporting. Instead, each writer was assigned an area of expertise which remained his throughout the year. The policy shift seemed responsible for the loss of a top writer in national news, about which Martin grumbled to several key executives in the magazine.

People are naturally fearful of change, and now that they had a real problem to worry about, Roland was badgered by several board members who were anxious that *Today* might no longer be able to improve its competitive position with the industry leader, as it had been doing over the past ten years. Quickly, their anxieties became his.

Ed Roland is a charming and elusive man of thirty-nine. He had hired Jake in the full blush of idealism. No longer would *Today* look and sound identical to its competitors. When his father was still in charge and Ed Roland was impatient for change, he never anticipated the effect that seemingly minor financial anxieties might have on him once he took over. But now that he was responsible for all that money and being closely watched with every dip in the graph, his boldness flagged.

Roland would like to be known for having overseen an important journalistic innovation. But he does not want to be remembered as the feckless son who ruined the empire his father built. He knows that while sophisticated people will applaud him as a man of rare vision and character if he dares to take a major risk and wins, the same people will bury him in scorn if he takes that risk and loses. And so he has become very sensitive to the feedback he is getting throughout the institution.

But Roland is torn. During their first two and half years together, Roland's respect for and belief in Jake had grown. Jake had attracted several extraordinary talents to the magazine. Under his leadership *Today* won important awards. Team spirit was stronger than at any other time in the past fifteen years. How could Roland now express reservations about the policies that he and Jake had agreed upon when Jake accepted the job?

Roland had promised Jake full editorial control and every ounce of his support. Although he felt he was going back on his commitment, in this, as we've seen, he was being unfair to himself. He was simply worried, and he didn't know how to share his worry with Jake or to reassure himself that Jake was sensitive to his concerns. He had been stung by fear, shameful, unleaderly fear. Unable to express it, he became subtly estranged from Jake. He eagerly accepted Martin's argument that the reforms should be tried first in the "soft news" section of the book, and, in a move that stung Jake deeply, he gave Martin the ability to stall the implementation of bylines in national and international news.

A Failure to Communicate

Anxiety soon lay just beneath the deceptive informality between the two men. They went abroad together on a promotional tour and visited foreign bureaus. They took an occasional jaunt in Roland's private jet. They discussed future issues of the magazine over dinner. But always now there was the sense of something being avoided. Jake attributed the disharmony to his own fears and doubts, and so he became a party to the silence.

Having failed to express his anxiety to Jake, having failed to get Jake's feedback, Roland began to see Jake as a reckless reformer. He viewed him as rigidly committed to going his own way and insensitive to the practical matter of keeping up with *Time*. He believed that Jake was aware of his fears and was calmly riding roughshod over them. (Jake thinks I'm still a kid! He thinks he's still my teacher! He thinks he can ignore me!)

Although he sensed that his anger was not justified, Roland was nonetheless unable to keep it from emerging in small ways. He started getting more involved in the editorial process. Jake, meanwhile, upset by Roland's innuendoes and convinced that Roland was purposefully whittling away at his pledge of non-interference, became more prideful and aloof and retreated more into himself, thereby reinforcing Roland's adversary assumptions.

Shortly before the editorial meeting that began our story, the two men were in the back seat of Roland's limousine returning from a closed circuit hook-up with their Teheran bureau which had been granted an exclusive interview with the Ayatollah Khomeini. All the appropriate expressions of high spirits and the popping of champagne only emphasized the gap that had grown between the old friends.

"This is the sort of thing we need more of, Jake!" said Roland heartily. Jake smiled faintly, nodded, and quipped, "You mean Khomeini or the champagne?" to conceal his discomfort.

"What does he think!" Jake shouted later at Grace. "That I'm withholding exclusive interviews with world leaders? That scoops are knocking on the door and I won't let them in?"

Then came the disastrous meeting, where in the banter with Martin, Jake came off the fool, and for the first time Roland clearly noticed that there was something off about Jake. *Aha,* he thought, Jake's so immersed in his plans, he's losing the handle. Gee, I'd better help him. Perhaps I'll suggest that he postpone the reforms if that will make things easier for him.

Seeing a sign of weakness in Jake gave a reassuring boost to Roland's identity. He no longer experienced himself as the embodiment of anxious inexperience, and he came to believe that his fears had been mainly for Jake's sake all along. If he hadn't spoken his mind about them, it was only because he didn't want to undermine Jake's morale. He had to give Jake a chance to solve his managerial problems first.

By these inner turns and rationalizations, Roland was finally able to slip out of his role of Jake's admiring student, a role that naturally embarrassed him, and into his proper role as leader.

Another month went by and a tiny drop in circulation gripped Roland by the throat. His fear turned momentarily to anger, which he quickly acted out. Visiting the Rome office, he promised the bureau chief a switch to London without first consulting Jake.

"Ed, you can't expect me to run this show if you're going to undermine my authority."

"Cool off, Jake, you're taking it too seriously."

"This is serious."

"Rome? Peterson? Serious? Come on."

Although Jake's feelings were storming, he held the point without escalating. "Ed, you know as well as I do, it's a question of authority."

"Well, I hope we don't have to discuss this all morning," Roland said, glancing conspicuously at his calendar.

"You think about it, Ed," Jake said and walked out, planning his resignation. Two hours later, returning from lunch, he found on his desk a toy bathtub gondola and a joking note that could only be interpreted as an apology.

Such were the seesawing tensions.

A Power Vacuum

A power vacuum has a natural tendency to expand, so that if you don't correct the imbalance now, you find yourself facing a greater imbalance later. Through a simple failure to struggle on his own behalf, Jake is on the way to turning a decent boss into a monster who will second-guess his every move, check all his personnel decisions, choose Jake's cover stories, and put flunkies over him to monitor his performance.

If a power vacuum can turn a boss into a tyrant, it can also turn guppies into piranhas. In the last two months, Jake has found himself needled with ill-intentioned questions from the staff about the need for strong editorial leadership and the dangers of giving writers too much authority. While he was on vacation a minor gaff in a story in the culture section, edited by his old friend, Kevin Collins, was openly blamed on confusion over the guidelines. A simple and embarrassing failure to check a fact became the subject of countless overheated discussions.

Jake's colleagues—like the science editor who didn't think it "necessary" to alert Jake to the arrival of the new photos, although he casually showed them to Martin in the hall—have reason to respect and stand by him. How can a few strategic lapses negate three years as managing editor? But they are conditioned to interpret everything strategically, and when everyone thinks that everyone else thinks that something signifies collapse, the slightest move in that direction is perceived as the onset of an avalanche—and as a result it often is.

A few grains of doubt, unexamined and left to fester, have thus grown into an enormous liability. And now, as Martin becomes convinced that he is dealing with a man on the edge of defeat, he becomes more ruthless in his attacks.

Blunder, Confusion, Defeat

The tension and instability reached a symbolic peak earlier this month over a decision to print a photograph. It was a photograph of the murdered federal court judge, Maxwell Browne, taken by an amateur photographer who happened upon the scene moments before Judge Browne died. Rather than run immediately for help, she paused to shoot a picture of the poor man while pathetic horror was still written on his bloodied face.

After carefully removing himself from the decision-making process, Martin made sure that word of the photograph and the large sum Jake had approved for it reached the judge's widow. A prominent novelist with many journalist friends, Arlene Browne immediately called Jake to protest. She didn't ask Jake to reconsider, she ordered him to. Jake felt violated and politely stood his ground. She accused him of sensationalism, yellow journalism, exploitation, invasion of privacy, promoting a craven hustler. She called him a Grub Street bastard and a corrupt little slug. She warned him of legal action and the loss of his job. She poured into her denunciation and threats all the pain and powerlessness she felt over her terrible loss. Jake had no defense. How could he fight back against this respected and bereaved figure? He felt as if he'd been thrown into the ring with his hands tied behind his back. He took the beating of his life.

For several days, as protests came in from all over, Jake reconsidered his decision. He felt caged in his office and went home at night in an ulcerous state of doubt. *The New York Times* reported the dispute, including Arlene Browne's denunciations. Roland phoned to assure Jake of his support either way, but he did not sound wholehearted. Jake felt more isolated than at any time in his professional life.

If Jake were to change his mind, it would look as if he'd backed down under pressure, the last thing he needed now. If he stood his ground, he might be acting in the wrong for the sole purpose of saving face. This was the worst way to have to decide a question of journalistic ethics. After consultations with his closest friends and advisors, Jake decided not to run the photograph. He issued a short statement defending its purchase, but explained that it added little to the story and would probably cause the family grief. "We ate crow, Lester," he told Chase when it was over.

The incident made Jake acutely aware of his vulnerability. He had jumped for an exclusive of dubious worth—"Shabby really," now that he thought about it—because of the pressure he felt from Roland. It wasn't like him to want to please so much he lost his judgment. Where did all this fear and insecurity come from? Where had he gone wrong?

"Grace," says Jake one evening after dinner, "I'm thinking of postponing the changes. Indefinitely. I think I acted prematurely."

"It's Grodin."

"Yes and no," he sighs. "It's everything. My reflexes don't feel right. That Browne photo. That stupid article in Culture this summer. And Collins—he should have been on top of that."

"You should *dump* Collins. Why didn't he keep it in the department?"

Jake shrugs.

"Let's suppose you made some mistakes," Grace says. "There's nothing wrong with what you're trying to do. If you cut your losses now and back off, I don't know if you'll ever recover your standing in the company. They'll see you as a tarnished entity. You'll *feel* like a tarnished entity."

Jake shakes his head. "Everything was great for two and a half years, and now that I've begun to try to institute those changes, it's all falling apart. Doesn't that tell you something? Maybe this just isn't the right time. Or maybe I'm just not the man for the job. Roland's been backpedalling. I can see it in his eyes. I can hear it in his voice. The signs are everywhere: *Back off. Back off.*"

"But you know what Roland's like. If you had all the arms properly twisted and all the heads nodding, you could turn *Today* into *Yesterday,* and Roland would say, 'Wow, groovy!'"

"I know, I know. But it's more than that really," says Jake. "For the life of me, I can't remember why I wanted to start this whole thing. What was it all about?"

20.

Martin—The Subject's Story

The secret life of Mr. Right. How his parents shaped him to be a winner. The dreams and losses of his childhood and youth. The tragic hole at the center of his being. His need for Georgette.

TO BE AN EQUAL is to be vulnerable to the influence of another—his feelings, his criticism, his love, his rejection, his maneuvers, his idiosyncrasies, any of which may be painful or threatening. To be one-up is never to risk that vulnerability.

For Martin being one-up is a great pleasure. He gets push-button responses from subordinates. Friends and associates show him undiluted respect. No idea he utters, no matter how wrong, is ever the cause for humiliation. The humor that is directed at him in his presence is never derisive. When he is in a bad mood, he can relieve himself with ill-tempered aggression and escape with a display of charm. He does not have to admit to faults or failings unless he derives some political advantage from doing so. He knows that being one-up means never having to say you're sorry.

Anyone can be addicted to such comforts and pleasures—a Christian, a socialist, a psychiatrist, a truck driver. It really doesn't matter what your religious training or political beliefs, how many decades of psychoanalysis you've endured, how deep your knowledge or great your charitable works. In the hidden realm of interpersonal politics, winning may be your primary commitment. And any system of ideas, from Buddhism to neo-conservatism, can be used to shame someone and bolster a winning hand.

The Subject's Game: Find the Weakness, Make the Judgment, Play for Advantage

Martin was raised by Catholic parents in an upper-middle-class Protestant community, by a father who was ashamed of how hard he had to work to keep up with his neighbors, and by a mother who believed that status was self-esteem. Their home was a training ground for making oneself invulnerable. Martin was ridiculed when he allowed pain and disappointment to show. He was rewarded with inclusion and approval when he was able to rise above hurt feelings and imitate his parents' strategic talents. The training was Spartan but effective, and Martin was early initiated in the subtleties of image, evasive humor, wry self-deprecation, aggressive posture, and spotting and exploiting the weaknesses in others.

Martin's mother was a manipulative and somewhat bitter woman who felt damaged by poverty, class prejudice, and lost opportunities. She had great dreams for her princely son. She saw in him an aristocracy lacking in her hard-pressed husband. She cherished his virtues. She had a way of talking about his brilliance, his appearance, his grades, his talents as if she were fondling gold coins. Such gloating was the only way she could bring herself to express her love, even to Martin himself, and so, through the subtle vehicle of praise, she fed off him. She made Martin into a doll, a conquering hero doll, and, thus, an object.

Martin did not feel worthy of his mother's love simply for being himself. As a child he could feel the burden of her expectations. Occasionally, he sought sympathy from her in such a way that clearly implied he was not invulnerable or that he lacked some quality she cherished. He was testing to see whether he would be allowed to tolerate that lack within himself, whether he would be accepted and loved anyway. But each time the iciness of her response ("If you feel weak, then you'll be weak") proved that if he was not what she expected, he was nothing. His fear of experimentation, his inability to tolerate doubt, his need to put personal advancement ahead of everything else are all built on that intense kernel of object experience.

When Martin had conflicts with other children or with teachers, his mother never asked him to examine his own responsibility for what had happened. She had only one agenda at such times—to make sure that her boy was not hurt or taken advantage of as she felt she had been. She trained him never to admit being wrong and to respond to all criticism as if it were unfair and selfishly motivated. Find the weakness. Make the judgment. Play for advantage. The adversary posture she taught him was deepened by his experiences with her; for she always assumed ill motives on the part of anyone who opposed her, including Martin himself.

When Martin, criticized by his tenth grade pals for letting his popularity go to his head, began to doubt whether he should run for class president, Mrs. Grodin would hear nothing of it. It was not in her to ask her son, "Martin, do you think if you were elected class president you might feel you'd become better than your friends?" A question like that would have given him something legitimate to struggle with. But it would not have paved over his vulnerability, and that was what she wanted to do. She told him that small and fearful people are always envious of the talented and the strong, and that he should never allow them to trim his sails. Meanwhile, she was thinking, as Martin too was learning to think, "class president" will look great on his record.

Martin's father held traditional views about coming down in the world. Certain people, because of their social status, were beneath him, and he felt unclean whenever he sensed he was getting too close to them. Mrs. Grodin held a more modern view. She would happily associate with criminals and poor artists if she detected a winning personality; and she secretly despised a person of great accomplishment if she could detect his vulnerability. To her, coming down in the world meant becoming associated with vulnerability of any kind.

She had laser eyes for weakness, and when weaknesses were discussed at the dinner table, Martin understood them to be qualities that made the people who bore them worthy of his complete dismissal. He found himself measuring his friends, teachers, relatives, and girlfriends by his mother's standards. He was always testing in subtle ways, testing the limits of each person's self-respect and learning to eliminate those who proved defective. Only losers associate with losers.

This process of eliminating people was painful to Martin, for he was often fond of those he rejected and felt as if he were cutting away a part of himself. It was a numbing process that made it easier for him to do much harsher things to people he didn't know and had no reason to care about.

By the time Martin reached junior high school, many of the smooth, discreet gestures that characterize him today had already been perfected. But uncertainty still showed on him. Some adults were still able to make him squirm, and he was still conscious of vulnerability, which, by the standards of his upbringing, was the most despicable of all qualities.

During his adolescent years, when confronted with the painful intensity of peer relations, Martin launched a semi-conscious struggle to conquer vulnerability and achieve a firmer grip on the interpersonal confidence and air of superiority that were the key to self-worth in his home. His "shoulds" told him to be prepared for every moment, to never be caught off-guard and embarrassed. Martin devoted himself to strategic thinking the way others his age devoted themselves to conformity or rebellion.

As a teenager, Martin discovered that when he felt like a million dollars—when his report card was excellent, when he won an important tennis match, when the prettiest girl necked with him at a party—everything he did and said communicated that million-dollar feeling. Why, he asked himself, can't I always communicate that feeling? He began to carefully watch his behavior and the behavior of others, collecting the tiniest specimens of what struck him as winning and losing qualities. Words, gestures, clothes, twists of the mouth, turns of a phrase, squints of the eye, tones of voice. Gradually, he hit upon a formula that seemed perfect for his abilities and the values of his community—to appear invulnerable, yet thoughtful and sensitive; strong but not hypermasculine. And there could be no doubt about the impact. No matter what he felt inside, if he looked and acted like a winner, he was treated like a winner.

Martin discovered that the less he revealed the safer he was; and even when he had the urge to tell all, to share secrets, to get close, he learned to stifle it. Why relinquish his one-up status? He discovered that if he didn't seem to need people, people would come to him; and no matter how badly he hurt and wanted to seek out a friend for comfort, he found he was able to suppress it. Why blow his carefully crafted image? He discovered that the surest way to become one-down in any relationship and to start feeling that illicit vulnerability again was to care too much about keeping the relationship alive; and even when he cared very much, he managed never to show it.

He came to many of his recognitions through experience, some of it big and painful, some of it small and unmemorable. He reached for the hand of his date as they walked to his car after a movie. Holding her hand, he thought, She may not be enjoying this, she may be just acting polite. The shame aroused by this thought ("Drip!" "Pathetic Worm!" "Horny Toad!") was more intense than it might have been for another boy because for Martin vulnerability was off-limits, and he therefore could never examine or come to terms with it in any way.

He casually dropped the girl's hand and when she did not start reaching for him, he dropped her. He found more demonstrative girls, and he saw that they responded positively to reticence, self-containment, and control.

Martin's extreme anxiety about vulnerability reinforced his tendency to view the world through adversary glasses; and maintaining a slight advantage with those people he saw as strong seemed crucial to feeling secure. Quick to spot the slightest self-doubt, he could not resist toying with it. But even when self-doubt emerged from people who seemed weak and unthreatening, he was still drawn to needle it—because their doubt reminded him of something he wanted to forget. And so, one way or the other, he played the subject and maneuvered to stay on top.

Once Martin had his advantage, he could be generous, supportive, entertaining, and attentive. He thus saw himself as a loyal and selfless friend and felt hurt and misunderstood when anyone abandoned him. But there were always enough people who liked and respected him. If they felt a little inadequate in his presence, they attributed it to envy, insecurity, or some other personal shortcoming.

During his high school years, Martin became a scientist of interpersonal relations. He recognized that both containing vulnerability and achieving strategic power begin with propriety. If he always appeared to stay within a certain circle of appropriate feelings, behaviors, and attitudes, he was safe from criticism. He took pleasure in deciphering what was appropriate in each of his roles—Friend, Student, Son, Guest, Newcomer, Prizewinner, Employee. He saw each new role as a challenge of adaptation, learning just the right mixture of humility, pride, obedience, initiative, warmth, and distance for every social situation. Because his main interest was social acceptance, achievement, and power, he did not mind burying many of his feelings in order to play his roles to optimum advantage. And he enjoyed watching, in each new context, as people with power began to nod their heads approvingly—even as his thoughts were already beyond them.

The Power Addition

Because vulnerability immediately triggered intense anxiety in Martin, the anxiety of a little child who is about to be shamed and rejected by his parents, much of what he taught himself represented an adolescent's struggle for survival. But his struggle to survive was too successful for his own good. He got lost in the power process and addicted to its security and pleasures. When he hungered for emotional nourishment, when he was hurt or depressed or needing love, he fed himself on conquest and achievement. He used power the way a food addict uses food, feeding his emotional needs with the wrong ingredients to make the needs subside. Soon Martin had no interest in any activity that didn't have some opportunity or ego purpose built into it, and today the thought of a passive, Georgette-style vacation is unbearable.

As a teenager Martin rediscovered in a slightly more conscious way something he'd always known: if he treated people with a touch of disdain, they would like him anyway and often raise their estimation of his worth. He made some calculated experiments and was amazed and in one case saddened by how well they worked.

There was a piano teacher, Doug, an older man without children, who had been an inspiration to Martin. Gentle, philosophical, very different from Martin's family, Doug had talked to Martin about ambition, failure, girls, books. He'd told Martin to read Dostoyevsky and had given him a copy of *Steppenwolf*, which became the favorite book of Martin's high school years. He'd seen in Martin a brightness and earnestness that he wanted to cultivate, and he'd given him some of the affection he wished he could give a son of his own.

One day Martin's mother said something disparaging about Doug, and although Martin was unaware of the connection, he soon found himself testing Doug by acting a little cutting and aloof.

The impact was immediate. Doug, surprised and hurt, asked him what was wrong, asked if he had hurt Martin's feelings, and so forth. As Martin dodged him, Doug behaved like an object, reaching and reaching to no avail, and the more he did so, the weaker and smaller he looked and the more conclusively he failed Martin's test. He said things to Martin he'd never said before—how important Martin was to him, how much their friendship meant to him. It was all very flattering and touching, but Martin could no longer respect Doug or imagine using him as a mentor. His mother's medicine was stronger.

Martin kept alive the dream of a true friend, a man with whom he could share ideas, a man from whom he perhaps could learn. The only men he would consider were thoughtful, gentle people, but they could not generally match his strategic power, and, once tested and found wanting, they lost their appeal. Today, his old chum Frank Caruso is his only friend, and the dream of deeper friendships is receding.

Martin was sorry over the loss of Doug, but he also felt very powerful. He felt marked for survival, favored by destiny. The whole world still lay before him, and he would find everything he needed there.

In high school Martin began to perfect a style of punishment he had learned from his father: the mocking eyebrow, the gentle sarcasm, the infinitesimal smirk, the borderline quip (is it good-natured or is it a dig?)—punishment that was so subtle he could hardly be called on it and which the recipient could barely resist the temptation of letting go. He thought of it as his "style," and if someone felt bruised by it, he shrugged and said, "I guess you don't like my style."

At the same time he was developing equally subtle rewards, which played at least as big a part of his winning formula. He watched people closely in order to understand how to appeal to them. He could say something flattering in so unassuming a way that the recipient would never guess at Martin's intent. He could make very astute people like and respect him without ever being suspected of ingratiation. And although obvious ingratiation on the part of others disgusts him *(bootlicker, wimp),* his own brand of refined ingratiation, built on hours and hours of calculation, is a chief aspect of his successful personality.

Martin refined his strategic skills through constant, careful thought. When he was embarrassed in any way, he would figure out what went wrong down to the finest point. While almost everyone goes through this process of analyzing the moves, Martin was exceptionally good at it. Because both of his parents were very strategic, he was never torn, as many others are, between strategic success and human connection, or between strategic success and inner truth. He was able to concentrate all his intelligence on deciphering the complexities of propriety and advantage. His strategic skill became so good, it was able to get him everything he needed in the way of success and adoration. Meanwhile, the more powerful he became, the more he saw the turmoil of self-doubt as the disgusting drudgery of lesser beings.

Perfecting the Winning Posture

As a young man Martin concluded that there was no point in confronting people. If they acted petty, arrogant, or foolish, he simply kept track so he would know what to expect. He didn't believe people could change; he was not about to go out on a limb with his observations or disappointments; so he acted pleasantly and remembered everything.

He found himself interested in politics. Not in the sense of choosing sides or debating issues, but in observing the winning process. Even in his teens, it seemed clear to him that politics was very theatrical and that it usually had more to do with maneuvers than with issues. In politics, it rarely seemed to matter what you did, only how you talked about it. Voters didn't line up according to what they believed in; the candidate who controlled the debate was the candidate who won. The more Martin thought about these things, the more he was able to apply them to arguments with his parents, to job interviews, to college grades. Why be nervous when speaking in class about what you don't understand, when nervousness gets you a D or an F while confidence gets you at least a B? His early political articles captured the essence of this process, and he soon acquired a reputation for political acuity.

As he applied this acuity to his own life, it contributed to his streamlined perfection. The measured gestures that thrill and intimidate the younger men at *Today*—the well-tempered nod; the knowing smile; the regulated eyebrows; the considered examination of his watch; his overt and calculated way of straightening his tie, brushing out a crease, or arranging his hair so that he never appears self-consciously vain; his ability to maintain a bullet-proof shield around the otherwise most intimate of acts—are all the result of years of study and training with the best coach in the business, himself. Nothing about him was spontaneous any more and very little took him by surprise, for he never stopped playing interpersonal chess and he was always thinking several moves ahead. By the time he reached his late twenties, success had carried him away from almost all contact with his deeper feelings. His vulnerability—the self-doubts, the longings, the shame, the true human substance—became a distant, forgotten thing. He thought less and less about his ideals and dreams as they progressively lost relevance to the life he had chosen. His dedication to winning constituted a train that sped him away from those abandoned aspects of himself.

The Wrong League

Although the depths of experience are now sealed off to him, Martin finds the life of a winner very absorbing. There are always new trophies to attain, new applause to receive. He feels good to be batting .320 and still better about the possibility of raising his average in the future. And yet, in some sense, Martin knows he is batting in the wrong league, for he is neglecting his greatest skill.

Martin has the rare mind that is both receptive and skeptical. He is quick to see through shoddy thinking or sleight of hand and is able to accurately unravel the way it works. He sees the way the speaker moves the crowd, he sees the changes in the crowd's chemistry, but, although Martin experiences the chemical reactions, he is not captured by them. He is not confused by appeals to emotion, by popular prejudice, by dogma, or by his own desires to believe. He is able to return and report his observations in a way that sharpens everyone's understanding of social phenomena.

But from the moment his mother placed him on his pedestal, Martin's subject qualities have been at war with his analytic gift. His early writings often focused sharply on injustice and exploitation in public life. But there were certain aspects of himself and his relationships that he could not allow himself to examine too closely for fear of exposing the emotional exploitation upon which his security is based. As a young man he'd developed two sets of standards: He reserved his penetrating eye for the political world he wrote about and lived his private life blindly, as if governed by a mystical doctrine that could never be spoken or observed.

As the inequality of his relationships became more pronounced, Martin found it harder to deny the inconsistency between his public and private values. His enthusiasm for political analysis waned. The power relationships of social groups, the insidious privileges and injustices, resonated with his own insidious privileges and struck him as inevitable. Sensing his loss of objectivity, he felt the juice being sapped from his most vital quality.

His interest in winning and applause, however, did not wane. Indeed, it took up the slack. His success in journalism, instead of being used as a vehicle to ask more penetrating social questions, was now turned into a quest for institutional power. He wants to be a leader. But leadership is not Martin's talent. He has little sense of what leadership means beyond having control and sitting atop the heap. Because he doesn't understand that leadership is essentially a position of service, because he is drawn to it largely as an outgrowth of his subject orientation, life there always feels hollow to him. As he drifts away from reporting and into management, the hollowness makes him a little more desperate and a little more destructive in his quest to get ahead.

More and more, beneath the layer of strategic prowess is a vast and disturbing unknown, and anyone who threatens to pierce his armor and make him experience that void—anyone who is unhappy with second-class citizenship, who demands more from him or who is equally bent on being one-up—must be eliminated from Martin's life. And with the whole world telling him how perfect he is, why shouldn't he weed out the neurotics, the malcontents, the egotrippers? A brother, a parent, a girlfriend, a job, a pet, anyone or anything that doesn't fit the requirements of his streamlined life is abandoned. Except Georgette.

It's not just weakness, as Martin tends to think, or that Georgette is a magnificent trophy, or that he's grown accustomed to having her there. She is the only one whose respect and caring for him is not based purely on fear, dazzlement, or opportunism. She's the only one who values something deeper in him than his image and his talent for winning. She's made a connection to some part of his hidden self, and he's grown dependent on that connection. Despite the trouble she causes him, she is, for him, a perfect combination of the docile and dynamic.

Although Martin is never quite aware of it, Georgette gives him something very important. And whenever she has left or threatened to leave, he has panicked. For he is frightened that without her, he wouldn't feel like such a superstar, that he might lose a hundred points off his average in the first year.

21.

Georgette—The Object's Story

How a spirited woman let her marriage go off the tracks by neglecting her power. How she came to feel like a "need machine," and now wonders, "Where did my marriage go wrong?"

"PEOPLE ARE ALWAYS telling you how much they think you're worth. By how often they call, by the tone they use, by how well they listen, by whether they're late or on time. If your stock is high, you get thank yous, apologies, acknowledgements. If your stock is low, you get nods, pats evasions.

"I had a boyfriend in college who thought the sun rose at my feet. I can hear him telling my mother what a wonderful pianist I was, what a genius at chemistry, that I had the greatest legs since Betty Grable. My mother could never understand why I didn't marry him. And it's not that I didn't love Irv. I did. I still do.

"I had more fun with Irv than anyone I've ever known. Whether it was time, money, or emotions, he couldn't be bothered measuring who gave what to whom. There wasn't a stingy, chiseling, paranoid bone in his body. I could cook for him, chauffeur him, tell him secrets—and never worry about being taken advantage of. The only thing I had to worry about with Irv was taking advantage of him.

"I realize now that I didn't reject Irv *because* he adored me. It had nothing to do with the old saw about never joining a club that would have me for a member. I rejected Irv because I lost respect for him, and I lost respect for him because one day I began to withdraw and Irv did nothing about it.

"I was young. This was my first big relationship. And I began to have doubts. What was I getting into? Was Irv the man I wanted to marry? Was I ready for such a commitment? I used to tell Irv everything, but when these thoughts entered my mind, I felt guilty and I clammed up. I wasn't mature enough to understand what was happening or to be able to express it to Irv. I was ashamed of my inconstancy, as if all the loving things I'd said to him were now lies. But clamming up only made it worse. It was as if a glowing spot within me started to shrink and grow cold. I wish I could have told Irv what I was feeling. I wish he could have forced me to tell him. But it didn't work that way.

"There must have been a moment when I acted as if Irv was not a very important person to me, and he let it pass. There must have been a moment when he dreamed aloud about our future while I acted silly or dreamed silently about another man, and he let that pass. There must have been a hundred times when Irv said the complimentary things that once meant so much to me and I despised him for it. I began to act out my disrespect in obnoxious ways, like a wicked little girl, hating myself for being that way and hating him for allowing it.

"As it turned out, I never did have to ask myself any of those questions about commitment or what I was ready for or what I wanted in life. Because once I lost respect for Irv, the only issue that existed between us was his inadequacies. I became absurdly secure in the relationship, like a queen with her valet. I had a terrible sense of power, as if I was watching Irv on a TV screen and evaluating him. My entire perception of him changed. Whereas once I thought him bright and original, I now thought him abstruse and impractical. Whereas once I thought him earnest and idealistic, I now thought him dull. Any Joe Lockerroom seemed more significant and interesting. His mannerisms lost their charm. He seemed pedantic; that made me impatient. Oh, I tormented him. Even his physical qualities changed. If he had a mole or a twitch, it became magnified. Day by day, he became a collection of ugly features, a monster. It wasn't too long until, for the life of me, I couldn't figure out what I'd seen in him.

"In the past year I've fallen into that position with Martin, the one Irv was in with me. For a couple of months now we've been doing an insane dance. We have fights, we make nice, I try to get things from him, he tries to appease me. What he gets me for my birthday, the amount of time he spends at work, his every 'please,' his every smile I measure. I feel like I'm standing over him with a stick. But it's all a charade. I make him guilty to no purpose. Because I still don't feel like an equal. I feel like a valet in revolt. A rebellious waterboy."

Giving Protection

"I've always protected Martin from embarrassment. I don't know how I got into that habit—maybe I do it with everybody. I've never wanted to let him look bad. I'm thinking now of the days before we got married. I might say something that threatened him, like, 'Let's take a cab.' Martin would grin and say, 'Never heard of the subway, Vassar girl?' And I'd smile and let it pass, because I knew money was a hot issue for him.

"We both knew very well I wasn't a Vassar princess and I had to struggle for every cent I had. But each little incident like that built an attitude into our relationship. Martin would start getting slightly paternalistic, and I'd find myself acting girlish. Gradually, that became the given: He was Daddy and I was the little girl. If you try to act like an adult now, you're breaking the contract. You push a little harder, and you're starting a fight. And I *would* start fights. But the girlishness had become such a prominent part of my way of relating to him that I would fight girlishly. While Martin seemed like a moderate, reasonable adult.

"When we first started talking about getting married, I told Martin I wanted to keep my maiden name. Martin's attitude was, 'Well, in that case, why don't we forget about my marriage and just keep living together?' I said, 'Well, what about children?' And he said, 'We'll cross that bridge when we come to it.' I thought, maybe he doesn't want a wife named Stepanchin, or maybe he'd be threatened if his wife didn't take his name. Now I think he was simply hurt. Taking his name was a symbol of my love for him. But he couldn't tell me that. He would have felt like a beggar. And I certainly didn't know how to get him to tell me or how much I needed to hear it. What a different complexion it would have put on everything, if Martin could have given me that, if he could have said, 'I'd like you to take my name, Georgette. It tells me that you love me.' Instead it was, 'No name change, no marriage,' and I knuckled under. In the end I felt crummy about my family's name, crummy about being different from other women, crummy about knuckling under.

"I got even with him. I always did. After enough incidents like that, I'd harden and walk out. Martin would send flowers and spout poetry and remember my favorite things, and I'd say to myself, 'Look, he loves me, there are just some things he can't give.' So I'd return. And the cycle would resume."

The Emperor's Napkins

"When I first met Martin, he had more poise, more confidence, more sense of his own destiny than any man I'd known. He was exciting to be with. He had a way of making me feel special. He had an ability to see through people and to capture something about the hidden workings of things that I've never encountered in another person. And when I saw through him, it was particularly touching because this was a man the whole world believed was perfect. I was going to be the one to share his secrets.

"One morning, a few months after we started going together, I was at his place up by Columbia, reading the Sunday *Times* while Martin cleaned up breakfast. I noticed him slinking toward the cupboard and doing something covert. I said, 'Martin, what are you doing there?' He said, 'Nothing.' So I walked over and saw that he was folding the paper towels we'd used for napkins. I said, 'What are you doing with the paper towels?' He looked peculiar, jittery, as if I'd caught him at something. He said, 'Well, they've hardly been used.' 'Oh,' I said, teasing, 'So you're going to, what, save them for lunch?'

"He looked at me as if he was being unmasked. I thought one more question and he's going to faint. I said, 'Why are you so upset?' He shrugged and said, 'I don't know, it's absurd.' And then he turned and resumed his cleaning.

"I couldn't imagine why he was in such a state. I teased him some more. I said, 'It's fine with me if you save the paper towels—I just want you to make sure I get the same one for lunch I had for breakfast.' He didn't think that was funny. He kept shuffling about, putting away dishes, wiping and rewiping the counter until I got the impression that if I didn't leave him alone he would explode.

"Well, Martin is Mr. Neat, and the only things out of place in the kitchen now were those two folded, used paper towels. I don't know what made me do it, but just then I opened the cabinet above the sink. And there they were. A *hundred* neatly folded, used paper towels. Martin squeaked. A little 'UH' lurched out of his throat. I could not stop laughing. 'Oh, Martin,' I said, 'you really are such a sickie!' I was in stitches; I could barely hold myself up. Martin looked embalmed. He turned away and said officiously, 'Are you going to see me again?' I slid to the floor laughing myself silly. Martin stepped over me and marched out of the apartment, and didn't come back for twenty minutes.

"When he walked in, I said, 'Some host you are!' I could see by the set of his mouth that he wasn't sure whether to get angry all over again or apologize or make a joke. Before he could speak, I said, 'Look, Martin, it's nothing to be so upset about. So you're a little neurotic. I still like you. I'd like you even if you were the bull goose looney of a Hundredth and Fourteenth Street.'

"'All right,' Martin sniffed. 'But it's not *neurosis*. I just don't happen to believe in unnecessary waste.'

"'*Oh*, I suppose you save little pieces of string. And used envelopes. And styrofoam cups. Let's open a few more of these closets. God knows what we're going to find—old newspapers, broken umbrellas, used condoms. . . . Do you wash out your coffee filters and save them too?' By this time Martin was beginning to see the humor of the situation, and he was laughing and kissing me and making funny faces.

"We spent the rest of the day together. It was one of those timeless days, when it didn't matter what we did. I remember lying on the grass in Riverside Park, laughing about the kitchen incident, Martin's telling me about his father (a real skinflint), his favorite aunt, lots of childhood stuff about money and scrimping. I still remember what it was like that night in bed.

"But then something very typically Martin happened. He could not forget those paper towels. I saw the whole thing as a foible. I was relieved to see he *had* one. I loved him a little more for it. But some devil inside Martin told him I had the goods on him and unless he did something about it, he was going to fall under my control. As if I was going to make him throw away all his paper towels or start taking cabs!

"Periodically over the next few weeks he interrogated me about my attitude toward money. Eventually we agreed that my relative freedom with money, and material things in general, represented a kind of irresponsibility, and after that he was appeased. Pretty soon he was folding those used paper towels and putting them in the cupboard with the same erect, precise movements he used for everything else. And for years afterwards, if I went to throw out the breakfast napkins, Martin would raise one eyebrow and say, 'Waste not, want not,' at which point, like a jerk, I'd fold them up for him."

The Dissatisfaction Neurosis

"Whenever I've felt unhappy with Martin, I've always dreamed of his changing—becoming less neurotic about money, more able to show appreciation, less threatened by my relationship with Marge, less obsessed with becoming famous. I've looked at things in terms of his hang-ups; but I don't look at things that way any more. The way I relate to him is the problem. The way I give, as Irv did, like a constant 'on' faucet, regardless of what I get or don't get in return. Shielding him from embarrassment, indulging his obsessions, accepting his name, letting him off the hook, all without the slightest mindfulness.

"They say that giving is better than getting. They say that life is better if you don't measure. But at a certain point you have to ask yourself, 'Why do I keep giving if it hurts?' It's one thing to give if you truly feel like giving. Then it's the most exhilarating experience in the world. But it's another if you keep giving because you're afraid of what will happen if you stop. Or if you can't demand what you need because you're afraid of feeling selfish. Or if you can't drive a fair bargain because you're afraid of getting dumped. Certainly that's not what Jesus or Buddha or any of them had in mind when they proclaimed the beauty of selflessness.

"It was nice going to bed with Martin after his fight with Marge in April. I could see he wanted to make up and that he was in a highly demonstrative mood, to say the least. But here was another case where I let something go by. I needed him to admit he'd behaved badly. He'd made my best friend feel unwelcome in our home. How could I let that stand? How could I give him forgiveness without getting an apology? Isn't that the usual rate of exchange? But I sensed that if I pushed for an apology, his heart would have hardened, and I didn't want to risk that. I didn't want to jeopardize the moment. I wanted to be connected to him and I wanted him to want me, and I guess I was willing to pay the price. So I told myself I was being picayune in holding on to this apology thing, and I ended up with a vague feeling of dissatisfaction, which months later I still feel.

"Martin has never been able to understand my 'dissatisfaction neurosis.' And neither have I. Here is a man who is intelligent, energetic, attentive in numerous ways, a concerned father, and yet I'm never satisfied. He gives me vases and I want a coat. How selfish! How ungrateful! And yet that's the way I feel. The dissatisfaction neurosis, *it's clear to me now*, is a symptom of the poor rate of exchange I've been getting. It's like an unpaid debt. And now it's gotten to the point where I don't know if I want to collect."

Review 5

1. The willingness to give credence to your self-doubts—"Maybe I'm not doing this right," "Maybe they have reason to be angry"—keeps you open and flexible. Martin's unwillingness to entertain such questions is part of his rigid subject orientation. Jake, on the other hand, by giving such questions too much credence, undermines himself.

2. A power vacuum may start as a tiny bubble, but if left uncorrected, it will expand into an enormous liability. As the powerphobic hesitates to act, the judgments made against him grow firmer, the self-doubts of others recede to nothingness, his own self-doubts become thunderous, and possibility of correction grows more remote.

3. Domination is not the only means by which a subject maintains his invulnerability. He also eliminates those who refuse to play his game. Martin reveals his underlying humanity by his inability to abandon a troublesome Georgette.

4. Georgette tends to seek relationships in which she can play out her object quality. But her sense of self-worth eventually makes her fed up and determined to leave. What she lacks is the faith that she can stay and make a change.

VI.

THE REPLAY

Making Fundamental Change

22.

Georgette Revisited

How Georgette can tackle Martin by learning to *balance the giving and the getting*. Driving harder bargains, smoking out feelings, being assertive, rebuilding the old contract.

When you give more than you get, and do so out of weakness, you suffer. And the pain you experience raises questions that preoccupy your mind.

Do I care more than he cares? Why am I always the one to call? Why are the gifts I give always bigger? Am I doing something wrong? Can they smell my flaws? Am I hung up on things other people take in their stride?

For the power to be balanced in any relationship, the giving and getting must be balanced. Not in the sense of making everything tit for tat, but in the sense that both people care equally and give equally of themselves, so that neither takes the other for granted.

If Georgette wants a certain type of vacation, will Martin accommodate her? Will he make an effort to understand her when she's upset? Will he try to adjust to her changing needs? Each answer reveals something about the value he places on her, and at the moment the answers do not look good.

Martin is unaware of all he gets from Georgette. He does not realize that he feels good about himself partly because Georgette nourishes him. And unless Georgette makes an effort to get the appreciation she deserves, she will be doing herself, Martin, and the relationship a disservice. In the end, she may get fed up, walk out, and never come back, and Martin won't have the slightest idea why.

Georgette has to do four things to transform this relationship. One, of course, is not to put up with any abuse. The rest have to do with giving and getting. She has to make firm and consistent demands. She has to speak up more about her feelings and press Martin to do the same. And she has to make a declaration of independence in a crucial area where her dependency on him has become unhealthy. Let's see how she can bring this about.

I. Driving Harder Bargains

In some relationships you can get what you need from others by manipulating them with rewards. That's what Georgette has managed with mixed results with Carmen. In others you can be direct: "Look, this is how things are, and this is what I'm not getting." But in Georgette's marriage neither of these techniques will work. She has to drive harder bargains by applying persistent pressure. Although driving bargains activates her shame about being selfish, she must suffer with that and do it all the same:

• "When are we going to celebrate my birthday? . . . It's important to me. . . . We don't have to do it on the right night. . . Don't you like it when we celebrate your birthday?"

• "Don't be cute, Martin, I'm pissed off. . . . I don't want to talk about that. . . . I'm not interested in what Marge did; I'm interested in what you did." And so on until he says, "Sorry."

Georgette hates this process. She feels it shouldn't be so hard to get her husband to please her. She thinks, "Knowing how hard I had to work for it will kill its value when I get it." Such bargaining may indeed kill her fantasy of the ideal marriage, but when she gets the apology, she'll feel good about it; and when her birthday comes, and Martin's there, she'll be happy to have him.

Georgette has to *retrain* Martin, as odd as that may sound. During the first ten years of their marriage she's trained him to believe he didn't have to give much to get by. Now, through persistent and patient demands, she has to get him used to a new regime.

Some of this will require negotiation. You want me to keep cooking, despite the fact that I work full-time; well, this is what I expect from you. Martin is prepared for this. Yes, he may put up some resistance. Why change a good deal, after all? But because he knows Georgette is right, he'll cave in as soon as he's sure she's not willing to bend.

Because they have developed an unequal contract, Georgette has to keep measuring. She has to make demands, make deals, negotiate a new position. If she feels some self-doubt over this ("Petty!" "Legalistic!" "Princess!"), she'll have to shove these doubts aside, not let them show on her face, in body language, or in her voice, and not let them weaken her resolve to go forward. And, if, in the process, she occasionally has to withhold what she's given unconditionally in the past, Martin may come to value it that much more.

II. Smoking Out: Getting to Martin's Feelings

Georgette never tries hard enough to get Martin to open up. Even at his most passionate, he will rarely say, "I love you," "I need you," or "I think you're wonderful." When he's been nasty, she can get an apology at times, but she never gets an explanation beyond his claim that he was suffering from a headache or was overwhelmed by work. She is forever guessing and interpreting.

Smoking out is a way of questioning someone in order to get to what he's feeling. Getting feelings out from between the lines neutralizes innuendoes, barbed humor, and evasions, and it helps make responsibility clear.

Strong Smoking Out. 1) When Martin argues with her about hanging her lithograph in the bedroom, Georgette immediately makes premature assumptions about his dictatorial intentions. The simplest way to perform a reality check is to question him evenly. "Why are you so adamant about the living room?" "Are you sure you'd be unhappy if we hung it here?" "What if we hung it in the bedroom for a trial period?" Such an approach is much better than flying off the handle, which distracts from the subject at hand.

The basic skills of smoking out are the ability a) to ask short, forthright questions; b) to be patient and to tolerate silence; c) to repeat oneself when confronted by diversionary and irrelevant responses; d) to control the emotional content of one's tone; and e) to withstand accusations of being hypersensitive or overanalytical. The process can squeeze out information that, once spoken, eliminates subtle, hidden threats.

There is something essentially *wrong* about Martin's position. How can he oppose Georgette on the disposition of this gift, especially when it hasn't been like him in the past? If Georgette can keep her irrational assumptions under control and get off her liberationist fervor ("No more shit from you!"), she'll avoid making a wrong move and Martin will be kept on the hot seat.

Eventually Martin will have to yield in some way: "I don't know why I'm getting like this. Would it be all right with you if we put it aside till tomorrow?" Or perhaps he'll find some face-saving diplomacy to get them both off the hook. In the best of all possible worlds, he'd go to the real source of his distress and start talking about how he's been feeling about Georgette lately—about her depression, overeating, and defeatism. Either way, the power will be balanced and a sense of equal partnership will prevail.

2) Smoking out can sometimes make a hidden abuse backfire. When Martin makes a nasty comment about the fur coat and 57th Street, Georgette doesn't need to counterattack viciously. All she has to do is get him to pick up his bloody stiletto and stand there holding it for a while.

Georgette: "So what are you saying? You don't want to buy me a coat?"

Martin: "Well, I don't really think you need it."

This is a good start; already the balance is beginning to shift.

Georgette: "Well, what do you honestly think about it, Martin? Don't joke, I'd like to know. Would you ever buy me a fur coat? What if we had more money? You don't feel our stereo is extravagant? What about the rent we pay? What about the car? We didn't have to buy a BMW. We didn't really need the leather upholstery. I don't care what the Friends of Animals says. What do you say? Do *you* disapprove of my wanting a fur coat?"

Martin: "No, I don't disapprove, I just find it kind of statusy and extravagant."

Georgette: "It sounds as if you disapprove."

Martin: "Well, maybe. It does seem unnecessary."

Georgette (with a touch of anger): "It's necessary to me." Exit.

Notice that Georgette may compromise the whole operation if she tells Martin what he's thinking, ("So, you think I just want a fur coat to keep with the Joneses!") or makes furious accusations ("How thrifty you are whenever it comes to me!"). She can't risk allowing her interpretations to become the issue. When dealing with a very strategic person, asking questions is much safer.

Georgette will also be strategically weak if she puts more cards on the table by arguing for her right to the coat or trying to convince Martin that she deserves it. She will only walk away feeling worse.

Georgette has asked the questions in the spirit of wanting to get things straight, and now she's gotten her answers. She hasn't gotten the coat (more about that shortly), but strategically speaking, she's achieved a great deal.

Having been forced to state his case and climb through some of its logical inconsistencies, Martin has weakened his position. Instead of walking away confident (My dopey wife wants a mink), he's left doubting and troubled (I asked my wife what she wanted for her birthday, she told me, and I've refused. Am I in trouble with her? Am I being stingy?).

Weak Smoking Out. Smoking out can be a very giving process at times and one has to guard against giving too much. When Martin is gnawing over a hurt, he is unable to go to Georgette for help. Instead, he acts sullen and rejecting, almost like a pouting child, anticipating that Georgette will eventually become so uncomfortable that she'll come to his aid. And, indeed, this is what she does. She expends a lot of energy asking a lot of questions, until the source of Martin's frustration emerges. Martin is able to get from her without asking, without actively cooperating, without ever giving Georgette credit for what she's done.

Georgette would be better off following Grace Donohue's example. When Jake becomes pouty and unpleasant, Grace grows cooler and cooler. It isn't so much a punishment as a quiet sort of disappearing act, which makes Jake realize that if he is going to get her to help him, he'll have to stop being petulant and ill-humored and ask for help.

Personal Power and Smoking Out Combined: Eliciting the Deeper Feelings

The Grodin marriage suffers from a lack of straight talk about differences, disagreements, and dissatisfactions. Martin has Georgette convinced that her dissatisfactions are a neurosis of some sort, but if Georgette is going to save her marriage, not to mention her self-worth, she has to get past her suspicion that Martin is right. She must speak up about her dissatisfactions in as persistent and agreeable a way as she can.

Martin has to know that she is not happy about the way the details of the marriage have been worked out, that she can't tolerate some aspects of his behavior, that there are times when she doesn't respect him. He can't be allowed to walk through life with his fantasies about himself and the marriage unchallenged.

In addition to exercising her personal power this way, Georgette also needs to get Martin to exercise his. Sometimes her expressions of dissatisfaction will cause him to get angry and express some of his own. That will be all to the good. But often he will simply become cold and distant, and she will have to start a campaign to bring him out. Some of the factors:

1. *Relentless pressure*. Martin is like a man hiding in a tent, who must be invited to join Georgette in an open talk about something that he's ashamed of. Georgette first has to convince Martin that the ground outside the tent is safe. She must convey that he has a right to his feelings, whatever they are, and that she will not make him sorry for expressing them. And then she must begin to make life inside the tent uncomfortable—by shooting arrows into it, by cutting off supplies, by continuous pressure. She must make Martin know that life cannot go on as usual until he steps outside and talks to her about what's going on within him.

Keep in mind the difference between punishing Martin for refusing to be honest and punishing him for what he feels. If Georgette cries or makes Martin feel guilty because he says something that upsets her, he will be doubly afraid of venturing that way again. His honesty should be rewarded, not punished. Her position should be not, "How dare you harbor such feelings about me!" but rather, "I'm not going to allow you to dodge me about something so important to both of us."

2. *Do good feelings have to be spoken?* At least some of the time, yes. If Martin only acts loving, never says anything about why she's so important to him, Georgette is being robbed of essential nourishment that could elevate her sense of importance. After the Marge incident, Georgette accepted the petting without the words. If she had smoked Martin out about his abuse of Marge, she might have discovered that Martin had been feeling lonely and blue and that he wanted her for himself. How long has it been since he's opened up to her that way, since she's seen that he has vulnerabilities and that he needs her?

3. *What about the bad feelings?* Let's suppose Georgette gets Martin to open up about some of his obnoxious behavior in the last few weeks. And let's suppose Martin says, "I feel disgusted with you when you become depressed and overeat." Is learning this worth her effort?

Very much so. For one, Georgette will no longer be in the dark about Martin's feelings. She will be free of the extreme fear and uncertainty that is the worst part of worrying about what someone you love is feeling. She may also learn something about herself. Martin knows her very well, after all, and if he is losing respect, there may be a good reason for it. An honest talk with him could get her going again.

Remember that Martin, by exposing what he feels in an open, nonstrategic way, will be forfeiting his upper hand. If he speaks openly and respectfully of his disrespectful feelings, it will be a turning point. Something *equal* is happening between them.

4. *The long-term effect.* The campaign to smoke Martin out about his feelings may be a long one. Georgette will have to be patient and guard against falling into the role of nag or shrew. She'll have to watch for various punishments and other maneuvers that Martin will label "just expressing my feelings." And she will have to recognize that even a successful campaign to balance the power will not necessarily result in perfect harmony.

But the levels of exposure must nevertheless become more balanced, and Georgette should not give up until Martin is willing to speak—even if she has to raise the subject twice a week for three months and live a slightly estranged marriage for the duration.

III. Rebuilding the Old Contract: A Declaration of Independence

Subjects and objects live by a double standard. If Georgette forgets Martin's birthday, that's a hurtful, almost inexplicable oversight, a virtual crime. But if Martin forgets Georgette's birthday, it's boyish irresponsibility, it's the prerogative of an important man, it's something that can be brushed aside with a display of charm. The double standard has its origins in their training.

Martin is still living in the family system he grew up with, still a little prince in his closest relationships. Georgette's object training—give, give, give!—folds neatly into his expectations. She too is living in her family system. Their childhood attitudes were built into the contract of the relationship early on and it soon seemed impossible to imagine things any other way.

Martin's tendency is to structure everything to suit his needs. He is able to convince himself (with Georgette's passive collusion) that Georgette's needs are satisfied, too. Then, periodically, seemingly out of nowhere, her eruptions of dissatisfaction turn his world upside down.

Georgette tells herself that she is neurotic, but she knows in her bones that she gives a lot to Martin and does not get an equal measure in return. Out of that bone-level knowledge comes the desire for a major symbolic gift, a fur coat.

The coat is a healthy expectation on Georgette's part, but Martin doesn't want to give such a gift in the context of his disrespectful feelings. He won't even talk about it in a respectful way. He and

Georgette are trapped, and a simple, straightforward solution, is not immediately possible.

Now, it is possible that by smoking him out Georgette can create a balance in the way they *talk* about the coat, but chances are she still won't get the coat. What is she to do? Georgette may be furious. She may want to put nails in his soup. But generally it is a mistake to try to balance the giving and getting by punishing. The most powerful strategic action Georgette can take is to buy the coat with her own money.

True, there is something punishing and guilt-inducing in this, but more important, it is a declaration of independence, much like her trip to Greece many years ago. With one act she tells Martin that he cannot take her for granted, that she is a separate person, that the assumptions upon which he's based his contented view of the world are not sound. The purchase recreates the balance between them by symbolically reducing the emotional commitment on her end. This would be essential to her self-respect even if it had no impact on Martin.

But of course it does have an impact on Martin. One of the great falsities created by an imbalance in giving and getting (aside from the sense that one person is superior to the other) is a skewered sense of dependency. Georgette feels desperately needy because Martin is always beyond her grasp. In reality, Martin is as dependent on her as she is on him, but because she is so blatantly, almost slavishly, available, he barely notices his need for her. Never hungry, never failing to get what he wants, he walks through life as if he has no needs at all.

But suddenly the sight of that fur coat on Georgette is very unsettling to Martin. He feels a hunger and an insecurity that surprises him. He reaches for Georgette, and, as he does, the opportunity arises for them to come closer on a more equal footing. If Georgette thinks about the process like this, buying the coat becomes a goal worthy of a major commitment, of scrimping, saving, even borrowing.

But buying the coat is only a step. If, afterwards, she goes back to sleep, much as she did after her trip to Greece, the opportunity will be squandered.

Guidelines for a Declaration of Independence

1. *Don't confuse balancing with retribution*. Georgette has to keep in mind that her goal is to balance the giving and getting and not to

get revenge or to end eight years of dissatisfaction with one blow. If Martin feels attacked, the more subtle effect of regulating the giving and getting is lost, and a new layer of power struggle is imposed on the old.

2. *Keep it clean*. The basic rule of keeping any strategy tempered is to avoid becoming one with it. Buy the coat, get it over with, go on to other things. Something will change.

Georgette should neither cover up her declaration of independence with false lightness nor make too much of it. Above all she should not let Martin maneuver her into revealing the strategic implications of the purchase. ("Are you trying to tell me something with this coat?" "No, it's just something I've wanted for a long time.") Exposing her hand is weak if Martin is still maneuvering. Meanwhile, if he begins to give more, she can accept his giving safely and without resentment.

3. *Don't worry about how much he understands*. The ungiving person does not necessarily know that he's ungiving, nor does he have to be made to know. He just has to give.

Conclusion

One of the obstacles the reforming object faces, like the reforming alcoholic, are people who expect her to go on being what she was. Martin's superior position is pleasantly addictive. He doesn't like his prerogatives taken away. He doesn't like to have to worry about Georgette's problems or to bend to Georgette's needs, especially when he is accustomed to having her bend to his. The imbalance also causes him to feel down a bit on Georgette, and for this reason, too, he will resist efforts toward equality. It would be a nuisance and an inconvenience, and, besides, equality with a slightly inferior person is never especially appealing. As long as he is conveniently unconscious of all this, he'll defend this status quo with vehemence, angrily denouncing her for wanting to "change the rules in the middle of the game." Any one of us might behave the same way.

So Georgette has her work cut out for her. But if she continues to make demands, express her dissatisfactions, smoke him out, and if she declares her independence by purchasing the coat, she will balance the power and end her object role. Ultimately, she and Martin will either talk seriously about the marriage and their dissatisfactions with it or Georgette will have to accept that Martin is beyond her reach.

23.

Jake Revisited

The responsibilities of leadership. How Jake can solve his problems 1) by using *Creative Power* to build a cooperative relationship with Roland and 2) by *asserting legitimate authority* with Martin.

PEOPLE ARE SELFISH. What could be more natural? They want what they believe is best for themselves, even though they are not always enlightened in choosing it. Chuck wants an exciting night in bed; Marge wants to get off a sexual express that feels out of control. Jake wants journalistic innovation; Roland wants businesslike caution. Martin wants to put all his time into climbing his mountain; Georgette wants him to give more of himself to her.

The *realpolitik* mentality says that in each case only one person can be satisfied and that he can gain satisfaction only through strategic maneuver. The creative mentality says that somewhere in each situation exists a solution that will meet the best interests of both and that it can be approached cooperatively, as equal partners. Creative power is the capacity to identify and implement such solutions.

Look at the two most common ways in which good ideas go bad:

• If you're a subject, like Carmen, you try to institute change by fiat, and no matter how good you idea is, you're seen as a dictator and quietly resented. Carmen's husband, children, subordinates go along with her great new suggestions, because it's easier to say yes than negotiate with a hyperactive tank; but they drag their feet and never become committed.

• If you're an object like Georgette, you can talk brilliantly about change, but you are seen as a dreamer and not taken seriously. Occasionally Georgette does manage to get Martin's attention by making him feel guilty, by threatening to leave him, or by earnestly appealing to his better judgment. And, as a result, Martin agrees to a change. He says, "Okay, honey. No more using Cindy, work, or sex as a political football. From now on we'll confront each other more openly instead. And we'll put aside a little time each night to do nothing but be together."

But Martin's assent is meaningless because he's not truly committed to making changes. He either doesn't fully understand what it's all about, or he agrees because he thinks he ought to, or he harbors resistance of which he is unaware, or he's just humoring Georgette. And so the agreed-upon change—intelligent though it may be—is merely a surface gloss of openness over the customary strategic maneuvers, now operating at a subtler level.

So the first point to be understood about creative influence is that the power must be balanced before any genuine change can take place. If you're the slightest bit one-up or one-down, a cooperative effort is impossible. And the second point is that for a new avenue of growth to be successfully explored in any relationship, both people must be equally invested in making it work.

As we've seen on many occasions, the *realpolitik* mentality is often correct. Martin will never make common cause with Jake, and for Jake to try to be creative with him is folly. But with Roland, Jake has had a thriving and trustful relationship, only recently become murky. Creative leadership is needed to turn it around.

Part I. Tackling Roland: The Inner Aspect of Creative Power

Creative power depends on several skills. One is the ability to identify solutions. Another is the ability to offer the solution in such a way that power is shared and your idea becomes the equal property of yourself and the other person. Underlying these two capacities are two deeper capacities:

1. *Empathy.* Jake may want the struggle with Roland to end, but can he really offer peace and cooperation to a man whose motives he is

unable comprehend? Probably not. That's why he must get beyond his own sense of hurt and injustice and put himself in Roland's shoes.

To identify superficially—to be able to say, "Yes, I can see that Roland is in a tough spot, that he has to assert his authority"—is not enough. Jake has to really get inside his skin. To do so he has to remember a difficult time when he himself was in authority and couldn't speak his mind.

Picture Jake having a drink one evening—absent-mindedly watching the news, cursing the plight of a managing editor whose national news editor—the hideous Grodin!—is not completely under his control. What an ass I was to take the job under such circumstances! What an ass I was not to have seen it! Imagine having to walk on eggs in order to deal with a subordinate! Imagine having to hesitate before giving feedback. . . .

Suddenly Roland comes to mind. The similarity hits him. God, Roland must have the same problem with me! It's difficult to be honest with someone you look up to and whose approval you want. Imagine the humiliation Roland must feel—being in charge of this big corporation and subtly diminished by a mentor-subordinate he's afraid to question.

This act of identification is the first step toward creative power.

The potential for achieving such identification is always present. Any one of us can find the basis for identifying with anyone else. Such is the universality of human experience. But it's a forbidding task because our defenses stand in the way. As soon as Jake identifies with Roland, he can no longer think of himself as pure. If he wants to come up with a truly useful solution, though, he will have to be able to view Roland's self-interest with the same intensity as his own.

2. *Taking Responsibility.* The second component of the creative frame of mind, closely linked to empathy, is the ability to see one's own responsibility for all that has occurred. It, too, depends on abandoning defensive thoughts.

Jake is peeved by Roland's cavalier style of criticism, his intruding on editorial meetings, his failure to be straight. He wants to say, To hell with him!, tell him to shove his job, and walk away from the whole mess. He can't understand how a self-respecting, thoughtful person can act with so little awareness of the infantile and destructive things he does.

But if Jake takes a harder look, he can see that he has helped create this maneuvering atmosphere. Hasn't he, after all, played into Roland's fears? Hasn't he played the elder statesman role to the hilt? Hasn't he, in his friendly way, signaled that criticism is not really necessary or welcome? Hasn't he always been aware of how impressed Roland is with him; and hasn't he, out of a desire to make things easy for himself, encouraged Roland's hands-off, worshipful attitude? By recognizing his responsibility, Jake has a little less reason to feel wronged and a little more reason to accommodate.

Jake also has reasons to be proud. For he has consistently dampened strategic vibrations that might otherwise have led to full-scale conflict. He has struggled to keep the door open. He has resisted taking an adversarial position. Jake has to recognize his substantial positive responsibility, as well, or he won't feel good enough about himself to make a new contribution.

Establishing the Conditions for Creative Power

Jake now sees the solution. Both he and his boss need a systematic means by which Roland can, without apology, give Jake his feedback. Such a system would free Roland to speak his feeling rather than act them out in ways that undermine Jake. It seems so obvious now! If all along they'd had periodic meetings for this purpose, they'd surely be on better footing today.

Balancing the Power. Hitting upon a solution like this is one thing. But implementing it is something else. What's to stop Roland from going along without any real understanding or commitment? What's to stop him from viewing this as another act of weakness and using the new meetings to gain some more leverage? Whatever he does, he will certainly not, based on a mere suggestion, suddenly feel free to express his thoughts honestly, drop all his strategies, and act like a changed man. So Jake must first balance the power and clear the maneuvering atmosphere.

Jake and Roland have a reservoir of trust. Jake can rely on that to get Roland to talk about what's on his mind; but he has to convince Roland that the truth will be welcome.

Because Roland is in evasive gear, Jake's timing matters. It will be important to catch Roland in the right mood. When Roland was afraid that Jake would resign and sent him the toy gondola and apologetic note, that was one opportunity. An even better one arose after the Khoumeni interview when Jake's stock was high and he could have confidently suggested a private dinner. But, even then, how do you get someone to admit what he hasn't been willing to volunteer for months?

Jake: *"Ed, have you begun to have doubts about all those changes we spoke of so ardently three months ago?"*

The touch of humor ("so ardently") suggests, "Don't worry, I don't consider your word at that time sacrosanct." If Jake had said, "changes you agreed to," he might have increased Roland's rigidity by appearing to insist on the contract.

Roland: *"No, no, I wouldn't say 'doubts.' No, I hope you don't think that. Maybe some timing considerations, but, uh. . . ."* He shakes his head, shrugs, puffs his bottom lip, all to suggest, "No big deal."

Jake: *"Tell me about the timing considerations, Ed."*

What Jake is doing here is going after the slight opening Roland has allowed. He doesn't want to challenge. He doesn't want to arouse Roland's skittishness or adversary feelings. He draws him out a little at a time.

As Roland talks about the timing, he naturally mentions something about ad revenue or subscriptions. Jake is sympathetic. He wants to know all about it, and he wants to show Roland he considers it important. Once Roland is speaking freely about his anxieties, Jake has accomplished the first step. The subterranean messages have been dampened, expression has become freer, and the power between the two is more balanced.

An open exchange of views. But for creative power to work, a renewed sense of mutual respect is not enough. All the cards must be out on the table. Jake has to ask Roland why he hasn't spoken up before. He has to hear Roland say how uncomfortable he's been, that because of Jake's experience, he has difficulty being critical of Jake's plans. And Jake has to assure him that he respects Roland's role and needs his input.

By the end of the conversation both men need to experience what a frustrating period this has been for each of them, and both need to feel fully understood. There must be a complete exchange of personal power, so that by the time they're done, there's no sense of anything being hidden any more. They have full information and a united desire to change things. That is when Jake can open a new door and suggest that he and Roland walk through it together.

The door Jake opens is an agreement to meet regularly and share more information, so that they no longer operate in the dark about each other's motives or intentions. Such an arrangement is not something that Roland agrees to for Jake's sake, or vice versa. It is something they are each doing for themselves, that they each see as a solution to this problem, that they are each fully committed to and equally invested in. As a result, a fundamental change will take place in their relationship. Instead of communication by symbols and strategic gestures that was leading them toward a break, they will communicate openly.

Clearly, the future of the magazine has not been resolved. But the means for resolution now exist. Jake has gone into the core of the interpersonal machinery and restabilized a skidding relationship.

Part II. Tackling Martin: Asserting Legitimate Authority

Jake's decline at *Today* derives as much from his failure to punish Martin as his negligence with Roland and the worse matters get with Martin, the more insoluble all his problems seem. Many of the staff believe that Jake's defeat is inevitable, that Martin always held an unbeatable hand, or that despite his rank, Jake is helpless because he is simply too nice or too ineffectual. Jake is currently caught up in his powerphobic inhibitions, but if he awakens to the challenge, he can still master this conflict.

Jake has no problem demoting, reassigning, or firing for what he considers legitimate reasons, such as poor performance. But he sees Martin as a *personal* problem: "I resent him because I've been ordered to groom him." "I'm taking out on Martin hostility that should be directed at Roland." "I'm feeling insecure because of my doubts about the reforms." "I can't tolerate not having total, unquestioned control." Such are the thoughts that fuel Jake's inhibitions.

All the reservations and cautions that distinguish a decent person are over-developed in Jake. To punish Martin by loading him with unpleasant tasks or by taking away some of his favorite responsibilities strikes Jake as an abuse of authority, like the desperate act of a weak man who cannot endure opposition. But he is wrong. No one in authority can suffer insubordination and continue to function.

As managing editor, Jake has immense power to reward and punish. If he decides to use it, the only question he should trouble himself with is how to be sure he's not abusing his power or making a wrong move that will bring Roland into the picture.

If a worker is insubordinate, there are essentially four steps any manager can take to bring him into line:

STEP ONE. *State position.* Jake should reaffirm for Martin's benefit exactly what his editorial goals are and what he expects of Martin both as a senior editor and a key subordinate. He must leave no room for misunderstanding. This can be accomplished in a superficially friendly meeting between the two.

STEP TWO. *Express dissatisfaction*. If Martin's behavior does not change, Jake cannot overlook his lack of compliance, even in small things. He must state that he is dissatisfied and ask Martin whether he has any grievances.

Early in the game Jake has no way of knowing where Martin's rebelliousness stems from, and he cannot afford to rely on his own assumptions. If Martin speaks up and voices legitimate grievances, each man will have an opportunity to express his views. They can then work toward an accommodation or at least an understanding.

Of course, we know that no such reconciliation will take place. Martin will maneuver and deny everything, because he is playing to win. But by going through this step Jake can be satisfied that he's covered himself, that he's allowed for an open discussion, and that he's made his dissatisfaction known. Also, having watched Martin do his little dance, he will have a surer sense that his initial assumptions were not irrational.

STEP THREE. *Issue a warning*. The next time Martin is ever so slightly insubordinate, Jake must threaten him. Martin should be made to realize now that continued opposition to Jake, even in small ways, is going to cost him something. In most manager-subordinate conflicts this can be stated directly. But because Martin has higher connections of his own, a veiled threat is needed. Martin might be interested to learn, for example, that Jake is considering a reorganization that would ease Martin's burden somewhat by giving the new assistant managing editor some of Martin's most coveted tasks. It's obviously a threat, but the thin cover story ("The magazine will run more efficiently this way") operates as a shield to keep Roland from getting involved.

A threat in time may cause Martin to rethink his subversion, which was all along based on his perception that Jake was a pushover. The warning stage is thus very important. It represents an opportunity for positions to soften before the institution is burdened with internal war.

STEP FOUR. *Punish*. If Martin persists, Jake can decide that Martin must now share his monthly column with the psychology editor and the assistant managing editor, two of Jake's staunch allies to whom Roland is also positively disposed.

If Martin subsequently evinces a willingness to cooperate, Jake should let him out of the doghouse with a series of small rewards.

Such a combination of rewards and punishments is the most powerful device at Jake's disposal.

It's important to remember that Martin has hardened into his posture precisely because of the power vacuum Jake has presented. Yes, Martin is very ambitious. Yes, he is capable of being ruthless. Yes, he believes Jake's job was rightfully his.

But Martin is also smart. He respects power, he accommodates, he rarely causes trouble for those above him or commits himself to battles he can't win. True, he has an unusual relationship with Ed Roland, which makes him harder to control. But that only requires that Jake calculate his disciplinary moves more carefully.

The Question of Selfishness

Because Jake is so preoccupied with the destructive power of selfishness, we should point out that in this imaginary replay with Martin, Jake has indeed acted selfishly. But by taking legitimate steps to see that his authority is respected, he has also acted in the best interests of the institution he serves.

Selfishness exists even in creative power. A structured form of periodic feedback is every bit as much in Jake's interest as Roland's. But in creative power, the selfishness is taken to a higher level, because it is expanded to encompass the needs of the relationship rather than Jake's needs alone.

24.

Martin Revisited

The skills and awarenesses needed to break the habit of winning. How Martin could balance the power from the top and change his life.

It has long been said that masters are slaves, too, and that is true, but the average slave owner, living in the big plantation house, accustomed to service and cleanliness, eating fine food, entertained in the evenings and fanned in the heat, seeing his children coddled and educated, and happily deluded by the smiles and respectful attitudes of the lower beings around him, may think his life rather agreeable. The thought, if it should occur, that he is in some way diminished by the master-slave relationship, that it diverts him from his true destiny, is not likely to cause him to throw open the doors and invite the unwashed multitudes inside to share his linen, his silver, and his fine tobacco.

So, in some respects, there is little point in addressing the issue of how the subject can change. It may not be what he has in mind. Nevertheless, subjects do sometimes have a sense of the costs—and they can be severe— of being one-up. Many of us are only part-time subjects and not at all committed to staying that way. Even Martin, who manages so much control across the board, is dissatisfied by certain things and makes stabs at changing them.

He knows, for instance, that Georgette constantly gets back at him, with her damned petulance, forgetfulness, argumentativeness, lack of enthusiasm, and other nuisance acts of revenge. Might she be as open with him as she is with Marge if he were a little easier on her?

Wouldn't there be a little more zap in their sex if she felt more his equal? True, it's nice to be feared and respected at work, but Martin never knows whether he's liked or whether anyone is really pulling for him. And why doesn't he have any close friends? Could it be something in him? Even Martin has his moments when he considers making a change.

But when Martin thinks about change, he rarely thinks in terms of relinquishing advantage. Even if he thinks about changing himself (rather than, say, finding a new wife or putting his present one on tranquilizers), he dreams mainly about altering his feelings. He wonders whether he shouldn't be less judgmental, more tolerant, less self-involved, less possessive. But there's not much he can do about his feelings. Once he's become one-up, there's no way he can prevent himself from feeling disrespectful and making negative judgments. That comes with the territory. What Martin could change is his commitment to putting security above all else and the inevitable corollary of playing for advantage in order to feel secure. What he could change is the way in which he unthinkingly strikes at the vulnerability in others.

The Subject's Trap

Martin feels impotent to do anything about Georgette's dissatisfactions. "Why does the fact that I want to live in a certain style—high speed, ambitious, unemotional—have to make her feel compromised? Why does the fact that I am not interested in soul-searching conversations make her feel one-down?"

From his point of view Georgette is a queen—if she would only let herself be one. He can't understand why she doubts herself or why she drags herself through the mud of depression. If he knew that she felt like a second-class citizen with him, he would account for such feelings by citing her hesitations, weaknesses, and fears. He has no sense of his own responsibility.

And yet, here and there, he does make an effort. Sometimes, from out of his massive armamentarium, Martin sends a goodwill message, like a paper plane amidst the drone of his drums and engines. It may consist of the porcelain vases he bought for Georgette for her birthday, a gift into which he put a lot of care and thought, or an offer of assistance to a colleague he wants to befriend. The recipients of such good-will messages may not appreciate that the drums and engines are Martin's constant background hum and that the paper airplane is the significant gesture. So they remain cautious and perhaps a little fearful. But, for Martin, tossing the paper plane was like going way out on a limb. He feels as if he offered his hand and no one took it. He is hurt and feels belittled. The drums get louder and the bombers start rolling down the runway.

Because they are incomplete and ineffective, the secret stabs Martin takes at being a different person leave him slightly shaken and regretful and more confirmed in his way of life.

Stepping off the Pedestal

The key experiment Martin must make is to place himself more in the open—to express his feelings in an unprotected way, to bare some of his fears and shameful impulses, to risk experiencing just a little more anxiety, insecurity, and doubt than he is now willing to tolerate.

He has to try a little harder to trust that as he approaches Georgette without his armor of image and defensive maneuvers, she will not make the judgments his mother would. That if she responds to him more warmly when he's down, it's not because she can only love him in that condition. In short, he has to slowly reopen the vulnerability he has spent much of his life sealing up. If he can hang on through the initial pain and tumult, he may discover that top-dog privileges can be abandoned without creating a new reign of reverse exploitation.

How much he can open up—and how much he can do on his own, without therapeutic assistance—we do not know. For he must not only be willing to speak his vulnerable feelings, he has to know what they are. And after a lifetime of repression, of keeping the focus off himself, of automatically avoiding his own self-doubts by judging others, he will find it difficult now to reverse that process and know what he really feels. But, alone or with help, he will have to make the effort. And the key effort for him is in the realm of personal power. He must learn to be more direct about his desires and dissatisfactions, even if that cancels his subtle advantage.

He also needs to spend more time getting in touch with himself. Outside of therapy, the best way to do that is through an intimate connection. Georgette is the ideal person, but it might help to have another, as well, especially when he and his wife are feuding. He needs intimacy if he is going to expand the ground for his personal power—that is, if he is going to be able to speak certain feelings without being overwhelmed by shame and driven into protective maneuvers.

In the end, the more forthright Martin is, the less he will be burdened by the soul-destroying consequences of winning.

Would Martin *want* to do any of this? Perhaps not. The subject's way of life is the only security he knows. Although he often acts as if he were born with the rights of princes, Martin does not truly believe he has a right to feel what he feels and want what he wants, and so he is dependent on dominating others. The only legitimacy he knows is that which he gains from being on top. The force of repression, of old habits, of the contracts he makes keeps him riveted to this place. (Even some of the objects who surround him may discourage him from changing and punish him if he tries.) Martin might take a chance, might even seek help if he were suffering greatly. But, as it is, we have to doubt that a man like this could put aside his strategies in order to gain access to feelings that have been useless to him for so long.

But one never knows; people are surprising. And so let's imagine a slightly different Martin Grodin. He has all the same feelings, but he's willing to risk some insecurity, he's a little more aware of himself, and he has a better idea of what his options are. Granted, his habits are deeply ingrained and the journey may be hard, but if he wanted to take a step toward growth, this is how some of his best efforts might look.

A Forthright Martin Grodin

At the start our replay, Martin apologizes to Georgette for the way he walked out on her the morning after her birthday. Georgette responds by asking what got into him. At this point Martin can dodge ("I was in a bad mood, honey—please let's forget it happened") and reward (kiss, make nice, tell her he loves her), or he can struggle to be more honest.

Martin: "I was furious. I can't stand when you're depressed. I try not to say anything about it, because it feels like hitting you when you're down. But after two weeks of this, I'm ready to kill. I'm sorry. I should have said something sooner."

Martin is still turned off by Georgette's behavior. But he's out in the open. He's not controlling her.

Georgette: "But why get angry at me! I don't choose to get depressed."

Georgette's defensiveness is to be predicted. After all, at any moment Martin might put a subtle spin on his words and try to prove that she was the problem after all and that his brutality did have some justice.

What is Martin to do? Disagreements, questions, signs of mistrust, defensiveness of any kind tend to push him back toward his adversary assumptions (She's out to get me! She's saying I'm the cause of her depression! She wants total surrender!) or down into his self-hatred (Oh, why am I such a loathsome wretch?). He may start explaining himself and setting Georgette up as the judge ("I was so preoccupied, it just slipped out, it wasn't directed at you, you know I'm neurotic. . . ."). He may get drawn into contention ("I'm not *accusing* you of anything, I'm just trying to tell you where I'm at"). He may give in to temptation and reach ever so gently for control ("Well, didn't you say your brother also has trouble with your moods?").

If he does any of these things, his personal power will be dead. And so he must stay in touch with his central feeling and persist. He must try to have faith that Georgette's shield is only an inch or two thick, and not a mile wide as it now seems.

"It makes me angry. I can't help it. It's not as if you've got a disease or a broken leg. It has something to do with *us*. It's as if you're constantly telling me, *Look what you've done*. And I feel helpless to do anything about it. This morning"—he shakes his head remembering—"you seemed beyond my reach."

"But, Martin, that's when I really need you."

Georgette's defensive tone tells Martin he's missed a step somewhere. She has a hidden objection. Is she afraid that if she softens, she will in effect, condone his abusiveness?

"Georgette, I hope you understand. Nothing I'm saying now justifies the way I acted this morning. That was rotten, and that's all there is to it. I mean that."

"You do?"

"Yes. Absolutely."

"Well, I was crushed! I felt as if I'd been run over by a tractor! You could have taken me to Bellevue and slipped me under the goddamned emergency room door! I felt like a discarded piece of trash! You ruined my whole fucking morning! How can you be such a pig!"

Now things are looking up. Martin apologizes once more.

"Okay, okay, okay," she says. "So tell me again why you acted like that."

As Georgette becomes more receptive, Martin feels less anxious. His own defensive shield recedes and he has a heightened sense of his true motivations. "I'm a person who is trying to push a lot of things into a very small space," he says. "I want to do everything, and I don't like slowing down. Every second of my life is tightly organized and accounted for. I don't mind your feelings down once in a while. But when you get into one of your depressions, it's like a ball and chain. I know that doesn't sound very nice. But I feel as if I'm running down the road, balancing all my acts, feeling good about myself, when I look back to the side of the road and see that you've come to a complete stop. And I'm not an idiot. I know it has something to do with me. And that makes me hate it all the more. I feel, oh shit, now my life is going to come to a complete stop, too."

"Why a complete stop just because I'm depressed?"

"Just take this morning. I couldn't pretend you weren't miserable. But it was either deal with that or go play squash. And—this sounds terrible but—I really look forward to playing squash on Sunday mornings."

"But who told you not to play squash?"

"You didn't tell me not to play, but, you know, come on. Didn't you want me to stay home and comfort you?"

"Sure I would have liked it. But that wasn't the only thing you could have done. You could have said something sweet and promised to be back in a few hours. That would have been all right. But the anger. . . ."

"It was my guilt."

"And you made me feel like shit so you wouldn't feel guilty."

"More or less."

"More!"

"But I don't *feel* like saying something sweet when you're like this. I hate it. It's like you're an *invalid.*"

The word just came out. Georgette is stunned. An invalid. Yes, that's what she's been like. In a flash, she knows something about Martin's feelings that never occurred to her before. But she also feels hurt and doesn't know if she can speak.

"And," he adds, a little softer this time, "I feel as if you're punishing me with it. How would you like it if I shut you out and never spoke to you?"

Goals

Martin is trying to influence Georgette, but solely by making his point real to her. He wants forgiveness, but he's not angling for it between the lines. His words are potent, but they do not clutch, tickle, pet, or strike. There is a respectful distance between them. He allows her the freedom of her reactions.

With personal power Martin is able to talk about his feelings of disrespect in a respectful way. He can talk about his self-doubts without acting them out. He can speak his feelings without riding them.

The conversation may now go in any number of directions. They've shared some important information, but they are dealing with hot issues, extreme sensitivities, and a history of conflict. At any moment the whole process could fall apart. Georgette may hear the word "invalid" and lash out with anger. Martin will then have to overcome his rage and figure out what his responsibility was for whatever went wrong. But whatever he's done up till the break will not have been wasted.

Martin's immediate goal—to put his cards on the table in a clear and compelling way—has been accomplished. Naturally, he would like more.

His medium-range goal is a feeling of complete reconciliation between himself and Georgette. Here, success may be more elusive, the lack of resolution more frustrating, and the temptation to turn his frustration into assault ("I said I was sorry—what more do you want!") irresistible. But Martin has to remember that in whatever he does he is setting a tone. Every time he reaches for control, he makes it that much harder to prove that it's safe for Georgette to be open with him.

As for long-range goals, Martin may not yet know what they are. But there are benefits to be had from equality, such as the contributions a self-confident Georgette could bring to the relationship.

To make life easier for himself as he attempts these changes, Martin should remember how large the task is. Their marriage is not going to straighten out overnight. But if he is determined and persistent, Georgette will eventually cooperate. Meanwhile, he has to try to be patient and consistent, keep his frustrations from boiling over into venom, and do whatever he can to dampen the long-established strategic vibrations.

Dissolving the Knots

If we could compress into one idealized conversation communication that may take months to complete, we would see the range of feelings Martin and Georgette could share without tipping things into conflict. Along the way, they would each abandon certain strategic fortifications as they take responsibility for the things they do.

Georgette: "Okay, I do blame you when I get depressed. You're so damned unapproachable. You talk about running down the road and having to stop for me. But long before I come to a stop, I'm calling out to you and you don't hear."

Martin: "I do hear you. I hear you when you talk about us becoming a one-parent family. But there's only one way I can change things. And that's to stop thinking about getting to the top at *Today* and concentrate more on the family. And the truth is, I'd walk over my mother to become managing editor. So what am I supposed to say? There's no way I can defend that position. It makes me feel guilty to even think about it."

"You don't realize, Martin, but I feel guilty, too. I mean, what right do I have to keep you from your work? You never signed anything that said you'd be home at six. As for Cindy, it's true, I don't feel you spend enough time with her, but we're *not* a one-parent family. It wasn't fair of me to say that. But I've built up such horrible resentments and I feel so unable to get you to take me seriously, that she sometimes seems like the only tool I have."

Martin is taken aback. "I had no idea you were so angry."

Georgette softens. "I'm not aware of it either a lot of the time." She pauses. "Martin, do you really have to work as much as you do?"

Martin thinks about it. This is the first time he's had the opportunity to speak with Georgette about the amount of time he spends at the magazine without worrying about the tactical consequences of every word.

"The way it works is this: Only the men who are willing to commit themselves totally have a chance of going all the way. It doesn't matter how good you are. You're labeled right at the outset. You're either a technician or someone with a future. And if you want to keep having a future, you have to watch your rear all the time.

"There are some excellent editors at *Today* who take shit from people who don't have one-tenth their talent. But their talent doesn't help them, because they're not committed to playing the game. They think they can just do a good job and forget the politics. But if you forget the politics, eventually you can't even do a good job. Oh, you'll be respected at first, if your work is really good. But as you start slipping down the pecking order, everyone's got a line to you, and they all know how to tug it. You thought you were just going to do your job and be aloof from the bullshit, but now walking down the hall becomes a political act. You're drowning in the bullshit. That's what's happened to a lot of these guys. And it shows on them. It's worse than death. I tell you, if someone's going to be holding the leash, it's going to be *me*."

Georgette is speechless. For the first time she realizes what she's up against. The man's ambition, zeal, and his stark, Machiavellian view of the world is stunning and seems unlikely to change. There's no question of blaming herself. This is the way he is. And for the first time a neutral, dispassionate spark of doubt questions the viability of her marriage. All the same, to hear Martin speaking from where he really lives excites her and makes her realize how much she has to give him.

"But you know," Martin continues, "there are a lot of days when I'm more eager to get to work than I am to come home. Work is manageable for me. This isn't. It wears me down."

"What wears you down?"

"Sometimes I think I'm just not cut out for family life. I think, you know, maybe it's not going to work out. Maybe I'll leave you. Maybe I'll find somebody else. But then if you start withdrawing from me and I think I may lose you, I panic. Is it just a security thing? I mean, nothing personal, but why do I need you in order to feel whole? And yet if I begin to suspect you don't love me, I feel terrible, Georgette, even worse because I feel I'm getting what I deserve. You see how inconsistent the whole thing is? I may have problems at work. But I enjoy them. They're all clear problems of the military variety. The enemy is moving in on the budget front, or trying to place an ally in your department, or about to make a big splash at your expense—head him off at the pass. That sort of thing."

Again Georgette is struck by the vivid self-portrait Martin is painting. The man is a child. He has no understanding of how to live with his feelings. She swells with a desire to help him, but cautions herself.

"Do you know I'm jealous of Cindy?" Martin says one day.

"*What?*"

"Because you eat with her a lot nowadays instead of waiting for me. You used to make such nice meals for us."

"And that was important to you?"

"Yeah, it was like coming home and being taken care of."

All this is very hard for Martin to say. Not only is he acknowledging a disgusting need, but Georgette might attack him for expecting her to cook when she has a full-time job. Besides, to acknowledge wanting something from someone you may wish to escape from is, strategically speaking, to be heading in the wrong direction. What if Georgette offers to cook again and a few months later he decides he can't hack the marriage after all. What sort of blackguard will he be then?

But as he becomes comfortable with his feelings and with expressing them, he is less fearful of strategic implications. If he can establish a legitimate context today, tomorrow, if his feelings change, he'll be able to do it again.

Georgette: "Well, if you were upset, why didn't you say anything?"

"I didn't think it would be smart."

"Oh, Martin, you are a sickie!" Georgette laughs her unbuttoned laugh. Martin smiles and is stirred by love in a way that he was years ago.

"Well, tell me, why did you stop cooking?"

"Cooking used to be a pleasure. But one day I realized it was just one more thing I had to do, and if Lisa can do it while watching Cindy, then fine. I need the time."

"You're sure it has nothing to do with your resentment toward me?"

"No, it's just, hell, Carmen keeps me late, I often have to take work home. . . ."

"I don't believe you."

"Okay, why should I cook for you? Give me one good reason? Besides, invalids don't cook. Not once they realize what invalids they are. When you're running down your heroic road and I'm chugging along behind you with a frying pan, I don't feel so good about myself. I feel like a waterboy! And I hate it! I hate it!" Georgette sobs.

Martin feels an awful twinge but knows that her crying is not an attack. In the aftermath of this talk, there is a growing awareness in both of them that Georgette's invalidism is part of the complex pattern of the relationship, and that they each "benefit" from it and are invested in it in subtle ways. Her incapacity gives Martin a legitimacy, comfort, and security he would not have otherwise. It settles all arguments by implying that she's the problem. At the same time, it gives Georgette a weapon to keep him feeling guilty.

Exchanges like this between Martin and Georgette will not necessarily solve their problems with working, cooking, giving and getting. But their talks feel good, they engender trust, they establish a sense of equality. As they drift into intimacy, and Martin talks more about his secret self, he may come to terms with some of the key issues of his life. And as Georgette gains strength and feels less need for her pathetic tools, she may inject creative power into the relationship, bringing her closer to the marriage she wants.

A Deeper Kind of Power

The gift that Martin gives to himself in all this is freedom. Until now the role of Husband has been like a cage, barred all around with taboos and restrictions. He's had many strong feelings that he's been unable to express (except through innuendo, humor, and uncontrolled outbursts). He can't say no to the coat, because a Husband is supposed to give. He can't say he hates Georgette's depression, because a Husband is supposed to be sympathetic. He can't say he feels distant and uninvolved, because a Husband is supposed to be loving. Unable to express or to feel his forbidden feelings, he is unable to feel at all. The role of Husband is a prison that constantly forces him to deny who he is. It's hard to think of a man in this condition as powerful.

But when Martin speaks to Georgette as he has here, two important things happen. First he loosens his straitjacket, and his range of movement soars. That is growth. Second, he causes Georgette to see that his point of view, however much it may distress her, has a validity she must deal with. That is power.

The Powerful Father

The same process could carry over into his relationship with his daughter, with whom he tends to get stuck and guilty and unable to stop being a subject.

Cindy does a number of things, like sniffing the lieutenant governor's gloves at the beginning of our story, that upset Martin. But he is not direct with his disapproval. Eager to hide his own anxieties and lacking the confidence to assert his parental authority openly, Martin pulls a trick from his bag of maneuvers. He may divert Cindy with a piece of candy and a false smile. Lecture her about hygiene or respecting the property of others. Control her with a slap, a sharp tone, or a reproachful glance. But whatever he does, his dread of abnormality and his wish to impress an important guest will mix with his self-doubts to send a painful message to the girl. Cindy ends up feeling not only that it's repugnant to sniff someone else's property, but that she is repugnant, for she has an unnatural urge to do so.

In disciplining Cindy, Martin has to be able to say to himself, "Yes, I have doubts about my position. Yes, I'm afraid it reflects my own hang-ups. Yes, I know that I helped develop in her many of the things that bother me now. But it's important to me that she wipe her nose, it's important to me that she eat with a fork, it's important to me that she stop chattering when I'm trying to think, it's important to me that she not sniff the lieutenant governor's gloves."

When Martin is able to allow his personal truth to live this way, complete with doubt and unbolstered by moral certainties, he will feel both freer and kinder. He may still be unfair at times or set peculiar rules, but he will be able to make demands on Cindy without burdening her with shame. He will be able to convey, "I love you very much, but this is what I require as your father."

The Secret Object

Ultimately, every subject is an object, albeit a privileged one. As Martin foregoes the comforts of advantage in each of his relationships, he will inevitably begin to feel the insecurity he's always evaded by being one-up. The long-buried object quality will heat up within him, and he will have to deal with the same problems of balancing the power that other objects face.

In the early stages he may be painfully object-prone and inclined to interpret every no, every rejection, every criticism as an act of subjugation. He may discover a full set of object issues within himself. And he may learn how his extreme fear of judgment and rejection fuel his compulsion to win or to lose.

At times Martin may hesitate to stand firm in his own behalf. Ashamed of having been a subject, he may become powerphobic, and it may be hard to resist behaving as if others are better and have the right to lord it over him. And so he will have to make an effort to remind himself of certain things:

First, that he will never be able to abandon his domineering habits if the alternative is his own humiliation. Second, that the complicity of objects has almost always played a part in his unequal relations. Third, that he has other qualities, fine qualities, that deserve his focus. Fourth, that even if he feels guilty about something he's done, suffers for it, and wants to make amends, there's no atonement in discarding his own dignity. And, finally, he must remember that, like everyone else, he has a right to be treated with respect.

Review 6

The skills of combat are opposite to the skills of intimacy. That is why we have Martins on the one hand who are brilliant at covering their rears, timing their moves, keeping the interpersonal accounts, spotting the opportunity for victory, but who are incapable of a single unguarded moment; and Georgettes, on the other, who can bare their hearts with the trustingness of young love but are nearly defenseless against guile. We would not choose Martin to join us on a quiet walk through our private joys and sorrows. Nor would we choose Georgette to lead a diplomatic mission, to head a collective bargaining unit, or to oversee forces in combat.

It is important to understand, though, that these two opposite capacities, as well as others that lie between, can co-exist within one person. The muscles are all there; but for various reasons—having to do with culture, habit, and training—some of them have not developed.

Most of us operate according to conditioned responses. The waitress gives Georgette an exasperated look, and she starts apologizing for having asked the same question twice. The waitress gives Martin an exasperated look, and he makes her feel like two cents. Neither Georgette nor Martin is fully aware of the dynamics of the moment. Neither one makes a conscious choice about how to respond in a way that both demands and accords respect. And, of course, neither produces an optimal outcome. They are habituated to certain styles and unaware of their options.

Of all our characters, Jake has the greatest range of sensitivities and interpersonal skills, and as a result he is usually able to give respect and get it in return. But even Jake's skills are not adequate to every occasion. He's unable to use some vital tools, and that inability is just now causing him great trouble. Aggressiveness, openness, ruthlessness, tenderness, creativity, are all vital to the multiple tasks of life. Achieving dignity and self-respect; persuading others of your point of view; being effective in a highly competitive world; becoming intimate with another person; avoiding the temptations of winning—to do all that you can't afford to let any of your skills lie fallow.

In this section, we've covered four new themes. Let's review them now.

1. *Balancing the emotional giving and getting* is an important aspect of balancing the power. To do so with Martin, Georgette must patiently overcome the contract they've established, which calls for her to give more than she gets. Techniques at her disposal include driving harder bargains, smoking out Martin's feelings, and declaring a degree of independence by buying the coat she wants herself.

No matter how hard Martin resists her, if Georgette succeeds in balancing the power with him, he will be grateful. For she will have brought him into the truly related way of being with another person that he's always longed for. That's what his fantasy of deep friendship is all about.

2. *Creative power* is the ability to change a relationship for the better by bringing the other person along in a fully cooperative effort. This subtle form of power depends on vision, empathy, and the capacity to look honestly at your own responsibility for what's happened to date. It also entails a willingness to give up control—so that your vision for change now belongs to both people.

Creative power can only take place between equals. It cannot succeed unless everyone's cards are on the table.

3. If you hold a position of authority, your authority must be respected. And so you have to punish insubordination. To be sure that you're not abusing your power, there are four steps you can take in *asserting legitimate authority:* a) clearly state what you expect from your subordinate, b) express dissatisfaction if he continues to fail you, c) issue a warning, and d) punish.

4. *Breaking the habit of winning* is at least as hard as breaking the habit of losing. If Martin wants to bring equality into his relationship with Georgette, he will have to make himself more vulnerable with

her. Intimacy and personal power are his key behavioral tasks. But getting to know what he really feels may be his hardest job. If he succeeds in opening up both himself and the relationship, he will be rewarded with a new Georgette. She will be straighter with him, stop her annoying maneuvers, and enhance the relationship with her creativity.

Quiz

PROBLEM. Jake talks politely to the dead judge's wife, trying to explain his reasons for purchasing the photograph of her dying husband. But he finds his reason faltering, his head fogging, his faith in himself evaporating. Mrs. Browne has no respect for his words and no intention to listen or be moved. She simply attacks him with a barrage of insults. The power Jake normally has as a speaker, his ability to convey his ideas forcefully, dissolves under her onslaught. If you were Jake, what would you do?

1. I'd think back to when I'd suffered a similar loss and let her know I could empathize with what she was going through.
2. I would stop explaining. I'd just say, "I'm sorry for your loss, but you cannot speak to me this way and expect me to respond."
3. I'd put her on hold and then have my secretary tell her that something urgent had come up and that I'd get back to her.
4. At a certain point, I'd have to sting her in order to make her back off. I'd let her know that the average person does not have the power to tell the press what to print and that she is abusing the privilege of celebrity.

SOLUTION: 1. This is very touching, but she doesn't want your empathy, she wants you not to print the photo. 2. The most dignified and effective response. It's considerate, it's forthright, it announces your intention to withdraw. It gets to the heart of the matter by establishing that bereavement does not legitimize abuse. 3. The smarmy way out. 4. A huge and irrelevant manipulation that continues an argument you want to end.

PROBLEM. You're the head of daytime programming at a small television studio that is rife with internal conflict. Over the years you've promoted Nancy to be your top associate in the department. You've always liked her and been on good terms with her, but lately you've been irritated by her lateness with reports and her manner of dressing at board meetings. Whenever you've broached these subjects, she's managed to have the last word, insisting, correctly, that she always gets her work done, that the department has not lost any of its key battles since she's been your associate, and that you've let the anxiety of the place get to your head. What do you do?

1. I've given Nancy adequate warning. I would now demote or fire her. My survival and peace of mind is my first priority.

2. Nancy is obviously a good worker. I would try to smoke out her feelings, see if anything in my style is offensive to her, and try to get as open a conversation as possible. Perhaps I'd then find an avenue for creative power.

3. I would speak openly about the pressures on me and the strong need I have at this time for an extremely airtight operation.

4. The next time Nancy resisted doing things my way or pooh-poohed my concerns, I'd let her know that her tenure depended on compliance.

5. I'd remind Nancy that I brought her up through the ranks, and now I have to demand compliance from her.

SOLUTION. This is a case for the assertion of authority. Nancy is using your closeness as a means of insubordination. 1) You've never really given Nancy a warning. This is premature. 2) In this case, smoking out may well be a continuation of the weakness you've shown with her. You're not ready to be thinking of creative power. 3) Probably too nice. 4) This is the most logical next step. You have to let Nancy know she's dealing with a boss. 5) This guilt strategy is not direct enough for a person in authority. You don't have to manipulate.

PROBLEM. It's Sunday morning and you're trying to catch up on some reading for work. Your husband and his son, who's visiting for the weekend, are in the next room watching TV. It's a small apartment, and the TV noise is distracting. You resent it—first, because you've already asked them to keep it down, and, second, because it's a cheap game show, typical of the way your husband wastes his few weekend hours with his son. You're getting a headache. You're tempted to go out, but you loathe being driven from your home. You're tempted to explode at them, but, in fact, it is hard to make the TV soft enough in this space, and you don't want to play wicked stepmother. What do you do?

1. I'd buy them a pair of headphones for the TV.

2. I'd try to talk to my husband about the way he spends his time with his son.

3. I'd tell them I have to work and suggest they go out.

4. I'd go to the library.

5. I'd suggest we all go to a museum.

SOLUTION. Like most relationship problems that cause headaches, this is complex, with many issues stretching back over the months and, perhaps, years. Do you like the son? Do you feel your husband has low-brow taste and doesn't spend enough time in museums? Is he intimidated by your values and judgments? Are you disgusted with the parenting style of him and his first wife? Does that affect how you feel about the potential of having a child with him? Do you feel it's your husband's fault that you live in a small apartment where it's impossible for one person to read while others watch TV? Does he not earn as much as you think he should? Do you feel his son controls him in the same way his boss does? Do you tend to be a subject with him?

Any and all these issues may come into play when you finally decide how to react to your predicament on Sunday morning, and so you'd better be on top of them and know what you're really feeling. If you try to ignore one thing ("I can't stand what an ignoramus he is!") and concentrate on something else ("I need silence"), the ignored feeling may bleed through. Once that happens, subterranean issues will take control and subject-object tendencies will move to the fore.

1) Excellent. It doesn't touch any of the deeper issues that may be involved, but it takes care of the immediate problem in a warm-hearted way that avoids sticky entanglements. 2) Yes, but not just now. You mustn't let your anger over the TV noise get confused with your disapproval of your husband's parenting. Also, when you do talk, keep open the possibility that you still may be working from a hidden agenda. That is, don't try to be helpful about his parenting style when you're really upset with the way he is with you. Finally, entertain the possibility that you may come in for some legitimate criticism, too. He, for instance, may not enjoy living under your critical gun. If the talk goes well, the situation will be ripe for creative power. 3) Depends. Can you do it without being rejecting? Can you keep it clean? 4) Perhaps this time—until you work out a better long-term solution. 5) Fine, as long as it's something you and they might really want to do.

Further Exercises for Self-Awareness

• Can you put yourself in the other person's shoes? What is he really feeling when he does the things that bother you? Take some behaviors you disapprove of in people you know and see if you can find an analogy in your own life.

• What is your responsibility for the condition of your relationships? What are your positive and negative contributions?

• What is special about you? What do you have to give? Is there some area where you could be applying your creativity but hold back?

• Are you capable of balancing the power with someone you now treat as less than equal? Can you tell him what you want and need rather than become disappointed and act it out?

• Review failures and successes. What went right and what went wrong? Are you capable of assessing your failures objectively, as a scientist might, instead of turning against yourself like a prosecutor?

• Are you able to seek help? If personal power or intimacy is impossible for you or never quite seems satisfying, or if your life seems determined to run in place, are you willing to consider psychotherapy? In choosing a therapist, be sure that the person you see is properly credentialed and licensed. Consider whether the fit feels good to you, whether you find yourself opening up and trusting, and whether you begin to feel some changes. It is common and acceptable to interview a handful of therapists before choosing one. It is also acceptable to seek a consultation with a second therapist if things seem bogged down with the first.

A Final Review: The Flexible Response

Relating to others turns out to be quite complex once you break it down.

You have to measure moments: "Do I need to balance the power?" "What type of response is required, given the way I feel and the nature of this relationship?" "Have I achieved my purpose?" "Is it safe to drop all strategic considerations and open a direct exchange?"

You have to measure people: "Is this person ready to show me his hand?" "Is he someone who's open to change?" "Can we be intimate?"

And, most important, you have to know yourself: "What do I feel?" "What are my real purposes?" "What are my best interests?" "What are my weaknesses and skills?" "What are the irrational assumptions I tend to make?"

Fortunately, as you go into the machinery of your interpersonal style and replace old habit-ridden parts with more conscious and skillful modes of relating, the new styles become second nature and some of the mind-bending complexity recedes.

Strategic power is often essential in gaining respect from others, in establishing your authority, in being heard, in getting your due, in balancing the power, and, in many cases, paving the way to a truly open exchange. But to live mainly by strategies is to live a parched and lonely life.

Personal power is a lovely way of dealing with others and one of the most satisfying. But the person who relies strictly on forthrightness and never bothers to balance the giving and getting, to cover himself with image, to act defensively, or to retaliate when necessary, will find himself talking endlessly into the wind. He will be exhausted by people with half his stamina and feel stupid alongside those with half his brains.

Creative power is a true mark of leadership. But the person who relies strictly on creativity, trying to lead the way to better relations before he's mastered the strategic elements of the situation and before underlying fears, insecurities and other concerns have been openly aired, is deceiving himself. When speaking from a position of dominance, he can muscle through changes, but they will never be more than superficial. When speaking from a position of weakness, he will be laughed at, taken advantage of, and ignored. In the end, he himself feels like a fool ("Pollyanna!" "Do-gooder!" "Kook!"), and his creativity becomes a cause for shame.

Being intimate is one of the most rewarding, spiritual, and therapeutic things two people can do together. It's a tremendous promoter of growth. But the person who tries to be intimate all the time will be an object, easily humiliated and easily dismissed.

The question about power is: How can I be powerful without being a subject, without exploiting the vulnerabilities of others? The question about intimacy is: How can I expose my flaws and uncertainties without putting myself at a disadvantage? The answer to both questions lies in one's ability to respond to each situation with a variety of options and to move back and forth between them as needed.

VII.

CONCLUSION

"If Not Now, When?"

25.

The Beleaguered Prince

Georgette erupts, Jake mobilizes, Martin scrapes his knees. A surprising fall.

"SEPTEMBER THIS YEAR seemed full of omens. Cindy entering the first grade. Carmen losing the primary. We heard that Beth Billingham had been hospitalized. And, suddenly, boom-boom, my mother died and then the disaster with Martin.

"I always feel angry nowadays. I walk through the office, and the staff seems to part, like the Red Sea. I can't imagine what they think. It worries me being like this, but I can't shake it. Nor can I really say I want to. There are advantages to being angry. I think better, I have more energy, I don't get depressed, I don't take everything so personally. Somebody's ticked off and giving me the cold shoulder? Who *cares?* Screw 'em.

"My mother died on September tenth, about a week before the primary. She couldn't have picked a worse time. The culture editor at *Today* had just been fired, a guy who had once been very close to Jake Donohue. Martin was planning to deliver an important speech at a weekend conference of the top editors, a speech he was certain would finish Donohue off. Meanwhile everyone in our office was in a state of campaign fever, because the polls showed that the race would be a lot closer than expected.

"My mother's funeral came on a Thursday. Ever since I was a kid, my mother and I had had horrible fights, but we were close, and I was not prepared to lose her. I had been going through a period of ups and downs for about six months—ever since my birthday—which included an exhausting roller coaster existence with Martin. I depended on my mother being there. Even if I didn't actually use her in any way. Even if she was half-stewed most of the time. It's just that we had so much unfinished business. And then, there I was, staring into the casket, seeing her destiny written in the lines on her face, seeing the jaw that had once intimidated me looking so pitiable, remembering how fiercely those eyes once accused me of being selfish, and then the stupefying realization that some lives get no more resolved than this. The curtain comes down. The end.

"I stood over my mother, sobbed and thought, relived a thousand memories, tried to understand the wild range of my feelings, and then, mixed in with my crying, I started talking. I told my mother I would miss her. I told her I loved her. I told her I hated her. I remember saying, 'You were the selfish one, goddamnit, *you!*' When suddenly people rushed up and hustled me away. I hardly remember the rest of the funeral. I was in such pain. I was choking on it and frightened that it wouldn't stop.

"So now Martin had a basket case on his hands. And he had the conference that weekend at which he was going to make his big speech. He was torn, to put the bitterest light on it, torn between me and his speech.

"I'll never forget the look on Jon Reiss's face when he came by to see me at my brother and sister-in-law's that Saturday. Jon is a friend of my brother who's always flirted with me. Whenever Martin and I were on the rocks, I'd hung out with Jon and several times come close to having an affair. 'What are you *on!*' he said. Martin had gotten a doctor friend to prescribe Meloril, a heavy tranquilizer they use for psychotics. I felt and looked like a zombie. 'Stop taking that poison,' Jon said. 'You're not a looney. Your mother just died!'

"It was a turning point for me. I almost said, 'No, Jon, you don't understand. I'm defective. I have to get fixed.' But there was Cindy in the next room, worried about her mom. There was my mother dead of alcohol. How could I let myself become nonfunctional? How could I give up on myself? Who were the perfect people, the *together ones,* whom I could aspire to be like if I were only fixed? Carmen? Carmen the Invincible, who just lost a primary to a haberdasher after outspending him sixteen to one? Martin? Martin whose worklife is such an addiction he can't even see his own marriage decomposing? Take the Meloril now and next they'll hospitalize you. You'll be right behind Beth on the road to destruction.

"Suddenly I saw that I'd been giving up on myself and it seemed obscene. I wanted to scream, I was so angry. But I couldn't scream, because the Meloril was lying across my emotions like a lead blanket.

"So Jon and I took a long walk, I flung the drugs into a waste bin downtown, and I knew that something was going to happen between us. Anyway, when Martin came back from doing whatever he did to Jake Donohue, I told him I wanted to separate."

Jake

In the months after the incident over the slain judge's photograph, Jake managed a political holding operation at *Today*, but his bearings were badly shaken. His occasional exceptions to his no-drinking resolution became less occasional, as did his spats with Grace. When he wasn't feeling depressed and aimless, a rage came over him that made him afraid he would attack and kill the next Walkman-wearing research assistant who bumped into him in the hallway. Every disagreement, every petty power struggle pierced Jake, and everyone who rubbed him the wrong way became the subject of a violent fantasy.

The morning after Labor Day, Jake awoke in his usual disgruntled state. A nagging image made him pause to recall a dream. All he could pull from his scattered mixture of vague sensations and mental pictures was the vibrant presence of a large bottle of vodka. The bottle, with its label in full color, filled his field of vision with such three-dimensional brilliance it almost seemed to glow. Jake didn't have to think about what the commanding presence of the bottle meant. He knew he stood at a fork in the road. To turn away and forget that dream would be to accept defeat in his hard-won victory against alcoholism.

"I have to slam the door on this thing," he thought. Riding into Manhattan on the Long Island Railroad, staring through the forest of uplifted newspapers, he decided he would slam the door. As the train slipped through the North Shore suburbs, his resolve grew harder and stronger. And as it did, he forgot about the booze and turned his attention to his flailing authority as managing editor.

For the first time since his troubles began, Jake did not think about the imperfections in his proposed reforms or about his own flaws or oversights and saw things as they really were. He was in a raw power struggle, nothing more. And unless he met the challenge of that struggle, the things that he stood for, right or wrong, farsighted or foolish, would never get a hearing. The ferocity with which he slammed the door on alcohol, the ferocity that had gone into his recent depressions and fantasies, was now aimed at its proper target: taking command at *Today*.

That week the editors noticed a steely purposefulness in everything Jake did. Devoid of his usual flourishes of diplomacy, and with the humorlessness of a field surgeon, Jake nailed down commitments, nailed down deadlines, nailed down responsibilities. He showed little concern for how his commands were received; his manner stressed the fact of his authority. Strategic considerations became a more prominent component of Jake's talks with his top aides; the power struggle with Grodin was more openly acknowledged. And because no one could ignore the enormous rewards and punishments still at Jake's disposal, the senior editors, whatever their sympathies, began to show a stronger interest in Jake's approval. "Just as it should be," he thought.

The first bump in Jake's road was the culture editor, his old pal Kevin Collins, who remained coy and elusive on a small matter Jake normally would have let pass. Collins had never known Jake to punish him, and, despite the change in Jake's countenance, he was not about to "play sycophant," as he thought of it. The gaff in the culture section earlier in the summer, which Collins had failed to contain within the department, and Grace's interpretation ("He *screwed* you") combined now with Collins' vague air of insubordination in a way that gripped Jake's mind. On Thursday morning he marched into Collins' office.

"Jake, come on, that's ancient history now."

"That was a blunder, Kevin. I don't want another one."

"I don't get it. First you tell me to follow the letter of the law. We have new guidelines. We're going to reform journalism. The millennium is coming. Then you tell me to cover your ass. It's not always possible to do both, old buddy."

Jake turned to the door in momentary confusion. There was some logic to what Collins was saying. He paced slowly like a man who was choosing his words. In that pose, he reconnected with his own logic. "Let's make it simple, Kevin. I want to know where you stand. Behind me or not."

Kevin pursed his lips and nodded, a facial display that could have been interpreted as acquiescence. Jake refused to let it go at that. He would not leave until Collins gave him a clear commitment, a signed contract. Jake spoke softly, his face flaccid and weary, but his eyes clear and intense. "Where do you stand, Kevin?"

"Jake, I get the picture. You took some heat. You don't want it to happen again."

"No. You made an error in judgment. That's what I don't want to happen again."

Collins still would not sign. "Look," he kidded, "it happened when you were on vacation. We shouldn't have to worry about it for another year. In the meantime, I don't think you need a loyalty oath from me. I mean we've only known each other most of our lives."

"Kevin?"

Collins looked up.

"Do you like working here?"

A combination of disbelief that Jake would fire him and self-destructive pride kept Collins dodging. "Look, *Jake*, I hear you," he said and turned away.

Jake was about to press him again, when he realized his position was becoming untenable. He was up against a wall and would be making a fool of himself to press on. The best he could get from Collins was a contract signed with a smirk. But he knew quite clearly that he had succeeded in something else, something he had not anticipated. He had flushed Collins out, seen his colors. For the first time since Grace suggested it, Jake could plainly see that Collins was treacherous.

"I'm glad you hear me," Jake said and left. The next morning Collins received a formal note announcing that he was relieved of his duties as culture editor and that Jake hoped he would consider a position as deputy chief of the San Francisco bureau.

Martin

During that first week, Martin did not perceive the implications of Jake's behavior, except perhaps to see it as a symptom of increasing desperation. There had been a stalemate at the magazine since the previous spring, when Martin, with the tacit backing of Roland, had managed to postpone the implementation of bylines in national and foreign news. The bylines were a minor aspect of Jake's editorial plans, but they were an essential step and their postponement symbolized both Jake's weakness and Martin's strength. Jake, not feeling sure enough to press the issue with Roland, had allowed the stalemate to continue all summer, and everyone had grown accustomed to it.

Although the stalemate worked to Martin's advantage, Martin had nevertheless grown concerned that Roland might go on like this forever, tolerating a crippled captain at the helm. Surely, Roland was not happy with such leadership. Surely, he did not want to see the magazine go on forever with one editorial policy for hard news and a different policy for the back of the book. Surely, he knew that the absence of a clear editorial statement told the world that *Today* did not know what it stood for. And yet, as Martin saw it, Roland seemed to be allowing sentiment to paralyze him.

Martin decided that he had to make Roland grasp the significance of what was happening; make him see the necessity for dumping Jake and replacing him with someone stronger; but he had to do it shrewdly, for it must not look as if he were grinding his own axe. And then it struck him: "The Ram's Head conference is the thing wherein I'll catch the conscience of the king!"

Once a year the editors of *Today* are brought together at a rustic retreat for think sessions, team building seminars, and inspirational speeches. Martin decided that he would give one of those speeches, a speech about the importance of leadership, the strength it can give to an organization, and the strength it can sap. A reflective, intelligent, and calmly passionate speech. Roland, who did not attend the retreats, would read the speech the following Tuesday in the solitude of his office, give little thought to the possibility that it had been planted there for the purpose of influencing him, and be captured by it.

Martin prepared the speech carefully for several weeks, and he kept adding fresh touches even as he helped with the burial arrangements for his mother-in-law. He was so committed to it, had put so much stock in it, was so pleased with it, and was so keyed up with pride and anticipation that he easily convinced himself that Georgette would survive the weekend without him.

By the time Jake heard Martin's speech that Sunday, he was already six days into his bitter drive for control. He listened coldly, understood completely the meaning of Martin's act and the impression it would have on Roland. On Monday morning when the minutes came to Jake's office for editing, he struck Martin's speech from the record.

Martin's first reaction when he saw the minutes was that an error had been made, and he was on the verge of jumping up to set matters straight when he realized that the omission was not an error. He eased back into his chair, felt an uneasy combination of disdain and confusion, and remembered, with pain, his separation from Georgette.

News of the edited minutes, following so quickly on Collins' dismissal, created a tremor of anxiety and rumors. In the weeks that followed, editors began to rush, bump, and slip into line any way they could. A covert, joke-shrouded obsequiousness crept into their behavior at editorial meetings, and in subtle ways, which only men with their experience would recognize, they climbed over each other to impress Jake with their devotion.

Jake, meanwhile, spent less and less time at the meetings himself. He came in—occasionally with Roland in tow—for several minutes at a time, when important decisions were being made. His lieutenants were instructed to play tackle and guard to Jake's quarterback during that time, cutting off any suspicious dissent with sharp opposition, so that Jake was free to remain amiable and conciliatory throughout. He departed early, leaving the other editors with a heightened sense of the gulf between his power and theirs.

Roland

"Jake, it's a sensational fete," Roland said. "It's like a who's who of New York intelligentsia."

The party, a large fortieth birthday celebration for Roland, was another strategic move. Jake had thrown it solely for political purposes, with barely a touch of real affection or joy. The party served several purposes: it accelerated Jake's momentum; it reminded Roland of Jake's standing among the people they both respected; it tied Roland's hands slightly, by way of an enormous reward, making it difficult for Roland to make any sudden moves at Jake's expense; and it gave Jake the certain ability to extract one small assurance.

"Come here for a minute, Ed. This is no time to talk shop, but something's just come up. We've got that special on the defense industry in the pipeline, and I want to send Grodin to Houston to supervise. I'm not going to have a problem there?"

"Hell, I don't see why."

"Well, when you're dealing with prima donnas. . . ."

"Oh, *hell*, Jake, you worry too much."

"Okay, Ed. Just wanted to touch base with you on it. You know Senator Moynihan, don't you? Pat!"

While Martin was out of the way in Houston, bylines began appearing in national and foreign news. Roland was stunned.

True, he'd long ago given his stamp of approval to the idea of bylines—and everything else Jake wanted—and had never reversed himself. But he'd grown accustomed to the stalemate and to the certainty that as long as Martin was there to stall, he'd have time to reconsider the whole idea. Now he was slapped with a *fait accompli*.

Roland had mixed feelings. On the one hand, he'd like the change he'd seen in Jake lately and was more comfortable about putting a piece of his fate in Jake's hands. On the other hand, he was still unconvinced of the wisdom of all that Jake wanted to do and angry at having been outmaneuvered. Above all, he still could not bear the thought of admitting that he'd gotten cold feet and wanted to reconsider the changes he'd so bravely agreed to when he'd shaken hands with Jake three years ago.

He called Jake into his office and asked him what the hell he thought he was doing.

"I'd like to show you something," Jake said. He pulled a neatly folded manuscript from his inside jacket pocket. "It's a speech Grodin gave at Ram's Head two months ago. He talks about leadership. About decisiveness. And how the fate of an organization can hang on small matters."

Roland read the speech, sensed Jake's posture of command, and smiled as if to say, "*Touché*." The chemistry of the moment was magical. For the first time in months the power felt balanced between the two men.

"Ed," Jake said, "why don't we sit down next Monday and talk about the direction this whole thing is going—put a lot of cards on the table."

"It's a date."

From the Perspective of Victory

Early that December, Jake and Roland developed a system of regular feedback and exchanges, so that Roland could carefully monitor and consider all future editorial changes. At the same time Roland agreed to stop attending editorial meetings. Jake was satisfied. His authority was secure.

Jake now began to relax his military measures with the staff and to reduce the strategic content of his thought and behavior. Reduce but not eliminate. He remained a little more aloof than he'd been before and found to his surprise that this felt quite comfortable and correct.

As he stripped away much of his wartime armor and momentum, feelings that he could not afford to experience before now possessed him. Exuberance, sadness, regret, resentment, hope, humility, and love each took him by turns. At times he enjoyed talking out his analysis of everything that had happened, and Grace, who was normally the bigger talker, became the listener.

"In the beginning I wanted to kill Grodin," Jake said, "and that surprised me. I'd been so involved in agonizing over what I'd done right and what I'd done wrong that I had no idea that such hatred was building inside me. All I felt was *self*-hatred. But halfway into Grodin's speech, when I made up my mind that I would delete it, I knew I had crossed the line. I was through with self-evaluation. I was ready to get down there in the mud and slug it out. And I was a little frightened, because I had no idea how vicious I might become.

"Once I'd neutralized Grodin, though, I knew he was finished. How could he compete with me for the job? He's bright, he's a damn good journalist, he can be very charming, but what has he got as a manager? Or as a leader? What kind of vision can he offer? The substance isn't there. And at the same time, by the same logic, I knew who I was again. And the more secure I felt about that, the less I wanted to kill Grodin. He wasn't that important.

"When I first met Grodin, I thought, *I can handle this guy.* I could see he was into power, and I knew he would test me, but I didn't really consider him a challenge. But when things started going against me, I became frightened of him, and I was ashamed of that. All those doubts I felt about myself, right down to the size of my balls—*starting* with the size of my balls—they all seemed so real. I didn't realize, didn't want to realize, what a tough predicament I'd gotten myself into. I was like a man in a tux and a top hat walking properly down the road while Grodin, and Roland, and Collins, and then half the god-damn staff were throwing tomatoes.

"Over and over again, I've asked myself, why do I always let this happen? Fifty-five years of accommodating, bending over backwards, tormenting myself with useless introspection—and all for what? To make life easier for people I don't respect. If someone broke into our house right now and pointed a gun at me, I'd wonder what I could have done to offend him. God forbid I should harm him—or even let myself hate him—without first considering that factor."

"That's exactly what you did with Collins," Grace said. "The more he shit on you the harder you tried to understand him."

"Yeah, but Collins is a special case. The literary boy wonder who never made good, the lousy marriage, the drinking, *everything*, and then, of course, our families being so close, my Pulitzers, the constant comparisons. . . ."

"There you go! There you go! You're doing it right now! Don't you think the guy who barges in here with a gun is a special case? Don't you think he had a rough childhood? *Hitler* had a rough childhood!"

Jake laughed. He began thinking again about his editorial plans, the once beloved reforms that had become a hated deformity. "I'm getting back to that stuff now, but I'm doing everything more slowly this time. I took Roland too much for granted before."

"But he gave you his okay. You had a deal."

"But I knew he was uncomfortable. I can't pretend I didn't. Something was bugging him, and he was afraid to tell me, and I conveniently ignored how hard it was for him to confront his brilliant former mentor. I wanted him to have confidence, to realize how good the whole thing was going to be. I didn't want to have to waste my energy on his worries. But he was worried, and he is worried, and if I were in his spot, I might be worried too."

"So the love affair is on again?"

"No, not exactly. I still haven't sorted out all my feelings about him. I'm still pissed about a lot of things that happened last year. I can't help resenting him for being such a prick. On the surface the relationship is what it was before—we get along well, we enjoy each other—but in my gut I'm standing an inch or two further back."

"I think it'll work better that way," said Grace.

A Horrible Stillness

As Jake swept through *Today,* making personal, procedural, and substantive changes that buttressed his authority, Martin's hands were tied. At first he hoped Jake would stumble or that Roland would wake up and oppose him. But, when in early November, Roland failed to pick up Martin's plain displeasure over being pressed into duty in Houston, Martin's hopes sank.

The tighter Jake's grip became, the more paralyzed and humiliated Martin felt, even though no action had been taken against him (and, indeed, none was planned). If Jake was generally too slow to make an adversary interpretation of events, Martin's adversary assumption was hyperactive, and now he was certain he'd been targeted for ouster.

Because of his need to be on top, the pause in Martin's momentum occasioned a troubling stillness filled with apprehension and doubts. Add to this Georgette's "abandonment," as he was inclined to call it, and Martin panicked. He felt like a victim. He began to sink.

Martin could not turn off his mind. The smallest incident—the failure to approach in intimidatingly attractive woman, an elevator ride with a student lugging a cello, an unsatisfying afternoon with his daughter—became the occasion for tormenting questions. Suddenly he saw holes in his life. I never learned how to be on my own. I forgot all about music. How could that have happened? I don't know my own child. And for every lack he saw, he punished himself ceaselessly. Because self-doubt and pain are themselves so shameful to Martin, symbolizing a defectiveness akin to leprosy, his descent had a built-in acceleration, one piece of shame automatically bringing on another in an endless snowballing mass. He saw himself sinking, sinking to the bottom of the cauldron where losers flounder in their disgusting pain and inadequacy. This image was followed by one in which he plunged a knife into his chest three times in succession.

Being at work was torture. To maintain his image in the context of such vulnerability was an unbearable burden. But something interesting was happening. He saw everyone around him in a different light now, as if for the first time he was looking past the categories he'd created for them. The staff seemed to react to him in one of three ways. Some remained very gamey and clearly responded only to Martin's capacity to maneuver and dominate. But because he did not feel that capacity now, their smiles and semantic jockeying seemed wasted and irrelevant. They persisted, however, and it troubled him to think that that was all they could see of him, even when it wasn't there.

The meeker of his colleagues also struck him in a new light. Yes, he could still see their layers of fear and the object clues that made it so easy for him to dominate them. He still saw them acting out their disrespect for themselves—in their facial expressions, their diction, their dress, their apologetic ways. But that only saddened him now. Their powerlessness was not something he wanted to exploit. For the first time other qualities seemed more important. Eliot the Stutterer was also a magnificent and erudite copy editor. Alice the Yenta knew Washington arcana inside out and could always be depended on for the right bureaucratic source. It saddened him to think that they lived a devalued life. Or did they?

He wanted to reach out to them, to talk to them, to touch them, to give them some sign that he had changed, that he was not a machine, that he was human. But the distance was too great; they were locked into an object pattern with him, and he could not change eight years in an instant. They apologized too often, they put a premium on his approval, they continued to defer and to walk around him. What was he to do? Punish them for being objects?

A few people fit yet another category. The secretary of one of his subordinates, the proofreader with whom he had chatted once or twice at the water cooler—unlike everyone else, they seemed to sense that he had been wounded. They appeared uninvolved in such questions as whether he had been right or wrong, whether he deserved what he'd gotten, or whether he had a right to feel wounded. They simply responded to the wound. A cup of coffee appeared on his desk. A warm smile slipped into an impersonal conversation. An invitation to lunch. Could he believe this? He wanted to cry; he felt unworthy of their caring. Would they hate him even now if he confessed how little they'd meant to him until today?

For a few days he felt he was on the verge of a religious experience. He thought he understood the meaning of "universal love." He wondered about the phrase "born again." The understanding was elusive, and he ran after it. For a time, he felt very pious, and his self-esteem climbed again; but then he jeered at himself for using humility to reinflate his damaged identity, and his little stack of ego cards collapsed.

This winter was the first time in his adult life he had been both without Georgette and without the sense that he was in control of events. Not since he was twelve or thirteen had he felt such yearnings for connection. He wondered if he should confide in his old buddy, Frank Caruso—maybe next Sunday after squash. Did Frank ever feel like this? Could this be an acceptable part of being human? He remembered his childhood piano teacher—where was Doug now?—and considered looking him up. As Christmas approached, he thought of going to a church and speaking to a priest. Or perhaps the psychology editor would recommend a therapist—a good one, a discreet one, not a nut.

But Martin had reservations about the slightest step toward intimacy or exposure. He was still hoping he could beat this rap, that his present condition was a temporary aberration that would disappear without a trace. He feared that to put his self-doubts into words might give them a life they would not otherwise have had. Once other people knew about them, they wouldn't be his to deny. And once he'd sought help, would he ever be able to say he'd been a self-reliant man, that he'd done it alone?

There were other problems. Martin had had almost no experience with intimacy, and he tended to think of it in terms that were either too timid or too extreme. To make little hints to Frank Caruso about being down lately would never lead to an intimate exchange. They would swap a few platitudes and jokes, and Martin would feel worse than when he started. It would never occur to him to say, "I want to talk to you about something, Frank. I want to tell you about feelings I've never mentioned before." To Martin real openness was a primal scream. It meant a total acting out of his pain. His limited perceptions limited his options.

Martin's sudden envelopment in pain and vulnerability, like Jake's dream, represented a fork in the road. It was an opportunity to become a larger person—less ruled by fear, more grounded in his feelings, more truly self-reliant, less addicted to the power treadmill, more capable of establishing equal connections. But in order to take advantage of that opportunity, he had to be willing to accept vulnerability as a more constant factor in his life. He would have had to face the fact that he was not Mr. Strong, Mr. Happy, Mr. Clean, Mr. Right from the nucleus of his being to the crispness of his shirt. But Martin had no way of accepting so much as a wrinkle in his status without seeing himself succumbing utterly to pain and defeat. And so, as his vulnerability persisted, the opportunity faded, and his choices narrowed to two—be destroyed by the pain or find a way back into the winning groove.

Christmas week was the worst. He phoned Georgette. "I want to see you" "I don't know, Martin." "Please," Each time he entered the apartment, he scoured the place for evidence of her boyfriend. He saw changes she'd made since he'd left. The controversial lithograph hung above the bed where he threw his coat. He looked at the thighs of the woman in the picture, but could not for the life of him remember why they'd so possessed him.

After dinner, Georgette tried to get Martin to talk, but he couldn't. She was tender, she was sympathetic, but she was not his. *My fault, my fault,* he thought. The distance she maintained accentuated his agony. He felt paralyzed, speechless. The best he could do was ask her to reconsider the separation. She would not. She wasn't ready to think about that, she said.

He felt blinded by one overriding desire—get Georgette back. But Georgette was imagining what life would be like with Martin back in the driver's seat again. He said, "We'll work that out." But to her it was not so simple. He became bitter and left.

Martin began to feel like a mean little man in his relationship with Georgette, a paranoid, peering into her garden through the window of his fortress. He tried to make her feel guilty. She hung up on him. He became insanely jealous and thought of hiring a detective. He would get the goods on her! Divorce her! Take custody of the kid! These fantasies occupied him a great deal. And the more vicious his thoughts became, the worse he felt about himself. He spent a night with a woman he didn't respect. His life felt small and cruddy.

And then one day he said: What the hell do I need to be in the dumps for? So the schoolboy publisher wants to hand the magazine over to his teacher. Great, let him have it. So my wife has gotten her ear bent in two by her jerkwater, bra-burning friend. Great, let them have each other. He began making calls and setting up appointments. The energy returned to his step, and he remembered that he was born a prince.

The old Martin Grodin, the man who always seemed to have a little extra up his sleeve, began to re-emerge at *Today,* and, as he did, the people around him sank into their previous slots in his mind. Then, in mid-January, the *Times* reported that Grodin had accepted a major editorial position at *Forbes*. The humiliation was over, the wound was sealed.

26.

"Good Girls Don't Want Power"

Georgette reviews her jobs, her relationships, herself, and her year.

"THE DAY AFTER Carmen lost the primary last September, Garfield Hughes, the Manhattan Borough President called and offered me a job heading his community liaison office. It turned out to be only one of several calls like that from people in city government.

"The first thing I thought when I got those offers is why did I cringe for so long? Why didn't I know how good I was? Why was I so afraid to confront Carmen about what I wanted? In Garfield's office I'm treated like a legitimate professional. It brings tears to my eyes even now—all these people valuing me so highly and I didn't value myself.

"The second thought I had was, Oh gosh, with that title and that salary I'm really going to have to *perform*. As long as I was unimportant they couldn't expect much. But now that I have more authority, the fact is I'm eating it up. I'm so tired of being frightened and behaving like a little person.

"Eli Kaufman is one of Garfield's top assistants, and when he retires next year, I'm going to apply for his job. It's not so important whether I get it. I just want to keep alive that I'm not the office sweetheart, that I'm executive material. I'm never going to be a Marge, but I hate having held myself back in order to please everyone and to never be thought of as too aggressive. 'Good girls' aren't aggressive. They don't need authority. They don't want power.

"Last Thursday an amazingly insignificant but somehow nevertheless important thing happened that sums up how I've felt lately. I went into a store to buy a new lamp, and I was in a rush. They didn't have the one I wanted, so I had to order it. They wanted fifty percent down. It turned out I was short of cash that day and didn't have my cards because I'd left my wallet home. I had a store credit that was worth thirty dollars and the price of the lamp was eighty. I thought, okay they want forty dollars down, I'll give them the credit slip—that's thirty—and ten in cash. But the man starts doing some figures on paper and says he needs twenty-five fifty in cash. I thought, oh, I must have figured it wrong. I could feel the heat going to my cheeks, and, somewhat embarrassed, I said, 'Gosh, I don't believe it! I don't even have the twenty-five dollars!'

"He said patronizingly, 'So what have you got, twenty?' Actually, I had almost twenty, but I didn't want to give it to him, because I needed some of that money for groceries. So I said, 'Could I see how you figured that?'

"He gave me an impatient look, and ordinarily I would have left it at that. I would have died before I'd put myself in a position of challenging someone else's figures and making a fool of myself. And I felt particularly untogether for having forgotten my wallet. This one dishevelled person holding up a whole line of solid citizens. But I didn't have the time to come back and forth to this place—and, you know, there's something about being a single parent that makes you feel, Goddamn it, I have my rights!

"So, anyway, I saw what he did. He'd subtracted my thirty dollar credit from the total price, which meant I owed fifty for the lamp, and then divided that in half to come up with the downpayment of twenty-five.

"I said, 'Wait a second, you subtracted the credit slip from the total. You should subtract it from the half that I owe you.' He looked at me as if I was the biggest pain in the ass he'd ever had. He rolled his head and told me he knew how to add and subtract, and I should not keep his other customers waiting.

"I said, 'Look, you want me to pay you fifty percent up front, right?' He grunted. I said, 'Okay, fifty percent of eighty is forty. I owe you forty dollars. Here's ten in cash and here's a credit for thirty.

"He said, 'Oh, now you're juggling with pennies, we don't juggle with pennies here.'

"Well, I was ready to kill. I pointed my finger at him and said, 'You do too juggle with pennies and don't you forget it!' I can't remember the last time I spoke to anyone like that. It felt terrific. His partner, who was standing nearby, leaned over and whispered something to him, and they went ahead and did it my way. And to think that five minutes earlier I'd been afraid to ask the kid in the back of the shop who'd been searching for my lamp to please check the stock room!

"The whole thing was such a revelation. These people who seem so intimidating—half of them are just bluffing their way through. After the primary, Carmen told me she was going to be joining the National Organization for Women in January and wanted me to come with her. Well, you just should have seen her solicitude when I told her I was considering an offer from Garfield Hughes. Suddenly she had more time for me than I knew what to do with. And not a sign of the big bad bully. No, it was a little love-fest, with Carmen telling me that I was the best staff member she'd ever had, that in the new job there'd be none of the little problems that seemed to have irked me before. And, of course, I'm lapping it all up. But at least I was smart enough not to commit myself one way or the other, and when I went home, it was obvious what I would do.

"I thought back to those times Martin had said that all I needed was to speak to Carmen forcefully about what I wanted and expect to get it. But I just couldn't get past my fear. So this fall I said to myself, Georgette, you just had a lucky break. You didn't do it for yourself, it got done for you. Now make it work.

"During the campaign I overheard a conversation between Carmen and David Brooks, who replaced Beth as press secretary. Carmen was holding up a speech he had written for her and saying, 'You really expect me to give this speech?' To which Brooks responded, 'You really expect me to answer that question?' And they circled around each other like that until Carmen gradually came up with some specific objections and they worked them out. I stood there with my mouth open. Because that's just the way you have to deal with her—and how did he know that? It's the kind of thing that some men seem to learn from age two. And it's so smart. Because with Beth Carmen would never be specific, Beth would entirely redo the speech, and then Carmen would still not be satisfied.

"All this stuff is so primed up in me right now! A weird thing just the other day at the hairdresser's. There's a nasty little bitch there named Wendel, one of several girls who wash your hair. It's impossible to get anything from her, and I can never prevail upon her to leave me a towel when she finishes. I ask and she takes it away. When I came in this time, I accidentally said, 'Hi, Meryl,' and she very quickly said, '*Wendel,*' and it struck—by God, this little jerk who never talks to me, she really cares that I get her name straight.

"Now, normally, when she treats me like shit, I think, Oh, damn, don't take it personally, these girls hardly make any money, they have a right to have a chip on their shoulder. And so I just sit there and stew. But this time I thought, God damn it, I don't care what her problems are—I treat her with respect and I want to be treated with respect in return. So I did something very unlike me. When she started taking the towel away, I said, 'Leave it, Meryl.' I didn't look at her, so I didn't see her reaction, but for the first time the towel stayed. There was an immediate understanding. If she's rude, I'm going to call her 'Meryl.' It spoke volumes.

"And, you know, I don't care if she likes me. I don't even care if she respects me. Let her just treat me with respect—let her fake it."

The Home Front

"Well, I'm going to be thirty-six this weekend, and Jon is coming over for dinner. Things were very exciting with Jon for a few weeks, but I knew I wasn't ready to start a serious relationship. I'm still too emotionally involved with Martin. Being with Jon was a great way not to feel any pain. And also, I have to admit, to make Martin feel some. I don't want to use Jon that way. It's nice to be dating other men, it's great for my ego, but I think about Martin all the time.

"I see Martin almost every weekend now, when he picks up and delivers Cindy, and from this distance it's much easier to appreciate his good qualities. He's almost always on time for Cindy, he doesn't play games with child-support money. And I do miss having him around. Just in terms of Cindy, there was always another person to take the heat off. I thought I would hate him for the rest of my life. But it's not like that at all; it's much more complicated. We've even been to bed together a few times. It seems that as long as I really don't care or hope too much, everything just falls into place between the two of us.

"He's still Martin. He looks at me funny. He'd like to know things, but he doesn't ask. He was humiliated too much when we first broke up by displaying his jealousy the way he did. Sometimes he acts like an injured party, as if he's telling me through his little sneers and postures that I destroyed the marriage. He looks at me quizzically as if to ask if I'm happy with the mess I've made. And all of his little tactics, they get to me. I keep wanting to respond, to argue with him. And, oh, that is so Martin. To get me to argue with something he'll deny ever having implied. So I just bite my tongue. And then he looks at me some more. He has that angular penetration that seems to say,

'So what do you think you're up to now? I know you're holding something back.' It's unnerving.

"There's something about powerful men like Martin. The attraction is so strong it's beyond reason. I've always felt anything that strong has to be right. At first it just seems like a very good place to be. Why not live with a prince? It's never boring. But then you feel put down. It's something about their confidence and your insecurity. You want to know, How can they be so sure of themselves? And at the same time you feel they've got your number, and that makes you obsessed with working it out. You think, 'This is home, this is where you belong, this is the problem you have to crack.' You can feel horribly persecuted and at the same time intent on getting to the bottom of it. It's almost like being with my mother.

"I wanted to change Martin, to make him softer, but I also wanted to share some of his invulnerability; I wanted some of his magic to rub off on me. If I could have been his equal, if I could have just won those arguments, then I'd have worked out some deep dark problem of my own. What a waste. I was so wrapped up in my obsessions that I never gave the relationship a fair chance.

"I never gave *Martin* a fair chance. I was never persistent. All he had to do was make the littlest growl and I'd scamper away. I cried, I made accusations. I got depressed and put on weight. But I never made a sustained effort to confront him as an equal. I look back at the way I behaved with him when we lived together, and I think, if I knew then what I know now, I never would have—but that's ridiculous. What I did then was the sum total of what I was. What frightens me is that I might do it all again.

"Martin used to accuse me of wanting to be stroked. I never said, 'Martin , it's not stroking that I want. I want more emotional involvement. Talking to you is wonderful when we're talking about culture or politics or a movie. You're alive and smart. But you rarely talk about your feelings and when you do you're boring. Your heart is not really in it.' It's so clear to me now. But when I'm with him, something fogs over.

"I've had such a skewed view of him. That always becomes so apparent to me when he's depressed and the facade slips away. I was talking to Marge the other day about the way he is with Cindy. He can be so stiff. And he gets into such absurd stand-offs with her, all of which makes me not respect Martin. But the whole time we were living together it never occurred to me that there was anything I didn't respect about him. Even when it came to Cindy, I was more worried about what he thought about me. If he said she was getting too dependent on me, I went into a big introspective tizzy. Marge said I should have been helping Martin in his relationship with Cindy. But how was little me going to help big him?

"I was always afraid of putting the marriage in jeopardy. I used to think, how could I do that to Cindy? She'd never forgive me for estranging her father. She'd grow up and say, 'Because of *your* Dissatisfaction Neurosis I only saw my dad on weekends!' Well, now she only sees him on weekends and I never took the risks.

"But I have learned this, and that is that the most important thing I can do for Cindy is to provide her with a good role model, and not let her grow up believing that a woman has to always be bending herself out of shape to please a man. I don't want her to be afraid of being selfish and to harbor secret resentments she acts out in obnoxious ways.

"Would Martin have come around if I'd been stronger and more persistent? I don't know. Sometimes I think it would take a delicate genius to get to him. Maybe I just didn't have it. Maybe no one does. Certainly the *teenagers* he's going out with now don't have it.

"It was my energy that made our marriage burn with whatever intensity it had. I fueled it. I know that. And when my fuel ran low, the marriage ran low. I did a little better, I think, each time I broke up and went back. But I never gave it the kind of energy I feel right now. Once fear crept into my joints, I started playing it safe. Just as I did with Carmen. I have to change that if I'm ever going to be a happy person.

"Sometimes I wonder: If it doesn't work with Martin, will I find another one just like him? Will I reject another man because he's too nice? That would scare me. That would definitely make me get some help.

"It hurts to be without him. I feel a hollow pain in my chest sometimes. And then I want to say, 'Martin, what are we doing? We belong together.' Neither one of us breathes a word about it, though. I think he went as far out on a limb as he's going to go. And I—I feel I have myself back, and I don't know yet if I can keep myself and Martin too."

Fear

"We had a good talk, Marge and I, the other day. We'd gotten into an argument about the personal ads in *New York* magazine, one of those tense little snits where every negative feeling we ever had about each other seemed to be writhing in and out of each sentence, when suddenly Marge said, 'Would you stop patronizing me!' I was stunned. Me patronize Marge? But it turns out that she feels I lord it over her when it comes to anything regarding men. That I'm smug about being married and having a child while she's still slugging it out in the singles scene.

"And it's true. It gives me some leverage to be the expert on relationships, as ridiculous as that may sound at the moment. I told her that I often feel I need some leverage, because she can be so abrupt and critical. I still remembered the way she treated me on my last birthday.

"She said, 'Look, Georgette, I need someone to tell me when I get that way. If you don't tell me, who will? But don't write me off and just assume that's the way I am. And don't make me feel like shit for being single. I already feel like shit for being single.' I loved her for that.

"It's hard to believe that my disastrous thirty-fifth birthday was just one year ago. The thing I remember most is that Thursday night when Martin and I 'made love.' Before he came home, I was like two people. One person was going about the house straightening up, lighting candles, fixing my hair, preparing to lure him into bed. Mirabel Morgan would have been proud. The other was cringing and frightened because something didn't feel right. I didn't know what is was and I didn't want to know.

"My mother used to say that fear takes forty percent right off the top. As a kid, you hear something like that and you just shake your head and wonder. But I know what she meant now. She must have been so frightened, especially after my father died. She was getting older, and she had us two kids, and she didn't know if she could do it. She was very alive and she could be ever so funny, and I really never doubted that she loved me. But she had such doubts about herself. And she was always tiptoeing around them, terrified that they'd spring to life and grab her. Without her fear about what she was and what she was doing to us, she could have been so much freer, more natural, and fun to be with. It probably cut her down by *at least* forty percent. I know she hated herself for all the drinking she did, but it killed off the fear for a little while.

"About a month ago, I was sitting at my desk when I had an experience I must have had a million times before. A flutter of fear whispered through me. And an hour later I found myself struggling against an undertow of despair. Normally the next step is I go out looking for some coffee and a Danish. But this time I stopped and asked myself what I was running from. I remembered that morning I had mentioned something to Garfield about a bill that was coming up before the Board of Estimate regarding shelters for the homeless, and he abruptly cooled off. He said he was late for lunch and had to go. I forgot the incident the moment it happened because it brought back all my fears about being a small person who has no business meddling in important affairs.

"It was a struggle to get the memory back. But once I did, it was a relief, as if I'd coughed up a bone. A wave of relaxation swept through me. Because what was really going on had nothing to do with what that little fear inside me said. Garfield was stuck between two opposing campaign pledges—to help the homeless and to keep city government costs down—and he hates to be reminded of the jams he's in. Garfield respects my expertise. And he doesn't want me burdening his conscience when he's about to make what might be construed as a shabby, pragmatic decision. But if I hadn't thought this through, I would have gone into the office the next day a little smaller.

"I try very hard to remember this: that no matter how frightening my feelings are, I've got to look at them—whether they come up in a tense moment in the office, or in a discussion with Marge that gets a little abrasive, or when I'm watching Martin's eyebrow start to rise. Otherwise the fear is going to win. I'm going to turn against myself and not even know it.

"Nowadays, if I feel gripped by anxiety and about to cave in, I try to hold out a little longer. I want to pause just long enough to get back to my center and remember who I am.

"I like sitting here looking at the river. It seems like this little space between Cindy's bedtime and mine is the only moment I have nowadays to reflect. I get flooded with such feelings. My love for that little girl tucked away in there. A whole new sense of power and, what is the word?—*efficacy*—since getting this new job. My sadness about Martin, mixed there, too, with love and a kind of boiling resentment. A sense that maybe I can do things I never thought possible before. And then, right at the bottom of it all my awareness that despite everything I know and everything I've learned in the last few months, there are still doubts. And I wonder, if Martin and I do get together again, will I be able to do it better?

"One thing I do know, though, is that it's much easier to be really in touch—with the good stuff as well as the bad—when I have some basis for feeling okay about myself. I keep trying to build on that and not let fear take too much off the top."

THE END

Acknowledgments

WHEN I first conceived of Georgette she was five years older than me. Now I am five years her senior. In the course of such a long project, there are inevitably many people who come to an author's assistance. Without their support, it's hard to imagine how this book could have been written.

I am very much indebted to my father for standing by me with financial support when I could not have continued the work without it. For her long and unwavering championing of this book, for her continuous reading and rereading of the manuscript in its various stages and incarnations, and for her sweet presence in my life, I am most lovingly thankful to Thaleia Christidis. It is a pleasure also to thank my agent (and friend), Evan Marshall, who believed in the book and did yeoman work from beginning to end; Judy Bloomfield for her wisdom, loyalty, and priceless friendship; Jon Koslow for his brotherly devotion and keen reading of the manuscript; my good friend and literary comrade, Jane Merrill; and Paul Wachtel, a fine thinker and teacher, who responded with enthusiasm to the book and was kind enough to write the foreword.

I am also indebted to George Coleman, who acquired the book for Donald I. Fine, Inc.; Deborah Chiel, my skillful editor; and Stuart Krichevsky for his timely relief pitching at the Sterling Lord Agency.

Lois Morris, Alicia Fortinberry, Emily Greenspan, and Dianne Partie not only gave me valuable feedback and encouragement, but were like a family to me during two memorable summers on Long Island when I was working on the manuscript. I will always think of them in conjunction with this book.

Others whose help has meant a great deal to me are Wendy Lipkind, Ralph Rosenblum, Barbara Creaturo, Michael Lipson, Holly Pittman, Katherine Coker, Nancy Slater, Barbara Wasserman, Lise Leipmann, Michelle Arnot, Sandra Kunhardt, Angela Bonavoglia, Walt Bode, Bob Lashaw, Bob Gould, Mary Anne Frank, Linda Lee, Chuck Stickney, and Charles and Elizabeth Crandall, who generously allowed me to use their tranquil Shelter Island kitchen one summer as an office-retreat.

Finally, I wish to thank my mother, my step-mother, and my brother-in-law Ken Stuart for their support during this period, and my darling sister Wendy, my biggest booster, who's always wanted to be in my acknowledgments.

Index of Key Concepts